ANGELA B. HUGHES

ELANOR
AND THE
SONG OF THE BARD

THE ONCE & FUTURE CHRONICLES
BOOK ONE

SQUARE TREE PUBLISHING
www.squaretreepublishing.com

IMAGINE NOW PUBLISHING
www.angelarhughes.com

For more information about bulk purchases, please contact Square Tree Publishing at info@squaretreepublishing.com.

Cover design by www.100Covers.com

Cover design by Sharon Marta, www.sharonmarta.com

ISBN 978-1-7369186-3-0 (Paperback)
ISBN 978-1-7362443-0-2 (Hardback)
Library of Congress Control Number: 2021906744

Angela Hughes, a storyteller champion, has written a masterpiece! *Elanor and the Song of the Bard* is a game-changer for the legendary story of King Arthur and Merlin. Hughes introduces a new Arthurian adventure that captures the heart of the reader and keeps them enthralled from beginning to end. *Elanor and the Song of the Bard* sweeps us into a fantastical realm, inspiring each of us through powerful symbolism to look deeper into our own present-day story.

Elanor and the Song of the Bard is bound to become another beloved and timeless classic. I wholeheartedly endorse this book.

Arthurian lovers, prepare your heart to step into a magnificent adventure!

Are you ready?

—Brae Wyckoff, Director of Kingdom Writers Association and award-winning Amazon best-selling author

Dedicated to my husband...
who knew I had stories to tell before I did.

And to Arthur, King of the Britons...
The Welsh bards would have said that you lived and were not just a legend. The prose of the French would have said that you ended in tragedy. I instead choose to believe that there was more to the story, and less of the legend. And that what was left behind was hope, and not death.

TABLE OF CONTENTS

PRONUNCIATION GUIDE

PROLOGUE: Arthur's End

PART ONE

PART TWO

ACKNOWLEDGMENTS

ABOUT THE AUTHOR

Cymry (Welsh) Pronunciation Guide

Aeron: AY-ron

Badon: BAY-don

Balek: BAY-lek

Bedwyr: BED-wir

Beltaine (Season/between Spring and Summer): BEL-tane

Bevon: Be-VON

Bors: BORS

Bram: BRAM

Brynn: BRIN

Caer (Citadel): K-air

Caer Lial: K-air LEE-ol

Cai: KY

Camlan: KAM-lan

Celyddon: Kel-ee-thon

Cilaen: KY-lee-An

Cormach: KOR-mak

Croighcat: KROY-cat

Cymry (Welsh): KIM-ree

The proper Welsh word for Welsh is Cymraeg. However, for continuity and flow for non-Welsh-speaking people in this Historical Fantasy Fiction, I have used Cymry (Wales) to represent the Welsh nation of 500 AD.

Dunnoc: DUN-ock

Dyved: DIE-fed

Ector: EK-tore

Eddna: ee-TH-nuh

Elian: EL-ee-AN

Emrys: EM-ris

Filidh (Druid Pupil/Poet): FIL-id

Ganieda: gan-AY-duh

Gwain: guh-WANE

Gwalahad: guh-WAL-uh-had

Gwenddydd: guh-WEN-thid-th

Grwyrthrhodd (Spoken Word): gruh-EERTH-rode

Gwylir Aures Draigen (Guardian Golden Dragon): guh-WILE-eer AWE-ress DRAE-gen

Gwynevere: guh-WEN-e-veer

Haldin: HAL-den

Haleth: HAL-eth

Halok: HOE-lok

Hwyddan: hu-WY-than

Lugh: loo

Lugnasadh (Season/beginning of Harvest): loog-NAH-sad

Llyonesse: LIE-own-ess

Mordred: MOR-dred

Morgan: MOR-gan

Morguese: MOR-goes

Murrian: mur-REE-an

Myrddin (Merlin): MER-thin

Ogham (Early Celtic Alphabet): OH-gam

Olham (Elder Druid): OH-lam

Osian: OH-see-an

Peredur: PER-aye-DUR

Prydain: PRY-dan

Ranok: RAN-uk

Samhain (Season/beginning of winter): SAM-ane

Thangul: THAN-gul

Thanul: THAN-ool

Thul: THOOL

Vortigern: VOR-tee-gurn

Wyllt (Wild): WIH-lt

PRYDAIN
LAND OF
THE
BRITONS

Picti Land

Great Wall

Caer Eoyn
King Bram

King Lot

Caer Lial

Celyddon
King Thul

Isle of Avalon

Éire

King Crioghcat

RIVER TOWN

Dyfed

South Lands

Narrow Pass

Caer Myrddyn
King Cormach

Lindonium

King Lugh

Llyonesse

N
W   E
S

PROLOGUE

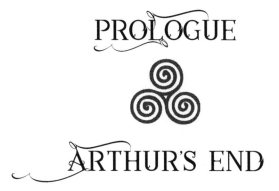

ARTHUR'S END

Mordred had captured Gwynevere and Merlin. He bound them and dragged them along behind his horses to the fields of Camlan. Glaring at their miserable faces, he felt a twisted sense of pride, knowing he had done what no other could. Mordred had successfully set a trap for Arthur and itched for his arrival.

It had been so easy, deceiving them all. While Arthur was away seeking the Holy Cup, Mordred was welcomed through the gates of Caer Lial without a single thought. Gwynevere and the Palisade were caught unaware, unable to see through his guise into his treacherous sorcery.

Merlin had his suspicions of Mordred but had never imagined this level of depravity. His mother, Morgan, had taught him well in the art of deceit. The Great Merlin, with all his powers, was trapped, unable to break free as Mordred released his havoc—capturing and murdering all within the walls of what should have been their protection.

Now at Camlan, Mordred smiled with confidence, knowing he had made his mother proud. He had usurped the kingdom, right out from underneath Arthur's long arm. With Merlin and Gwynevere in his clutches, Arthur would be like putty in his hands when he saw Mordred's knife pressed against their throats.

"He will kill you, Mordred!" Gwynevere shouted. A tear rolled down her dirt-smudged face as she shook with anger. "You have no idea the force he will have against you when he sees what you have done."

Mordred pointed the tip of his knife at her face. "Here, Arthur will watch me kill you as soon as he crests that hill."

Merlin's lips curled as he stood, brooding in silence, the wind blowing his dark brown hair across his face.

"And you…the Great Merlin! No plans of escape? No magic in your pocket?" Mordred taunted. "No one has dared face you, yet here you are at my mercy. You never divined I had sorcery, nor that I could be strong enough to bind you. You in all your wisdom never suspected I was Morgan's son…Fool!" Mordred struck Merlin's head with the handle of his blade, laughing as sparks of madness glinted in his eyes. He spat, "You will both die, and there is nothing you can do to stop it."

Arthur finally appeared on the horizon. At his left and right appeared his greatest champions, Bedwyr and Cai, with Gwalahad, Gwain, Bors, and Peredur following closely behind. It would be the seven of them facing Mordred and his small army of a hundred men.

An army of this size could not hinder Arthur and his mightiest, but for the knife's edge that lay pressed against Gwynevere's throat.

"Arthur!" Mordred called out. "Watch this day as I kill your queen and your dear Merlin. My knife is keen to slit her throat and spill her precious blood to the ground. Your kingdom I now rip from you, and I leave you with nothing but death!"

Arthur hesitated, gazing across the field at the spectacle before him. Despite the distressing scene, a sliver of hope emerged when he saw no fear in Merlin's eyes. His brazen stare bolstered Arthur's confidence. He knew that lilt of Merlin's chin and familiar glint in his eye meant he was not beaten. The intimidating scene Mordred tried to display only made the dauntless king rise in his fury. He rode forth, refusing to be cornered by this worm, and would not stand by while those he loved were slaughtered before him.

Recovering his strength, Merlin steadily worked to wriggle his hands free from his bonds, overcoming Mordred's weak enchantment. He had only to wait for the right moment.

As Mordred lifted his knife, Merlin released a sound that vibrated with a loud CRACK. Before Mordred a flame burst, knocking him to the ground.

Quickly, Merlin snatched Gwynevere out of danger as he grappled with one of Mordred's men—wrestling him to the ground, taking a sword, and cutting Gwynevere free.

"Run!" he yelled, ready to block any men from stopping her.

Mordred's men were taken off guard as Arthur's men drove in like a mighty battering ram. A clash of spears and swords ensued as Mordred's men found their footing and faced their opposition. Just in time, Peredur lifted Gwynevere out of the frenzy onto his horse's back and fled from the battle to secure her to safety.

Arthur's men stabbed into the fray, knocking three men down at each blow, but the enemy's numbers gained them the advantage.

The battle froze as Arthur's eyes captured the first of his men to fall. Gwain fought bravely, slicing through his foes with the grace of the wind. Men fell at each of his strokes, but there were too many. An enemy warrior caught him from behind, piercing a sword through Gwain's chest.

"NO!" Arthur reeled. His confidence faltered as Gwain fell to the ground, dead. Rage beset him. His eyes raced back and forth, searching to find where Mordred stood. He would not escape the wrath he had incurred.

Arthur pressed through men, knocking them over like a charging bull. The rain of swords and spears, however, prevented him from finding his foe and forced him to stand in the fray, slicing and ripping through flesh.

Pain scourged Arthur's skull as iron struck his helm—knocking it free— dizzying his stance and blurring his eyes. He could barely see the large warrior and the tip of his spear barreling toward him. Arthur deflected with his shield, just in time to stay the blow, but was knocked off his feet. His vision clearing, Arthur rolled from the second blow and swept his sword at the enemy's feet. As his foe lay helpless on the ground, he stood to deliver the killing blow just as another enemy swiftly arced his sword toward Arthur's back.

CLANG! Rang the sound of Cai's sword, clashing against the enemy, saving Arthur from the attack. Now both men fought back-to-back, cutting down men as though they were grass. Blood staining the ground, they smiled at each other—brothers—fighting together as formidable warriors.

Red-haired and fierce, Cai fought with a sword in each hand, the weapons mere extensions of his arms. As he swung, heads rolled to the ground as if he were an indomitable god. The enemy surrounded them, rallying their strength to stop them. Cai's wild eyes intimidated the enemy, reinforcing Arthur's strength.

Yet in one weak moment as Cai maneuvered around an enemy's shield, he was struck. A spear planted into the muscle of his calf, and another found its way into his side. The mighty Cai—with all his strength—swung his swords into the air, and with a loud yell, dove them into the midst of the enemy. Foes enveloped him, cutting him down one piece at a time.

Arthur's heart was rent in anguish as he plunged into the red and black fury of iron. The scent of death invaded his nostrils, and hopelessness berated his heart. These men had been with him, in and out of many battles, but always they had lived.

Suddenly, a horn sounded. Cresting the hill from the east was King Ector and fifty of his Cymbrogi warriors, charging down the ridge. The sight lifted Arthur's spirit and sent Mordred's men into a panic. They scattered, loosening their ranks.

Renewed, Arthur looked up, and this time he spotted his enemy with tangled strains of black hair stuck to the sweat on his brow. Mordred stood with a black sword in his hand and his eyes widened as Arthur set upon him.

With the frenzy of battle upon him, Arthur roared wildly toward Mordred. Their swords met with the sound of shattering metal. Arthur, the superior warrior, knocked Mordred to the ground, his sword hitting the earth beside him. Quickly, he rolled and captured his sword in time to block the hammer that plummeted toward his head. Terror filled him, knowing he was no match for Arthur.

Mordred stood to his feet and, like the coward he was, ran, glancing over his shoulder to see Arthur charging after him. Then, he was struck by what felt like an iron wall. Stunned, he saw Merlin above him, who had stopped him with a supernatural force.

Merlin grabbed Mordred and turned him to face Arthur. Shoving him forward in distaste, Merlin shouted, "Face him, you coward!"

Mordred flung his sword up, and Arthur struck it once, twice, three times with the strength of a bear. Arthur lifted his sword high to bring it down again, but Mordred turned, swinging his sword to the side, slicing Arthur's torso, causing him to stumble back. Seizing his moment, Mordred raised his sword with both hands, thirsty for the kill. Arthur swiftly grabbed Mordred's hands, stopping the arc of his sword. With his free hand, Arthur rammed his own sword through Mordred's gut.

Mordred's face grew red, realizing his own mortality was slipping away. He fell to the ground. The life drained from his face. He shook, panting heavily. Then, his body fell limp. Mordred was dead.

PROLOGUE

Breathless, Arthur stared at the treacherous remains of his foe, whose
fingers remained tightly wrapped around the hilt of his sword.

"Traitor!" Arthur shouted with the full force of his anger.

The death of Mordred took the wind out of his few men that were left,
and soon the clanging of swords and battle cries were no more. Arthur and Merlin
stood in the silence, side by side, scanning the field for any who still remained.

Arthur triumphed over Mordred, but at what cost? The field lay strewn
with red. Through the midst of mangled bodies, they found Gwalahad, Cai,
Gwain, and Bors slain, leaving only Bedwyr and Peredur, the remnant of all the
mighty men who had sailed in the glory of Arthur's mighty hand. Even King
Ector had been found amongst the bodies of the fallen.

As Arthur sighed in grief, he touched his side where he had been cut
and fell to his knees. Drawing his hand away, he took a painful breath, staring at
the blood. The cut was not deep, but something insidious was happening in his
body. The simple slice of Mordred's blade had proved more effective than he
had thought. For as Merlin quickly discovered, Arthur himself had been mortally
wounded. Mordred's sword had been tipped with poison, and Arthur's sorrow,
mingled with the venom, were far too strong for Merlin to heal.

Arthur struggled to hold on to life. Merlin felt Arthur's only hope lay
with the Christian monks on the Isle of Avalon. It was said they had great powers
of healing.

Alas, even there, no power could heal poor Arthur, and he died. The
monks placed him inside the very boat Merlin had sailed him in, laying his sword,
Excalibur, at his side. He lay as if he were but asleep and was sailed back to Caer
Lial. He was buried inside the Hill of the Kings, marked by a cairn with a stone
marker that read, "Arthur, King and Battle Chief of the Britons." Under one
banner Arthur had brought all the minor kings and battle chiefs together, and a
peace like no other time remembered had been established. But now his death
left all of Prydain to grief, and a darkness fell over them all. All hope seemed to
have left the world.

Merlin knew his aid would be needed in the unsettled time, but in his
grief he could not return. He wanted to diminish. So, he stayed in Avalon, not
knowing where else he should go, or who else he should be. He thought that
maybe, just as Arthur, his time had come to an end.

Magically, Merlin placed a veil of mist around the island, knowing
that others would seek him. The mist shrouded the island, the grey matching

the clouds as they met the horizon of the sea. In this way, Merlin could hide himself and disappear into his misery. He was lost to the world of men. Purposeless and conquered.

PART ONE

IT BEGINS WITH THE DREAMS

Four Years Later

"**M**erlin...Merlin!" *she called out, desperately reaching out toward him. Like a ghost he could see her standing across the chasm, her arms outstretched and her raven black hair blowing behind her in the wildness of the wind.*

"Please, Elanor!" Merlin cried out to her. "Elanor!"

He couldn't lose her this time. This time, he would reach her. This time, he would grip her hands and not let go. The wind tore violently between them, like an angry beast threatening to separate them.

Meanwhile, the mighty sounds of the drums of battle rang in Merlin's ears. Is that Arthur...upon the hill...with his Cymbrogi armed with spear and sword?

"Arthur! Arthur!" he called out frantically. "Arthur..."

Merlin was violently shaken awake. Great drops of sweat fell as he gasped for breath, his face pale. The dream had come once again, a torment in his sleep. Furiously, he gritted his teeth and stood to wipe his brow.

"Not again! Will these dreams never abate?"

He mechanically made his way toward the water basin but stopped abruptly, caught by the sight of his own reflection. His long, dark curls twisted in strands across his face; his golden eyes were sunken and dull. He splashed his hand into the water and crumpled to the floor, his forehead sinking into his palms. He hated how old he appeared, ragged and forsaken. In truth, he was still a man, strong, in his prime. Though, through grief, his face reflected something different.

His magical life wasn't the result of sorcery, but a reality of an older time. His golden eyes, his mother said, were given to him because the Great God desired him to see more deeply. But now, it was all fading.

Four long years he dwelt in Avalon, where the waves of time could not touch him. The sting of the memories of Camlan still burned in his mind. Alone he sat in a small, stone chamber, listening to the voices of the monks outside. He ate little and drank less. Trance-like he remained within his own mind, daring his life to be taken from him.

It was here these mysterious dreams began.

They invaded Merlin's sleep, even breaking into his waking mind, disturbing his dark solace. As one who knew the ways of the druids and bards of old, he recognized signs from the stars, nature, and dreams. These visions were not just dreams. For the first time in the years of his self-banishment, he knew that something was being set in motion. But for what, he did not know.

Desperately, he tried to ignore the dreams, but they kept coming relentlessly, night after night. With each dream, their reality drew nearer. He could feel it deep in his bones: a calling to come back awake to the world that needed him.

"Merlin! Merlin!" the mysterious woman in his dream had called to him. She reached for him as if trying to save him from something. His heart yearned to save her, too. But a mighty wind always pulled them apart as they struggled, reaching for each other. She was always in his mind, her beautiful eyes haunting him, and when he woke, her voice called to him, yet the brokenness of his heart resisted her.

"Who are you? Why are you disturbing me?" he'd seethe, but in the dream, he would call back, "Elanor!" Stretching to reach for her, he felt there was something more he should want.

He knew well the meaning of the dream, but he did not care. He had already resigned himself to nothingness; however, the dreams refused to give him that peace as they pointed a finger, judging his complacency and despair.

He shouted at the sky, "Choose someone else! I am done hoping for a new beginning that never comes, or once comes, dies like a flower in the cold of winter."

He was forced to leave his chamber of stone and stormed about the isle in anger. It was the only way he hoped to clear the damned things from his mind.

Chapter One

"No! I do not want to see their faces! I should have stopped Arthur from leaving! I should have stayed to help them, but I ran away! I do not want to go back!"

In the dreams, he saw Arthur, tall upon his black horse. He held his standard high of red and gold, pointing at two stars brightly gleaming in the sky. The reminder of Arthur's glory tore open the wound of Merlin's great loss.

Merlin tossed and turned within his chamber while a solitary candle burned slowly down to its wax in a small corner of the room, its light barely a flicker in the darkness. He mumbled as he wrestled on his mat, his voice increasing in the darkness.

"No...no!" Merlin groaned. Then, he shot straight up and shouted, "I will not go!" His outburst startled a young monk, causing him to drop the milk and bread he had brought for Merlin. The loud clang of the metal cup hitting the floor woke Merlin fully, causing an angry fire to burn in his eyes. "What are you doing in here?"

The monk stood silently, shaken by Merlin's aggressive tone. He placed his hand upon his chest and breathed out. Composing himself, he bent down to clean the mess from the floor and lit a new candle.

"This one has nearly gone out," the monk said. "As you are now awake you may have need of a new light. Were you dreaming?"

Merlin snapped, "I can make a candle burn without need of new! Are you the one they call Rian?"

The young monk busied himself about the room.

"I have seen and heard you about my chambers," Merlin continued.

Rian bowed. "Yes, my lord."

"I am nobody's lord!" Merlin growled, looking at the floor.

"You are Merlin! And you are one of the lords of Prydain's great kingdom."

Merlin sprang toward the young monk and grabbed him by the front of his robe, pulling him close enough to look him in the eye. "You know nothing. Leave me!" he commanded, tossing Rian to the floor.

The monk stood up meekly, dusted off his robe, then boldly remarked, "I have not forgotten you, my lord, though you may have worked hard to forget yourself." Then he turned and left the room.

Merlin felt like a fool. "What does he know?" He said aloud as he threw himself back onto his mat. "He of so few years, calling me out by my name, as if he has any understanding of all that has been done. He knows nothing."

Flashes of the woman calling him from his dreams were still fresh in his mind, and he wrestled within himself, unable to find peace for his efforts. The memory of her face and sound of her voice pointed him toward the mainland—calling him home.

He spent the entirety of the next day shouting at the Great God in the sky, ignoring the dreams as loudly as he could on the black rocks of the shore, flailing his arms, and accusing the wind. "I have nothing left to give them. They will never forgive me. The magic you have given me did not stop the evils from doing their work. And, oh, how I tried. I tried and failed. I will try no longer. Where was your hand to stop Mordred? Why did you not come?" he yelled, exhausting his emotions. He was furious that the only reply he received was a gentle breeze and the sound of the water slapping at the shore.

Merlin sighed deeply and returned to another fitful night of sleep. He saw Arthur again rising up over the hill behind him, a legion of Cymbrogi warriors, armed with spears pointed high. Even as the scene unfolded before him, fits of grief and anguish rolled over him. All that could have been, now gone. The glorious scene tortured his mind, forcing him to believe for something that had already been dead and buried.

"Why?" he mumbled, in his sleep. "Why?"

Then, something changed as he dreamt. He felt a sensation, like when the sun warms the skin after emerging from behind a cloud. He saw Arthur raise his sword and release a battle cry, and as the Cymbrogi roared, it shook Merlin completely, reaching deep into him and igniting his heart. He felt unable to stop it.

He awoke abruptly and found Rian sitting at the edge of his mat, hands upraised, silently praying.

"Why are you here praying like this?" Merlin demanded, perplexed and a bit annoyed to see him there. Rian said nothing. He sat in silence, his hands resting in his lap.

"It's these dreams! They persist and will not let me go. All of this magic," Merlin exclaimed, waving his hand as if shooing a fly. "I am working hard to ignore its stirrings! I am for it no longer."

Rian stood, bowed toward Merlin, then slipped quietly out of the chamber. Merlin rose and walked across the room to fill the emptiness of his stomach with the food Rian had left behind.

"You," he whispered, somberly. "Great giver of dreams, leave me to rest. The more I look at them, the more I cannot ignore them. Please take them from me."

For days this continued. Every day Merlin would shout, and in the evening he would find Rian at his feet in prayer. Finally, on the seventh day, Merlin said to Rian, "This does not help me, monk. Do I need to find somewhere else where I can be alone, and away from you?"

"Please do not, my lord," Rian finally spoke. "The Great God does not desire that you should be alone while He shakes you awake. He said that He must cause you to dream until you decide to wake."

"The Great God abandoned me and has left me here."

"No, my lord."

"But Arthur died. He's dead! It is over. I am done now. I…" Merlin stopped, gazing out across the room at the small flickering candlelight. His eyes flooded with tears and deep sorrow. "I left them. I do not want to see the disappointment. Arthur and I, we failed. We were the promise, and we did not fulfill it. The Great God—He left us. Arthur left us. I could not hold the kingdom in my hand alone"—he lifted his fists into the air—"nor could I keep Arthur alive." Merlin dropped his hands, as if he were letting pebbles fall to the floor. "Let someone else do it. I have become old, and I want to be finished."

Rian treaded carefully, "When you let yourself awaken, you will no longer feel this way. Though it will be hard to open your eyes. The strength is still in you; it only seems like you have lost it because you stopped moving forward."

Merlin turned toward Rian, a glare in his eyes as he hissed through his teeth, "You know nothing!" He stormed furiously out into the dark night, not stopping until he stood at the very edge of a rockface hanging over the sea. Only small glints of light could be seen reflecting off the ripples upon the water. Rian went after him but dared not approach. Angry and defeated, Merlin glared out at the sea, facing for the first time the choice that stood before him.

A vision of Elanor, the woman from his dream, took shape in the grey darkness before him. He struggled to resist her call. He knew he must leave and return once more to the world he had left behind. Day by day, little pieces of him were surrendering to the call, and he could deny it no longer.

"Rian!" Merlin shouted, turning to look behind him. "I know you are there. It is all right…come." He held his hand out to invite Rian forward. Slowly, Rian emerged and stood beside Merlin. "You are not the one to be blamed for these dreams and how they have disturbed me." Putting his hand on Rian's shoulder, Merlin admitted, "I am afraid, Rian." He turned to look once more at the blackness of the sea. Pointing his finger, he proclaimed, "I shall go to Caer Lial. Tomorrow I will lift this cursed mist that has concealed me, and you will be free. Then I shall sail and return to my home."

THE THRESHOLD OF DECISION

The faces of those he'd left behind in grief still haunted Merlin's mind, but Rian's presence steadied his heart as he prepared to set sail. In a silent goodbye, he boarded a boat, along with a horse for his travels. Merlin then sailed away, watching Rian's figure slowly disappear into the darkness of the still morning. He sailed on, cold and alone. Only the black silhouette of his horse could be seen ahead of him as he continued upon the waters.

He breathed in deeply, and waving his arms, the mist cleared, and the sky and water opened up before him. He turned to see the rocks of the isle behind him and the safety they had provided him fade, as he set forth toward the place of his pain.

As he approached the shore he knew within a fortnight, he'd be in Caer Lial.

The unknown stood before him. There was nothing left for him to do but to ride. He travelled like the wind upon his brown horse, not stopping for a moment's rest to collect his thoughts. He would travel onward until he reached the gates of the stronghold.

Caer Lial was where Arthur had established his kingship with Gwynevere and his mighty Cymry warriors. It was there the High Kingship had become established after the many battles with the Saecsan invaders, and it was there he hoped to find Gwynevere still queen.

Three days of hard journeying passed, and still Merlin rode on. He stopped only to camp for the night and water his horse. He feared if he stopped or lingered long in any place he might not continue on his route. Always there in the back of his mind was the thought of retreating. Finally, he could see the gates in the distance. He knew once he crossed through, he would not be able to turn back. He stopped to peer at them for a long while. He saw the face of an angry Gwynevere before him. How could he satisfy her with the explanation of why he left?

Then a worse thought entered his mind, of there being no Gwynevere at all, and the Caer left, cast into ruin without its king.

He sat upon his horse at the threshold of decision. Would he discover the misery that had damned these lands, or would he discover the moment of his accountability?

"I don't want to remember." Merlin cringed as thoughts ran through his mind of the bloody grounds of Camlan. He turned to look back at the forest behind him. It was calling to him to retreat.

"Aah!" Merlin shouted angrily. He yanked the reins of the horse, whipping around to run toward the forest. He did not want to face the pain gripping his heart. The persistent dreams seemed no longer important as he approached the forest, riding free into the sanctuary of the trees that seemed to be spreading their arms wide to welcome him.

But the further away he got, the more his mind sobered, remembering the torment of his dreams. No matter how long he stayed away or hid in the forest, the dreams would be there until he did what he knew was necessary.

Merlin brought his horse to a halt and sank his head down into his hands.

"Mordred," he growled, anger radiating deep into his chest. "How is it that one could so silently, and cunningly twist his way into the goodness of Arthur's kingdom? Rotting away all the beautiful and lovely strength it held." The venom of Mordred's bite remained in Merlin's veins. He hated that he was being forced to go where he desired not.

Memories of Mordred's treacherous smile invaded Merlin's mind. He had been one of them. Acting as a faithful Cymbrogi warrior, with strength and character. He had fought with them and honored Arthur. Morgan had been dead, along with her seductress daughter Morguese. The threat of witchcraft and sorcery had been dealt with. But as it turned out, Mordred was Morgan's final arrow, and he bided his time and built trust—causing all to drop their defenses—before attacking Arthur's kingdom while his back was turned.

Chapter Two

Merlin bit his lip as he remembered it. He had known something was not right, but he shrugged it away as the kingdom rose like a mountain, unconquerable.

"Please, I beg of you," he said with slumped shoulders, still holding his head, "choose someone else. I have done my part. I rode beside Arthur and raised him up high. I saw the brightness of his days. I established the promise. I have done it all. Why am I responsible for anything more? Why should I have any more part to play? They cannot want me to return." He lifted his head up to the sky, as if waiting for a response, for some final mercy to be poured out.

Hearing nothing, Merlin turned his horse back toward the Palisade, defeated. He rode until finally the great citadel came into his view once again. He moaned within himself, knowing that forward was the only direction he could go. He had no other option, and as much as his fear tried to convince him that he didn't care, deep down, he did. He cared deeply. The consequences of his decision to abandon them weighed heavily upon him, and he had no escape.

The sun was already beginning to set, and he could see lights shining from the citadel. He would not go further this day. At least he would have the delay of the night before he would have to ride to the gates.

Merlin did not want to be seen, so he found a small gathering of trees to conceal himself for the night and rested. Still, he had a full view of the expanse of Caer Lial, and the tall hill and Palisade to deepen his sullen thoughts throughout the night. In the morning, he would ride to the gates, and come what may, he would not retreat. He settled down beneath a tree, hoping to at least find some peace before the morning. As he closed his eyes, he began to hear her, the woman in his dream, calling, "Merlin! Merlin!"

THE RETURN OF MERLIN

Merlin woke as the sun was rising. Already his heart was pricked with the regret of what this day would bring. Turning his head, he focused on the view of the Palisade of Caer Lial looming on top of a hill afar off. The great Palisade of stone, so Roman, with the Great Hall rising up in front of it—wooden and rustic in the style of the ancient Cymry.

The high and fortified outer wall with its broad stones was still black in the dim morning light. Merlin knew that just beyond it could be a town still brimming with traditional round thatched homes, merchants, and iron forgers. On the other side of the town was a second gate, through which there were fields for the training Cymry warriors, and stable yards for horses. He stood to stretch his bones and wondered if it all still remained.

As the sun continued to rise, it alighted upon the Great Hall's pillars with their standards of gold and red blowing in the wind. The memories of the sweet-smelling apple orchard that surrounded the Palisade snuck into Merlin's mind, making him feel reminiscent.

There had been nothing like it before in all of Prydain, Great Isle of the Briton's. Many strongholds had been built before with their great halls, and even the Romans had their great houses and villas, but still none of them compared. With such freedom and passion, the Palisade of Caer Lial was built, and it was a glorious sight to see.

Climbing onto his horse, Merlin rode toward the stronghold. As he approached the outer gate, he could see many of the young warriors outside the gates running the horses while practicing with their spears and shields. Their liveliness and action fooled him into believing that things had remained unchanged.

Visions of Arthur seeing him from the ramparts of the walls shouting happy greetings to him welled up inside Merlin's mind. But as the visions faded, the bitterness settled back into his heart and the spirit amongst the men offended him. His face twisted as he approached the gate.

The men standing guard saw him drawing near and hurriedly scrambled. Before Merlin had even reached the gate, the Cymry had sent a rider to the Palisade.

The two warriors stationed at the gate were dressed in hard leather breast plates and helms. Brown breeches covered their legs, and soft leather boots tied up to the bottom of their knees. Around their shoulders, they wore colors of red and gold, draped and pinned with silver broaches—each with a spear in his hand. They bowed low, in awe, and ushered Merlin through the gate without uttering a word.

Merlin could see that they had recognized him. Curious at the seeming lack of change since his absence, he moved through the gates and up toward the Hall. A part of him wanted to be relieved at what appeared to be a thriving Caer, but the other, larger part wrestled with having been pressed to return. If all was well—what reason would he have needed to return?

Seeing the Cymbrogi warriors without Arthur rubbed salt into his wounds. Passing along the way, he saw the town and a marketplace full of people selling and buying. Through the second gate, men threw spears and cracked their swords together in the field. Already Merlin's imagined devastation of Caer Lial faded.

As he glanced around, the warriors halted training and silently stared at the Great Merlin as he rode past. Their eyes were full of hope at the sight of him.

"What are they hoping for?" he asked himself as he wrestled within his mind. "I have nothing to bring them. I am not the Merlin they once knew."

He tried not to look at their faces as he travelled up the hill and through the orchard to the front steps of the Great Hall.

A young boy came running down the steps, greeting him nervously with a bow. Gasping and out of breath, he said, "I am to lead you into the Hall to meet with the queen."

Merlin nodded. The thought of seeing Gwynevere made him nervous. He leapt down from his horse and immediately, a servant standing by grabbed the reins, bowed, and led Merlin's horse away to the stalls. Merlin stood amazed. The feeling that nothing had changed made him feel small, and he winced at his own arrogance. The sight of it all was forced down his throat like dry bread without water.

He followed the boy, who seemed very anxious and eager to complete his task. As Merlin walked through the wooden doors, he gazed behind him one last time, seeing the fullness of the Caer below, before the wooden doors shut. There could be nothing now to stop the events he dreaded from unfolding before him.

The Hall was a large room with a row of pillars on each side that matched the great whorled pillars outside. Each side of the room was lined with long tables, and in the center of the room was a hearth where fires were lit, and a golden cauldron beside where the ale was poured during feasting.

The boy walked at almost a skipping pace, which amused Merlin and lightened his mood momentarily. He was led up to a long table at the front of the room where behind sat several large chairs upon a higher platform. No one was in the Hall but Merlin and the boy, who fidgeted with his feet back and forth.

The emptiness of the room quickly changed as two men entered. Both stopped and stared in Merlin's direction. The air felt stale and heavy as Merlin recognized the newcomers, his abandoned companions and all that was left of Arthur's mighty men, Bedwyr and Peredur. Both walked slowly through the door, as if peering through a fog that was slowly lifting. Bedwyr's mouth fell open, and Peredur stood frozen.

Bedwyr slowly stepped toward Merlin with a look that was hard for him to read. "You are alive?" Bedwyr said sorrowfully. "We looked for you. We had need of you, my friend."

Peredur stood stoic and aloof, looking across at Merlin with tense eyes. "We went searching for the Isle, but it was not there," he muttered. "Hidden, it seemed."

Merlin could hear the accusation in Peredur's tone.

Bedwyr stepped closer to look Merlin in the eye and placed his hand upon his shoulder. His eyes were full of disbelief, as if he were staring at a ghost.

The gaze from both men was unnerving, yet Merlin was resolute in showing no care nor emotion in his face.

"Where have you been?" Peredur sternly demanded, causing the boy beside Merlin to twitch slightly.

Bedwyr shook his head at Peredur and waved his hand to cool his temper. His eyes formed tears as he embraced Merlin, squeezing each of his arms in his hands. The heaviness of Merlin's heart was moved by Bedwyr's warmth, but his eyes wandered back to look upon Peredur, who continued to stand back grimly in the shadows of the doorway.

Peredur pressed, "What have you to say?"

"Peredur, he has come to us now," Bedwyr said, turning to face him. "Can we not be happy that at least he has returned? Have we all not paid enough penance?"

Merlin's eyes stayed locked with Peredur's, unsure how to respond. He was not yet willing to explain his absence.

Bedwyr continued, "I am overcome with amazement! We dared to hope, but thought you were dead." Then, in a tone more serious, he asked, "What has kept you away from us, friend? I want to be angry, but my relief of seeing you has overruled it."

Peredur's eyes were wild as he stared Merlin squarely in the face. He was known for his strength, and his stature toward Merlin was threatening.

Finally, Merlin said, "Peredur, I meant no ill toward you in staying away." He felt unsure he deserved the chance to defend himself, however his words seemed to soften Peredur, revealing the hurt in his eyes as he cast his gaze to the floor, forcing Merlin to consider what his absence had created.

Peredur clenched his hands at his side and lifted his chin a bit higher. "When Arthur's time came, I was at least consoled that you would be here to guide us. Never did I dream we would lose you both," he snapped, locking his strong jaw. He scanned Merlin's face, as if looking to find something in his eyes that would give him a clue. Merlin remained unmoved, and Peredur could see that his need for answers was falling flat on the floor. His shoulders slumped downward and unclenched his hands as the fight began to leave him. "Boy!" Peredur called, waving his hand at the young lad. "What are you doing just standing there in the shadows? Bring the welcome cup. Go!" The boy left and returned quickly with a large bowl full of ale, tripping and splashing some over the sides and onto the floor. "Slow down, boy, or you'll spill!" Peredur yelled, yanking the bowl out of the boy's hands and shoving it into Merlin's chest. Ale spilt over onto Merlin's tunic as Peredur demanded, "Drink!"

Merlin stood still, unable to swallow any of the sweet ale offered him by his friend. He felt like he was being tested. Then, as if caught like a thief, Merlin stiffened as Gwynevere walked into the Hall. Her presence struck Merlin to his core, and he quickly turned to set the bowl down beside him. His every fear rose to the surface. The air in the room was tense and thick as she stood before him, beautiful and commanding.

She lifted her chin high, her eyes fierce.

Merlin saw very quickly; this was not the Gwynevere he had left behind. This Gwynevere was high queen, and her presence was severe and lofty. She walked lightly toward Merlin as though gliding on water. Her hair was long and raven, and the dress she wore flowed about her with regal authority. She came to stand in front of Merlin, the very air of her presence intimidating. Merlin could see that she was holding tears back as she pressed her lips into a thin, tense line. Grief and anger passed in waves over her face.

Unsure of what to say, Merlin stared at the floor, unable to hold her gaze any longer. Timidly, he said, "I am sorry, Gwynevere."

Without warning, her hand flew, quick like a viper's strike, leaving a sting of pain across his face. The shock of the slap struck his heart, forcing him to steady himself on the inside as well as the outside.

A tear slipped from Gwynevere's eye as she seethed, "Not a word from you?" Her whole body trembled. "You were not supposed to leave with him and never return. You..." She paused to gather herself and took a deep breath. "I knew Arthur would die when you left. I saw it in his eyes as you sailed him away, though I dared not believe it," she gasped as she stilled her breathing to keep her emotions still inside her chest. "I needed your help. What has kept you away?"

Merlin knew nothing he could say would justify his choice to stay away. As he spoke, he felt the flood of emotion toiling within him. "Grief. I had come to my end. I will not ask your forgiveness for that." His chin quivered with the anguish unlocking within him.

Gwynevere stepped back and peered into Merlin's face. "I do not understand your meaning," she replied sharply. "I wanted to hide away. I had to continue on... all the while I have felt death and despair. I had to do what was before me, many times feeling as little as I could. I picked up the crown so that all would not fall into ruin. I couldn't hide away."

Her rebuke was a blade to his heart, and it made him feel the shame he had wished to evade.

"The kings of these lands have been silent, and I know not if they have accepted my rulership. I have felt strongly that I am only biding my time until I am overthrown." Her hand pointed to both Bedwyr, and Peredur. "I only still rule because of these men here. They are loyal to me and have stood by my side. What have you?" she asked, her eyes wide.

Gwynevere's words pulled a string of guilt within Merlin. He had never considered that his actions would have been interpreted as disloyalty. He had been justified within his own mind and believed grief was owed him. How could she not understand that something had died inside him? That he had nothing to give, and still was unsure if there was any value in his return.

"I have had nowhere to escape to," she continued. "Nowhere to hide. I wanted to be Arthur's queen, not high ruler of these lands. Though if I had not ruled, then all that Arthur had fought for would be in ruins. It is still in threat... What of you, Merlin?" Gwynevere asked again. Her face drew nearer, her eyes not allowing him to look away.

He now felt the shame he knew would come and was struggling to resist it. It pressed upon him like a dam unable to hold back the reservoir. It was what he had expected when he chose to return. It was what he did not want to face, but now here he was.

Gazing at the mighty queen, he swallowed the hard knot that had formed in his throat. "I can say nothing of my choice, my lady. I have owed you more. I felt my life was forfeit, and I could not find myself. Every purpose within me died. I had become old and useless."

She shook her head, refusing his excuse. "Useless are never any of the deeds of Merlin." She lifted the welcome cup and handed it back to Merlin, holding it firmly into his chest.

Merlin knew drinking from this cup meant that he had been welcomed in, but it also meant that he would have to give a greater account for himself. Drinking from the cup meant he could not abandon them again. It meant there was no turning back.

"We have all suffered much in grief. The years have been enough of a burden, and I will not add to it for any of us." With that, she stepped back and opened her arms, inviting Bedwyr and Peredur closer in. "Drink, Merlin. Your return has awakened much grief, though it has also offered us hope."

Merlin slowly lifted the great bowl to his lips, feeling the great humility of his welcome. He then passed the cup to Peredur, and they all partook, one by one, until the cup was drained. As they drank, Peredur began to smile, and both he and Bedwyr placed their hands upon Merlin welcoming their mystic brother home.

34

"Uri!" Gwynevere called to the servant boy. "Have a fire set and food brought up from the kitchens. We must talk together. There is much that needs to be said."

4

CILAEN

"**M**erlin!" came a shout from across the Hall. "I knew you'd come back to us. I always believed we would see you again." Merlin's spirit lifted as he recognized the young man's voice. Through a dark corridor in the back of the Hall he stood, tall and lanky, wearing a red healer's robe over his shirt and breaches. His brown curly hair was tied neatly behind his head, and his smile lit up the whole of the room.

It was Cilaen.

Cilaen was Merlin's young friend and filidh pupil. Merlin had been training him in the bardic arts and healing ways of the druids. He was only thirteen when Merlin took him in, and nineteen when Merlin left. His brown eyes were bright and always full of promise. It seemed nothing had changed in him, except that now he was much more a man.

It saddened Merlin that he had so easily forgotten Cilaen in his grief. How easily he had forgotten about all of them.

Giving Merlin a whole-hearted embrace, Cilaen said, "I am happy to see you, brother."

Merlin's eyes dampened as he placed his hands on both sides of Cilaen's face. "How did you know I would return, when I knew not whether I would myself?" Merlin asked with genuine happiness for the first time in years.

"I knew the Great Merlin would return," Cilaen said with a wide smile, looking up. "I never doubted."

A smile stretched across Merlin's face. "Well, my brother, I have to admit, seeing you has brought me a most joyful heart."

"Join us!" Peredur shouted as they sat down at the board, while food and drink were being set before them. Merlin wrapped his arm around Cilaen, pulling him along with him to the table.

Merlin ate until he was full, feeling truly warm and satisfied. Food and good company made his heart ache as he felt the loss of time and companionship he had denied himself.

After the clamor of eating and drinking settled, the queen leaned in. "Merlin. What has brought you home?"

He hesitated as all eyes set upon him, each begging to hear something true. Merlin glanced at each of them, considering what to say.

"I have resisted, my lady," Merlin said, pausing to gather his thoughts. "Only, I began to dream a dream that will not let me go. It is not a passing dream, but a dream of knowing. A dream of prophecy. I have not dreamt in this way since before I sailed away, nor did I expect that I ever would again." As he spoke, an authority settled upon him. The strange spark of prophecy that had evaded him these four long years flowed out. "Something is shifting."

The atmosphere of the room shifted at his words, becoming ecstatic with magic and hope. All of them leaned in.

"There will come a promised one! I do not know when, or for what reason, but I know that she is important. She calls to me in my dreams, and her call is one of awakening and choice. When she comes to us, I believe it will set both good and evil in motion." He glanced at Gwynevere. "It has to do with Arthur, but I know not how. We must establish the New Way once more. Though our obedience will provoke the darkness to manifest…it is already rising…I can feel it! The promise is the very gift Arthur brought, being offered again."

"Arthur?" Gwynevere said, taken aback.

"Something is amiss, Gwynevere, but the promised kingdom may yet come. The woman I have dreamt of is in my mind much like Arthur was before he was born. She is somehow far away and has not been meant to be. Things may have a chance to be put right…" As Merlin spoke, he was surprised by his own hope.

It was as though someone else spoke through him. For he still did not want to believe in anything. But even as he prophesied, the shifting began, and he became aware that there was nothing he could do to stop his involvement in what followed.

"How are we to know her?" Gwynevere asked. "Do we search for her?"

"I will know her. I know her face. I believe she will be easily found, and the time is soon. For it is imminent in my sight."

"This is a strange word you bring us, but there is a feeling of expectation in what you say," Gwynevere admitted, staring deeply at him. "Does this mean you have come back to us to stay?"

Merlin simply replied, "I have no other direction to go."

"You and Arthur were the bearers of the New Ways. Establishing the new kingdom and uniting our lands. Arthur thought the Holy Cup would be the signet of the new age, but he did not find it, and in searching almost lost the kingdom." Gwynevere pursed her lips bitterly then continued, "And now what is to be our hope? A mysterious woman? She will be our guide? No, Merlin, it needs to be you. You are the one that stood by Arthur. You are the one that raised him up. You are the Kingmaker in these lands, and those troublesome kings of the south know it. Now that you have returned, maybe the unsteadiness of this kingdom will become strong. They know the authority you carry and may not cast their gaze so lightly at Arthur's queen."

The day wore on unto night. Gwynevere retired to her chambers while Peredur and Bedwyr had successfully drunk themselves asleep at the long table. The young servant boy Uri had also fallen asleep by the hearth fire, snuggled up against one of the Palisade hounds. Merlin and Cilaen had passed from conversation into deep thought, side by side staring into the flames.

While the fire light danced in Cilaen's eyes, he said, "I did know you'd come back."

Merlin shook his head, wondering what had made Cilaen so confident in him. "I had no intention of returning. Still Avalon calls me," Merlin replied. The sweet songs the monks rang in his memory as he remembered hoping they would take him to his death one day. As Merlin glanced at Cilaen, and then at Peredur and Bedwyr, he felt regret. "I am afraid I had all but forgotten you, until now. I had let you all go."

"The way I saw it," Cilaen said with a short, dull laugh, "whether you knew it or not, what grace of magic you held inside of you was still needed in this world. One way or another, we would find you here again."

"You put too much trust in me."

"Maybe so. But the truth is, you have come back," Cilaen said, gazing at Merlin from the corner of his eye. "And with a promise. No one else has done such a thing in the years you have been gone. All has been grievously silent."

Merlin did not want to tell Cilaen that he did not want to be what Prydain needed. He did not want to be the one with purpose or promises; to be the kingmaker, or the one Prydain relied upon once again. This was what he was running from. The disappointment of trying again still heavy upon him, yet he felt forced to do it anyway. He wanted to be grateful that Cilaen believed in him, but the look in Gwynevere's eyes at the sight of him was proof that one day, Cilaen would also look at him that way. Angry and disappointed.

"I still have your harp and your things. They have all been saved in your old chamber next to mine. I have stayed here, having learned much of the art of healing, and the queen employs me as a healer."

Merlin smiled, patting Cilaen's back. "This is good. I am proud. You were always talented at healing. I am sure the queen has been lucky to have your gifts."

"I may have healed the queen and many of the people of the Palisade, but in the depths of their hearts, they remain wounded. Their spirit is broken. Festivals and celebrations are rare, and only held in obligated tradition."

"Strange that you say this," Merlin remarked, "for as I came riding it seemed Caer Lial was as alive as it has ever been."

Cilaen shook his head. "It is not as it seems. Truly, all have been in dark despair. They move and go about their business, but in lifelessness. Your appearance today seemed to shake them." He paused briefly. "The warriors, thanks to Peredur and Bedwyr, have always been at the ready, always training, as if they have been waiting for Arthur to command them again. The kings of the Southlands do not support Gwynevere as queen and have become increasingly menacing. They fight amongst themselves and stomp over the settlements and villages as they go. They have been an increasing threat, and an anxiety to us all. Peace has been exchanged for instability. The High Kingship Arthur had over all the land's rulers has not rested upon Gwynevere." He turned to look at Merlin. "The whole of Prydain has been waiting for you—or Arthur, or someone." Cilaen halted, seeing Merlin lost in his thoughts. "Come, let us turn into our beds. I am sure there will be much for us both to do come morning."

Chapter Four

Merlin followed Cilaen up a set of stairs leading out of the Hall. They entered a passage just above the courtyard to the door of the very chamber where Merlin had once lived. Memories raced through his mind as they pressed open the door and into the room, his thoughts now full of the times he held counsel with Arthur within this chamber. Herbs and bottles now lined the room, along with Cilaen's tablets and books, which lay about the floor and on the shelves.

Pressing through the memories, Merlin walked to the back of the room, through a door where he entered his very own room, kept in the very same way he had left it. His harp leaned against a wall, his table and chair still piled with his books and parchments. A large urn sat beside the table with scrolls filled with his writings. In the center of the table lay his golden brooch of two emerald-eyed horses twisted together, and the silver torc he once wore. Both were tokens of his long past of council with kings and lords of war.

In that moment, Merlin remembered taking them off before he sailed away with Arthur, already deciding that he would not return. Now they sat there glaring at him, making him feel bitter, as if life itself were mocking him.

Merlin ran his fingers through his hair, gripping handfuls of it in frustration. He sank down onto a small bed that sat at the back of the room as a cool breeze blew in from the window just above him. He could see the stars. A tired peace began to settle upon him. Now, for the first time since he had left on his journey from Avalon, Merlin allowed himself to feel his weariness. Sleep began to call him, and he hoped he would rest in a place where no more dreams would find him.

5

ELANOR

Beep! Beep! Beep! Beep!

The irritating sound of Elanor's alarm clock woke her up. She groaned, reaching blindly for the alarm, finally slapping the snooze button with her fingers. Her eyes slowly focused to see that it was 6:00 a.m. Normally Elanor had no trouble with mornings, always finding it easy to rise and shine. But today was different. She lay in bed, blinking at the ceiling, considering whether or not to make an excuse to stay in bed. She had to be to work by 8:00 a.m., so she could do nothing but get ready.

Today was her twenty-third birthday, and she preferred to be alone. Her birthday was definitely not a special event for her—only an annual reminder of her unimportance. Her mother made sure of this. Growing up, this day was deliberately forgotten—never a present or cake to celebrate. Her father often snuck her treats and gifts, but it only made things worse. If her mother discovered the gifts, she would take them away and berate her father for it.

Now that she was grown and was living in the city, her father would drive in to have lunch with her, but in recent years, she was lucky to receive a phone call.

"I hate birthdays," Elanor groaned, rubbing her eyes before getting out of bed. She half-heartedly determined not to be beaten by this day. *I will just treat today as any other day.* Pressing a button on her coffee maker, she listened to the machine whir as coffee dripped into the pot. She poured the warm, aromatic drink into her favorite mug, sipping it carefully as she stood in front of her painting.

Elanor was an artist and made a habit of sitting in front of her canvas each morning when her mind was fresh, adding a few strokes and lines to her work in progress.

Cocking her head sideways, she stared at the blurry portrait she had been working on. It was the face of a man she had been seeing in her dreams, night after night, over the past few months. She hoped she could capture his details so she could clearly see him. His brown curled hair and soft eye lashes. The curve of his long nose, and the tilt at the corner of his mouth. Most mysteriously, he had beautiful, golden-colored eyes that glowed like the eyes of a hawk.

She dipped her brush into the paint, adding more yellow to the brightness of his eyes. There was something about him; something about this dream. He seemed so real, and Elanor wanted—almost needed—to know him. Taking another sip of coffee, she squinted at the details. Maybe this man she painted would not see her as a shadow.

"Oh, Elanor, such the romantic," she said, half laughing, half sighing.

Elanor was unknown by all the people in her life. A fact that should have made her sad, but she was used to it; she lived hidden behind a veil, deep down knowing that there was something inside of her she could never quite let out. Like a treasure waiting to be revealed, yet there was no map.

Adding some final touches to the canvas with her brush, she knew it was time to get ready. Elanor stood and began to sing. She liked to sing while she got ready in the morning; the sound of her voice reverberating in the shower made her feel happy. Her favorite songs to sing were tunes she used to listen to with her father while he played outside in the garden as a child. No one bothered them out there.

She looked at herself in the mirror as she hummed, one last look before she headed out the door for work. Her shiny, dark brown hair was tied up in a pony and her blue eyes sparkled as she smiled in approval of her outfit.

Elanor worked as an intern for an advertising firm as a graphic designer in cold and windy Cardiff, a bustling city in the South of Wales. She was one of a team of six. She didn't love it, but it was the only career she could find that fit her as an artist. Her mother thought her art was stupid and refused to pay for her schooling. "I refuse to invest in a 'poor, starving artist,'" she'd once said. Still, the job had its perks. She could be creative, and even as an intern she was getting paid something.

Chapter Five

The sky was clear and the air was cool as she left her flat to walk to work. Her office wasn't far from where she lived. She pulled her sweater closer as she went, for the chill was sinking in. On the way, she stopped at her favorite café. She loved how they frothed the milk just right in her latte, and their homemade cinnamon twists were delectable.

"Elanor?" Bill called out as she walked in the door. "I've got your coffee on the counter, dear. Oh, and I almost forgot to mention, a man has been asking about one of your paintings. He wants to know what price you've put on it. He left me his number, and I told him I'd call him and let him know what you'd said."

Bill was the owner of The Cuppa Café. He loved his customers, and he loved that Elanor was one of his regulars. He was short, red-headed and balding. Once in his café, Bill always had a smile and a story. While his employees busied themselves with customers and cleaning the shop, he was found leaning over the counter, greeting everyone as they came in. He never forgot a face, and people loved that about him. For Elanor, he always had a cup to go when she came in the morning, and a cup of tea upon her return in the evenings. Sometimes, she would sit and sketch a while in one of the corner chairs before returning home.

"Which painting?" Elanor asked.

Bill pointed across the room. "Oh, that one there with the dragon-looking creature on it." Everyone in the café turned to look, and Elanor's cheeks reddened with embarrassment. She didn't like people knowing the paintings were hers.

"Oh, Bill, I am not sure I could sell it. Could someone really be all that interested?"

Shouting loudly for all to hear, he said, "This man was certain. At the right price, he seemed he might want to buy the whole lot."

The spectacle Bill made over her paintings while the other patrons overheard was almost unbearable. Elanor never really liked having much attention anyway, and it hadn't been her idea to have her work on display. Were it not for Bill, they wouldn't have been there at all.

Oh, but Bill loved them! It all started one day with one of her sketches, as she sat sipping tea in the back corner of the café. Bill was puttering around with too few customers around to tell his stories to, so he sneaked over to spy in on Elanor as she drew.

"Oh, what's this?" Bill asked, leaning his head over her sketch as though it weren't an intrusion.

"This?" Elanor said, surprised. She brought her drawing pad in flat against her chest to conceal it. "It's just a doodle. It's nothing."

"Nothing?" Bill chided. "Hah! Let me see."

Reluctantly, Elanor let her drawing be revealed and nervously looked up at Bill as he examined her art. She hated the vulnerable feeling of her art being seen.

With a genuine sparkle in his eye, he said, "Aih! These whorls and patterns! The horses! Elanor, you are a wonderful artist! Do you have more, my dear? Any large paintings I could hang up here in the shop?"

"Oh, Bill, I couldn't."

"Haven't you even one painting I could display?"

Bill worked on her for weeks. He began making a habit of looking over her shoulder to see whatever she was working on, and finally, the flattery had gotten to her. Against her better judgement, Elanor brought one of her paintings in. That was how it all began, with the enthusiastic café owner's compliments. One at a time, slowly, more and more of her art hung on the walls, but always Elanor was at peace that at least no one knew they were hers.

That was until this morning, as Bill so loudly pointed them out to be hers in front of everyone in the café. Their eyes looked upon her, then turned to look at her paintings. She could see in some of the faces a mix of opinions as they peered at her strange creations. She cringed on the inside as a lady turned to her husband and said, "These are rather odd, don't you think?" The woman obviously did not realize how far her voice carried.

Elanor put her coins on the counter and grabbed her coffee. "Thank you, Bill. I will let you know."

Bill shouted after her with a smile, "Alright, dearie, see you this evenin' for tea!"

Elanor walked out the café as quickly as she could.

She loved her paintings, but even she felt them to be rather odd and was unsure why anyone would want to buy one of them. She painted images she never could clearly see, because that was how her memories were: strangely faded pictures with blended colors and hazy lines.

Her favorite was a painting of only the bottom half of a horse. Its white legs ran gracefully through tall, green grass, but there was no head or top half. It was like she had seen the horse before, a memory struggling to rise to the surface. She could feel the fresh air and hear the horse's hooves beating the ground. She could even smell the grass. Had she been there? She had never even ridden a horse before.

Faces and landscapes were the same; she would grasp to recall them, but they were always faded and far away. For Elanor, that is how she saw pictures in her mind, and she painted them like that on purpose. All of them, half there, just like she was. Painting helped her make sense of her world, and whether anybody else got the chance to see them mattered very little to her.

As she entered the office, every eye turned in her direction. Even those of Demetri Palmer. Quickly, Elanor turned and took a sip of her coffee as if she didn't notice him.

Demetri was a piece of work, and he had an irritating habit of follow-ing her around the office, determined to con her into a date. He was handsome and mighty proud of his athletic build; he clearly believed himself to be God's gift to women.

Elanor couldn't stand him, finding him to be a weasel. Unfortunately, her indifference only made him more persistent.

"Elanor!" he shouted as he dashed across the office to walk alongside her. "Good morning, gorgeous," he said with a wink. "It's Friday! I could ditch the lads after work and take you for a pint instead?"

Dismissively, she said, "No, thanks, Demetri." She sped up to reach her desk where she knew she would have the backup of her desk mate and friend Jess. Jess gave a knowing look as she saw Elanor dashing toward her desk with Demetri on her tail.

"Good morning, Demetri!" Jess said, stepping around her desk just in time to come between them. "Good morning, Elanor"—she leaned in and shoved Elanor with her elbow—"and happy birthday!"

"Ack! Jess! Please don't...you know I do not like the attention."

"Birthday?!" Demetri exclaimed, leaning onto Elanor's desk. "Now you have to let me take you out. Come on; it would be fun. You know you want to... what else are you going to do? Sit at home alone?"

Jess positioned herself more forcefully between them and said, "She has plans with me, Demetri, and you are not invited." Demetri looked at both girls skeptically, then finally said to Elanor, "Call me when you come to your senses." He walked away then, turning around once more, held his hand to his ear like a phone, mouthing, "Call me."

Relieved, Elanor plopped onto her chair. "Thanks for that!"

Jess smiled and then asked with a lowered voice, "What are you going to do tonight? We could hang out...I mean, it's your birthday."

"Listen, Jess, I am just not that into birthdays, alright? We can hang out some other time. Besides, I do have a sort of plan," she said, turning to her computer and starting it up.

"Okay, you know you can't leave me with that. What plan?"

Elanor sighed loudly. "Fine. You know that dream I've been having?"

"You're still having that dream? The one with Merlin, the Great Wizard of Camelot?"

"No! Er…I mean, yes. I mean—" Elanor's face flushed with embarrassment. "Yes, the dream with a person *called* Merlin. But no, not the Great Wizard of Camelot. Whatever that means. Maybe it sounds a bit silly to you, but these dreams just won't go away. The only thing I understand about them is this person, Merlin. And, well…I thought maybe it would help if I actually read about the only Merlin I have ever heard of. I don't know, I guess I thought I would go to a bookstore on my way home and see if I could find a book about King Arthur and Merlin, or something. All I know about him is what I've seen in movies. An old wizard in a blue pointy hat, and that is not the person I have been dreaming of. Still, I'm curious what the stories might say about him."

Jess gave a knowing smile. "Oh, so the Merlin in your dreams has no pointy hat, but might give Demetri a run for his money, eh?"

"Jess!" Elanor exclaimed, snagging a paper clip and throwing it at her friend.

"Okay, okay!" Jess giggled. "So, your plan is to spend the whole weekend reading about King Arthur and his non-pointy-hatted friend?"

"Well, yes. And maybe drink some wine," Elanor said with a smile.

The bookstore wasn't far from where Elanor lived, and the walk in the cool of the evening helped her clear her mind from the day's mundane tasks at work. Her thoughts eventually drifted to Merlin—he was the only thing she could think of since the dreams had begun. She had to keep reminding herself that he was not an actual person. He was just a dream. But it didn't feel like a dream. This idea, as crazy as Jess thought it was, was the best one Elanor had. In many ways, she felt like an obsessed teenager, but she was only going down this strange path for the weekend. At least that is what she told herself.

The bell on the door of the old bookstore jingled as she walked in. She headed to the back of the shop to where she knew the fiction books were kept.

"Fiction?" she asked herself.

She wasn't quite sure if the book she was looking for would be in fiction, or in some special section for legends and such. She was familiar with the bookshop, as she loved to read, and was sure she had seen some books about King Arthur along those shelves.

As she rounded the corner, she saw that the section was already occupied by an older gentleman scanning the pages of a book he held in his hands. *King Arthur and His Knights.* Elanor was surprised at the coincidence. As she walked deeper into the aisle, he looked up from his book, smiled tenderly, and said, "Hello…"

MAGIC

"Hi..." Elanor said hesitantly, never one for small talk with strangers. While in public, she preferred not to be bothered, yet this old man had captured her attention.

He nodded at her and continued perusing his book, thumbing through the pages of the very book she had been looking for. Her curiosity grew as she observed the elderly man. He appeared a gentle and friendly sort of man, so pursuing a bit of conversation with him seemed harmless.

He gave her a sideways glance as she smiled and asked, "King Arthur, huh?"

"King Arthur? Oh, uh...yes," he bumbled as if caught by the question. "Is that the sort of book you are looking for? Maybe something with magic?"

She laughed. "I suppose, yes." She scanned the bookshelves, as if waiting for another book about King Arthur to jump out at her. "The thing is...I had a dream, and I am doing a bit of research." She shook her head, wondering why she was telling him this. "Not that books about magic should help me discover anything. Not even really sure I am looking in the right place." She shrugged. "Though books with a bit of magic are always the best kind."

He leaned in a little, his eyes inquisitive. "Do you have magic, I wonder?"

"What? Me have magic?" she laughed, rolling her eyes. What an absurd question. Then she began to feel strange, as if the question begged to unearth something trapped within her. "That is a very strange question."

"Is it?" the man responded, watching her closely.

Elanor was a bit floored by his response. "When a strange man in a book shop asks me if I have magic, I should think he's crazy and find a new section of books to browse."

Already this conversation had taken her places she wouldn't normally tread, yet the old man's face seemed so safe, almost familiar. That alone urged her to continue speaking to him. Somehow, she was drawn in; be it from the book he held or his knowing smile, something told her that to turn around and leave would be a terrible mistake.

"Okay," she finally said. "As a child, I use to believe I had magic." She waited for his reaction.

Curiously enough, there was no change. His eyes shone a deep interest and a barely discernible smile fell across his lips.

"My father told me it wasn't good to keep pretending I had magic. I didn't know I was only pretending." A strange pang of sadness struck her heart as she spoke. "But I remember…" Her voice trailed off.

"What do you remember?" the man kindly urged.

"Feeling sad…" Elanor said, her words now just above a whisper.

"Elanor, I told you to stop with this idea of magic. It is only going to get you in trouble," her father said severely, smacking a flower out of a young Elanor's hand.

The memory struck Elanor deeply. She couldn't remember what it was that she was doing with the flower, but she could remember her hurt and how confused she'd felt. What had she done that was so bad?

"I haven't thought about any of this for a long time. Maybe my father was right. I mean, it probably was just my imagination anyway."

"What was the magic you were supposed to have imagined?" he continued, coaxing her thoughts to the surface.

Elanor stopped and thought for a moment. "I…I knew things. I thought I could look at someone and see them. *Really* see them. I could know their mind and feelings…sometimes even know who they would be. It was just my imagination, as my father had said." She shook her head. "I think I even imagined healing a bird once. It had flown into the window, unaware of the glass." She stopped for a second, lost in memory. "Once revived, my father said it had probably just been unconscious. There was more, I think...I don't remember."

The old man listened intently. His calm gaze did not make her feel what she shared had been foolish. "I think," he said, "that you must still have magic, or else why are you talking to me? I am just a strange old man you happened upon in this book shop. But you felt something—a pull, a sense, a feeling, and so you talked with me." He paused, looking at her intently. "Listen, would you do this old mad man a favor? Would you look into my eyes and tell me what you see? Just like you did when you were a child?"

Elanor stiffened, suddenly uncomfortable. Her mind sobered at his request. This was all too strange. Was she really going to look into the eyes of this stranger and hope for something to happen? Though, something inside coaxed her to press into this mysterious moment.

"I don't know why I am doing this..." she replied reluctantly. "No guarantees."

She stepped closer and looked deep into his eyes. Only a second passed before she began to feel absolutely foolish.

She shook her head and stepped back. "What am I doing? I'm sorry, I am not sure where all of this is leading, and this is all getting a little strange. I almost convinced myself for a second that something was going to happen." She sighed, rubbing her forehead, and turned to leave.

"Elanor!" The urgency in the old man's voice stopped her cold. Her heart raced as she tried to remember whether or not she had told him her name. "Do not run away. Come back," he said, so tenderly that she immediately felt somehow safe.

Elanor turned around slowly. "How do you know my..."

"Try again," he encouraged as he held his hand out to her. "You will remember. It will come to you. The magic is there."

She let out a deep breath, still unsure whether his request wasn't entirely crazy, and approached him once again. Grabbing hold of his hand, she gazed up into his eyes.

"Peer into my eyes, and then see beyond them. It's there. In the thoughts and memories within your heart and mind."

Who is this old man? He was making her understand that their meeting in this book shop was not by chance. He was there intentionally for her. *But why?* she wondered. *Who am I? Who is he?*

Emotions rose within her heart—emotions that were not her own.

The old man's eyes seemed to fade away, and in their place lurked a deep sadness. Within moments, images swiftly passed through her mind. Like photographs, Elanor saw people and places she did not recognize, and they moved so quickly, she hardly had the chance to single one out. She could feel deep love, great loss, and finally she saw what appeared to be a white dove flying away. She swore she heard its wings as it flew by, and then out of her thoughts. All the while, a fire burned inside her chest.

Suddenly, all she saw were the tender, beautiful eyes of the stranger whose hand she held.

"Do I know you?" she asked, struck by his odd familiarity.

"I cannot say," he said with a knowing smile. "What did you see?"

"You are grieved." Emotions swelled in her throat as she spoke. "You have lost someone you loved. Perhaps many, I think. You have seen many things in your life."

Tears welled up into the old man's eyes.

"But I feel the loss is almost over. Somehow things are changing for you now. You will not be alone much longer."

The old man let out a breath of emotion. He placed his hands over his eyes as tears rolled down his cheeks. "So, you see? You do have magic." He wiped his eyes. "Thank you for that. You cannot know what this has meant." Gathering himself, he took a moment before speaking again. "I have something I would like to give you, to say thank you for humoring an old man." He held a leather satchel, and out of it he pulled a little blue book. "Faery stories." He pointed at the cover. "It is very old, and you will not be able to read the words. They are in an older language, but there are beautiful pictures within it. This book is very special; it belonged to someone important to me."

Elanor's eyes widened. "I cannot take your book."

"Please," he insisted with a pained look.

Elanor took the book from his hands. She began to open the book to look inside.

"Oh, no, no, no! Do not open it here. It is very old. Take it home and open it there. There you will be able to look at it better. Not now."

She nodded, placing the blue book in her bag. "I do not know what to say. Thank you?"

"Your father should not have told you that you didn't have magic."

His words reached an aching place within her heart. It was as if she had been waiting for someone to say that to her for a very long time. She placed her hand over her heart, her eyes glistening with tears. Elanor looked up, wishing to know who this mysterious man was.

"King Arthur was not a fiction," he said, handing her the book he had been holding. "And you ought to be careful believing what they have written down in these books about him. They are mistaken."

"Mistaken?"

"Yes, mistaken," he said firmly with a curious smile.

She grabbed the book. "Well, I am not reading the book to learn about Arthur."

"No?"

Elanor nodded. "I am reading it to learn about Merlin."

The old man smiled at this, and as he did, Elanor hesitated a moment, then turned to go. The moment was over, and she could feel it.

"It was nice to meet you," she said, waving over her shoulder. She felt awkward leaving but continued walking anyway.

She bought her book and walked out, the bell jingling a goodbye as she found herself, once again, back out on the street. Suddenly mystified by the whole encounter, she peered down at the book in her hands, realizing something important: She had never mentioned to the mysterious old man her intention to buy a book about King Arthur, nor did she tell him her name.

Walking into her flat, Elanor shut the door and stood leaning against it.

"What a strange thing that was," she said to herself.

She kept thinking about the old man and his eyes. Taking a deep breath, she placed her bags and the book down on the counter, ready to move on.

Elanor's flat was an upstairs, one room studio, with the kitchen at the entrance, and opened up into a large room. There was a bed directly across from the kitchen. To the left, a bathroom, a closet, and then a beautifully decorated floral dressing screen. Then to the right of her bed was a small sofa facing two windows overlooking the street. Within that small space was a stool with her canvas and paints. It was a perfect downtown flat. Perfect because it was small enough to keep her from feeling too lonely in her solitary life, and it helped her to keep things just so in her steady routine and not think too deeply about the cracks in her heart.

Reading was her escape, and her favorite spot to read was on her bed where she could see the whole space.

After a warm shower, she slid into some comfortable night clothes and put the kettle on for some tea. She remembered the little blue book the old man had given her and grabbed her bag to pull it out.

She was curious to take a closer look. It was leather and blue with beautiful crawling vines all along the sides of the cover. It had a strange smell to it, like cedar oil and clove. There were no words on the cover or sides, just a small group of flowers imprinted on the front. She could tell it was a very old and rare book, for she had never seen one quite like it.

The kettle whistled to her. With a steaming hot mug of her favorite tea, she took both books and headed over to her bed, excited to read and investigate more intently.

As Elanor opened the cover to look at the first few pages, her eyes became blurry, and she couldn't quite focus on the pages. She rubbed her eyes and tried again, but it was no better. In fact, now everything in the room looked cloudy. The book suddenly felt quite heavy, and her head began to feel heavy, too. Before she could really give any of this much thought, she had fallen back onto her pillows and fell asleep.

"Elanor!" she heard him call her, like she always did.

The call was distant, but grew slowly clearer, like light piercing through the fog when the sun begins to rise. She heard the hoof beats of a horse approaching, as she had so many times in her dream. She turned to see the horse and its rider. The horse, black and sleek like satin, was armored and beautifully decorated in gold, red, and green. Upon the horse's back was a man, tall and broad. His hair was wavy and golden, and his face, chiseled and intense. He wore a leather breast plate and held in his hand a standard. As he lifted the standard, he pointed toward two stars that sparkled brightly in the sky. His voice thundered as if sounding a battle cry. She could see in the mist behind him the faint shadow of men rising up to follow, holding their spears high. The man upon the horse drew a long sword from its sheath, its metallic ring echoing loudly. The army and their commander were ready for battle.

As this scene unfolded, Elanor was merely a witness, the way it sometimes happens in dreams. She stood afar off in a misty blur of colors and lights. Although she could still hear that familiar voice calling her, she could now see his dark figure moving out of the fog.

"Elanor!" he continued to call.

"Merlin!" she called back.

She longed to reach him, but she never could. A terrible wind would always come and with it, a loud tearing sound so fierce and loud that once it began, it swallowed the sounds of their voices. She could never get any closer before she'd wake up.

Here they were once again. She could see him standing there, both of them looking across this grey, misty chasm.

"Elanor, take my hands." He reached out desperately.

Merlin rushed forward, his eyes fixed upon her. She started toward him, still waiting for the wind to come at any moment.

But something surprising occurred. Reaching each other for the first time, they stood close enough for Elanor to take his hands. Nervously, she gazed up into his eyes. They were golden and beautiful. Everything was quiet; she could hear his breath. His hands still laid open before her, and tentatively, she lifted her hands just above his and stopped.

She had hoped for this moment in every dream and now here it was, yet why wasn't she taking his hands? She had never been this close, and part of her wasn't prepared for things to change. She could hear her heart thumping in her ears as his outstretched hands were just inches beneath hers. She let out a long breath that echoed loudly as she dropped her hands to meet his.

For a short moment, she felt the warmth of his skin on her fingertips, before a bright, white light sprang up around them, blinding them both. Amid the light, she could feel his fingers wrapping around hers. Whatever earth was beneath their feet seemed to crumble away, leaving Elanor to feel like she was floating, disoriented, not knowing which way was up or down.

Finally, her feet alighted on what felt like soft, damp earth. What had been only the sound of her breath and heart beating became a beautiful chorus of leaves rustling and birdsong. The harsh light slowly diminished into pleasant greens and blues, blending together like watercolors.

Elanor blinked as her eyes adjusted to see what was being revealed around her. The colors turned to blue sky and golden-brown meadows of oak and willow. The trees moved with the breeze to welcome her as their branches swayed. The meadow was in the bloom of springtime, and white flowers dotted the grass beneath her. She could smell the fresh scent of earth, flowers, and damp wood.

The warmth of the sun was on her skin, the air moist from a fresh rain. Everything was vivid and alive—real and tangible—not at all like a dream. Lights danced through the air. She now realized her hands were still locked within Merlin's grasp.

Merlin had held her hands tight, his eyes staying upon her. She glanced at him and saw that he, too, was mystified. They had never been to this place before now. They had always been unable to reach one another, however, something had finally happened to change all this.

He placed his hand upon Elanor's cheek and, for the first time, seemed to see her. She leaned into his hand, his touch drawing her in. And suddenly, there stood between them a sense of rightness she had never felt before.

Leaning closer to her ear, Merlin said, "Now, don't let go."

She looked back at him, confused. Within an instant, the terrible wind had returned, filling her with disappointment and dread. She did not want to be taken away from him, not now that she had finally reached him. She wrapped her arms around him tightly, unwilling to let him go. He squeezed her tightly into himself as the wind tore and ripped. The force of the wind slapped and struck, making fools of them both for thinking they could ever truly be in each other's arms. The wind increased, stinging every exposed piece of skin like needles.

Still Elanor held on. Then came a crack and a pulling sensation. Their feet were torn off the ground in two different directions. It felt as if her skin were being pulled from her body.

"Merlin!" she screamed. "Don't let go!" Their hands barely held on, their fingers slowly pulling apart. Panicking, she thought, *Why am I not waking?* She had never had a dream so painful; her heart remained steadfast to hold on. A loud CRACK like lighting ripped through the sky while Elanor's body felt torn to pieces. She no longer knew if she had Merlin in her grip, or if he had her in his. The very air shook and vibrated. Unbearable sounds of thundering and slashing met her ears. They rolled in waves which would suddenly stop and resume again, making her feel as though she had gone deaf. The percussive booming and shredding made it seem as if the very mountains were crumbling. All she could feel was pain searing into every nerve and muscle. Elanor screamed, but she could not hear her own voice, nor could she feel her body beneath her. Until all went dark.

THE DREAM IS OVER

CRACK! The loud sound woke Merlin up, and he was instantly sitting up in his bed. Was he still dreaming, or had he awoken? He looked across the room, and there, just before the edge of his bed, stood the woman from his dream. His eyes widened. Before he had a moment to process her presence, Cilaen bolted through the door.

"Are you well? I heard a loud…" Cilaen halted, seeing a strange woman standing before Merlin. Shocked, he looked at Merlin, and then at the woman.

They both froze, unaware of what to do.

Elanor stood in disbelief, completely disoriented. "Merlin?" she said strangely, feeling weak and unsteady. "Where am I? Am I still dreaming?" The moment she spoke, stinging sensations rapidly filled every part of her body, and she began to tremble. Slowly at first, and then more violently. She threw her head back, clenching her teeth as pain shot through her. Her back arched, and Merlin sprang to catch her as she collapsed. He reached her just in time as she fell into his arms, her eyelashes fluttering and her body seizing. "It hurts so much!" she squeaked out, tears of pain rolling down her cheeks.

Merlin held her close, still perplexed by what was happening. One moment he was dreaming, the next she was here. *Did I do this? Did my magic bring her here?* He didn't know. His heart rent as he watched painful tremors surge through her body.

"Cilaen!" Merlin shouted, shaking him out of his frozen confusion. "Help me. We need to move her to the bed."

"Of course!" Cilaen jumped into action, cradling Elanor's legs under his arms and helping Merlin move her to his bed.

Merlin placed his hand upon her brow, sighing out a long deep breath. Swiftly, he whispered in the old tongue druidic words of healing. *"Iachad fod, codi, llawnder...Iachad fod, codi, llawnder."* His brow perspired with the intensity of his effort.

Cilaen watched as her body continued to shake and convulse. But as Merlin pressed his hand on her forehead, releasing his magic to heal her, her shaking melted into light tremblings. Merlin's anxious whisperings grew calm, and slowly Elanor's body relaxed. She closed her eyes and passed back into sleep. Merlin breathed out intensely, exhausted by his effort. He slid to the floor and sat in a bewildered daze, his eyes transfixed on Elanor.

"Who is she?" Cilaen asked, stunned.

"She...she's the woman from my dream," Merlin voiced in amazement.

"The woman from your dream?"

In utter disbelief, he held his hands out toward her. "Never did I imagine this! This...this is extraordinary."

"What happened?"

"I do not know," Merlin said, closing his eyes to think. "I was dreaming that same dream again, but this time the dream was different. I was able to get to her. I have never been able to in my past dreams. I don't even know why I needed to get to her so badly. I always felt the dream was showing me symbols of her importance. That is why I thought I had always seen myself calling to her. Just symbols." He opened his eyes, looking confused. "I told her not to let go of me, and there was a loud sound, and I awoke to find her standing in front of my bed...In all my life of miracles, I have never seen this. I do not know what has happened."

Cilaen's mouth hung open. He did not know what to think as he glanced over at the stranger laying before him. As he looked, he observed the furrow in her brow and the quickness of her breath.

With urgency Cilaen said, "She still does not look right." Within those few moments, she had turned white as a sheet, her forehead beaded with sweat. Cilaen placed his hand upon her head. "She is hot with fever. We need to get this fever down."

Cilaen hurried from the chamber and returned with a water bowl and some cloth. He laid the bowl next to the bed and handed the cloth to Merlin.

"I must make a poultice." He raced back out of the room.

Merlin looked at the cloth in his hand, and then over at the woman who lay struggling in front of him. The reflection of Arthur struggling from his poisoned wound surged within his thoughts. He dabbed Elanor's forehead with the dampened cloth, then her chest and arms. He had done what he could with magic, and now it was up to Cilaen and his medicines.

"I hope I did not do this to you," he said to her softly. It felt unreal that she could be laying there before him. The responsibility of her presence weighed heavy upon him.

It was just a dream of symbols, he thought, as if trying to convince himself. He had always believed that this Elanor represented a real person, but he did not imagine this would be the way he would come to know her. Her purpose was still not entirely clear. But what bothered him most was how he had felt about her in the dream. The moment he was able to truly see her, it roused his heart. Maybe this feeling had a deeper, other meaning, like his need for hope. Love was not something he wanted. Love always disappointed. Love always led to loss. His life and purpose were beyond these sorts of distractions. Besides, his time for life in this way had passed. Yet he could not deny, now that she was in front of him, literally pulled out of his dream, that there was something real between them. Surely it was just the shock of all these strange events. He would feel more sobered by the rising of the sun.

Cilaen returned with the poultice, and throughout the rest of the night, they aided Elanor in hopes that her fever would break. After several hours, Cilaen grew tired and fell asleep, slumped over in the chair next to Merlin. But Merlin could not rest. His eyes stayed upon Elanor. His thoughts mulled over her every detail—this unexplainable woman. Her manner of clothing neither he nor Cilaen had ever seen before, and she murmured things foreign to them. Everything was baffling. Where had she come from? He would have no answers until she awoke.

Upon the morning, she remained feverish and in a dark sleep.

"She can't have come to us so miraculously, only to become ill and die. What would have been the purpose?" Cilaen encouraged, seeing the anxiousness on Merlin's face.

But Merlin was wrestling with the guilt. He felt the circumstance of Elanor's illness to be his own fault, however unintentional. He felt as he did when he was a boy when he had gone hunting with his grandfather. He was too cavalier and hasty, shooting at a stag, wounding it, but not killing it. His heart broke as he followed the trail of blood, but never did he find the animal. This woman was no stag, and far more valuable besides.

He could not shake the feeling that if his magic had brought her here and killed her, he should have somehow known better. He could not justify that he had no control over his dream, nor the magical result of it. But if he was not to blame, then the blame leaned toward the one who gave the dream.

Each hour she laid there, Merlin's heart longed for her to be well and speak to him once again. He was sure these longings were the result of a desire to see her well, and only that. Her waking would surely clear the cobwebs of his confusion and bring balance into what was happening inside of him.

By the next morning, some change had finally come. Cilaen woke to find the fever had gone. The color had returned to her face, and her cheeks were rosy. Her breathing had returned to normal, and she appeared completely at rest and tranquil, no longer struggling and sick.

"Wake up," Cilaen said, shaking Merlin. "Her fever has gone. She looks well."

Merlin hastened to see the good report for himself. There she laid, looking beautiful and well. One glimpse, and he saw she was entirely changed. He sighed in relief as the stress and worry fell from his shoulders.

Moving into action, Merlin said, "I must see the queen. She will want to know that the girl is improving."

Merlin had informed the queen the very first morning of Elanor's magical arrival and had been ordered to keep her aware of any changes.

He readied himself, splashing his face with water, and threw his leather vest over his tunic. He patted his side, nodded to Cilaen, and walked out the door.

Cilaen warmed a mixture he had prepared in the event that Elanor should wake. As he was busy about his work, adding herbs and roots, he heard a faint moan come from Merlin's bed chamber. It was Elanor. Her eyes flickered slowly, squinting against the bright light coming in through the window. She moved her head and arms ever so slightly as Cilaen now stood by her bedside. It was then that Merlin returned.

Cilaen motioned silently with his arms for Merlin to come see this exciting moment. They both stood before her as she opened her eyes, and they could see the brightness of the blue in them.

She peered back and forth between them. Merlin noticed a flash of recognition in her eyes as she saw him. She sat up suddenly, then grabbed her head and collapsed forward.

"Hush!" Cilaen said gently. "You have been sick. You are not ready for such movement." Merlin helped lay her back down and placed a pillow behind her head while Cilaen retrieved the mixture he had made, knowing she may need some to mend.

Cilaen returned with a bowl in his hands and sat near her. "Here, drink this. It will help."

She scowled at him strangely. Merlin helped her to sit up as she took a sip from the bowl.

"Slowly!" Cilaen encouraged.

She stopped drinking. Confused, she said, "I do not understand your language. Where am I?"

Struck by the sound of her words, Cilaen said to Merlin, "She does not speak our Cymry tongue. What language is that? It is not Latin. Is it a form of Saecsan speech?"

"I do not know what you speak of," Merlin said, surprised. "I understand her words perfectly."

"I can understand what *you* say," Elanor said timidly to Merlin.

Merlin paused, trying to work out what was happening.

Cilaen pressed his brows together, befuddled. "You understand what she is saying?"

"Yes..." Merlin replied. *Was this another form of magic?* Gazing into her weary eyes, he said, "You are in Caer Lial. The Kingdom once ruled by the Pendragon, and now ruled by his queen, Gwynevere. This is my good friend, Cilaen. He is a healer, and you can trust him. I am Merlin. We… have never truly met."

Elanor laughed out loud. Her laughter caused her to wince in pain once again. "Is this a joke? You're Merlin, and we're in the kingdom ruled by Gwynevere?"

"She needs to lie down," Cilaen said, worried.

Laying back with her hands over her eyes, Elanor said, "Heh, next you're going to tell me there is a King Arthur and a Camelot. Maybe a Lancelot and a roundtable, too. I'm definitely delirious, and possibly hallucinating."

"You need to rest some more. We have excited you too much. I do not know what has brought you here, but I think you might be a long way from home. We can try to get you back home if that is what you want, but for now, just rest."

For a moment, Elanor studied Merlin with her eyes. She seemed comforted by his presence, and it wasn't long before she drifted back to sleep. Before she closed her eyes completely, however, she reached her hand to him.

As he cupped her hand in his, a white light flashed before his eyes. He was instantly in a vision. He had had visions like this before when the awen came upon him. The awen, a gift of sight to see into the realm of the spirit. This awen came at the touch of Elanor's hand, and suddenly he found himself standing on a hill in the Otherworld. A world where the enaid, spirits of this realm, would reveal signs and omens of the Great God.

In this vision he saw a great oak tree, but all around the light was so bright he saw nothing else. He raised his arm up over his head to shield his eyes. The light grew brighter. Walking up over the hill toward him was a man, but because of the brightness, all he could see was a dark silhouette. For a moment, Merlin wondered whether the light was around the man, or whether the light radiated from him. As the man came closer, he saw more details about his appearance. His eyes were bright, and he had a smile on his face. He wore a light blue tunic, but Merlin could not make out the detail of his face. The man in blue approached him and held out his hand. Merlin feared to not take the man's hand would be to his detriment, so he reached out and took it. And as he did, a fire went through his body, and all else faded away. He no longer saw the man in blue, the hill, or the tree, but he heard his voice.

The voice came from every direction, from in front, behind, and inside him, completely encompassing him. The voice reminded him of the sound of the great wind of the dream. The voice was much greater than he was, and the words were unknown to him. Merlin was ashamed, thinking himself a master of anything. He suddenly felt so small and helpless, and realized that he knew nothing. All the years Merlin had spent gaining in wisdom meant nothing as the light encompassed him within its great strength.

Then, the voice faded, and all became quiet and still. He found himself on the hill again, with the tree behind him. The radiating light had faded, but in his heart, he was overcome and humbled. Then, the voice came again. This time, it was gentle and warm, and this time, Merlin understood the words.

They echoed within his mind, "You have a splinter in your heart, Merlin. It must be removed. She can help you. She has healing, and she has hope within her. She is important. You need her to become whole. The coming darkness will not prevail against you if your heart is full."

In one swift moment, the awen had lifted. Merlin found himself in the room with Cilaen and Elanor. He looked at Elanor, mystified. He breathed heavily. The vision had shaken him greatly on the inside, and he felt as if he had withstood a windstorm.

"Are you alright, Merlin?" Cilaen asked. "The awen had taken you, I think. Was it a powerful vision?"

Merlin leaned forward and placed his hand on his chest before nodding. "I have never felt its like. I am undone."

"What did you see?"

"It is hard to explain," he said breathlessly. "There was a man in blue, and...." Merlin looked at Elanor, who lay there, breathing softy, calm and serene. "I was wrong, I think," he said finally. "Not about everything, but my understanding has been so limited. I still do not understand, except to say it is beyond me." He touched Elanor's arm. "She is important. I do not believe she knows it... but she needs to help me in some way. A darkness is coming, and I cannot be prepared for it without her."

WAKING ON THE OTHER SIDE

L ater that evening, Elanor awoke. Her head had stopped aching and spinning, and she could think more clearly. Her mind flooded with the impossibility before her. This place was definitely not her flat. She remembered returning home and sitting down to read. Her mind raced to remember what had happened after that. Slowly, she recalled the dream, and then the wind and the pain. Her heart pounded anxiously as she remembered that final moment of finding herself standing in this very room.

Then there was the confusion of waking, feeling very ill, and a strange man who spoke with unusual words. And Merlin…MERLIN! The very man from her dream had been sitting next to her—telling her that she was in a kingdom ruled by Gwynevere? She *had* to be dreaming…yet here she was in a cold stone chamber, surrounded by unfamiliar things.

Confused, Elanor recalled the strong pull she had felt for Merlin in the dream. Were her feelings real? She didn't know. She had never been quick to trust anyone. It had always just been Elanor, alone, with her paintings. What did all of this mean?

The door creaked open, and the strange young man from earlier entered the room. She sat up suspiciously, watching as he calmly approached her and offered her bread and a broth that smelled like mint and ginger. He did his best to make her feel comfortable, yet she felt unsettled. She stared at him uncertainly as she nibbled at the food.

Where was Merlin?

The strange man worked hard to communicate using hand motion, speaking very slowly.

He pointed to himself and said, "Cilaen," and continued to communicate using antics that made Elanor lighten, putting her at ease. His round, brown eyes were kind, and his youthful smile, sincere and friendly.

For the moment, Cilaen distracted her from feeling distressed. He brought out books, pointing at pictures and maps, many of them written in Latin. She recognized the letters and symbols from secondary school.

That night, Elanor went to bed feeling strangely comforted by her new friend. She closed her eyes, hoping that come morning, this would have all been just a strange dream.

But by the next morning, she was still met with the same cold stone wall. The disturbing awareness of where she was settled back in. She slowly stretched her legs over the side of the bed to work her way up to standing. Her legs wobbled weakly, but it felt good to stand.

She gazed out the window curiously. A high stone wall jutted out from the side of the window, and down below was a beautiful grove of trees. Far beyond was a town and a large field dotted with horses. The unfamiliar landscape stirred the anxiety she felt inside.

One thing had become very clear: This was no dream. As surreal as it seemed, this was completely real. All of this made her think the unimaginable. That maybe, by some strange phenomenon, she had somehow travelled through time. Which, of course, was impossible, but she didn't have any better way of explaining the situation she found herself in. The unfamiliar language, the appearance of the room, and the strange clothing.

Elanor felt dizzy.

Can this really be happening? Have I lost my mind?

The door clicked open, and Cilaen entered. "Elanor!" he exclaimed, throwing his hands up, pleased to see her standing. He motioned toward another room in the greater part of the chamber. Her curiosity was piqued, and her eyes darted around at all the new surroundings while Cilaen sat her down at an archaic table before bringing her some cheese and warm porridge.

Books were piled high and scrolls lined shelves and were huddled in corners. Herbs, pots, and bottles decorated every surface.

How medieval, she thought, though still not sure where in time she might be. "Where is Merlin?" she asked. "Me-r-r-r-lin?" she repeated more slowly.

Cilaen understood, shook his head, pointed to the door, and then held both hands in front of him as if to say, "Wait." She took this to mean that Merlin would be back soon. With that knowledge, she began to eat.

Then, Cilaen headed toward the door and began the same strange sign language. The head nod, then pointing to the door, and then wait. She was beginning to think that maybe he meant he was leaving, and she needed to stay and wait. She nodded, hoping that she understood as he grabbed a red jacket and bowed before turning to leave.

Elanor waited silently, her curiosity finally getting the best of her. She hurriedly finished her breakfast and explored the room for all its treasures. It was the books that drew her interest the most. Picking one up from a nearby table, she scanned through its pages. This one was also in Latin. She looked at the letters and worked to remember the Latin alphabet. *"The Systems of Nature,"* she deciphered as the title.

She placed the book down and marveled at all the different jars and vials. Many of them contained herbs inside liquids. She found a mortar and pestle coated with a yellow, powdery substance. At the back of the room in the corner sat a little bed with a small pile of straw. On the opposite side was an ancient iron stove with a huge steaming pot left unattended.

As she continued through, Elanor's eyes were drawn to some more books on the floor. At the top of the pile was a small, green book. It was in the same fashion as the little blue book she had been given at the book shop. Eagerly, she picked it up, looking at the cover and designs in-layed in the leather. This one also had a picture of a small bundle of dandelions.

She discovered a bench just underneath a high window and settled down on it, keen to look more closely at the book. Fresh air blew through the window, and she leaned back and opened the book.

Inside were pictures of different plants and flowers, all of them beautifully detailed with handwritten letters and drawings. Her own artistic nature pricked with appreciation. She was amazed by the excellence and time it must have taken to create such a fine work of art.

She wondered if the blue book she had left behind looked anything like this one on the inside. The old man had said that there were pictures. She remembered that she opened the book, but never got to see what was inside before she found herself dreaming.

Still weary, feeling the wind upon her face, Elanor closed her eyes.

Merlin saw Elanor sitting asleep under the window with a book in her lap. He needed to speak to her but hated to disturb her peace. He carefully sat down next to her. The wind blew, brushing a few of her hairs gently across her face. Seeing her serene beauty evoked feelings of longing, igniting within him the power to resist her. Still, just like in the dream, the sight of her called to him, "Merlin! Merlin!" But now, the dream was over, and he had the choice to not answer that call. He knew better. Love was not promised him and would never be. He hesitated, then lightly touched her arm to awaken her.

Elanor opened her eyes and delicately smiled at him. "The fresh air felt nice," she whispered.

The pleasant sound of her voice brought peace to Merlin's thoughts. "Cilaen told me you were awake. I did not mean to disturb you."

"I am not disturbed." Curiously, Elanor asked, "Where have you been?"

"There has been much to prepare. Your coming here has been quite a shock, and I have had to do a lot of explaining to the people who need to know about you."

She sat up a little more attentively. "Who needs to know about me? Do you know what has happened to me? How have I come here?"

"It is a mystery, my lady. I was hoping you could tell me." He hung his head slightly, and then, lifting his eyes, squinted inquisitively. "Can you tell me about where you come from?"

"You said we are in Caer Lial, and Cilaen has tried to show me where we are using maps and pictures. He said that this is Prydain. Is this right?"

Merlin nodded with a smile, pleased that Cilaen had served her well and worked to bring her understanding as best he could.

"Well…" Elanor began uncertainly. "I think my home would be just south of here. Only…my home is not here…not in this time." Confused, she shook her head. "What I mean to say is…Where I come from, this place is no longer Prydain. This place appears to be hundreds, if not a thousand years or more in the past."

Merlin leaned back, perplexed by her revelation. His thoughts raced.

"How could I be here? Everything looks like ancient history…And then there's you," she said, pointing her finger at him. "Merlin? Hah! And Gwynevere? Listen, from where I come from your names are renowned, but as *legend*. Just stories in books. I'm probably not making any sense. This is all so confusing. If it didn't all feel so real, I would think I was still dreaming. It has to be a dream. How is any of this possible?"

Merlin was dumbstruck. "You are from a future time?"

"If all that I see is true, then, yes. From far, far in the future."

"And there are stories written of us?"

"Well, if you are the Merlin of King Arthur. Are you? You said Gwynevere was queen?"

The mention of Arthur stung him. "Arthur was my lord, and friend." He turned his gaze painfully toward the window. Then, he said harshly, "He is dead."

"Oh…" Elanor considered sadly, seeing his pain. "I did not know. This is all so strange."

"Time traveler," he breathed, almost as if talking to himself. He was wrestling through his rational thoughts, trying to put together how any of this could be possible. Still peering away from her, Merlin said, "Tell me…if what you say is true…what does the future look like?"

"It would be hard for me to explain. So much is different. We have technology. Mobile phones, cars, and television…" Elanor trailed off, realizing Merlin would have no grasp of modern inventions. She thought hard for a moment. "I wish I could just show you. For instance, I assume that you travel mostly using horses?" She stopped for Merlin's confirmation, but he made no reply, so she continued. "Where I am from, we do not use horses to travel anymore, at least not over long distances. We have cars that travel fast down roads, and airplanes that travel in the sky." She swooped her arm up over her head. His confused gaze told her she wasn't doing a good job explaining. "We have these special machines that…no"—she stopped to think of a better word— "tools, called phones. You can use them to speak to people that live far away." She shook her head. "None of this makes sense. Just trust me, not a whole lot remains the same as it is now."

"This is all very strange for you then?"

"Well, leaving this room would tell me a great deal more about what it is like here. I wish I could show you what my world looks like. It would probably shock you to see it," she laughed. A memory came into her mind, and then something ignited within her. Her desire to show Merlin the future felt like a key being turned in a lock. The old man's words from the book shop kept running through her mind. "*Your father should have never told you that you didn't have magic.*"

Merlin could see she was spinning. "Are you well?"

Elanor peered into his eyes and felt a switch inside of her fully click into place. A sudden flash of yellow light sparked in her eyes.

"What was that?" he asked curiously, pressing closer.

"I looked at you and I could see…" She paused. "I could see you." And then, gazing closer, she said, "You are conflicted."

He gasped, "How do you know my mind?"

"I believe, maybe…I can show you what it looks like where I am from. I do not know how I know this, but if you'll trust me." She put out her hands for him to take. "I feel like I am remembering something I have always known to do but have just forgotten. I think it has something to do with you."

Merlin could feel the stirring, too. There was something magical happening, and it felt familiar to him. These stirrings he thought were unique to him; he had never felt them from another person. Magic that flowed like nature, moving and bending like grass blown in the breeze. He took Elanor's hands and instantly, his mind was transported. Like a waking dream, he saw flashings of memories that were not his own—they were hers. He felt her in every one of them as if he were peering through her eyes.

Many pictures and moments flashed through his mind before coming into focus on one. Suddenly, he stood on the corner of what seemed an active center. He was amazed as people sped by in extraordinary ways. Everything looked so bizarre. One young boy sailed passed him on a flat board with wheels, and then he saw the road roaring with what could only be described as iron chariots, moving without horses. They rumbled loudly as they sped past. People walked by on both sides of him, as if they were all rushing toward something. Structures loomed large, all of them great fortresses. Colorful fronts with large loud, flashing letters. The people wore curious clothing, and many of them held small rectangular boxes that they stared at and talked into. He could hear strange music and voices coming from them. So much noise and movement all around. He wanted to cover his ears but forced himself to observe instead.

The memory switched, and Merlin stood in what he thought must be Elanor's home. She moved about the room, humming to herself. The room appeared strange with lots of lines and angular shapes—not at all like the homes he was familiar with. He watched her walk over to a water-spout and fill a cup with water, and then come to stand in front of a box where he could see smaller people, somehow moving about and speaking to one another. Lights magically glowed on the ceiling and on the tables without candles or torches. So many sights and sounds to baffle him, and before he could absorb any of it, it stopped.

Elanor let go of his hand. "Did it work? Did you see the memories?"

"How did you do that?" Merlin asked in disbelief, a little frightened.

"I've never done that before," she said, gazing down at her hands, confounded. "At least I don't think I have."

"You have magic?"

"I don't know," she said as worry lined her face.

"Did no one teach you?"

"Teach me? I don't know anything about magic. I was told when I was a child it was a pretend thing. A pretend thing I needed to forget. Or so I was just recently reminded." She frowned. "Everything is so strange and turned upside down." Her emotions began to escalate as she considered the impossibility of it all. "What is happening to me? Where am I? How did I get here? Ever since these dreams started...and then that old man in the book shop—I must be losing my mind."

"The old man?"

"It's a long story," she said, turning away from him.

Merlin stared at Elanor, astonished. He couldn't believe it. He sensed her magic, though it appeared she did not know it herself. A magic that wasn't learned or developed, in all its purity, untainted by the world or darkness. His perplexity was giving way, and his heart fluttered in the healing thought that he was not alone.

Just then, Cilaen came crashing in. "Have you told her?"

"No, no...not yet," Merlin said, holding up his hand. He shook his head, bothered by the intrusion. "We have had many other things we've been sorting out." He glanced tenderly at her. "Elanor, tomorrow the queen is prepared to meet you."

His statement sent alarm radiating through her.

"A handmaid will be here tomorrow to help you prepare."

Panic shot across Elanor's face. She had no idea what a queen would expect of her. Especially in a world so foreign.

"Elanor," Merlin said. Seeing her distress, he placed his hand lightly on her shoulder. "You have nothing to fear. I will be there with you."

She wanted to feel encouraged by Merlin's assurance, but who was he to her? How did she know that he was safe and could be relied upon? He was only a stranger, made familiar by a dream.

Samara was a young handmaid about the same age as Elanor. She had her dark hair tied up tightly with blue linen that wrapped around her head. Her brown eyes were small and pleasing, and her fair skin was dotted with small freckles along her nose.

She talked while she filled a basin with water and sang while helping Elanor step into the small tub. Samara flailed her arms while expressively babbling in words foreign to Elanor, splashing water out onto the floor. This whole experience was very awkward for Elanor, but she wasn't about to make a fuss. She knew she would have to get used to things being different until she was home again. Wherever home was from here.

Cool air blew in from the window as Elanor rose out of the tub, and Samara quickly wrapped her in a linen. Moving Elanor to a seat, she commenced brushing through her hair.

The humming sound of Samara's voice as the brush moved through Elanor's hair struck a painful chord in her heart. She had never been touched like this. She never realized there was a loss inside her, of the intimacy she should've had with her mother. Samara's fingers were warm as they tenderly twisted through Elanor's hair. She hated being reminded of the rejection she felt. She always worked hard to forget it, pretending the pain did not exist.

Samara perfected Elanor's tendrils, then stood in front of her. She placed her hands on her hips, pleased with her work. Then, she stood Elanor up and removed the linen wrapped around her, making Elanor feel exposed. Quickly, she drew her hands up to cover herself. Samara seemed not to care as she mumbled to herself, grabbing up a green dress and other garments from where they laid waiting. Over Elanor's head went a sheer white gown, and then over the top, the green dress. Samara laced it up tightly in the back. Over the dress, a lighter, green-colored tunic flowed that gathered around her waist with a gold sash that hung on the side, beneath her hip.

Elanor felt odd in the unfamiliar garments.

Samara bowed, timidly smiling.

Immediately Elanor wished her to stand. She didn't know what to do with the feeling created by Samara's stare and attention.

Then, Samara began pulling her toward the door. Elanor's anxiousness rose, knowing she was about to meet the queen. Now she wished she could stay with Samara and pulled back against Samara's leading. Samara turned and gazed at her. She nodded knowingly, as if to say, "It will be okay," then gripped her hand to pull her forward.

What if the queen decides to have my head cut off, or have me burnt at the stake? Did they do that sort of thing here?

She tried to push out of her mind all the thoughts of ruthless kings and queens she had seen in the movies. Things were probably not at all like she was imagining them. Not romantic heroes nor raging tyrants. Maybe it was somewhere in between.

Meeting the queen of England in her time would be scary enough, with all its finery and politeness, but here she would be meeting Gwynevere, in a place she imagined was definitely more rugged and wild. Having only been within these small rooms, she had no idea what this new world would be like. She had no way of preparing for what was going to happen next.

She walked through the door to stand before Merlin and Cilaen. She grappled with the side of her dress, nervously twisting her fingers around the fringes and trying to calm her breathing so she could appear confident.

9

GWYNEVERE QUEEN OF THE CYMRY

Merlin watched Elanor gracefully glide out of the room, carrying herself like a woman of great nobility. He was captured by the shape of her in the green dress and the flash of her eyes as she glanced his way. Quickly, he turned his back to her, facing the door, refusing his heart to quicken. He was sure everyone who saw her would be taken by her—thinking her a lady of high and noble birth. There was no disguising that her movements and grace were unlike most common women.

Nervously, Elanor brushed the front of her dress and tried not to stand too awkwardly.

"The queen will be pleased," Merlin said, clearing his throat. Still facing away, he extended his arm for her to take.

Elanor gazed up at his profile, hoping that the strength of his out-stretched arm would protect her. Nervously, she breathed as Merlin led her out of the room and out along a high walkway with a balustrade above a courtyard. On her right, she could see a long line of doorways extending the length of the passage.

Below, flowering trees and tresses covered the courtyard, with great stones set with whorls and knots etched into them. Directly across from the yard, she could see another balustrade in front of a row of doors. In the center, above the courtyard, it opened up into a beautiful sky.

It must be spring, she thought.

They went down a staircase leading into an archway, then through to another hallway, which widened until a large round room opened up before them, with tall ceilings, high pillars, and a large, grand staircase.

The floors were decorated with intricately laid tiles. And in the very center, the tiles created large circular patterns around a great bear standing on its hind legs with its teeth bared. Surrounding the bear within smaller circles were warriors, all in different poses. One warrior had a two-headed serpent in one hand, with a spear in his other, stabbing through the snake. Another held the severed head of a giant, while still another held three swords in his right hand and three spears in his left. One by one, warriors all unique wrapped around the bear, each portraying a mighty feat.

This mighty design she knew had a deep, rich meaning, but she hardly had a chance to look any closer as Merlin pulled her forward. Her mouth hung open, wishing they could stop for just one moment to take it all in. Beautiful carvings on wooden pillars. Large tapestries with chariots, depicting naked warriors on horseback.

The corridor was lined with torches, awaiting the flames of the evening, black and silent. Merlin led her past door after door silently, and Elanor wished he would acknowledge her. Then ahead, she saw a final door, guarded by a strong, sturdy man with a spear in his hand.

The guard glanced at her but did not smile. He was dressed like an ancient Celtic warrior, wearing a great torc of silver around his neck. He was broad and tall, but his eyes were soft and the color of chestnuts. He wore his long brown hair tied up in a braid, with a trim beard on his chin. He nodded knowingly at Merlin and opened the door.

As Elanor entered the room, her hand squeezed Merlin's arm. Her heart pounded wildly, and her face flushed. A woman sat on a high-backed chair in front of a large hearth, and beside her stood another guard, his hand upon the hilt of his sword. He was dressed just as the other had been, only this man was taller. Like a Roman centurion, he had trimmed hair and a strong, clean-shaven chin. He too had no welcome in his eyes.

She felt both guards' eyes upon her as the guard at the door had entered along with them. She peered at Merlin, but he only gazed straight ahead at the queen, which gave her no consolation.

Merlin bowed. "My queen, I have brought you Elanor."

The queen stood, gazing at Elanor from across the room. Anxiously, Elanor stood still, holding her breath and waiting for the queen to move or to speak. Slowly, Gwynevere moved toward her. Her eyes observed Elanor with intrigue.

Fear tightened Elanor's throat, and she could barely swallow. The queen intimidated in her beauty, standing tall and regal in a gold and red dress. She wore a circlet of gold around her head, and a beautiful, delicate gold torc around her neck. Her hair was dark, and her green eyes pierced from just above her slender, long nose and small, rose-colored lips. Altogether, she was splendidly powerful, and there was no mistaking her presence and authority.

Elanor's knees trembled as the queen stood before her. She had never felt more fragile or out of place. She wanted to run, but where? She was helpless. Completely unknown to this world—knowing nothing and no one. Vulnerable and weak.

The queen's eyes passed over Elanor's face, and a look of deep astonishment came over her. She lifted one hand to her mouth and slowly lifted the other toward Elanor's face. In silence, the queen stared deeply at Elanor, as if shocked by what she saw.

Merlin stepped aside, observing Gwynevere's strange reaction. The queen had seen something, but what? Just before touching Elanor's cheek, she snapped out of her strange trance and straightened up. A look of confusion fell upon the faces of everyone in the room, unsure of what made the queen take such attention.

The queen commanded the guards, waving her arms. Elanor watched as the two of them hesitated, then swiftly exited the room. Then, the queen turned to speak very rapidly to Merlin. Elanor understood nothing. Concern grew in her mind, and she hoped that the queen hadn't seen something wrong. Perhaps the guards leaving the room was a good sign.

The queen remained in front of Elanor, making her afraid to move, or even breathe. Cold sweat formed on her neck and behind her knees.

Finally, Merlin nodded to the queen, then motioned to Elanor. "The queen invites you to sit with her."

The queen turned to Elanor inquisitively. She smiled lightly as she beckoned for Elanor to follow her and led her to a chair across from her own. As the queen reclined, she began talking to Merlin once again. Elanor, feeling oddly ignored, distracted herself by scanning the large room. At its center was a long table with chairs. In the back corner of the room stood a bed, beautifully draped, making her realize that she had been invited to the queen's private chambers.

Merlin spoke, bringing Elanor back to attention. "The queen is curious. My words of counsel in regard to your identity have not entirely eased her mind about you. What powers you possessed to show me the future, she would like to see for herself. She cannot so easily believe that you have come here from another time."

Elanor couldn't believe her ears. The queen's eyes were piercing as she waited for her response. She sat up taller in her chair, not sure what to say. She could scarce believe she had traveled through time herself.

"I have only ever done it once before…" She paused, glancing uncomfortably at Merlin as if he should have known better. How could he have put her in this position? She didn't even know how she did it the first time, let alone how she could replicate it for the queen. "I can only try…"

Merlin gripped her arm with a serious gaze. "This act may help put Gwynevere at ease about you. You must try. This is important, Elanor. I know this magic resides within you." He encouraged, "Just try."

This whole moment felt unsettlingly reminiscent of the book shop. Trembling, she said, "I will try." When she had done this before, she had a feeling, a sort of sensation and knowing. She did not know if that was what was required in order to do it again. It had just sort of happened the first time.

She put both of her hands forward for Gwynevere to take. Elanor took a deep breath and tried to connect with how she felt the day before. She remembered how much she wanted to show Merlin her world. Her desire to show him was what seemed to quicken the moment. So, she focused, urging herself, to do as she had done before. She thought about her home and the coffee shop. Her heart warmed at the thought of Bill's smile, and suddenly the magic kindled. Her eyes flashed with light as they had the time before, surprising Gwynevere, but she did not pull away.

Memories swirled. Elanor knew that Gwynevere could see them. The street corner and her flat. Only this time, it was hard to control how the memories formed, or how long they lasted. She tried to focus on the memories that had naturally come to her with Merlin, but it was harder this time. For some reason, her mind wanted to wander to other places and memories. The thought of her father gripped her. She couldn't help thinking of him. Without being able to stop it, she was there, in the memory.

"Elanor! Elanor, come down from there."

A ten-year-old Elanor hid up in the branches of the apple tree in the back garden of her house. Her cheeks were covered in the dried salt lines of her tears. Why was he calling her down? She just wanted to be alone. This was her secret refuge. Coming down meant she had to go back where words stung and she was forsaken.

Elanor tried to ignore the compassionate face of her father as he reached up toward her, begging her to come down.

"Elanor! You have been up there long enough. It's time to come inside," he pleaded. "Please do not make me climb up there and get you."

Elanor gasped as she tried to stop the memory, shaking herself and Gwynevere out of the connection. Elanor released Gwynevere's hands and quickly turned away, unsure and flustered.

Gwynevere took a deep breath. The revelation of what she had just seen danced across her face as she began softly conferring with Merlin. She leaned toward Elanor, placing her hand on her knee.

This unexpected touch jarred Elanor, as she was already reeling over having shared such a vulnerable memory.

"The queen said that she could feel your loneliness like it was her own, when she saw you in the apple tree…She would like to know who the dark-skinned man was who was trying to call you down."

"I did not mean to show her that…I couldn't seem to help it," she confessed, peering up at Merlin. She hesitated a moment, staring at the floor. "That man was my father." Elanor glanced at the queen to see her response and was baffled that she did not appear more rattled. The queen had been there with her in the memories. She had the ability to feel her feelings, and she could feel hers. She knew that the queen had been astounded and disbelieving—her curiosity and amazement translated into Elanor's thoughts. Yet the queen's confusion and compassion in that final memory gave Elanor a comfort that made her disconcerted.

Gwynevere responded, and Merlin translated, "You do not look like your father. You are so fair and blue eyed. He is a dark-skinned man with dark eyes."

Elanor remained silent. She was still working to get a hold of herself. Why had that memory come up?

Gwynevere rose, glancing down at Merlin with authority. She spoke, and Merlin voiced her words. "The queen will have us return later this evening to dine while she holds council. For now, she needs time to think."

THE GREAT PALISADE OF CAER LIAL

On the other side of the door, Elanor let out a huge sigh, placing her hand on her stomach and breathing deeply. She wasn't going to get her head cut off today, but there still remained the anxiety of the queen's council later that evening.

"The queen was pleased," Merlin encouraged.

"Oh," Elanor responded with a tremble in her voice.

"The test is over. Please be at rest. She is not a tyrant, and certainly claims no lordship over me. I trust her. She is noble and kind. She only tests you to know that you mean us no evil. She has known evil to manipulate and destroy, and she is careful to know her friends from her enemies. She does not believe you to be an enemy. Just a mystery, as do we all." He put his arm toward her to take. "Come…let me show you the Palisade. I think by how pulled you were by every sight on the way, that you would be happy to see more."

Lightness returned to Elanor's eyes and excitement sparked. "Even the little I have seen is remarkable. No one I have ever known will have the opportunity to see this. In my world, this is now all in ruins. The tiles I saw downstairs, I have seen similar things like this, small pieces, aged and chipped in museums. Now I see them, and they are vibrant and new."

"A museum?"

"Oh…uh…" She laughed. "A museum is a place where you can view old relics and what remains from the past. It is a way to learn about those that went before us."

Merlin replied thoughtfully, "We also have ways of remembering our past. Our past is preserved for us in verse and song." Then, with a cheeky grin and a twinkle in his eye, he said, "Let us go see all that is not in a museum."

Merlin's warmness settled her, and she nodded, taking his arm.

He led her down passageways and corridors. Her wonder at every turn quickened Merlin's heart. He felt young, fresh, and alive in her presence.

What magic is this? he pondered.

He had forgotten the feeling of joy. The weight of the world was threatening to fall off his shoulders as he watched her dance at every step. Instead of her vitality offending him, making him recoil, it enticed him. Each laugh and movement challenged him to live in a way he had refused to. He forgot himself for small moments, captured by the move of her neck when she turned, or the tone of her voice when she spoke.

They wandered all the way up to the very top of the Palisade where it opened into a large terrace that jutted out above the whole citadel. The terrace's edge was lined with a large stone parapet wall.

Approaching the stone edge, they could view not only the entire stronghold, but far beyond and into the countryside of pointed forests and grey, snow-capped mountains.

Elanor leaned out over the edge, taking in the fullness of the sight. "This is a beautiful place. It feels like there are no boundaries. So untouched and wild." The wind blew up all around her. "If I lived here…I would never stay hulled up in my flat on the weekends."

Merlin curiously asked, "Is it always so noisy in your world?"

She smiled. "No. I only showed you places that were near my home. The city is always very loud and busy, but there is countryside and quiet places. Though fewer quiet places than here, I should think. I grew up in a house near the country. It was always quiet in my father's garden."

Touching his fingers to his chin and leaning against the parapet, Merlin asked curiously, "There are stories of me in your future time?"

"Many different stories," Elanor said, an amused smile on her lips. "The stories of King Arthur and Merlin are very famous where I'm from. There is hardly a person that hasn't heard a tale or two. Some stories say you are a magical wizard that wears blue pointy hats. Or at least that is the Merlin depicted in the version told to children. Some say you turned Arthur into different animals to teach him lessons about being king." She observed Merlin's face change at her mention of Arthur. "Some stories, I believe, say that you were a faithful aid to Arthur, and that it is because of your wisdom that he conquered many of his enemies. Some say you raised Arthur up, and it was you that made him king. Strangely enough, I was about to read one of the versions of the story right before I ended up here. Which is what really makes me think I am just going mad," she sighed, turning back toward the view.

"Blue pointy hat?" he chuffed.

Elanor nodded. "And you are always very, very old, with a long white beard."

Merlin laughed, enjoying the thought. Then he leaned in. "I am very old," he said mysteriously. "I may not look it, but I have lived long before even Arthur drew his first breath."

Elanor straightened. "How can that be when you stand before me a tall vibrant man in his prime? Is it magic?"

"No, not magic."

Elanor's brows turned up in wonder. "Without magic? Are you immortal?"

Merlin glanced at her, feeling her eyes upon him. She was struggling to understand. Her eyes intensified, and then flashed.

In a snap, he grabbed her by the wrist. "What did you see?"

Startled, Elanor yanked her wrist free. She gripped it to her chest and gazed at Merlin, frightened and angry.

"I am sorry," he said quickly, not realizing the violence of his grip.

Elanor stepped back distrustfully. "I did not mean to."

"No...no." He shook his head. "I...I did not mean to. I saw the flash in your eye and hoped to understand. I did not mean to frighten you..."

"I wasn't trying to pry. I didn't know that would happen. I am not sure I know how to control this."

"I meant only to understand. I did not feel you intruded. I want to help you, Elanor," he said, gently offering his hand. "You did nothing wrong. Please tell me, what did you see?"

She glanced down at his hand hesitantly, then said, "I'm not sure." She clasped her hands anxiously in front of her. "I just saw a glimpse. It was confusing. In your eyes, I saw years of burdens that had worn you. Your eyes seemed old, but then I saw your eyes change. You were old, and then you were not."

"Curious?" He folded his arms across his chest, setting his mouth as he thought. "Well, I am not immortal. I am just a man," he said, gazing intently at her, trying to surmise what she had just seen. It was strange to him how completely unaware she was of her own magic. "I will tell you more about myself another time, but never fear me, Elanor. I only aim to understand. I can only help as you trust me."

Elanor bit her lip, her eyes moistening with tears. "I want to know what's going on. What in the world is happening to me? It's all so…so…surreal!" She sighed, rubbing her forehead as her chin quivered. "Your face is so familiar to me. I have been dreaming of you for so long." Moving toward him, she reached her hand and almost touched his face. "I even painted your likeness." Then, she swiftly turned away. "I am not sad I have come to finally know you. Those dreams were beginning to drive me crazy. Months I had them, night after night. You had them too?"

He breathed, giving her a small smile. "Those dreams were very bothersome. I did all I could think of to stop them, understand them, release them, and nothing. Nothing until finally that last dream brought you here. Now I can once more sleep. All will come. I am sure of it, Elanor. I knew you'd come, and you did. Now we will have to take each piece as it comes to us." He nodded, then said, "There are some small truths in the stories you've heard, I think. It is almost too much to think that our names have been remembered hundreds of years from now. Maybe we did truly change things more than we thought, Arthur and I."

A slight smile formed in the corner of Elanor's mouth, and together they peered out over the parapets, quietly observing the world below.

"I want to show you something," he said.

Supporting her arm, Merlin led her around the back of the terrace and down a set of spiraling stairs. At the bottom, they entered a room that had the tranquility of a chapel. It was a round room with several small, diamond windows lining the upper walls. Beams of light filtered into the chamber, crisscrossing one another onto the floor. The beams highlighted two large bumpy stones in the center of the room. The rough shapes became figures laying on top of rectangular slabs.

"This is the Chamber of the Pendragons, and these are memorial stones. The farthest one over there," Merlin said, pointing to the stone in the back, "is Uther."

"And this"—he placed his hand on the stone in front of him—"is Arthur. They have been buried, along with Aurelius, within the Hill of the Kings, but these memorial stones have been placed here at the top of the Palisade for our remembrance."

Elanor stepped closer and peered at the face of the stone king. He was naked with a torc around his neck and a sword in his hands, the hilt across his chest. She became suddenly aware of Merlin's heavy sadness. The lightness had gone from his eyes. His face appeared old and sunken. Grief emanated from him, weighing in the tragedy of Arthur's death.

Elanor placed her hand upon the cold stone face of Arthur. "You should not have died," she said, not meaning to speak aloud.

Her words surprised Merlin and shook him out of his somberness. Soothed by her remark, he glanced at her inquisitively. "This is not the point of our day." He smiled and held out his hand. "Let us go and not take the dead with us."

Merlin scooped his arm around Elanor's, leading her back out of the room. His closeness surprised her, and yet, a yearning in her heart coaxed her to lean into him. She resisted.

They quietly strolled back through all the places they had been, until they reached two large doors that led into the courtyard.

The courtyard seemed much larger than it did when she was peering down upon it. Around the perimeter of the yard were more doors underneath stone pillars holding up the balustrades above. Now in the yard, she was swallowed up by the trees and flowering vines. Around the garden's edges were large stones cut to create great chairs and benches. This was true for all except one stone, with etchings of warriors carved into it, that sat in the middle of the courtyard like a memorial.

"Peaceful," Elanor chimed. The yard was every inch how she imagined the gardens of a Roman villa would have looked, only the stones reminded her of old Celtic ruins.

"This place, Arthur built as a refuge for his men. Their minds could be so fitful from the battles, and here, there is only safety and open sky. Many a healing conversation has been had in this yard," Merlin said while brushing his hands across a stone chair. "These doors," he pointed to each side of the yard, "have been occupied by many of Arthur's greatest warriors. Many now sit empty. Gwynevere has not sought to fill them anew." He took a deep breath. "So, the peacefulness of the yard has not been utilized to its fullest need, I fear. I think much of that to be my own fault." Merlin lost himself in thought for a moment, then turned to notice Elanor gazing at him. Their eyes locked, and Elanor's heart quickened. She swiftly shifted her glance. Merlin shook his head, then ushered her forward to enter into the Great Hall.

The Hall was large, and the voices of several men echoed as they sat boisterously eating and drinking at the long tables set in rows. A young boy looked up when they entered and came running toward them, his feet patting loudly on the floor.

He stopped before them, a boy of maybe twelve years of age. "Can I get a cup for my lord? Food? The kitchen is ready with bread and stew."

"No, Uri," Merlin said, placing his hand on the young boy's head and messing his hair. "I have only come to show this fine lady our hall. We will not need anything."

The boy glanced at Elanor, fidgeting anxiously. He regarded her a great lady and bowed. "My lady," he said with wide eyes. "Ca…can I get the lady a cup?"

"She does not understand." Merlin smiled, amused by Uri's wonder of her. "She does not speak the language of our people."

"Oh." Uri stared.

"We do not need any refreshments. Now run along!" Merlin laughed, shooing him away.

Elanor watched the boy run off, before realizing that the chatter of the men had stopped. "Why are they all staring at me?"

"They think you must be a great lady. Mostly only serving women are seen in here, unless there are festivals or feastings. The queen is usually the only other woman to come into this room. These men are the Cymbrogi—warriors of Caer Lial. They only wonder who you are. You have been given very fine clothes to wear, and you carry yourself upright like a woman of noble bearing."

"Maybe we should go," Elanor said, uncomfortable by the attention. Elanor turned to walk toward the door and nearly bumped into a man that was coming in behind her.

The man stopped, startled. She recognized that it was the same man she had seen earlier that morning guarding the queen's door. This time, he bowed toward Elanor in greeting, and then toward Merlin. He put his hand forward, taking

Elanor's hand, then bowed once more, almost resting his forehead on the top of her hand. As he lifted his head, he smiled broadly.

Elanor quickly pulled her hand from his grip.

"This, Elanor, is Bedwyr. One of Arthur's mightiest warriors and closest of friends."

His brown eyes were kind and handsome, and his teeth shined white as he smiled. He seemed now gentle and not at all intimidating or forceful.

Bedwyr looked at Merlin and said, "Please apologize if I frightened the lady. She is a friend to Merlin, and so then is my friend also."

Merlin relayed the message to Elanor, and she smiled, bending back in his direction.

"She is a beautiful lady," Bedwyr said, elbowing Merlin.

Merlin laughed, "Should I tell her that as well?"

Both men laughed together, and Bedwyr slapped Merlin's side. They began a jovial exchange, and Elanor stood awkwardly, understanding only half of what was being said.

The Hall seemed more rustic and alive than the rest of the places she had seen. It was wooden, and the ceiling was high and domed. The large hearth in the middle of the room was inviting. Two grey hounds came bounding in from the front doors and down the center. They scampered over to the side, yelping as they wrestled into some hay.

The men dining in the Hall were still turning to stare at Elanor, but they had at least returned to their conversations, making her fell less uneasy. She watched as Uri ran from group to group with a pitcher of ale, refreshing the men's cups.

All of this was a far more Celtic and more ancient time then the stories she had been told of Arthur. There were no knights in shining armor, or vast, high castles. Though the Palisade was grand, it was not the medieval castle that had been commonly thought to house King Arthur's Courts. The Palisade was round and circular, spiraling up to the terrace above.

Merlin leaned close to Elanor. "The queen gathers her most trusted council at her table. It will be important for us all to hear what she has decided."

Elanor breathed nervously, feeling increasingly overwhelmed as they headed toward the queen's chamber, now with Bedwyr and Cilaen in tow.

Cilaen pressed in, distracting Merlin. He felt Elanor's forehead, then turned to Merlin, speaking severely.

"She is well, Cilaen. No need to fuss. I have taken good care of her. She has shown no sign of weariness."

Bedwyr nudged Merlin. "What do you think the queen will decide about the girl?"

"I know she is careful to pay attention to all I have said. None of this has been a coincidence."

"The very lark that has been calling to you in your dreams. Aih! The strangeness of it all. Do you truly believe she has come from another time?"

"Yes—but only because of what her magic revealed, and there being no other explanation for her."

Bedwyr's brows furrowed. "Could it be sorcery? The dream? All of it?"

"No. It is not dark magic. The difference between the magic of light and darkness can be hard to discern, but only when there is fear or ignorance. It is clear to me. She is only caught up, just as I have been. She is no agent of evil."

"Hah! You just love the sparkle in her eyes, brother," Bedwyr jested.

No guards greeted them at the door, but instead two servants with blue head wrappings stood just inside. Both women held silver pitchers, peering down at the floor.

Gwynevere stood, ready to receive them at the head of the table, nodding at Merlin and Bedwyr. Then, she stopped to gaze at Elanor with an unsure stare. Silently, Merlin escorted her to sit beside Gwynevere at the table.

Merlin sat across from Elanor on the queen's right. Cilaen was positioned next to Elanor, and Bedwyr across from him. As they situated around the table, another man entered the room. It was the other guard Elanor had seen earlier that morning, likely another of Arthur's men of high stature. She hoped that maybe, like Bedwyr, he would offer a warmer greeting, but that was not the case; he stood large and menacing in the doorway. His eyes rested suspiciously upon Elanor. The man took his seat next to Cilaen, where Elanor was relieved she wouldn't have to bear his intimidating stare.

Merlin gave her a knowing look and mouthed, "Be at peace."

The servants poured a golden, milky-looking liquid into their cups. Next, they served hot food from a large brass tureen in the center of the table. It was a stewed meat and broth, which filled the room with its juicy, comforting aroma. Bread and cheese were also served, that the men gladly tore large chunks from as it passed around the table.

All spoke loudly, back and forth, while they ate. Elanor felt strange; she couldn't understand anyone except Merlin. It made her feel more a stranger than she had in the Great Hall. It was apparent that they all knew each other intimately and she did not belong. She wished she could escape back to her world.

Elanor felt a soft hand grab hers. Startled, she was surprised to see the queen was glancing at her kindly.

Gwynevere spoke softly to Merlin, and he peered over, seeing Elanor's distressed countenance. "Gwynevere would like to know why you aren't eating."

"Please tell her not to feel shy," Gwynevere said encouragingly. "I know this all must feel very strange."

Elanor was taken aback by the queen's compassion, unsure what she had done to earn it. She smiled and took the cup in front of her, first lifting it toward the queen before taking a sip. The liquid was strange and had a sour, bitter taste as it flowed over her tongue. Her lips puckered, but she quickly tried to hide her reaction, pretending she enjoyed it.

Gwynevere laughed, delighted by Elanor's effort. She motioned her hand toward Elanor's plate, encouraging her to eat. Elanor tried to ignore the fact that all eyes were on her and began to eat. The food tasted good, and suddenly she remembered that she hadn't eaten since the morning. Hungrily, she dove into her food. She knew everyone was likely talking about her, as each person at the table stared at her in turn as they spoke.

The servants rushed around the table, cleaning up the food and dishes as they finished and refilled their cups. This drink was different and had a pleasant blend of spices that warmed Elanor.

The queen placed her hands on the table, stood, and cleared her throat. All fell silent, giving Gwynevere their attention. She waved her hand to dismiss the two servants that had been waiting on them, then gazed at Elanor and then Merlin.

"Now we come to why I have gathered you all. This company alone knows of these mysterious happenings surrounding this young woman," she said, pointing to Elanor. "Elanor has come to us in a way that no one can yet explain. I am still confounded, but I saw purity of heart when I encountered her. I am willing that she should stay here under our watchful eye until more understanding comes. However, I believe we must keep the people's questions at bay regarding her presence. As such, the people, including the servants, must be told that she is a relative of mine. It would not benefit them to know more than that. This decision I have made with regard to Merlin's prophecy." This announcement caused the table to stir. "I have ordered that Samara prepare Elanor a room here in my corridor and be her chamber maid. Samara is the only servant trusted with this secret." Gwynevere looked at her company intensely before her eyes settled on Elanor.

"Elanor will come to my chambers in the mornings, as I desire to understand her. She will need to be by my side in moments where her presence will be important as a relation to the queen. Cilaen, you will spend the early part of the day tutoring her. She must be taught how to speak our language, and she will need to understand how we live. Merlin will aid in all of this, keeping his discerning eye upon her."

Everyone sat silently as the queen's words sank in. Then, Merlin bowed to the queen and relayed the details to Elanor.

"Selfishly," Gwynevere said, "there is something about her that I need to understand. Something about her...her face is just like..." She dropped her head, then shook it, changing the subject. "She will refresh me from the tired company of men."

The stoic centurion stood abruptly, slamming his hands on the table. "How do we know this isn't some kind of deception? Mordred came slipping in the same way, finding favor with everyone. We were all hypnotized by his charms."

Merlin quickly stood. "Peredur!" His presence seemed to grow in the room as he loomed. "It wasn't I that was taken in. Have you so little faith in me now?"

"What of Morguese? The seductive daughter of Morgan, bent on deceiving you?" Peredur shouted back. "Were you not taken in by her schemes? I cannot suffer that loss once again."

"Aih! But I was not deceived, I was not paying attention. If it hadn't been for..." Merlin stopped and dropped down into his seat. "Arthur and I suffered our moments of great arrogance and pride. Neither time would we have been taken in by these deceivers if we had some humility."

Elanor grew alarmed, as it appeared that this intense moment had been created by her. She wished she could have been anywhere but there. She put her head down and closed her eyes to avoid the stares.

"No," Gwynevere scathed. "You. All of you have been deceived in past times. All of you, but never have I been. Peredur, I have made my decision. It is not for you to debate me." Leaning over the table she sighed., "I cannot explain to you what I know. I daresay Merlin would have a hard time explaining it as well. I have felt her mind and have seen her heart. She is not here to bring us evil. You will have to trust me and trust the words of prophecy Merlin spoke before all of this began."

Merlin extended his hand to Peredur. "It is the Great God that has His hand in this. Not dark spirits."

Peredur stared at Elanor. His eyes burned into her, and she dared not look at him. She did not know what he had said about her, but from Merlin's responses, it was clear Peredur feared she might have some evil intent. She had no way of defending herself. All she could do was sit and wait for it to all be over.

Peredur angrily slumped down in his chair, his demeanor increasing the thick, tense atmosphere of the room.

Bedwyr then stood slowly, leaning forward on his knuckles. "I believe we have all learned our lessons from the past. Merlin has returned, and with him has come hope. I will not abandon that hope to return to the painful remains of the past. I choose to believe this is a new day. Though deceivers have come, I refuse to live as though we will forever be ensnared by devils. There are those who will come that are trustworthy also. Our fear will not bring us wisdom." He nodded toward Merlin, then raised his cup to Elanor. "We welcome you, Elanor."

"But what of her magic?" Peredur said through his teeth.

"What of my magic?" Merlin said soberly. "I know that there has been evil done in the name of magic. Witchcraft, sorcery, and devilry. But there is magic of another kind. I have seen it in the druids and the monks of the Great God. I have felt it flow through me, and it is not the same as the darkness. She is not of that darkness."

"Morguese came as light!"

"No…no, Peredur, she did not. She came as a temptress, and though many loved her allure, she never came with a feeling of light."

Temptress! Elanor could only understand Merlin's words, and his stinging remark made her want to crawl under the table.

Cilaen interjected, "I was not here when Morguese deceived, though I did experience the devastating hand of Mordred. Still, I did not see him face to face, to know his deception. Maybe I am naive, but I have spent much time with Elanor. She has a forgiving way, a laughter and a smile that is like the flowers of Beltaine. She has not the words to deceive, for she is not Cymry. This alone has left her vulnerable. She has been at our mercy, and not the other way round." Cilaen lifted his cup while Peredur let out a disagreeable grunt.

With that, they each grabbed their cups and extended them to Elanor. Even Peredur begrudgingly raised his cup. The cups were drank, and the agreement was made.

"What is it, my lord? What has disturbed you?"

"The day of prophecy is upon us. Merlin has returned," the dark man spat as if poison rested upon his tongue, "and now all will need to begin. We have been preparing—for we knew this time would come. Already, my agents of fire have been weakening the southern forces." He snapped, "Merlin must die, and with him, all hope that the New Way will ever rise again…Donnuc?"

Trembling, Dunnoc bit into his lip. "Yes, lord?"

"It is time. Go to Caer Lial, in order that all will not fail. Merlin will rue the day he chose to come back. Death will come to Prydain, and the prophecy will not come to pass. Death and blood will cover these lands. They cannot stop what is coming." A seething, dark smile drew long across his greasy teeth.

"Has the promised one come?"

His smile sank at Donnuc's question. He glared through the darkness. "Keep your eye out, Dunnoc, for it will be for you to know it, and you to reveal to me all you learn. Keep your eyes low, and do not let yourself be revealed. The promised one will not be far from Merlin's side."

THE THORN

Merlin opened the door to Elanor's new chambers. The room was lit by the orange, flickering light of a warm fire. Samara stood waiting with a smile. She greeted Elanor, wrapping her arm around her waist and leading her in.

Merlin bowed. "This is where I leave you."

"So soon?" asked Elanor, anxiously looking about the strange new space.

"You will be well taken care of. Rest well. Goodnight." He hesitated a moment, and then left, shutting the door behind him.

Elanor stood silently, peering at the door. A sudden emptiness surrounded her.

Samara rubbed her back knowingly. She muttered and began untying the sash around Elanor's waist.

The room had a pleasant-looking bed with draperies. It was smaller, but similar to what she had seen of the queen's chamber. A dressing table was set beside a window, and in the middle of the room was a small table for dining where a pitcher and bowl of plums sat. Flames burned hotly on a hearth. Candles and lanterns lit the room, revealing a throw on the floor that created an inviting atmosphere.

After helping Elanor slip out of her clothes, Samara dipped a cloth into a bowl of water and placed the wet cloth over the fire with an iron rod. After it warmed, she handed it to Elanor to wash herself. The warm cloth was soothing, and as she finished, Samara returned with a sleeping gown and placed it over Elanor's head. Elanor watched Samara take her clothes, fold them, and place them in a trunk at the foot of the bed.

Reluctantly, Elanor turned to her bed as Samara drew back the covers.

The bed looked warm with a fur and a wool blanket draped over it. It felt firm and hard. It was less a bed and more of a wooden platform with a thin pad stuffed with feathers and straw.

As she laid down, Samara blew out the candles and lanterns, one by one. When she came to the small, clay lantern on the table beside the bed, Elanor held out her hand to stop her. Though there was still a fire dully lighting the chamber, the last thing she wanted was to be alone in the unfamiliar dark. Samara bowed in understanding, bid Elanor good night, and left the room.

Elanor lay there, completely alone. The silence forced her to ponder all that had transpired. She was a stranger in a world she didn't understand. She had strange magic abilities that confused her.

How can any of this be? Her mind wildly raced.

And then there was Merlin. Who was he to her? She didn't want to trust him, but she only felt safe when she was with him. Her heart beat with the uncertainty of her thoughts, and anxiety filled her. Every thought that came into her mind was scary. As far as she was concerned, she might as well have landed on Mars. There was nothing normal. Nothing familiar.

She closed her eyes, yearning for sleep. But that was just the problem. She lay there, yet sleep never came.

Frustrated, Elanor sat up and decided it was no use. The fire was getting lower, and the room was getting darker. How she wished she could make herself a warm cup of tea to bring herself some comfort! She thought what she might do to help herself reset. A walk in the brisk night air. Possibly that would help.

She found a red robe and a small pair of shoes that Samara had left for her. In the darkness of the corridors, she hoped she would remember the way to the terrace she had visited with Merlin earlier that day. Surely it would be alright to go up there. She wondered if the hallways were guarded at night and if it would be a problem if she was found wandering through them. She decided it was worth the risk and grabbed the lantern from her side table. It still had plenty of oil in it, and she trusted it would do a good job of lighting the way.

Timidly, Elanor opened her door, and it made a loud creaking noise. She cringed, hoping that the loud sound had not roused anyone. She took a deep breath and peered out into the corridor. One torch remained lit, so it was not entirely dark. She scooted out into the hallway as quietly as she could, moving nimbly as her heart pounded. It reminded her of the feeling of sneaking through her house as a child. Elanor smiled at the thought.

She was careful not to round any corners without looking first. Most of the corridors were dark, so she felt certain no one would be around. She turned to go up some stairs, having faith they would lead her in the right direction. The dark passages gave her the creepiest feeling, and she found it hard to control her imagination. Every turn made her think of haunted places, and she wondered if she should turn back. It seemed to be taking a long time. Had she lost her way?

Finally, the passage opened up, and Elanor could feel the wind from outside blowing down on her. The fear of demons in the dark was getting the best of her, so she quickened her pace. When she saw the opening to the outside, she burst into a run until she found herself out in the night air. She breathed a deep sigh of relief, bending over to catch her breath. Feeling silly about her panic, she laughed a little, then checked that her quick pace had not blown out her lantern.

The terrace was lit with bluish hue, and the sky was clear and full of stars. She could see clearly all around. It must have been a full moon, though she could not see it.

She walked to the edge of the parapet and looked out beyond at the blue world, searching the stars in the sky. The world around her might have been completely unfamiliar, but the stars had always been her friends. She pointed her hand up to the heavens to help her search the sky. She hoped that she would see it, and there, bright as ever, the three stars of the belt burned brightly. She dropped her hand and slowly sank to a seat on the stone floor beneath her, staring up at her constellation.

"What do you see?" said a voice from behind her. Elanor gasped and quickly twisted around. There she could see Merlin leaning against the wall not far behind her.

"Merlin," she whispered forcefully. "You frightened me."

He laughed and walked over to sit down beside her. "I was just as surprised to see you burst onto the terrace at a run. Made me jump nearly out of my skin. As soon as I realized it was you, I thought to say something, but then decided to wait. I am sorry I startled you. What are you doing out here at this late hour?"

"Honestly, I cannot believe I was able to find this place. Especially in the dark. I could not sleep, and I hoped getting some fresh night air might clear my mind."

"I have often come up here at night to settle myself. It is a good place for quiet. What did you need to clear your mind of?"

"I feel lost. Scared. Far from home. Nothing is known to me here. Nothing for me to find comfort in."

Merlin nodded in understanding. "What did you see just now? You were pointing at the sky."

"I was gazing at the stars. I thought at least they might bring me comfort. See that one?" she said, pointing up at the sky. "The row of three stars?"

"Oh, yes. I know the stars well. They have many stories to tell. That one is a warrior."

"Orion."

"I have heard it called other names."

"I always liked to look at the stars with my father. Late at night, we would sit and talk together and search for constellations. My favorite was this one. Partly because it was so easy to spot, and because I loved the stories my father told about the Great Hunter. He told me that the Great Hunter Orion would keep watch and hunt down the evil demons of the night. He said that Orion was looking down at me to keep me safe. I thought maybe it would make me feel better to catch a glimpse of him on this night."

The stars winked at them from high above. "The stars have many things they can tell us. Especially if our eyes are open and watchful," Merlin said quietly. "You sought comfort from them. I was seeking answers."

"What answers have you found?"

"None," he sighed, sounding a bit disappointed and weary. He pointed up to the heavens. "I have been seeking answers from them for four years. Nothing. I used to be able to see signs in the stars and in nature. Everything that I was seemed to die when…" He paused, his head hanging low into his chest. "But encountering your magic made me think, maybe…" His voice cracked with emotion.

Deep sadness radiated from Merlin like heat from a fire. Elanor longed to comfort him and see his pain healed. Though she doubted she had the capacity to even begin to understand how to help someone whose wounds might be older than she was. She did not want to be arrogant and assume she had the answer.

Slowly, she turned to face him.

Merlin looked longingly at her, as if hoping she could answer the cry that was in his heart.

Could I answer that longing? Could I help him live again?

Feeling drawn to his pain, Elanor placed her hand over Merlin's heart, hoping to bring him some peace. As she touched his chest, something inside her ignited like flame. She could hear an inner voice calling her, speaking to her, instructing her what to do. Magic began to kindle within her. Strangely, this magic felt mixed with compassion and love—a love far beyond her own.

She didn't understand, but the voice became louder. Cooperating with the voice, she repeated, "You still grieve Arthur's death deeply."

As Elanor spoke, heat began to fill Merlin's chest where her hand was laid. "There is a thorn in your heart," she continued. "Will you let me pull it out?" These words poured out from Elanor's mouth, but they were not her own.

Merlin felt as if hot fingers had reached into his chest and were sinking into his heart. Elanor's eyes reflected a golden glow as the hot fingers pressed deeper. Then, Merlin felt a prick of great grief and disappointment surge within. He felt the agony of watching Arthur close his eyes for the final time.

You cannot die! he raged, remembering the despair at the loss of his friend.

"It's my fault!" Merlin cried out.

"Why do you claim others' choices as your own? Others' failures as your judgement?" Elanor questioned, her eyes fierce.

The heat crept into Merlin's throat. It was like a pressure, dislodging a lump of pent-up emotion. It pressed and pressed and pressed.

"Because it was my destiny!" Now the heat flooded his face, and hot tears flowed from his eyes. "I was supposed to bring in the new day. The new kingdom of the sun! Arthur was to take it up, but he died. He wasn't supposed to die!"

As he opened his eyes, instead of Elanor, he saw the man in blue. His eyes sparked with the same golden light of Elanor's. Now it was the man who had his hand over Merlin's heart.

"I have given her the power to pull out this thorn, but you must forgive yourself." His words echoed deeply in Merlin's ears, and it felt like warm oil was running down into them.

"Who are you? Are you the Great God?" Merlin said, mystified. He waited for a response, and when he had none, he asked, "Do you forgive me?" His heart ached for the man in blue to respond with hope.

"I have always forgiven you, Merlin," the voice reverberated, shaking his insides.

These words melted away all the punishment Merlin had been inflicting on himself. "Then," he groaned weakly, "I can forgive myself." As Merlin spoke, something burst forth in his heart. Freedom. Joy leapt into his spirit, chasing thoughts of gladness. He had forgotten what it felt like to be unburdened. For so long, sorrow had pulled him down like a heavy anvil. Now, he was light, like a carefree child.

Instantly, Elanor's hand shot off of Merlin's chest with a great force. She gazed at him in wonder. Merlin sat with his head thrown back, tears streaming down his face as he laughed uncontrollably.

Elanor looked at her hand, expecting to see something there, some evidence of what she had just witnessed, but it was empty. "What happened?" she asked, grabbing his arms. "Are you alright? I didn't mean to."

Laughing, Merlin grabbed her and pulled her into his chest. His chest bounced up and down against Elanor's cheek as he laughed. Soon, she also began to laugh, swept up in his joy. He laughed so hard he rolled onto his back, pulling Elanor down with him.

"Merlin!" she said, quickly sitting up and smiling at him curiously.

As he lay there on his back, he slowly composed himself, wiping his eyes. He lifted his hand to her cheek. "I keep being reminded what a fool I am. I came looking for answers in the stars," Merlin said, still laughing to himself. He lifted himself up onto his elbows, leaning closer to Elanor. "Do you not know what has just happened? I am not sure I know myself. Tell me, what did you see?"

"I could sense your pain, and I wanted to bring you comfort," Elanor said timidly. "I didn't know how to help ease your pain, or even if it was my place to do so. But I thought I might console you, in some small way, so I reached over to touch you, and something began to happen…I felt love, and it was hot like fire…" She looked down, embarrassed. "This has to sound so ridiculous; it came from somewhere else. It wasn't my own. Then…I…I saw a thorn in your heart, and a man in blue. He helped you, I think."

"Do you know the man in blue?"

"No."

Merlin erupted in another long, loud bout of laughter. "Well, then, I guess we will both have to find out together." Calming down, he leaned closer to Elanor and stared at her tenderly. He gently brushed the hair out of her face, tucking it behind her ear. "You pulled the thorn out of my heart."

"I don't understand," she implored, confused. She stared at him, hoping for answers, but his undisturbed and gentle gaze made her want to move closer, so she leaned in until their noses nearly touched.

Caught by her eyes, he whispered, "I do not know the answers myself. It is something outside of us both. But," he breathed, "I do not think these things are just happening. We may not understand yet, but you are not here by accident. It seems to me things have been hidden from you. You have been brought here as much to understand as I..." Merlin paused, "am to understand you." Another surge of joy rose within him, and he collapsed back down with his hands over his face, trying to recover. "Heh! I sought the stars, but they had no answer," he said again, leaving Elanor completely confounded by his meaning. He shook his head, then rose to his feet. He reached out his hand to Elanor. "Come!"

Taking Elanor's hand, Merlin lifted her up and pulled her in close. The air stood quiet and still around them as the connection between them deepened. He smiled at her longingly, and Elanor saw the eyes of a young man full of joy, no longer seeing the mystical old Merlin. Maybe the laughter had chased the old man away.

Merlin shook his head, refusing to yield to the urge within him. He felt the same pull on his heart and lips that he had when he dreamt of her. So instead, he embraced her and kissed the top of her head. "Come now. I will walk you back to your chamber."

"Yes," she said, her ear against his chest.

Merlin released her, and she turned and grabbed her lantern from the ground. Leaning on one another, he led her back to her room. Quietly unhitching the metal latch on the door, Merlin turned to leave her to her sleep.

WHAT OF THE HEART?

Merlin crept into his chamber, his heart alight. He was almost drunk with joy. Thoughts of Elanor swirled in his mind. She was so lovely, beautifully contradicting everything he had worked so hard to believe. And then there was this man in blue.

Who was he?

He had appeared now twice. Both times at the touch of Elanor's hand, yet she did not know him.

Was he the one that sent the dreams?

Elanor's beaming, blue eyes made his heart yearn for her, but this could not be. She seemed so familiar, so known to him, yet they had only known each other for a short time. She drew him in, like every part of her was meant for him, but his rational mind forced her away.

He was Merlin. The Great Merlin. The one who had pressed through the fires of the ages. The fires of woe and battle. The bard of prophecy and the druid of wisdom and magic. Always he had been alone. That was his way. Decidedly so. In the times of Arthur, Merlin acted as a loyal aid, always by Arthur's side, and even acted as a brother and friend. But he always left, retreating to his solitude to seek his signs and remain unbothered. When he got close enough to let his heart love, he was punished for it. Loss and betrayal, always.

Something on the terrace had happened this night, and it seemed to heal his broken heart, ending his long-depressed season of grief—though he knew he could bring it back upon himself if he had so desired. Elanor's presence was setting him free, distracting him from his grief. The words he had heard from the man in blue ran through his head. "You need her in order to be whole."

I cannot let my heart long for her.

He wrestled as fear gripped him, thinking of all that could happen if he let her in.

Merlin didn't know what to think about the growing desire in his heart and his encounter with the man in blue. He wandered through Cilaen's side of the chamber, reaching for his door. When he grabbed at the iron handle, it rattled as he pulled the door open.

"Merlin?" he heard the raspy voice of Cilaen say, waking from his sleep as Merlin entered the chamber. In the dim light, he saw Cilaen walk around the corner, rubbing his eyes.

"It is only me," Merlin whispered. "You can go on back to your sleep. It is late."

Cilaen continued to wander toward him, lighting a lantern at a table nearby. Always Cilaen did this when Merlin disturbed his sleep. He remembered him as a much smaller boy, rubbing his eyes and hobbling around the corner because Merlin had awoken him. Cilaen had learned early that if his master was awake in the lost hours of the night, it was because he was seeking answers. He had also learned that Merlin was always willing to process his thoughts if he woke to listen.

Merlin loved that Cilaen wanted to be by his side at moments like this. Cilaen cared for him and desired to ease his mind. Most times, he would only sit and listen, having no understanding of Merlin's ramblings. Still, it warmed Merlin's heart every time he heard Cilaen's feet scuffling over to him from his bedside.

Cilaen poured them both a cup of water, and they sat at the table together.

"What has kept you so late?" Cilaen asked, his tired eyes focusing strangely on Merlin's face.

Noticing a puzzled look upon his servant's face, Merlin returned, "What is it?"

"Your face! You seem…changed. Your eyes look so bright, and, well…I don't know. Different."

Merlin placed his hands on his face, as if it would tell him something about what Cilaen had seen. "I have been up to the terrace. I couldn't sleep for I had too many questions, and…"

Chapter Twelve

"And?"

"Elanor was there," Merlin reminisced with a smile. "She...she said she could not sleep, and...then something extraordinary happened. An awen came that seemed to heal me, and she..." Confusion and excitement danced across Merlin's face.

"I do not believe I have ever seen you so flustered," Cilaen laughed. "Was it Elanor who has changed you?"

"I believe it was her. At least partly...and that is the very problem, isn't it?" Merlin said, rubbing his forehead.

"Why is that a problem? You said yourself that it is the Great God who has had His hand in this. So why would that be a problem? Your face! It radiates so much peace."

"I cannot love her, Cilaen!"

Cilaen leaned back, surprised by Merlin's outburst. He observed Merlin's conflicted thoughts as they passed over his countenance.

"I am not made for it. It cannot be this way." Merlin shook his head. "But when I am around her, curiosity pulls me in. The movement of her breath, the curve of her mouth. Everything about the way she speaks and moves. She is like the moon with the tide, and though I resist her with all my strength, I am weakened by her at every turn."

Cilaen smirked. "You love me, don't you?" he challenged.

"Hmmm? What?"

"You have been my master and my friend. You love me, and you loved Arthur. You love Gwynevere also. That is why her fierce and unhappy gaze makes you feel sick. And Bedwyr? And there is Peredur, also? All of us."

"Yes, I have love. Of course, I do. I would not be wise or good without it. But even my love for them, for you, costs me. My love for Arthur nearly cost me my sanity. Sanity I have not fully regained. But this kind of love..." He pointed in the direction of the Palisade where Elanor slept. "It would cost me more, and I would not be able to leave it as easily as I have you. That price is too high. What if the cost were so severe that I could not fulfill my purposes, my destiny, all be-cause of love? Because of her? Distraction, Cilaen. I am not as others are, free to have love and to marry."

"Ah!" Cilaen said. "Alone. Alone and secure to be important to the world, but untethered and free to run away as you please."

"What is this accusation? You speak as though you were an ollamh."

Cilaen smiled humbly. "I have spent many of my young years alongside the greatest of bards. I hope that has taught me something."

"Hah!" Merlin laughed. "Ha, ha, ha!" Laughter began to roll out of him, just as the laughter he had experienced on the terrace. "Perhaps you are right. I just...do not know what to do. She is all I can think of. I have never met someone who is like me. In all this lonely world, she is the first."

"Master, I do not know what you should do, only to say what I know about her to be true. She seems to have a pure heart. If she is the one who has shaken the Great Merlin back to himself, then she must be worthy above all others. For Prydain does need you, Merlin, and your gifts, if it is to be restored from its brokenness...I see your countenance transformed. There is life in you once more. I have never seen your eyes so bright, nor your smile lifted so high. If she has done this, then you should not run from her. You should not deny her your heart."

Cilaen's final sentiment sent Merlin into deep thought. Nodding his head, Merlin stood to retreat to his bed for the night. On his way, he paused to look upon his brooch and torc, the silver catching his eye. He had still not moved them from their place on the table, but now the events of the evening made him want to reach out to them. He grabbed the fine brooch, turning it around in his fingers and rubbing the emeralds to make them shine. Then, he took up his torc, with the many seasons of his life laid within its memory, and twisted it to once again to lay around his neck. There he stood, lifting his chest high.

Cilean gazed through the door and saw a spark of honor return. Merlin caught Cilaen's eye, nodded toward him, and shut his door.

FIRST DAY OF CHANGE

The next morning, Elanor rose to the sound of Samara singing. She sat up, rubbing her eyes. A strange feeling settled in from the night before. The sun shone through the shutters of her window, and she opened them to see what she couldn't in the darkness. Down below, the trees abounded with pink blossoms, and the air filled with their sweet aroma.

Samara took Elanor by the hand, babbling as she pulled her near the freshly lit fire. She dressed Elanor in a light blue dress that tied up in the back. The soft fabric of this dress featured a simpler design than the one from the day before.

Elanor's thoughts wandered to the vision of the man in blue and Merlin's laughter as Samara twisted her hair into braids that fell down her back. The memory of the laughter made her heart swell.

Samara clapped her hands, snapping Elanor out of her thoughts. It was time to see the queen.

Elanor couldn't keep her mind from drifting, floating in a sea of thoughts while she passed door after door on her way down to the queen's chamber. She didn't understand the events from last night, but it made her eager to see Merlin again. As she walked through the door, she saw him waiting next to the queen. He stood as she entered, and the calm lilt of his golden eyes alighted upon her. Elanor blushed, flustered with rising and falling emotions she was not ready to understand.

"The queen is anxious to know you," Merlin began as Elanor was welcomed in beside Gwynevere. A servant presented her with food.

The queen's eyes rested upon her, waiting for a reply, and Elanor breathed, "Please tell her I feel fortunate to be welcomed by her. I would tell her anything she would like to know."

"Gwynevere knows it will be a bit difficult until you have learned the language, but she wants you to feel comfortable. She wonders if you could tell her more about your family. Where you come from?"

Elanor nodded nervously. "I have a father and a mother. Both teach at university, though my father will be retiring soon. I have two older siblings. A sister Nancy, and a brother called Jack. I live on my own in the city away from them. I am an artist...a...uh...painter." Uncomfortably, she grimaced at Merlin, wondering if this was the sort of thing Gwynevere wanted to know. She struggled to find words to describe her life in a way that would make sense, and feared she was being interviewed to stay in the queen's favor. "I do not have a lot to say about my family. We all sort of have our own lives," she tried to explain. "I am just sort of... Oh, she can't really want to know this?" She glanced at Merlin, imploring him for help.

Merlin and the queen spoke back and forth for a moment, and Elanor ate a few bites of the small biscuits in front of her, wondering what to say next. She stared into the fire. Talking about her family made her think about her father.

"Elanor?" Merlin said calmly.

"Oh...uh."

"Are you well?"

She nodded. "The thought was just occurring to me...I wonder if my family even knows I am missing?"

Gwynevere asked through Merlin, "You are a long way away from them. Do you miss them?"

"My father...yes. I always miss him. I missed him before I was ever here. My father and I were very close. We still are—it's just that we see so little of each other anymore. We used to spend every day together in his back garden. He had a beautiful vegetable garden, and he loved to spend his days making it perfect in the spring and summer months. I would get my hands dirty helping him, and we would talk for hours and eat fresh strawberries." Elanor smiled, remembering the sweet taste and the look on her father's face. "I didn't spend much of my time inside with the rest of the family. Now I live in a flat by myself, and we don't talk as much. But I know he misses our conversations as much as I do." Elanor paused, placing her hand on Merlin's arm. "Do you think I will ever be able to go home?"

He gazed at Elanor, seeing the frightened, worried look in her eyes. "I do not know. I am sorry for that. If it gives you any peace, I believe this all has a purpose."

"All this talk about my father…What if I never see him again?" Pain and regret surged as she considered how she had neglected to tell him how she loved him. She lifted her chin with a sorrowful smile. "He used to always tell me I was not meant for his world."

Merlin's fingers stuttered to reach for her—to comfort her—but he pulled his hand back into a fist on his lap.

Gwynevere spoke. "My father was a Chieftain. He is gone now, as are my brothers. They joined in Arthur's fight against the Saecsans and did not survive the many battles." A pained expression crossed Gwynevere's face as she spoke, but it was quickly replaced with a smile. "My father was large and strong and had a laugh that could shake your bones. He was not gentle, but he loved his children."

"I am sorry."

"Yes." Gwynevere's eyes fluttered with emotion. "They were strong. Arthur was strong, and…now I have to be strong."

The room became tense as Gwynevere's eyes turned to Merlin. She spoke softly, but her tone was agitated. Merlin's face strained as she spoke.

"People are being attacked in the forests," Gwynevere said to Merlin. "I had heard rumors, but now distressed chieftains have been reaching out to me."

"Wildmen? Thieves?"

"No…no, the attacks are too direct. I believe it to be those wretched kings in the Southlands. They are in rebellion against me, Merlin. They are causing trouble to make me appear weak. They are gaining in strength."

"What is it that makes you believe it to be the southernly kings?"

Gwynevere shot Merlin a stinging glare. "You have not been here to know of the turmoil and the damage that has been done." Sighing, she regathered herself and leaned back. "Those attacked have not been just wanderers and vagrants…but Cymbrogi. Whole groups of them, left slaughtered. A display of my strength may be necessary, but I have no line to draw against the culprits. No evidence to support who is responsible…The time of need for the mighty Merlin to arise is immediate."

Merlin's head hung low, and he rubbed his forehead. "They will not be so eager to rise in rebellion once they know I have returned." Then, his eyes brightened. "Truly a new day has come and is already. Elanor has proved to show me there is hope."

Gwynevere pointed at his collar. "I see you have put your torc on once again. The men will be encouraged to see it. This will show them that you have taken back your authority. It will make them battle ready."

"Bore...ray...yah," Cilaen said slowly while dancing his finger in the air with the annunciation of the accent. "Boreauau." He lifted his hand, pointing to the sun through the window. Then, he pointed at Elanor to speak.

"Bore...ray..." Elanor shook her head with a smile. "...yah. Does that mean the sun?"

"Noh...sah," Cilaen continued. "Nosau." Pointing to the window, he brought his hand slowly down as if drawing the sun low.

"Night?" Elanor laughed, confused.

Cilaen was very attentive, making Elanor very fond of him. He moved through the words rapidly but remained patient. The room flooded with their laughter every time Elanor struggled to say a word clearly.

Merlin sat silently in an effort to stay out of Cilaen's way, but his face expressed his amusement as Elanor bungled the words. Sometimes she would reach out to him to help her understand, but he shook his head. "You cannot lean on me to interpret. You will not learn as quickly."

Cilaen began with the basics, and Elanor felt like a child as she repeated each word and syllable. The language was very difficult to learn, and she was confined to learning it by sound alone. It was not a written language, and there were no letters or words for her to reference. She worked diligently to retain as much as she could, as she was weary of not understanding anyone except Merlin.

Cilaen took to relaying many of the words through Latin, as Elanor had a basic understanding of the language, and it helped her to connect to the meanings of the words. The sound of the Cymry words were long and lovely. They had feeling and intention—no words were used flippantly.

Standing up, Cilaen brushed his hands together. "Gwblhau," he said in the Cymry tongue. The lesson was over, and Elanor was overjoyed that she understood what he'd said; they were finished.

"You are very fortunate," Merlin said to Elanor. "Books are rare, but Cilaen has many Roman texts. Many of them are mine. Some have been collected from old Roman settlements and travels I have taken. The Cymry do not write in books like the Romans do, and most all do not read; however, the druids teach their filidh to read and write in Latin. That is why we have so many books and scrolls here. I was taught Latin as a child, and I taught Arthur, and then Cilaen."

Curiously, Elanor asked, "Do the Cymry people keep a calendar? Surely in one of these books there could be a Roman calendar of some sort. I am curious. I want to know where in time I may be. I am guessing maybe somewhere in the sixth century, as you have said the Romans have recently gone, and what I know of history is helping me guess."

"Most would not know, but I know a way of discovering it. Though I am not sure our time keeping would be in line with the time keeping that would be known to you."

"To think, if I am somewhere in the fifth or sixth century! That... that would be..." Flabbergasted, Elanor tried to think. "That would be nearly fifteen-hundred years or more in the past." She laughed, astonished. "That is, if I haven't somehow stumbled into another world all together."

"What is it?" Cilaen asked, wondering what her laughter was about.

Merlin replied, "She seems to think it is possible that our world could be fifteen-hundred years from her time."

Cilaen threw his arms up astounded. "By the Great God! How can that be? Fifteen-hundred years?"

Merlin leaned over to Elanor. "The sun is still high. Let me take you riding. There is a place not far from here that I think you would like. It would be quite a sight for you to see the townspeople as we ride out of the stronghold."

"We would go now?"

"Right now, if I can get Cilaen to help prepare us some food and water." He nodded at Cilaen. "I will go out and ready our horses. And Cilaen...could you take Elanor to the Hall's entrance after all is ready? That is, if you would like to go?" He gave her a look that made her heart flutter.

"I do not know how to ride."

"You could ride with me."

"Well, then...I *would* love to see more of this new world..."

Merlin sat for a moment, peering over at her. His look was both of curiosity and fascination, and Elanor was intrigued. She watched as he left to get the horse ready.

Cilaen wrapped bread, apples, and cheese into a cloth, and placed them into a leather satchel. For the first time since the morning, Elanor's nervous feelings were returning.

MERLIN THE ENCHANTED

Cilaen turned to leave the room, indicating that he would return. Elanor distracted herself by repeating her new words. She rehearsed them repeatedly, trying to set them all to memory. This kept her mind occupied so she wouldn't have to think about the anxiety growing in the pit of her stomach. Before long, Cilaen had returned carrying over his arm a long, thin coat. He held the coat before Elanor, opening it to slide it over her shoulders, and she pulled her arms through. It was a beautiful, thinly-lined light green coat that was the length of her dress, embroidered in yellow and green thread.

"Samara has made!" Cilaen said simply for her to understand, putting his hands on his hips and nodding his head in approval.

He ushered her out through the Great Hall and onto the stone steps of the entrance. Elanor was amazed to see how the doors opened to such a grand view of the stronghold. It was a vantage point where all could be seen. She imagined what it must have been like for Arthur to stand on the steps of his Great Hall and look out above his citadel. He would have been seen by everyone, standing tall in all his grandeur on these great stone steps, the fields of warriors before him and the villages below. Elanor turned to look at the high pillars and the large, oak doors she had walked through, which contained carvings of warriors on their horses, spears in hand, in the action of battle.

"All is ready!" she heard a voice call to her from below, and there she saw Merlin, handsome and tall, at the bottom of the steps. He waited for her with the reins of a beautiful, brown horse in his hands.

Cilaen smiled with his arms crossed, then handed the leather satchel to Elanor. As she walked down the stairs to meet Merlin, Cilaen threw his arms into the air and shouted, "Bydded i'ch diwrnod gael ei fendithio!" Bowing low, he nodded to Elanor and left to return to his work.

Merlin waved. "Be blessed, my friend." Then, he held out his hand to invite Elanor close. She grabbed his hand and then reached the other to touch the nose of the majestic horse. The horse happily brushed his nose against her hand as Elanor gazed adoringly up into the animal's eyes. She had always loved horses, but this was probably the first time she had ever been close to one. She loved hearing it breathe and chuff as Merlin finished getting things tightened and ready.

"I don't know the first thing about riding a horse. You'll have to be patient. I don't even know how to get up onto one," Elanor said, smiling up at the horse's red-brown eyes.

"Elanor?" Merlin said, dropping his head uneasily while patting the horse on its side. "Have I assumed too much asking you to ride out with me? You seem to have…"

Elanor reached up and placed her hand upon his. Merlin peered down at her to see her eager smile. "Shall we go? I would love to see more of this beautiful place," Elanor said.

Merlin nodded and positioned himself to mount the horse. He noticed jitters on Elanor's face and said, "Don't worry. I will lift you up once I am settled. Just put your front leg up into the stirrup and grab hold of my hand."

He launched himself up over the horse with ease, and then reached a very confident hand down to her. Nervously, Elanor wrapped her hands tightly within his grip. Merlin was stronger than she expected, for she felt like a feather as he eased her up behind him.

"Well, that was easier than I thought it would be," she said with a surprised grin.

Merlin laughed, clucked to the horse, and they began forward down the path, first past the pink blossoming trees, and then downward onto the sloping road that led unto the fields. Elanor's eyes were wide as they passed the warriors tossing spears and practicing their war craft. Peredur was shouting at men as they slammed their swords painfully upon shields, groaning and grunting with each swing. Peredur glared over at Merlin and Elanor as they rode by, his distrusting gaze making her feel less than a speck of dirt. She wondered if there would ever be a way to show him that she wasn't a deceiver. Luckily, she did not have to bear his stare long, as they continued onto the road leading straight to an opening in the stone wall.

Merlin slowed as they approached it. Already Elanor could see movement bustling on the other side. People walked back and forth, busy and active. The iron gates stood open, and they crossed through into a great marketplace. The smell of fresh bread and manure filled Elanor's nostrils, and the sounds of stone, chains, and steel rattled in her ears. Wagons travelled down the roadway led by cattle, and children ran in and around the market stands. Smoke billowed out of the chimneys of round, thatched houses as people traded their goods and fabrics.

Both men and women stopped and stared as they saw Merlin and Elanor come through.

"Who is the great lady?" a child shouted. Women chattered, looking her way. Their faces were sad but teetered on the edge of hope.

Elanor leaned in, wishing she could disappear from their sight.

"It is not just you they are surprised to see," Merlin said. "It is also me they stare at. Really, the pair of us are making quite the spectacle. Just smile. It will encourage them. They think something exciting must be happening for a great lady like yourself to be amongst them."

"Great lady," Elanor snorted.

"Oh, I think you must be. You are a relation of the queen, remember? The queen is the greatest lady of the land. Soon, they will all know who you are, and after being seen in the towns, they will surely all be talking about you."

Elanor realized what the queen had done. Her plan to tell the people that she and Elanor were related made Elanor to be someone of importance. She hadn't been a great anything before, and the attention, whether it be in the Great Hall or out in the towns and villages, made her uncomfortable.

Elanor looked into the distance as they approached another wall. It towered so high that it came into view long before they reached it. They rode out of the market and into a space where homes now rested on a grassy plain. Here, there were many more thatched houses and little stone cottages. Cows and sheep scattered the fields of small farms. The fortress of Caer Lial was so much bigger and wider than it seemed when they were up on the terrace looking down.

They approached the wall, and the guards opened the gates for them to pass through. Out in the open, Merlin picked up their pace. Elanor began to jostle, having to tighten her grip around Merlin to hold on. The wind blew through her hair, exhilarating her as the green hills dotted with hedges of yellow flowers rolled out before them. Forest trees lined the edges of the landscape. It was beautiful, fresh, and wild.

Merlin guided the horse leftward toward the forest, slowing his pace as he carefully led the horse around the trees. They didn't pick their way long before the forest expanded into an open meadow, green and sweet-smelling from the sunshine. Across the meadow, they approached trees that created a natural archway, and there between them, Elanor could see the sparkle of the sun reflecting off of water.

Merlin dismounted and walked the horse over to a patch of grass to graze while Elanor remained on its back.

Elanor knew that Merlin intended to help her down, but as she considered the reins and the stirrups, she felt she could get down on her own. Leaning back, she tried to roll herself over the saddle; however, she slipped, and before she knew it, she was falling toward the earth. Bracing for impact, Elanor held her hands out and hit the ground, landing flat on her stomach. The fall knocked the wind out of her chest.

Hearing the sound, Merlin turned just in time to see Elanor hit the ground hard. "Elanor! Are you hurt?" he said, rushing over to her side.

Elanor laid with her head on her arms. Merlin watched as her back heaved up and down. Alarmed, he quickly rolled her over, and as he did, he was surprised to see Elanor laughing. She laughed and laughed. She laughed so hard she couldn't speak. Merlin sat down next to her, relieved she appeared to be fine, and chuckled to himself.

"I thought I could do it," she finally managed between fits of laughter. "I thought I could easily roll to the side and gracefully slide down to the ground. Horses are so much taller than I realized." She fell into another gleeful bout of giggles. Merlin helped her sit up, and she slowly relaxed. Staring up at the horse, she said, "I will not be trying that again without some assistance."

Merlin chuckled. "Or at least allow me the chance to teach you how to do it the right way."

Elanor raised her hand to her face to wipe the tears that had formed from her laughter and saw that both of her hands were bleeding. "Oh!" She bent to look closer while Merlin gripped her wrists to examine them. "Just a scratch," she said, a little embarrassed. Now that she had seen her hands, she could feel the sting of her wounds. She blew on her hands to alleviate the discomfort.

"There is cloth in the satchel," Merlin said, swiftly standing.

"No need," Elanor said as she climbed to her feet. "I saw water over there. I can just rinse them."

"The lake. Yes, that is what I have brought you here to see. The water will feel cool on your hands. I will still get the cloth."

Elanor walked through the arched trees and out to where they opened up to the shoreline of a small, tranquil lake. Behind the lake was a large, wooded hill, and beyond that led to the base of one of the mountains she had seen from the terrace. Taking in the scene, Elanor walked out onto the pebbled shore, forgetting her injured hands. It was breathtaking. The sun was warm, and the air was cool. It was like she had stumbled upon an enchanted lake, secret, safe, and hidden.

After tethering the horse to a tree and unloading some of the things he and Cilaen had prepared, Merlin walked through the trees to find Elanor standing on the shore, looking out at the lake. He set everything down by a long-fallen tree that lay in a grassy patch of the shore. "Have you not made it to the water to wash yet?"

Gazing down at her hands, she laughed. "I was taken in by this beautiful place and nearly forgot. If it weren't for the sting."

"Come," Merlin said, leading her by the arm to sit on a rock by the water's edge. He cupped water up into her hands and delicately washed the dirt away from the cuts. "I thought you'd like this place. I come here often to think. How are your hands?"

"You must think I am so clumsy. Clumsy and complicated," she said with amusement, poking fun at herself. Merlin dabbed Elanor's hands dry with the cloth and inspected them. "See. Just scratches. I am fine, I promise."

Merlin pressed on her hands and carefully wrapped them. "There. Now I am at least satisfied that you are well," he said, looking at her inquisitively.

Elanor wished she knew all the questions he was asking himself. Magic fluttered quickly in her heart, and she began to realize that the magic would come when she desired something greatly. She wanted to know his questions and desired to know him. And so, the magic roused.

Quickly, Elanor shut her eyes and turned away.

"Ah," Merlin said. "You're beginning to know the magic."

Elanor kept her eyes shut. "I wish I knew how to keep it from happening. There are things that are not for me to know. I do not wish to intrude where I haven't been invited."

"That is why you have the power and why others do not. If power does not come from a place of purity, then it twists and manipulates. The Great God gives strength and understanding, but many gain their power through dark arts and sacrifice to dark spirits. Their minds cannot be motivated out of love, and they only seek to control and destroy. That is what Morgan did." Merlin was lost in his thoughts for a moment. "You are not like her. But then, most are not like you and me. I did not create my power; I was born with a natural understanding of how the elements worked. I have never known another like me, until I met you." Touching her chin, he tenderly moved her face back toward him. "I can feel it. It feels the very same as my own…open your eyes and look around at the stillness of this place. Every bird and minnow here is at rest. Listen to the wind blowing through the trees. This place is in order with nature and the spirit." He leaned closer. "That is how I feel when I am with you."

Elanor opened her eyes and gazed out at the lake, listening to the sounds Merlin described. She deeply felt everything Merlin said, and she knew his words were true. "But I have not always been this way."

"I think you have, Elanor. Coming here has let loose the prisoner that has been chained."

She twisted her mouth, her emotions rising at his words. "How do you know that?"

"Look at me, Elanor, and do not be afraid." Merlin lifted her up to stand beside him. Then again, he said softly, "Look at me."

Slowly, she lifted her gaze, and her eyes flashed. Emotions rose deep within her, calling out with a loud resonance, like the sound of Merlin's voice when he called to her in the dream. The dream was so simple; she went where the dream led her. But this wasn't a dream. This was real. Could she answer the call? Already her heart called back to his. She could see his mind, and she could see that in it there was love. She did not want to resist. Merlin made her feel like she existed. For the first time, lost in a world she didn't understand, she was found. She belonged. She belonged to him.

As Elanor looked into Merlin's eyes, her fear melted away. His eyes were young and bright. She lifted herself onto her toes and pressed her lips against his.

Merlin wrapped Elanor in his arms, his warm lips taking her in. As they embraced, wind swirled and flower petals blew all around them. The trees seemed to applaud as they rustled in the breeze, and everything, just like in the dream, felt perfectly right. There was no doubt in Elanor's mind, nor any doubt in Merlin's.

Both chose to embrace whatever mysterious force had brought them together, and everything in that moment seemed to agree.

She uttered softly, "Is this wrong?"

"I never thought my heart could feel like this," Merlin said, unashamed. "I tried to resist it. I thought my life was over, and then you came, and I became young again. Destiny reborn. Last night on the terrace, I was changed. I cannot go back to what my life was. It seems so simple, but I am alive once more, and you are my very soul."

Elanor put her remaining questions to rest, placing her trust in Merlin. She had never done that before. She had only ever found safety in her father.

Merlin pulled out a wool blanket and laid it upon the ground. As they settled down onto the blanket, Elanor leaned back against Merlin's arm, and they quietly gazed out at the lake. Merlin waved his hand, and white petals flew up from the ground and twirled around in the air. His eyes flashed with yellow light, just as hers had, and the hovering petals took the shape of a great dragon that swirled and rolled in and out of itself. He let it dance before them for a while, then dropped his hands, allowing the petals to fall back to the earth, floating gently as they rained down.

"That was beautiful." Elanor leaned in closely. "How did you know you had magic?"

"It has always been with me. It would come in moments no one expected, like yours. When I was a child, things just seemed to occur. I do not actually believe it is magic, but there just seems no better word. I am not a sorcerer. There are things I can see and things I can do. It all comes from a stirring in my heart and spirit. There have been times when the magic came in times of great need, and times I cried out for it, and there would be nothing. I have asked the Great God to show me wisdom. He tells me when I should act and when I should not. I have assumed in the past that because I had great power, it was my right and responsibility to use my powers to help when I saw fit. Truly, I have been arrogant to assume I am great at all. I have made many mistakes believing I was the answer and have paid dearly. I have learned to sit and listen, and then obey.

"My mother told me my power came from my father. She said he had a similar strength. As a bard, he sang, and whole groups of people were moved by his voice. Their hearts would be healed, and he would speak truth to them. He died just after I was born. So, my mother sent me to learn from the druids, hoping to help me understand my gifts. I learned, as my father did, to hone magic and prophecy through the song of the bard. I would prophesy in this way.

"There came a time, when I was still very young, that the druids began fighting amongst themselves. Many of the order believed they had discovered the Great Triple God. That this God was the one they had been seeking in the sky and the earth. They cast off many of the dark traditions of the past and embraced the New Way. But some rebelled at this idea, going even deeper into the ways of dark arts and sacrifice to the priestesses of the earth. It was at this time a greater power rose within me. I believed it was the Great God calling to me, and I listened to Him. My mother had always said that my father spoke of a time a kingdom would come and never fade. This kingdom would bring peace and end wars. This was the kingdom I wanted to see, and the one I felt rising up in my bones. The ways of the past had to change, and the New Ways had to come. During this time, the old order of the druids split, and they have never returned to the way they once were. Divided now, many of the druids of the New Way stopped calling themselves druids, and the druids of the old ways have gone into hiding."

"You say you are old? But you are young," Elanor questioned.

"I am young again; I feel now that I have met you."

"How?"

Merlin laughed. "I am not immortal! No, no. My mother's people are of an older race. They travelled to these lands a long time ago. Some have called them the Fair Folk. Few remain of my mother's fair race. They were a tall people, graceful and strong. They age much more slowly than other races, but age they do. My father is a mystery, however. He hailed from a race of Cymry warriors, but they say he was different. Special in some way. He was brought up the son of a Cymry Chieftain and raised as a bard and warrior. So, I am not all Fair folk. I was born not quite ninety years ago, but as I have not aged the same as the others around me, age does not mean to me the same as it does for others. It has, however, made me feel very alone."

"All was building, you see, to this great kingdom. The kingdom I was meant to build. The Romans left, leaving us exposed to raiders that were overwhelming our lands. All those years, I waited for the king I would raise up. All those years, watching Arthur be a great battle chief and win over all of his enemies. All those years, and finally I saw him king, and a kingdom established, only to have it dashed to pieces." Merlin shook his head, remembering the anguish. "I thought I had died. Age had finally had its say, until I dreamt of you."

"What happened to Arthur?"

"He went chasing the holy cup. He thought the Great God had given him this cup as a symbol of the new kingdom age. So, he left all to seek it. Then, he arrogantly went chasing after the Romans in their own lands to lord over them. I counseled him to leave them. They were not long for this world anyway. An old, failing empire. Still, Arthur was on the rise and thought he was invincible. It would be too much to tell you how it all crumbled. Always there had been dark forces set against us, but always our Great God kept us steps ahead. They could not hinder us. But when Arthur left, it seemed the protection we had left with him. The kingdom was robbed and taken by Mordred, son of the slain sorceress Morgan. Her evil was treacherous. Arthur returned just in time, and there was a great battle on Camlan. There we won against the enemy, but such was the cost that we never recovered." Tears formed in Merlin's eyes. "Most of my dear friends died that day. Arthur was injured, but we thought he had been saved. The wound seemed like nothing. Only we did not know that Mordred had poisoned his blade. There was nothing I could do to save him."

He sighed a great breath. "None of that should have ever happened. But," Merlin said, pointing his finger into the air, "something more, I hope, has begun. I refused to hope for so long. I hated it with all my being, but one moment has made all my hopelessness seem like folly, or maybe it was a lot of little moments." He drifted off, looking out across the lake and biting his bottom lip as he thought. "The sun will be setting in a few hours. We must return." He grabbed Elanor's hand, kissed it, and stood up to stretch.

"I hate to leave this place," she said, peering out at the still water as she stood.

"We will come back."

They walked hand in hand over to the horse to prepare to leave, but Elanor stopped still, letting go of Merlin's hand. She took a deep breath, taking in the sweet fragrance of the air. A smile drew long across her face, and she peered all around as if to quickly spy something that would soon disappear.

"What is it?"

"Don't you smell it?" Finally, Elanor's eyes caught what she was looking for. "Primrose!" She dashed over to a patch of yellow flowers beautifully blooming just underneath the side of a tree. She knelt down to smell them, then closed her eyes and smiled. "I love the smell of primrose. They remind me of springtime when I was a small child. There was always primrose in the garden, and the warm evening sun would make their sweet smell fill the air." She picked a single flower from the patch. "I'll just take this one and leave the rest to grow."

"Primrose are a happy flower," Merlin said, kneeling next to Elanor.

Leaning over, Elanor softly kissed him. "I won't delay us any further."

Merlin was mystified by how quickly Elanor could move past sadness and confusion. He knew it was not naivety but strength, and it made him feel strong. She might not have known her own strength or magic, but that did not make her weak. She did not resist moving forward when faced with fear or the unknown. Everything about Elanor made him feel like there was more to life than he could have ever imagined. Every turn of her head, every look from her eyes, made his heart sing, yet it was what she said and did that drew him in. Truly he had never met another like her. Maybe in her future time, there were many like her, but here in this time, most carried weariness in their eyes. Elanor was like the primrose she'd picked, young and sweet with the beginnings of life upon its petals. Yes, this was what he felt too. Like a primrose. He was glad she had stopped for the flower, because she had become his rose and youth of spring. He hoped the love he felt for her was not as fragile as the delicate flower she now held in her hand.

They rode home, back through the forest, and out onto the green hills. Elanor leaned into him as they rode. Both of their hearts felt warm and new. Safe with each other, both hearts had found a home that had been missing.

BELTAINE

Merlin and Elanor kept their love secret from all but Cilaen. Keeping it hidden saved them from having to share it with anyone else. Elanor was less eager to know the mystery of time travel and magic now that she had found a place with Merlin. Unbeknownst to her, two full months had passed since first arriving in Caer Lial.

Because of her love for Merlin, Elanor no longer desired to go back home, though she never told him so. Sometimes, she worried she might go to sleep and wake up back in her flat. She worried that she would be whisked away just as unexpectedly as she had arrived. She pushed these thoughts away as often as they came, hoping that if she did not think about them, they would never be.

In her life before, everything was blurry and half there. Here, everything was clear and whole. She did not want to go back to a half-life. No matter how different or harsh things could be in this new place, this was a far kinder reality for her. Here, she was something to someone, and not just to Merlin. She had a growing friendship with Cilaen, and an affection for Samara.

And then there was Gwynevere.

Gwynevere had accepted her, though it seemed a mystery to Elanor as to why. As queen, Elanor thought Gwynevere should have been less trusting and suspicious, but she never was. Though the queen was severe with others, she was never like that with Elanor.

Preparations had begun for Beltaine, an important festival and feast to the people of these lands, and Elanor found that more than usual, people bustled around the Hall and Palisade in preparation for the season's eve. Yellow flowers and ribbons appeared, decorating the Hall and the town, and even some of the livestock had been moved into pens around the warriors' fields for the ceremony. The men and warriors set up new fenced arenas for games of strength and skill. For in just one day's time, there would be a bonfire and a great feast.

As the queen grew busy making preparation, Elanor saw less of her. Some of the people from surrounding villages would be coming, and many of the chieftains would be in attendance. The important nature of the festival pulled the queen away to oversee preparations. This fact also meant that Merlin would be busy.

Cilaen explained, "Merlin's presence will be important for the chieftains at the festival. The sight of him will make a significant impact for the people of lands outside Caer Lial."

Curious, Elanor wandered out to look over the balustrade and into the courtyard. Servants with arms full of ribbons and flowers moved back and forth between the Palisade and Great Hall. The excitement of the festivities permeated the air.

Contentedly she watched, when suddenly she became aware of a dark shape lingering, distracting her from the scene below. Elanor slowly turned to see the silhouette of a man watching her at the end of the passageway. In the shadow of the corner he stood, his frame hunched and ominous.

"Hello?" Elanor inquired. The figure did not respond and remained still. His lack of movement produced a creeping feeling in the pit of her stomach.

Maybe he doesn't know I am speaking to him, she thought, turning her body to face him. "Hello?" Her voice wavered nervously. She squinted to see him more clearly, then moved toward him.

Abruptly, he darted down the stairs. Without knowing why, Elanor chased after him. Down the stairs and toward the Great Hall, she rounded the corner. "Aaahhh!" Elanor screamed as she collided with a man just inside the door of the Hall.

Bedwyr grabbed hold of Elanor's shoulders to steady her. "Are you well, my lady?"

Elanor's eyes darted left and right, seeking the man she was chasing, but there was no sign of him; he'd been swallowed up by the bustle of so many people.

"My lady?"

"I'm sorry...I thought I saw someone," she admitted, embarrassed now that she had run into Bedwyr. She hoped her words came across in an under-standable manner.

"You are speaking very well," Bedwyr encouraged. "Are you helping with the preparations?"

"I wouldn't know where to start helping. I think I would just be in the way," Elanor said, still looking over her shoulder nervously.

"I, too, am in the way, I think." He gazed over at the center of the Great Hall and pointed to a very frustrated-looking woman who was shouting orders with an angry grimace on her face. "I am highly respected by my men, but appar-ently not by everyone," he laughed. "So, this is what we will do. I will show you all that is being built for the games and festival tomorrow's eve. We can ride horses down to the fields."

"Oh, I do not know how to ride."

"Haven't you been to the forest with Merlin and Cilaen?"

"Yes, but I have ridden with them, never on my own."

"Well, that will change today," Bedwyr said with excitement. "I have raised many of the horses and have equipped many a young rider. My role is to instruct the warriors on horseback, while Peredur instructs the footmen. I know just the horse with a good temperament for my lady." He bowed mildly with an enduring smile.

Bedwyr led Elanor to the stables that were just outside of the Hall. They were tall and beautifully built, painted in green and red. It was not a meagre building constructed just to hold animals; rather, the structure was built to honor the horses, with a high roof and pillars on the outside. Wooden faces of horses jutted out from the pillars, looking down on those who entered. Inside were many stalls along the length of the structure. Men moved in and out, cleaning, feeding, and brushing the horses. The horses neighed and puffed majestically as Elanor passed by.

"These are war horses. They are primed and ready for battle. Just like the warriors, they train daily and are well taken care of for their services. They are our legs and sometimes, our right hand in a battle, and so we treat them as an extension of ourselves."

Elanor could feel the respect and honor the men had for the horses. The horses themselves seemed to know they were important, their heads lifted high and regal.

"These horses back here," he said, pointing as they approached wider stalls at the end, "no longer go into battle. They are older and have served many years. Though they still have spirit, we honor them with rest and peace. They have seen enough seasons of battle." He lifted his hand up to a white and brown speckled horse with a similarly colored mane.

The horse nuzzled Bedwyr's hand as he came close. "This one is Brynn. She was my horse for many years. She's a good girl." Bedwyr patted her side and allowed the horse to nibble his fingers while rubbing her muzzle against his head. "Brynn will be a good horse for you to ride. She is steady and knows how to take care of her rider. She will not give you any surprises. Let her see you." He clasped Elanor's hand and drew her near the horse. "Place your hand on her nose. Let her smell you."

"She is such a marvelous horse."

"Aih, she is that," he said, looking his horse over.

Bedwyr prepared Brynn and another, darker brown horse with saddles before leading them both out of the stables. "This is Hwyddan. He is young and needs some exercise." Elanor felt a bit nervous about riding on her own, but Bedwyr put her at ease. He helped her put her foot into the stirrup and hoisted her up at the waist. He explained how to sit on the horse and properly hold the reins. "Brynn will follow my lead. You have but to hold the reins as I have shown you. I will instruct you as we go. Just stay relaxed; she will sense your anxiety."

Elanor was relaxed with Bedwyr by her side, instructing her calmly all the way down the hill to the field. Brynn gave Elanor no surprises, just as Bedwyr had promised.

Now on the field, Elanor watched the action as men trained for the games. Some tossed spears from horseback into rings on the ground, some wrestled hand-to-hand, while others fought with mallets and shields.

"They are preparing for tomorrow," Bedwyr said. "Each winner will be given a prize from the queen. Some will receive chickens or quail, while the winners of the larger events might be given a cup or weapon. Over here is where the queen will sit." He motioned to a hill set before a large arena. On top of the mound, a canopy was being constructed. "You will sit with the queen up there. As will Merlin, Peredur, and myself. Many will be wondering who the young lady is," he said with a wink. "Many will also be pleased to see that Merlin has indeed returned. This year will be a good festival and feasting."

After returning, Bedwyr helped lower Elanor down from her horse. "Thank you, Bedwyr," Elanor said. "It was lovely to ride Brynn and find a friend amidst all the goings on."

He bowed. "The pleasure was mine, my lady."

The next day started early. The day of Beltaine had come.

"You seem very excited," Elanor said with a grin as Samara hurried to prepare her for the procession to the fields.

"Oh, yes!" Samara replied. "This year feels like a real celebration. Preparations like these have not been made since before the king died. The good God smiles on us this day."

Merlin met Elanor at the door. He was dressed in the colors of Caer Lial, fastened together with his brooch. He looked handsome and bright. She wanted to rush to him, but she controlled herself and bowed.

"You look lovely," Merlin said, grabbing Elanor's hand and pressing it to his chest. "Bedwyr told me he took you riding yesterday. I am glad."

"Bedwyr was fine and wonderful company."

"It is very well that you spent the day the way you did, since you will be riding down with us into the fields. Bedwyr has made sure that Brynn has been made ready. The processional will be led by twenty Cymry warriors. Peredur will follow, then Gwynevere and I—side by side. Bringing up the rear will be you beside Bedwyr, and then another twenty Cymry. Once we have arrived at the mound, the queen will open the festivities. Now then, are you ready?"

Elanor had never been in a procession of any kind, let alone one for a queen. The idea of this was both nerve-wracking and exciting. Out in the yard, she could feel the anticipation. The warriors were already up on their horses, dressed in red and gold, holding their spears up high.

Peredur escorted Gwynevere past the Cymbrogi. Gwynevere was beautiful as she was lifted onto her horse. Her every movement carried authority with grace. Peredur still wore a stoic face, but at least no one doubted that he would protect the queen. In her gold dress she sat upon her horse, sovereign and noble.

How Elanor had found herself with such dignified people, she did not know.

The procession began, and the field crowded with people in expectancy. As the queen crested the hill, the people cheered. The immensity of the moment was nothing Elanor had ever experienced. She tingled in excitement, her face filled with wonder. Majestically down the hill the procession went, continuing out across the field. People waved yellow ribbons as they passed. Dismounting their horses, they climbed the mound, now set with a canopy and a row of high-backed chairs for each of them.

Gwynevere raised her arms and gazed out at the people. She exclaimed, "Cymry! Tonight is the eve of Beltaine. Tonight we light the fires that will light our lands. Our long season of mourning has passed. The cold has melted away and the sun has returned. Today we celebrate. Hope and new days have returned to us. Let the Games of Beltaine begin!" she concluded, throwing her arms down as the people cheered.

Three warriors on horseback catapulted across the field. They wore no tunics, but their tops were covered in blue woad. Paint swirled across their faces, torsos, and arms. They held their spears pointed forward like arrows, hollering and whooping as they rode past to begin the games.

The field became active. Cheers roared from every direction as children ran about with ribbons in their hands. The arena before them hosted a spear toss-ing event, and all three men sitting upon the mound vocalized their support for the champions as they sent their spears flying to the furthest point. Even Peredur was smiling as he shouted for his favorite man. This was the most enthusiastic Elanor had ever seen him.

Merlin could see Elanor's surprise. "This is the Peredur I know. You will know him also; just give him time."

"Why does he mistrust me so?"

"He is a follower of Esu. He is the same Great God of these lands, but Peredur grew up in a Roman home. Their belief in the Great God came with many fearful superstitions. There is no room for magic. The unexplainable is all of the dark realms. He worries you have come like Morgan to deceive us. Peredur is one of Arthur's strongest of men. He is tall, strong, and formidable, but he is also strong of heart and faith. He has the purest of hearts. He and Arthur zeal-ously sought the holy cup above all else."

"But you have magic."

"Yes, well, Peredur and I have had long history together. He knows my ways are different than the fallen, ruined ways of sorcery and dark druids, but he is not so willing to believe that of others. And his experience has affirmed his belief to be true. He will see that you are different."

"Aren't the festivals of Beltaine pagan?"

"Old and druidic, yes. Traditional mostly. Many things in this land have blended together over time. We are Cymry people, and this is how we have always honored the land and the changing of the season."

"I see."

Knowing this of Peredur made Elanor feel better about him. She realized that the reason for his prejudice was founded, and in truth, she was surprised that there hadn't been more suspicion in the others.

The games changed, one to another. There were battles with great clubs, and even combat with sword. The games on horseback were Elanor's favorite as she watched men aim at targets at full speed, and even a game where they attempted to unhorse their opponent with blunt poles the size of spears. It was almost like jousting, but on a much closer and smaller scale. The queen lit up every time she awarded a winner with a prize. Elanor admired how much she seemed to love her people. Their delight was her delight.

The day was long and full, and soon the sun would be setting. The games ended with a final prize being given to the highest champion: a bronze bowl, delicately designed and handsomely received.

Men had constructed a large, wooden pyre in the center of the arena, surrounding it with tall branches and brambles. Merlin had been gone from Elanor's side for a while, and now emerged walking into the arena toward the pyre. He had taken off his colors, now wearing a grey cloak, and carried with him a rowan staff—becoming the very wizard of the stories Elanor had heard as a child. Mystical and ancient. He stood before the pyre as men of the Caer came into the arena, leading their largest bull. Merlin lifted the staff above his head as the sun slipped down over the horizon.

"People of the Caer Lial," he exclaimed loudly. His voice boomed as if supernaturally amplified. "Beltaine is upon us, and we graciously thank the land for its continued bounty. Great God, bless us as we light the fires of Beltaine and carry its light into our homes and into our land."

Elanor heard him shout two words that were undecipherable, followed by a crack that sounded like several branches being broken all at once. The pyre sparked on the inside, and then slowly, the flames grew higher and higher until it was a fully ignited bonfire.

Merlin held his staff high as every man with a bull walked around the great fire in a sun wise circle. Around the fire once, then twice, and then after the third time around, they departed the arena with their animals in tow. The whole line had completed their rounds, and Merlin brought down his rowan staff.

A man from every family in the stronghold approached the bonfire and lit a torch within the fire, then carried the flame back to their homes. From Elanor's vantage point, she could see fires begin to light all over the citadel. The warriors and chieftains were next, and then lastly Elanor went down with the queen and lit the final torches.

The great procession of warriors and chieftains, led by the queen and her men, made their way back up the hill to the Great Hall, the hill alight with flame as they ascended. The ceremony was beautiful and mysterious.

The queen walked into the Hall and dropped her torch into the large hearth at the center of the room, instantly illuminating the space with orange and red light. The men shouted as the hearth fire began to burn and set their many torches upon walls, making the room even brighter for the evening's feast.

Merlin joined Elanor's side again, dressed once more in red and gold, with a bright smile on his face. He escorted her to sit next to the queen at the long table in the front of the Hall.

With the boards now heavy with meats, cheeses, and bread, Gwynevere stood, lifting her cup aloft. "And now to the feasting."

The men cheered wildly and sat down on their benches to commence in eating and drinking, laughing and boisterously sharing their stories.

Elanor leaned over to Gwynevere. "This has been a wonderful day!"

Gwynevere shouted over the men, "It truly has been. I am glad you are here, Elanor. Arthur would be glad to see his men celebrating so highly. It has been a long time."

Realizing that the loudness of the room made it impossible for a true conversation, she gave Gwynevere a simple nod.

After all ate and had become full, Bedwyr jumped up onto the table and shouted loudly, spilling his drink over his hand. "Listen, all you men! Let us not waste this time of drinking and fellowship without a song." He stomped his foot and the table shook with the force of his movement. He flung his arms open wide and sang a jubilant song about men, ale, and maidens.

The warriors swung their cups, singing along with him and eagerly drinking as they did. Bedwyr sat down, happy with himself for what he had started as the men continued to sing, round after round.

After a long while of happy song, a man standing far in the back began to sing a more sombre dirge of battle and woe, and the men sang along with their voices high and melodious. The men felt their song, creating an atmosphere of deep, contemplative sadness.

Woe, was that day—We stood strong upon the Bay. The ships sailing, forever hailing, but ready we were to enter the fray. We would defend the bay. Oh Woe, was that day.

Woe, was that day—When the enemy feet landed. We stood unafraid. The Bard's strong voice could lift us on, we would not be carried on. Oh Woe, was that day.

Woe, was the day—Our arrows and spears were true. The enemy fled, but we still bled. The enemy defeated, but we were depleted. All we had gained, we lost in men who would never an ale be quenched. Oh Woe, was that day.

The song ended and brought silence. Quietly, they sipped their ale, raising their cups to those lost. The Cymry spirit weighed heavy in the room. Gwynevere broke the silence. "It is time we now had a song from you, fair bard," she declared to Merlin.

Merlin looked at Gwynevere uncertainly. He hesitated a moment, and then replied, "It has been a long time, my queen, since this voice has sung, or these hands have graced the harp…" After another moment of deliberation, he said, "But maybe it is time. Cilaen, would you fetch me my harp?"

Cilaen eagerly delivered the beautiful instrument into Merlin's hands within moments. Merlin turned to stand on the platform behind them. Gazing at his instrument, he began brushing the strings gently. He took a deep breath and then closed his eyes. Every heart was silent and still as he stood. No one moved nor spoke, all patiently waiting for the bard's song to begin. A voice came ringing out from Merlin's throat, rich, strong, and gentle. The sound moved through the room like sunlight in the morning.

Elanor sat amazed, and instantly emotions welled inside her. This was the second time during the festivities that she felt her body tingle from head to toe. Elanor had never heard a voice more beautiful or pure.

Every word he sang pierced the hearts of everyone in the room. At first, it was only his voice, but as he went, he began to softly pluck at the strings of his instrument. His music was not just sound but magic itself. It moved and shaped the minds and thoughts of all who heard it.

Merlin sang a song of a warrior of old who had fought for his land and for his king. The warrior fell in love with a woman of the forest, but it was only at night in the reflection of the moon in the water that he saw her. Always he chased her image, so fair she was to him. Milky white was her skin like the moon, and golden was her hair like the stars. Night after night, he forgot the land, the kingdom, and even himself. Every night, he thought he got closer; but by day she was gone. Finally, one night she invited him to the water's edge, pulling him down into her watery world. Down, down, down she pulled him into the depths. She was so beautiful; his eyes fixed on hers as they sparkled back at him.

"I shall perish!" he said to her as the depths stole his breath, but still she pulled him down, smiling as she did. He realized then to have her meant to choose death. Would he choose to live forever with her in death, or live forever without her in life? He looked back up to the surface, to the life he had before. He could see the moon floating high above the surface of the water.

Have I forsaken all? he thought. *To chase the moon that has always been before me but never mine?*

Fighting for breath, he swam to reach the surface, but alas, it was too far. His last breath stolen, he died looking up at the moon. Some say that though the night had stolen him away, perhaps in the day he might awaken still.

A tear slipped from Elanor's eye. She knew Merlin's song was more than a story. Its truth saturated the room, and all who heard it understood. The gift of the bard to release a song was a power she had never encountered before. A great fire began to burn in Elanor's chest. The magic within her responded to the sound of the bardic harp and rhythm.

THE DARKNESS

Beltaine had not long ended, and days were becoming warmer and longer. Elanor had begun to live for the long evenings when she and Merlin could find reason to be together. Elanor was becoming quite proficient at helping Cilaen with his tasks, along with learning all she could from him. She scanned many of his books, gaining what she could from them. She grew fascinated by the books detailing the use of plants and herbs for healing. So much that had been forgotten; it seemed a pity that some of this basic knowledge had been lost through time.

She was enchanted by how Cilaen took the knowledge of medicines from his books, combined them with the art of druidic healing of plants, and then used words of power he had learned from Merlin.

One day as Elanor was looking through Cilaen's books, she stumbled upon a small blue book that looked strangely familiar. Eagerly, she picked it up and stared at it. Could it be the same book, or was it just another one like the book the old man had given her? She smelt it to see if it had a similar smell.

"Do you like faery stories?" Cilaen asked, observing Elanor's interest of the small book. He and Merlin had been sitting at a table in deep conversation. "It seems like you have found a treasure."

"Faery stories?" Elanor asked curiously. "I didn't know you had story books mixed in with all your books of learning."

"I have a few. There is one on beasts and spirits around here somewhere as well," he said, standing from the table to rifle around the room.

"What is it?" asked Merlin, noticing the look on Elanor's face was more than just curiosity.

Elanor glanced up at him as she swept her fingers over the cover, tracing the flowers and vines inlaid into the leather. "It's just that I have seen a book very much like this one before. It was a gift," she said, a nervous smile flickered on her lips. "I never had the chance to look inside it. I was told that the book contained faery stories, just like this one."

"Let me see it?" Merlin asked, taking the book from her hands. "This is a book of mine. It came from my mother. This one, and I think a few others, are from my mother's people. These books were rare because the Fair Folk wrote on scrolls, but very few created books such as these. Small and delicate. You would love the pictures, let me show you." Merlin opened the book to reveal the pages, and Elanor gasped and threw her arms up over her eyes.

Her panicked reaction made Merlin drop the book. "What is wrong?"

Elanor slowly brought her arms down to see that the book had fallen open on the floor. She could see colorful letters and a picture on the open pages. Curious, Merlin watched as she retrieved the book, staring deeply at the pages. She drew it onto her lap and ventured to look at the finely drawn picture of what appeared to be a sea serpent wrapping itself around a ship. "This language, what is it?"

"Elanor, what had you so frightened?"

Elanor looked at Merlin strangely. Her mouth twisted as she considered what to say. "This cannot be the same book. I wish I could remember clearly. It was a book just like this, and when I opened it to look inside…" She stopped, trying hard to remember what had happened that day. "I think the book was magic—enchanted—because it was as I opened the book…I was sent into the very dream that brought me here."

"Truly?" Merlin questioned, looking over at the book in her lap. "I can assure you that this book has no magic in it. You need not fear it."

She laughed uneasily. "Silly, really," she said as she flipped through the pages.

"Who was it that gave you this book?"

Just then, there was a loud knock at the door. Cilaen looked at the both of them, but before he could answer the door, Bedwyr barged urgently into the room. "Forgive the intrusion, but I must be quick. Merlin, Gwynevere needs you in the Hall at once. Three elders have come from the Southlands seeking help. Please, come immediately to hear their plight."

"Right away." Merlin quickly turned to leave. He looked at Elanor for a short moment, and then followed Bedwyr out the door.

Cilaen stood by Elanor, placing his hand on her shoulder. "I am sure it will all be fine," he said, more to comfort himself. "Saecsans have not raided these lands in years. Not since Arthur finally drove them out, and the Picti have left us undisturbed on their side of the wall in the north. I do hope it is not invaders of any kind. We have warriors prepared to remind them that these lands are not unprotected." Cilaen sat down, still looking toward the door. "Ah, well. We cannot worry about what we do not know. Merlin will be sure to tell us what we need to know. In the meantime, I will get us some food."

Elanor looked at the book in her hands, and then at the door that Merlin had departed through. She watched as Cilaen began unwrapping a cloth from some butter and placed some bread out on the table. She felt uneasy. She couldn't tell if it was Merlin's abrupt departure or Cilaen's words that had set her on edge. Perhaps it was her fear over having found the blue book. She had been afraid that opening the book was going to send her back home, and that would have broken her heart. She struggled to be at peace and put her mind at ease. Sitting down with Cilaen and eating didn't distract her, however. Both of them anxiously watched the door, waiting for Merlin to return to put their curiosity to rest.

"Merlin will be the best aid for a serious situation," Cilaen finally said. "He always knew how to bring wise counsel to the king in times of trouble. Not that I was there." Cilaen glanced at Elanor meekly. "I was so small a child when many of the battles were being fought. I have only really known the peace that was brought through Arthur, but the songs and stories have been told to me my whole life. I was, however, here at the Palisade when Mordred came. He locked me up with the servants for days without much food or water. Those of us who were locked inside knew little of the goings on outside. I became very fearful when I had heard that Mordred was leading Gwynevere and Merlin out to be executed, just as he knew the king would be sailing home. Mordred wanted the king to see his beloved wife and druid slaughtered. Though he had no such luck. Arthur did not fall into his hands. At least not entirely. Finally, the doors were unlocked, and we were set free. Never did anyone truly see Arthur again, or many of his faithful men. It was a very sad time. A time that seemed to last the many years of Merlin's absence. Merlin had disappeared, and we were left behind to rebuild." Cilaen trailed away, deep into his thoughts. Talk of Mordred and battles had not eased their minds.

It was early in the evening when finally, Merlin returned. He stood, looking at Elanor and Cilaen gravely.

"What happened to the villages?" Cilaen asked, unwilling to wait for Merlin to begin. "What did the elder men say? Were they attacked by Saecsans?"

Merlin sat across from Elanor. "Please come, Cilaen," he said, pointing to a seat next to him. He gripped Elanor's hands, and she could see from the look in his eyes that he was distressed. "I will tell you both. The news is not good. The villages were attacked, but not by Saecsans. They told us of eight men, all hooded, who terrorized three southern villages."

"Only eight men?" Cilaen asked, surprised.

Merlin held up his hand. "There were but eight hooded men, however, one of them wielded some kind of dark magic. They came into the villages on foot, which drew no immediate alarm, but then the dark sorcerer among them began throwing men with a wave of his hand, and no one could come near to stop them. The other hooded men moved through the villages with torches, burning all as they went. The warriors who protected the villages tried to rise up against them, but the dark sorcerer easily defeated them. They were completely helpless—the evil men killed as many of them as they wanted. They burned down homes and slaughtered many of the sheep and cattle with the sword. In one of the villages, they pulled the elder druid from his home and cut off his head. They killed all the young filidh, many of them children. They left the villages burnt to the ground, food destroyed, and their druids murdered. Nothing could be done to stop the devastation. The hooded men left no trace except for carnage and ash. The elders are very frightened and are seeking our aid. They believe more villages are in imminent danger. We must act quickly. They fear they have an enemy that they have no ability to fight."

"What defense could they have?" Elanor asked.

"Me," Merlin said, staring her straight in the eye. "Elanor, I must leave. Bedwyr and I will be leading some men to the villages at first light to help replenish their supplies and see if we can pick up the trail of these villains."

Elanor's heart dropped to the floor. She swallowed deeply, trying to keep tears from welling in her eyes. She did not want him to go. She knew she could not be selfish, but her heart was afraid to be parted from him.

"How long will you be gone?" she said, choking on her words as they came.

Merlin could see she was fighting inside herself. He knelt in front of her and placed his hands on her face, softly kissing her forehead. "I am sorry, Elanor. I do not know how long I will be gone. I hate to leave you, but these people need our help. Know that I will be safe, and I will return to you. Cilaen will care for you like a brother. You will not be alone. Gwynevere will need you, and that will bring you comfort also."

Elanor sat quietly, rationalizing all she had heard as she worked to calm her emotions. "I wish you did not have to go, but I will be alright. These men must be stopped."

"There are many things unknown. The only way to discover what will need to be done is to go."

"Sorcery!" said Cilaen finally. "I truly had been naïve to think that it had all been destroyed at last with Mordred's death." He slapped his hand on the table.

"We may discover the group and find that they are no more than terror-izers that can be stopped. This is my hope, and that is what we set out to accomplish; however, my heart tells me that these men are but another symptom. These are not the first dark happenings of late. Though sorcery like they have exhibited takes time and planning. It will likely have exhausted them, and they will not have regained much of their strength if we hurry. This kind of magic would have cost them." Merlin turned once again to Elanor. "I have much to prepare in a short amount of time. I will come see you before I leave. Have Samara ready for me to come, for it could be quite late."

Elanor quietly nodded, still working hard to stifle her rising emotions.

"I will walk you to your chamber," Cilaen offered.

Silently, Elanor nodded in response, feeling unsure. Merlin leaned in to kiss her and reluctantly left to his work. Cilaen sat down next to Elanor and wrapped his arm around her. As he helped her stand, she folded the blue book between her arms, taking it with her.

At her door, they were met by Samara, who had been waiting for Elanor. "What has kept you?" Cilaen jumped right in, telling Samara all that had transpired, relieving Elanor of the task while she moved to sit on her bed. The conversation between Cilaen and Samara became muffled and distant as she lost herself in thought.

What would it be like without Merlin? What if something were to happen to him?

She looked down at the blue book in her hands, examining the cover before laying it on the table beside her. As she thought, she resolved that she would be strong. She would not be weak, and she certainly wasn't going to allow this situation to make her feel disheartened.

She pressed through fearful thoughts that sought to overwhelm her. Desperately, she searched for reassurance. Elanor had never really thought much about a Great God before, though Merlin always spoke of him. When he talked of Him, it made her feel like He was real and tangible. *"The Great God was the source of the good magic,"* Merlin would say, *"the magic of purity and love. Not deceit and evil."* Merlin said that the Great God was the source that was within her and within him.

She didn't know how this could be. She had never believed in a god before, but she was beginning to believe in a lot of things she would have considered false until recent experience showed her otherwise. She closed her eyes and began to speak the name of the Great God within her heart. She hoped that if He was really there, He would strengthen her and keep Merlin, Bedwyr, and the men safe. Maybe it was the Great God who would do something to stop these terrible villains.

She opened her eyes to find Cilaen kneeling in front of her. "Are you alright?"

"Truly, yes. I…I was only thinking. Maybe the Great God could bring us hope," she put lightly.

"Aih! I do believe He could," Cilaen said with tender encouragement. "Elanor?" He placed his hands over hers. "If it would bring you comfort to know, I would gladly be to you as a brother is to a sister. We could take care of each other. It would be an easy thing for me to do."

"Thank you, Cilaen." Elanor was moved by the sincerity of his offer. Then, nodding, she said, "You are my brother, and I am your sister."

Smiling, Cilaen stood. "I will see you tomorrow then," he said as he turned and left.

The night went slowly as Elanor waited for Merlin to come. Samara had laid down on the long bench beside the hearth, and Elanor laid awake in her bed. She tried to sleep but couldn't. She was too anxious. She knew Merlin would come, but feared if she fell asleep, he might choose not to wake her.

Chapter Sixteen

Elanor laid in view of the window where she could still see the stars. The black of the sky was beginning to wane blue. It would soon be dawn.

Finally, there was a knock at the door. Samara leapt up, grabbing Elanor's robe, and draped it around her shoulders as she rushed to stand beside her bed. Samara scurried to the door to let Merlin in. Elanor's heart leapt inside her chest.

"Would you give us a short moment, Samara?" Merlin said quietly, his voice but a whisper.

Samara bowed, leaving the room.

Merlin stood at the door, staring at Elanor. He looked blue in the darkness. She wondered why he did not move but lingered silently. Then, he finally said, "I do not want to leave you, Elanor. I have gone out many times to do the work of these lands, but never with such heaviness in my heart."

"Please come over to me. You seem far away." Elanor extended her hand toward him.

He quickly came, grabbing her hand and kissing it longingly.

"Miss me," she said tenderly, "but do not worry for me. I cannot have you worrying for me when you have important things to do. I will miss you greatly, and I will try hard not to worry after you. A luxury of my time was that no matter how far someone was away from you, you could still speak to them. You could hear someone's voice that was miles away from you, and even see their face." Elanor breathed, "There is no such thing here. Just know I will be alright. I am not fragile, Merlin."

"I know you are not," he said, placing his hand on her cheek. "But it does give me peace hearing you speak this way."

"I hope we are not parted for a long time."

"It may be longer than I would like but know I will not delay returning to you longer than necessary. I believe we have only this season to track them. If we do not find them quickly, it will become too difficult."

Merlin glanced at the small clay lamp that sat on the table beside her bed, still lit. "This is what I will do." He held his hand over the flame, took a long slow breath, and then whispered. The flame danced up and down underneath his hand, and then flickered out. His hand stayed over the lamp for a moment more, and then the flame burst back, a green flame burning brightly.

Removing his hand, Merlin gazed at Elanor and smiled. "This flame will continue to burn bright as long as you pour oil into it every day and do not blow it out. The wool will never need to be changed. It will burn as long as I am alive and well. In this way, you will have peace. If the flame should go out, then you will know that something has happened to me."

Elanor watched the green flame dance in awe.

"Elanor, I need you to know that there are not many sorcerers, nor dark druids, that have power that matches my own. Likely, if they knew I was coming, they would flee. Not many would ever try to face me. Even Morgan dared not, and that is why she had to be cunning and deceptive. Even then, she was killed by her own kin. I will be fine. It is those I come after who must fear. This is where I must be wise and follow the Great God and not my own strength of action. Do you understand?"

Elanor nodded.

Merlin stayed, holding Elanor's hand. Neither of them wanted to let their time together end. He stroked her face and his eyes danced, peering at her elegant features. "I wish I could see your blue eyes in the light." He leaned over and gave her a long, tender kiss. His heart ached within him; he longed for her more, knowing that he had to go.

Merlin drew away reluctantly; he knew it was time. Hesitantly, he turned toward the door, letting Samara return.

Elanor stood beside Merlin to be near him while she could. To Samara, Merlin said, "I am sorry that you have had to stay here so that I could say good-bye to Elanor. She is important to me, and it would not have been right for me to see her without you nearby."

"I understand," Samara said, bowing her head.

"You see that green flame?" he pointed to the lamp. "It is a gift to Elanor. Never blow it out, only feed it the oil it needs to keep burning."

Samara looked at the lamp curiously and then, acknowledging Merlin, said, "I will make sure the flame never goes out."

RAIN AND APPLE TREES

Elanor awoke that next morning, tired and with an empty feeling in her chest.

Samara watched the reflection of Elanor's forlorn eyes in the brass mirror. She brushed Elanor's hair delicately and sang, hoping to bring her comfort, but the song seemed to have little effect. She stopped and gazed at Elanor as she remained unmoved, starring out the window.

The queen did not call for Elanor that day, nor the next. So Elanor spent much of her time helping Cilaen and taking her meals with him. As the sun set on those first few days of Merlin's absence, she stood on the terrace, looking out as far as she could see. Even though she knew Merlin was far away, she hoped that if she looked hard enough, she might see him returning on the horizon. The green flame at her bedside helped remind her that he was still with her.

But then, the weather began to shift. Rain fell relentlessly for days. For three weeks it poured. Elanor hoped that the endless rain hadn't made Merlin's plight harder. Trapped inside, she pined to find ways to busy herself. Cilaen had been helpful, finding some old parchments for her. Recognizing that parchment was in rare supply, Elanor gratefully set about delicately detailing her drawings upon them.

Cilaen wrote on brilliant wax tablets as he calculated his recipes for various medicines. Elanor loved to watch how he could rub out his writings in the wax, and then rewrite. Cilaen pursed his lips as he focused, making his piles of herbs and gathering vials of liquids while jotting down each and every detail. He truly was a very gifted chemist, mixing all his ingredients into potent potions that worked powerfully to heal. He explained that while each ingredient performed an important function, so did the hands that delivered them.

"Words have power and life to heal also, and that ingredient," he said, "is only learned through the awen." Lifting one eyebrow mysteriously, Cilaen left her with that.

Finally, after days of wetness, the morning sun rose and the rain stopped. Elanor woke to see that the bright sun was shining, and a warm, humid breeze blew through her window. Quickly, she put on her robe and shoes and set off to peer out over the terrace. She knew she wouldn't see Merlin riding out of the green, but still she had been aching to at least look. It made her feel better, as though gazing across the wide world connected them through the distance. She had been deprived this pleasure for too many days.

Elanor ran swiftly through the passages, up the stairs and out into the fresh morning air. The rain had left a sweet smell of earth as the sun warmed the ground. She reached the ledge of the turrets and gazed longingly at the hills. The blossoms on the trees below were all gone now, but the trees stood bright and green with dots of new, tiny green apples upon the branches. Spring had now begun to pass, and summer was beginning to shine brightly upon the fair Palisade.

"He will return, my lady," said a voice from behind. Startled, Elanor turned to see Peredur approaching from the stairwell. "You have nothing to fear. It will not be this day, but he will return home to you."

Elanor was surprised to see him. She wrapped her robe more tightly around herself, feeling exposed. Fumbling her words, she stammered, "Re...return to me?" She tried to sound indifferent, as though she did not know what he was referring to.

"I have known Merlin for many years, and I have never seen him like he is now. As much as he has never told me of his love for you, it is clear to me. I know you must miss him greatly." Peredur sighed, looking out with worry on his brow. "You should know," he said, his stoic demeanor returning, "that the men who are being chased have much more to fear than the ones doing the chasing.

He will return well, and hopefully, having found the scum that have given rise to such pain and death."

Elanor was mystified that Peredur was even speaking to her, let alone bringing her words of comfort. Maybe, she thought, it was as Merlin had said, and he was warming toward her. He did not seem to disapprove Merlin's choice of love.

"I went to your chamber, and Samara said you could be found up here." Lifting his chest, he smiled pleasantly. "It has finally stopped raining, and it will be a fine day."

Elanor had only seen Peredur smile a few times, but this time was up close. The brightness of his smile made her see him anew. His mouth parted lightly, making his strength seem noble and less intimidating. His prowess was still sturdy and unmovable, but now she also saw a slight glimmer emerging out of the corner of his eyes.

Peredur continued, "Gwynevere has been brightened by this lovely morning and would like to walk with you in the apple orchard."

"That would be lovely," Elanor said, her heart lifted by the idea.

Nodding, he dismissed himself with a grand bow, then quickly turned, leaving Elanor baffled by the short parlé.

Elanor laughed to herself and thought about all the wonderful things the sunshine had already brought on this day. With enthusiasm, she scampered back to her chamber to dress.

The orchards were alive with sunlight, making every drop of water on every leaf glow with its light. Though the grassy orchard was muddy from the rain, still there were pathways between the trees that were dry enough to traverse, and Elanor and Gwynevere walked carefully, skipping over the puddles and muddy patches. Rays of sun shone between the trees, creating a comforting warmth.

"You seem at ease," Elanor said to Gwynevere as they waltzed along the path.

Lifting her head toward the sun, Gwynevere said, "I am tired of worrying. The sun shining through my window as I woke helped me shake off the stale air. I have been hoping to have a message sent to me, but with the rain, I knew it was not possible. It is horrible to be responsible for so many and feel powerless to do much more than wait." She let out a long sigh and lifted her hands to the sky. "But today offered me hope that at least a messenger might now be sent. Merlin's return created security for us, and to have him gone again brings me an anxious heart."

Gwynevere's words made Elanor's heart sink and sent a vibration of fear through her.

Gwynevere observed the sudden change in Elanor's countenance and encouraged softly, "He does not have a reason to stay away as he did before. Don't allow my fears of the past to disturb you...Come!" She snatched Elanor's hand and pulled her toward large rocks that sat amidst the trees. "Enjoy the sun for a moment. It will dry up all the bad thoughts." She patted the smooth, warm rock next her. "When the men return, I shall throw a feast," Gwynevere said, looking to see if that would return the light to Elanor's eyes. Then, lifting her feet to examine the mud on her shoes, she said, "I worry what sort of news they will bring us."

"I thought you said the sun was supposed to dry up all the bad thoughts," Elanor said. "Let's go back to talking about the feast and the men returning with good news. Triumphantly finding those evil men and stopping them from hurting another settlement of good people."

"Ah...yes!" Gwynevere smiled, lightly patting Elanor on the back.

Falling into silence, they watched the wind blow through the leaves. For a moment, the peace stole away their thoughts.

"Tell me," Gwynevere wondered, her eyes fixed upon the apple trees, "what were you doing up in the apple tree that day your father was calling you?"

Elanor recalled the memory she had shared with Gwynevere upon their first meeting. "Well," Elanor hesitated, wondering at the question, "I used to hide there. It was my special place where no one could find me. Only my father ever sought me there."

"Why would you hide? I could feel your emotions that day you took me there. You were very sad and lonely. Why?"

Elanor paused to consider how she should answer. It was hard to resist the urge to conceal thoughts she preferred to keep hidden from even herself.

"I went there because my mother would not be bothered with me there. She never went outside into the garden. It was where I spent time with my father and could be alone. My father had a big, golden dog named Brando, and he would keep me company." The memory of the scruffy dog made her smile.

Chapter Seventeen

"My dad, Brando, and I would go for long walks down the lane from our house into the wooded areas…but even from the garden, sometimes I could still hear my mother from the window. The apple tree was farther away from the house." Elanor picked at the rock. "She didn't want me. I was a source of irritation to her. That's why I spent most of my time outside and away from her. Even in the rain, I sat on our covered porch with Brando and told him all my thoughts. If I came into the house, I would run straight to my room to avoid my mother's disapproving gaze. The very sight of me reminded her I existed. At least when I went away to school, I was no longer a nuisance to her." Elanor gave a pained laugh.

Speaking about her mother ignited hurtful emotions that churned within her heart. For years, she'd tried to conceal the memories from her mind, ignoring them whenever possible. But even still, she'd been powerless to absolve the rejection she had experienced from her mother. She'd desperately tried to trick herself into believing it didn't matter; but that was only a lie to shield herself from the truth. It mattered to her greatly.

"Show me?" Gwynevere asked, putting out her hand.

Elanor wasn't sure why Gwynevere was so curious about this part of her life. But it did bring her some comfort that the queen cared. It had always been her secret pain; a pain she swallowed down hard in hopes it would disappear altogether.

Elanor took Gwynevere's hand and closed her eyes, focusing on the memory. The past choked her as she remembered it. The memory swelled inside her and began to spur the magic.

And then, as if she were truly there, Gwynevere could see her. A small, ten-year-old girl, dark haired and blue eyed, curled up behind a rose bush just underneath a window. She could see through the window Elanor's father, with his dark skin and brown eyes, facing a woman who must have been Elanor's mother, with fiery red, frizzy hair and small green eyes.

Her hands were on her hips as she spoke. "Where is that little thing? She's out hiding in that garden of yours again? She is useless! It is beyond me as to why I have had to deal with her all these years. She's not my problem, she is yours. Get her, I need her to start supper."

"She is not a problem; she is our daughter," Elanor's father yelled back.

"She is not my daughter. I never wanted her, but you insisted. She is nothing. Nothing but a pain in my side. I feed her and give her a room to sleep in, for you," she shouted.

"Quiet! She will hear you. She is just outside."

"I do not care whether she hears me or not," she berated as she stormed away.

Elanor's father turned to look out the window and watched as Elanor stood up to peer inside, tears forming in her eyes. Then, she ran away toward the apple tree, tears streaming down her face.

Brando ran after her, barking at her heels. "Not now, Brando!" Elanor cried, climbing up the apple tree and away from the dog, who continued to leap up toward her. She curled up onto a long, sturdy branch of the tree, its rough arm cradling her—a comfort while she cried. She mumbled angry thoughts while leaning against its bark until, at last, her father came to fetch her, calling up to her from the ground.

The memory dissolved, and they were back in the apple orchard sitting on the rocks in the sunshine. Elanor looked away from Gwynevere. She did not want Gwynevere to see her struggle as the memories forced fresh emotions to emerge.

Staring at Elanor's back, Gwynevere said deliberately, "She was not your mother."

"No. She was not my mother, and she never wanted to be. I have never known my true mother, or my true father. My father, David, chose to adopt me as his own, but she would not. I was always grateful to them, but I never understood why she never wanted me. I...I have never shared this with anyone."

"I am sorry if I pried."

"No. You did not pry. Strangely, I feel relieved someone else knows. Even if all those memories are far away from me now."

Elanor and Gwynevere fell silent, the weight of Elanor's memory hovering heavily in the air between them.

"I never knew my mother," Gwynevere said quietly, finally breaking the silence. "She died when I was born. I missed knowing her. I always imagined what she might have been like. My father did not speak of her. He was a quiet, stoic man. That was his way. I wondered if I looked like her."

"Yes, I have wondered the same."

Gwynevere smiled serenely at Elanor, and then, changing her expression to a frown, she said sadly, "I think it would have been easier never knowing my mother, than to have one that did not want me."

"Well," Elanor said wistfully, "I have always tried to pretend the rejection didn't hurt. I put on a mask of happiness hoping that would make her love me. Maybe just naïve thoughts of a child, but it kept me from despair."

"Now I feel I know you, Elanor. At least a little more. You do not have to forge an inner strength for me to love you."

Elanor leaned her head onto Gwynevere's shoulder, and they continued to sit and enjoy the sunshine and each other's company long into the afternoon.

18

AT WIT'S END

Another week had passed, and Elanor had to work hard to not think about Merlin. With each passing day her frustration grew. Everything was bothersome and difficult without him, and there were fewer comforts to bring her peace. Slowly, an angst was building within her. The annoyance of bathing in a cold, small tub, the water stinging her senses awake—she missed warm showers. Even coffee or tea would be nice. Anything familiar that would create a sense of home. She was sick of the hard bed and the coldness of the stone that surrounded her.

There was nothing romantic about the everyday tasks that needed to be done, and Elanor felt it. Out of all the times in history, she was grateful she hadn't landed in a time of corsets and horribly irritating ribbed dresses. These dresses were itchy, but not uncomfortable, and the shoes were all made from a soft leather that laced up the leg. Still, she missed the soft suppleness of cotton. Sometimes, she wondered what had happened to her soft cardigan and the clothes she had worn when she arrived. Staying positive was her daily goal.

On this day, Cilaen had gone down to distribute some medicines and tinctures. He asked Elanor if she wanted to accompany him, but she decided to stay behind. She hoped she might be useful and make something nice for Cilaen while he was away on his errands. In her own time, she loved to cook and bake.

Elanor thought making a stew would be simple enough. Cilaen had hung a coney he had bought at the market, and there were carrots and onions. Plenty enough to make a nice stew. She knew where to find milled flour in the kitchens so she could bake a simple flour and egg bread that wouldn't need any yeast.

This would brighten her mood and would be a nice surprise for Cilaen. Since nothing in this new world came easy for her, Elanor hoped this would prove a special and useful skill. So, she set about finding all the ingredients from the kitchen and prepared them for the pot. She made the dough in a wooden bowl she had borrowed from the kitchen.

Now she faced her first real challenge: lighting the fire in the stove. The coals needed to burn hot enough to cook the meal and bake the bread. She had seen Cilaen and Merlin do it enough times and hoped it would be easy enough.

The wood sat beside the stove, and Elanor easily loaded it into the hole behind the iron cage. She placed one large piece inside, and then grabbed some of the smaller bits for kindling. After jamming them in, she tried to light the fire, striking the flint over and over, but no matter how many attempts she made, the fire would not light. Frustrated, she jerked the kindling out of the stove; perhaps rearranging it would help. Elanor pulled and shoved, but nothing came loose. Tired and sweaty, she angrily grabbed a stick and jabbed the pile in hopes that the log would loosen.

Finally, in a fit of rage, Elanor screamed and struck the stove. She forced her hands between the pieces of wood and began pulling with all her might. Her hand slipped against wood, cutting her, and sending several splinters into her fingers.

"AAAAhhhh!" she screamed, falling to the floor as she grabbed her wrist. Blood pooled from her palm. "That's it! I have had enough!"

She lost all grip she had on her emotions and began to weep. Her pent-up exasperation had finally peaked, now manifesting as tears ran out of Elanor's eyes onto her bleeding hand.

Just then, Cilaen walked through the door, finding Elanor on the floor. He rushed over, seeing her hand dripping with blood.

"Sshhh!" Carefully, he lifted her off the floor and gently set her onto a chair before examining her hand more closely. "It is a deep cut, but I can mend it. What happened?"

Elanor could not answer; the flood of tears could not be dammed. In silence, she sulked in her chair while tears dripped down her cheeks.

Chapter Eighteen

Cilaen saw the remains of flour on her face, now streaked with tears. The firewood and the food preparations sitting on the table behind her told him all he needed to know.

"Were you going to make our supper?" he asked with a slight smile. Cilaen clicked his tongue, slowly nodding his head. "Wait here." He drew some water and gathered supplies to dress Elanor's hand. "Ah...I see some splinters." He cleaned her hand, wiping the juice from a small plant on her palm. Then, he took a small knife out from his tunic and brought it toward Elanor's hand. She jerked her hand away with a look of panic.

"Trust me," Cilaen said. Falteringly, Elanor let her hand rest back in her lap, and quickly and tenderly, Cilaen removed each of the splinters without hardly a pinch before wrapping her hand. He closed her hands in his and gave her a look of understanding. "What happened, Elanor?"

She felt like a child. Her chest now heaved as she tried to speak. "I am just so angry," she finally said between her teeth. "I cannot do anything. Everything is different here. So much harder than in my time." Another sob rose from her throat. "It was easier when Merlin was here." Her chest bobbed, and she tried to settle her breathing, but the emotions welled up again as she continued. "I just wanted to do something nice for you. You have done so much for me. Cooking used to be so easy for me. I never had to light a *blasted* fire to cook back at home. We have electricity. Sometimes I just wish I could do something—*anything*—on my own. I feel so helpless."

"Electricity?" Cilaen's face scrunched in a confused smile.

"Yes. Electricity," Elanor growled. "It is a natural power. It is the great power you see in lightning, the small power that makes our bodies move and things grow. In my time, we have learned to harness it and use it to make things work on their own."

"Magic?" he said in surprise.

Elanor laughed. "No...not magic. It's science. Just like your healing medicines. It's just not something people of this time have figured out how to use yet."

"Well, I am glad you are laughing now. Even if it is at my ignorance. Now," Cilaen said, placing his forehead upon hers, "I will teach you how to light a proper fire, and soon you will be able to make me as many suppers as your heart desires. I am truly blessed that it was your intention to do so." He paused, then remarked tenderly, "It will not always be hard for you. You have had to learn so many things, and you have done so well. You have learned a new language and to live in a brand new way. Don't be so hard on yourself."

She smiled, laughing through her sniffs. "Sometimes I just want a cup of coffee."

"What is coffee?"

"Let's just say, it is a wonderful drink that makes getting up in the morning all the more worthwhile."

Cilaen showed Elanor how to properly strike the flint and create hot coals while turning the wood. Now that the oven was hot, she was able to prepare the stew. Before long, the stew was simmering and the bread was baking.

She and Cilaen waited as a pleasant aroma began to fill the room. Elanor felt strengthened and more accomplished now that things were cooking. Cilaen had even brought her some herbs and parsley to brighten up the stew's flavor.

Elanor opened the oven to see if the bread was golden. She watched as smoke came streaming out of the oven, swirling above her head. Quickly, she shut the oven before more smoke escaped, but was surprised to see that the smoke above her had not dissipated.

Curiously, the smoke continued hovering and swirling before taking the shape of a dragon that twisted and turned—just as the flower petals had the day she and Merlin had gone to the lake.

She gasped and threw her hands over her mouth, almost afraid to turn around. She looked over at Cilaen first, who smiled at her, nodding his head toward the door. In an instant, Elanor turned to see Merlin, fully bearded and quite disheveled, standing at the door. His arms open wide. Without a thought she ran to him, throwing her arms around him.

Elanor's eyes lit with joy. She didn't want to control the feelings or the magic that kindled within her. She saw in his eyes how much he had longed for her and missed her. She saw his travel-worn thoughts, but mostly, she saw his relief now that he was holding her in his arms.

"I missed you, too," she said, smiling in happy relief.

Merlin threw his head back and laughed, then bent her completely over backwards to kiss her. She grasped at his beard and pulled him in tight.

Cilaen laughed. "Well, I guess I had better take the bread out of the oven lest it burn."

"Oh," Elanor said, remembering her previous task.

"Elanor was cooking me a supper, Merlin. You've arrived just in time, almost missing the greatness of her meal."

"It smells wonderful." Not taking his eyes off Elanor, Merlin whispered, "I do not want to let you go. I fear if I do, you will be gone away from me, like you have these many days."

Elanor caressed his face and kissed him once more. "Well, I am sure I will not leave you. Let us eat, and I will sit next to you."

"That will have to do, I suppose," he said with a longing glance.

"Please tell us. How did you fare? Did you find the men?" Cilaen asked, placing out the bowls as he readied the meal.

"No. None of that right now. All will be told soon enough. For now, I am happy to be home resting with the ones my heart loves most. Bedwyr has gone straight to the queen, and the welcome cup will be poured tomorrow. Then, we will be altogether, and all will be made known. I am so hungry; I am happy I have come here first," Merlin said, shedding his dirty layers of clothing, all the way down to his tunic. He sat down and dove right into the stew. Bits of it rolled down his beard as he ate.

Cilaen scolded with a laugh, "Slow down, there is plenty more! Elanor put an entire coney in there."

"An entire coney?" Merlin laughed with surprise. "Well, it is an excellent stew, and definitely a hearty one. Thank you, Elanor, for putting in an entire rabbit." He winked. "We were all so anxious to be home that we did not stop for eating the whole day long, and it has felt like a very long day." He turned and smiled at Elanor. "Do not let my rudeness sway you, beautiful one."

"Oh, I have missed you. I daresay I have never missed anyone so much. Though I will be happy to sit closer to you after you have had a bath," Elanor said with a laugh.

"Hah! Yes. We have been riding long and hard, and I am afraid it has been some long days since I have bathed. Am I so despicable?"

"Never." She grinned.

The stew tasted wonderful, and the bread was soft. Elanor was once again feeling herself. Merlin had returned and—dirty or not—the sight of him was sweet. All the many weeks had begun to melt away in her mind, and now she was only glad for the time she had been with her friends, awaiting his return.

Merlin and Cilaen had settled into a conversation, but as Elanor listened, her chin cradled in her hands; her eyes grew heavy. She felt for the first time in weeks that she could truly unwind. She was glad to hear the voices of the two men as they spoke, though she was too tired to focus on their words. It felt like home to hear them. Back and forth they went until she found herself drifting off to sleep. Slowly, her head sank into the folds of her arms until she fell asleep.

Merlin, seeing Elanor's head finally fall into a resting position, stopped talking. Both men peered at her.

"She has had a very long day," Cilaen whispered to Merlin. "She has worked very hard at being strong while you were away. You couldn't have come home at a better time. She was beginning to break a bit. She didn't want anyone to know it, but she has suffered with you being away. This whole new world was a bit harder without you. Though she would hardly show it." Cilaen pointed to her other hand. "She cut her hand today trying to start a fire. She will not need as much help the next time."

Merlin placed his hand on her cheek. "I should take her back to her room." Softly, he patted her on the back. "Elanor." She opened her eyes and reached for him. "Let us take you back to your chamber."

She sat up, sleepily. "I'm sorry. I hadn't realized how tired I was. I do not have to go. I could stay. I've been weeks without you."

"I will be here in the morning; you are tired now."

She looked at Merlin, and then at Cilaen, who nodded his head encouragingly. Elanor conceded.

She leaned on Merlin's arm as they walked to her chamber. No words were spoken, and soon they were at her door.

"I have something for you," Merlin said quietly. "I saw it in a village. There was a woman that worked with stones." He lifted her hands together in front of her and then opened them. There, magically laying in her hands, was a blue stone in the shape of a tear drop. Wrapped around it were silver birds that twisted around each other, and it hung as a pendant on a silver chain.

Elanor's mouth grew wide. "It is beautiful."

Merlin opened the chain with his hands to slip down over her head. Elanor pulled her hair out over the necklace and placed her hand over the pendant where it rested on her chest.

"I do not know what to say," she said, looking up at Merlin's scruffy, unkempt face. "Only that I will treasure it and wear it always."

"So, you shall." He grinned with pleasure.

Elanor raised herself onto her toes and kissed him, then turned to enter her chamber. Merlin waited and watched her go in, closing the door slowly behind her.

Samara gasped as she caught a glimpse of Merlin as the door shut.

"Merlin has returned?" Samara clasped her hands and ran to embrace Elanor. Then, caught by the silver sheen around her neck, she said, "What have you got there?" Elanor released her hand from her chest, uncovering the blue stone.

"Oh my!" Samara breathed. "Only love gives such handsome gifts. Maybe now we could blow out the green flame. He has returned to you."

Elanor looked across the room at the green flame that still flickered by her bedside. "No. The flame is also a gift. If we have the oil to keep it burning, then let it continue to burn."

"It will be done," Samara said without a second word on the subject.

That night, Elanor slept deeply and soundly. She dreamt of a white bird soaring high in the sky. It flew higher and higher, and it gave her the feeling of falling from a tall height, though the bird soared upward. She wondered when it would change direction and level itself. She longed to see the land the bird was flying away from. Where had the bird come from, and where was it going? Forever it flew straight up, and then slowly faded as Elanor opened her eyes and it was morning.

THE WELCOME CUP OF RETURN

All morning, Elanor's hand squeezed tightly around the pendant that hung from her neck. She treasured it and loved it with every part of her that loved Merlin. She gazed at the blue stone with the silver birds circling their wings and tails, interlocking one another. The sight of it made her heart sing. She wondered if she should conceal the pendant, or if it should hang freely for all to see. Slowly, she chose to tuck it away into the bosom of her dress. With a deep breath, she raced down the corridor to Gwynevere's chamber where the full council had already gathered. The atmosphere was jovial due to the return of Merlin and Bedwyr.

"Bedwyr!" Elanor trumpeted happily. "I am overjoyed to see you."

Approaching her, Bedwyr said, "I am very relieved to have returned." He bowed low and kissed her hand. "You look lovely." He then pointed to her chest and whispered, "I see you have been given your gift. I am glad to see you wear it, as I know of the deep wish to give it. The moon might as well have been set upon the one it was intended for."

Elanor blushed, though she felt reassured by Bedwyr's happy acknowledgement of the pendant. He lifted her hand into the crook of his arm and led her into the midst of the others. Merlin and Elanor bowed to one another and acted as they always had. Though they were secret in their love, cautious to invite anyone into that part of their world, Elanor felt fully aware that it was likely not the secret they thought it was. Still, it felt comfortable to go on pretending, and everyone pretended along with them.

Gwynevere spread out her arms, bringing them all to attention. "I am eager to know what has been discovered. Your untroubled return has given me hope. Please…Merlin…tell us what we need to know."

Merlin remained standing as the others seated themselves in a circle. He was now finely trimmed and back in his fine clothing. His countenance was bright, causing all to be hopeful his report would be reassuring.

"To be true," he said, looking to Bedwyr, "the state of the villages was beyond what had been described by the elders. The villages were nothing but the remains of what had been homes, stable houses, and granaries. Many of their animals still laid in the blackened fields while birds picked at their flesh. The smell of fire and ash hovered in the air. There will be much for them to recover before harvest. The slain accounted for most of the ablebodied men. These hooded men were harbingers of death to these settlements. We were helpless to do much to aid them. Many spoke about the dangerous and powerful magic they had witnessed, and I am convinced that the sorcery has not been over-exaggerated. No one could tell me why they killed the druid and the young filidh. They did it without remark." Merlin noted the expression on the faces around him and continued.

"The rains came, making our efforts to track the hooded devils impossible. Our efforts were waylaid, but we remained motivated. We had heard reports that the villains had been seen moving north. So, we went northward, hoping for some sign or evidence that had withstood the incessant rain. En route, we came upon a tavern not far from the northernmost village, so we went to search there. The tavern owners—a man and his wife—were not much help. They only wanted coin from us and would have said anything out of greed. Still, they did tell us some men matching the number of eight had come through, but there was no event to their visit. Being that it had been good weather when they passed through, they had also seen a good many others. It was unreliable, but it was the only lead we had, so we followed the direction the men might have travelled. There was only one road, and the men were on foot, so they could have chosen not to travel by it—leading us nowhere. Finally, the rain lifted. Without seeing anything to lead us further north, we returned south hoping for fresh clues. No new attacks had taken place. Unfortunately, my queen, we searched in vain. We come back to you empty-handed with those wicked men still loose in Prydain."

"All of this time without you, and we have nothing more than when you left. No men caught, and the villages only helped a little," Gwynevere remarked. "Ah…that rain. Do you think you might have found them if it hadn't rained?"

"There is no way to tell."

Gwynevere scowled. "There have always been thieves and marauders along the dark paths of this land. What worries me is the power which these men wield. This small band has done the damage of an army of invaders. What should be done?"

Bedwyr stood. "Searching for them has done nothing. But from what I have seen, we should be alarmed. The kings and other chieftains should be made aware so they can be prepared. They cannot be left vulnerable."

"I agree," Gwynevere confirmed. "I sent riders the moment the rain dried up." She waved her hand angrily. "They seem protected by their dark magic. Since when have Arthur's men come home unable to find what they seek? It alarms me that we have been left mystified. Disarmed by an invisible enemy that sneaks away and cannot be found." She sighed loudly. "Great God help us." They all sat quietly, as if waiting for the answer. "Merlin, is there any wisdom to be had?"

Solemnly, Merlin replied, "This is not something we can ignore. Attention must be paid. Our enemy's intention was to be known. Their objective was to be deliberately on display. There will be more attacks—mark my words. It was wise to warn the kings, Gwynevere."

Gwynevere dropped her head, thinking in distressed silence. Then, slowly lifting her head, she sighed. "Well, maybe we are denied an answer today, and maybe we are denied the triumph of knowing that these men have been stopped. But I will not be denied welcoming my friends home. We have all been looking forward to your return. Even if the news is not what we had hoped for, you have all come home unharmed. You will be welcomed this night with the welcome cup and a feast. Arthur always welcomed his men home, and so shall I. The preparations have already begun. We will show the darkness the light of our friendship." Gwynevere smiled with an awkward tension. "Now go, Peredur and Bedwyr, and welcome your men to the feast. Bedwyr, your men and horses will be wanting to see you. Go!" She swished her hand to excuse them. "Merlin, you and Cilaen must busy yourselves with other matters. Maybe the matter of rest will become you, Merlin. Elanor must stay with me. We have some preparations we must make together."

Merlin looked at Elanor with disappointment in his eyes, reluctant to leave her, but bowed and left with Cilaen by his side.

"It is impossible to know how to navigate these strange devastations." Gwynevere placed her hand to her head, looking out the window with a furrowed brow.

Elanor stood quietly. She tried not to look downcast that she had been asked to stay.

Gwynevere shook her head. "All of that aside for the moment…" She approached Elanor, placing her hands on her shoulders. "I have something for you." Gwynevere called her maidservant and directed her to deliver Samara, who seemed to have already been waiting and ready. In her arms, she held the most beautiful garment of blue and gold fabric, embroidered all down the center with brightly-colored flowers of red and yellow, and green leafy vines intermingling around them. "I have asked Samara to make this gift for you over the past weeks. I wanted the feast day to be special for us all. She has specially made it for you." Then, Gwynevere leaned toward Elanor slyly. "Let me see it?" She pointed to the chain around Elanor's neck. "You cannot hide it from me. I can see the silver that wraps round your neck."

Elanor smiled and slowly pulled the blue pendant from her bosom. The blue stone sparkled in the light. "Ah…now this new dress will match perfectly. Merlin has given you a precious gift."

Elanor eyes flickered. Stunned, she said, "How did you…"

Gwynevere swished her hand, stopping Elanor, and pulled the dress from Samara's hands.

"It is beautiful," Elanor said, touching the stitching.

"Samara has done well."

Samara complemented the dress by putting a gold ringlet in Elanor's hair. Elanor felt a little ashamed to be wearing something that made her look in every way the queen's equal, but Gwynevere only seemed to delight in it.

Gwynevere herself was radiant, her dark hair cascading down her shoulders. Her green eyes sparkled against her gold dress.

Elanor glanced over into Gwynevere's long mirror. The dress shaped her perfectly. Standing beside Elanor, Gwynevere carefully lifted the blue pendant out from under her dress, setting it to hang visibly on top of the garment.

"It deserves to be seen."

Elanor said soberly, "I am not entitled to such gifts."

"Others believe you are." Placing her hand upon Elanor's shoulder, Gwynevere added, "You are related to the queen, and the people must see you as such. Be glad. The feast will be grand, and we will be its shining ladies."

Chapter Nineteen

Warriors crowded the Hall. Now, the long tables that occupied the Hall lined the walls, leaving a wide space down the center. During Beltaine, most of the townspeople had dispersed to light the flame in their homes and village centers; only the warriors and chieftains sat in the Great Hall. But now, there were many others of different rank in attendance, bringing their fine ladies along with them.

A minstrel sang, playing a harp while sitting on top of the long boards. Servants, including young Uri, dipped their pitchers into the great cauldron until they overflowed with ale. Uri was in his usual fashion, jumping from one foot to the other with a grand smile upon his face. He seemed happy to always be in the action, serving the warriors that loved him and treated him with kindness.

Merlin stood before the chairs on the platform, loudly greeting his warrior brothers as they eagerly awaited the queen to start the feast.

The Hall silenced as the queen entered in like a fine jewel, followed by Elanor, who seemed a sparkling star.

Indeed, it was so, as she captivated the room.

"She will not remain long unmarried, I think," said Peredur, slapping Bedwyr's back. "She will be stolen away if Merlin drags his feet."

Merlin smiled and pretended not to hear them, for he too was enthralled and could only agree. His heart swelled at the sight of her. If only he could whisk her away, he would that very moment. She was the picture of the desire in his heart.

Elanor gazed at him and smiled, unaware of the room. She cared only that Merlin was there.

Gwynevere had also captured the room, as a queen equal to Arthur in every way. She took her place in front of her tall, high-backed chair. "Bring me the welcome cup!" she declared loudly, and the bowl was brought before her. "We welcome back our men who have gone and returned to us. We welcome them in the style of the mighty Pendragon."

The returning men, along with Merlin and Bedwyr, moved to stand in a circle before her.

"We welcome you home and are glad you have returned to us." She passed the cup first to Merlin, then to Bedwyr, and so on around the circle as each one drank. As the bowl reached the final man, the people lifted their cups and shouted a cheer of welcome.

With the men now properly welcomed, the celebration had begun. The queen clapped her hands and the crowd parted. Musicians entered, playing their harps and flutes. Behind them followed a long line of barefoot women dancing, their hair sprinkled with flowers and green-leafed branches in their hands. The musicians stood in the center while the dancers circled around them. Hopping and skipping, they swept their branches on the floor and waved them over their heads.

The people joyously clapped until the dance ended. When the music began again, the crowd rushed in to dance, creating a circle within a circle, around and around. The dancers with the branches took to skipping around the crowd as they danced.

Elanor clapped her hands, enthused by how the people celebrated without timidity. So freely they danced, drank, and laughed.

Merlin bowed before her. "I will not allow another man to steal you away. Come and dance with me." His magical eyes twinkled as he gazed at her. Elanor placed both her hands in his, and before she could think about how the dance should go, Merlin had his hand around her waist, sending her skipping and jumping around the circle. They were swept up in each other's arms and no one else mattered as they gracefully moved across the floor.

Three dancers leapt around them, holding their branches high over their heads, creating an arch of spinning green leaves. The moment forced them to stop and gaze at one another. Time stopped as the green leaves twirled, both breathless from dancing, not wanting to let the other go. Then the dancers broke away to dance around another couple, bringing Merlin and Elanor back into the room once again.

"All this dancing has made my mouth dry," Elanor said between breaths.

"Then I shall get the lady a drink." Merlin bowed and left to find a beverage to quench their thirst.

The room continued dancing around her, and she turned to look at Gwynevere, who sat smiling at her from her chair. The emotion of friendship graced Elanor's heart as she returned a joyful glance to the queen. The spirit of the feast made her soar with thankfulness for being given the chance to be known by such nobility.

In that moment, Elanor felt an icy chill go through her spine. She whipped around and saw a servant filling a warrior's cup. The servant was a man with a pale face and long, stringy black hair. Her stomach instantly churned. She struggled to catch her breath, her mind racing as she tried to place him. She gazed at him curiously, wondering what it was that caused her to feel distressed. The memory of the slinking shadow she had seen in the passageway at Beltaine struck her mind. Elanor's heart quickened.

The man looked up and caught her eye. He bowed and smiled at her. His gaze made Elanor feel as though she had locked eyes with a hungry wolf. His smile filled her with dread. Then, he turned and walked away to fill another cup, disappearing as suddenly as he had appeared.

"Are you alright?" Merlin asked, returning to her. He noticed the frightened look upon her face.

"Oh…uh…I just felt something strange," Elanor said oddly. "There was a servant filling cups, and…" She paused to look around nervously, but in the crowd, he was nowhere to be found.

"What happened?" Merlin's eyes darted about the room as concern rose in him.

"Nothing. Truly, it might just have been all the excitement. I saw a man…a servant…his eyes were so foreboding. I think I have seen him before—watching me. I am sure he means no harm…only…his look was so unnerving."

"What did he look like?"

"I am sure it was nothing," she said, placing her hand on Merlin's chest. "Poor man is just doing his work. I probably just needed a drink." She laughed with an insecure air. "All is well."

Merlin agreed uneasily, still looking behind him for anything suspicious. Not so easily swayed, he warned, "It is wise to learn to pay attention in moments like these. No matter how small the moment."

Elanor nodded, turning back again to see if she could find the stranger.

"Come," Merlin said, pulling Elanor back to her seat.

She leaned back, taking long draughts from her cup. Cilaen joined them, and he and Merlin began to talk. Elanor could not follow the conversation over the noise of the room. It still took a level of concentration for her to understand the Cymry words and their meanings, and amid the noise, she found it too difficult. So instead, she watched to see if the ominous servant would reappear.

"I want to go riding in the morning!" Gwynevere said, leaning in and distracting Elanor from her search. "Would you come with me? It is wonderful riding in the first light of the morning. There is a beautiful meadow I'd like to show you."

Elanor shouted back above the din, "I am still not a strong rider, but if I could ride Brynn, I am sure it would be alright."

"Merlin!" Gwynevere shouted above the roar of joyous voices. "I want Elanor to go riding with me in the morning."

"Through the fields?" he inquired.

"No, to the lower meadow. It is not far."

Slightly alarmed, Merlin warned, "It is not safe. I have a bad feeling about the forest with these hooded men at large. You should ride about the fields only. Elanor is not a strong rider; both of you are not safe alone outside the walls."

"I will have Peredur and a few of his men accompany us. We cannot allow ourselves to be frightened away from the meadows outside our own walls."

"It is not fear to use wisdom, my lady," Merlin cautioned.

"This is truth, Merlin. We will not go to the meadow if you think it unsafe. I always heed your wisdom."

"I will keep them safe," Peredur replied, looking at Merlin. "I will ride out with two of my men, and we will not linger longer than the morning."

Merlin nodded warily. "You are queen. I would trust Peredur with my life, and I know he is an able protector."

Elanor turned to Merlin privately. "Why couldn't you come with us?" she asked. She forgot herself as she reached out and took his hand.

"I have not been invited, my dear one. And I believe Gwynevere knows that Peredur would leave the two of you alone, whereas I would not be as likely to. Like she said, it will only be for the morning."

Elanor nodded in reply.

The feast went late into the night. The dancing slowed, and many had drunk their fill. The Hall slowly cleared as people stumbled back to wherever it was they laid their heads.

"The stables will be scattered with drunken men sleeping upon the hay." Bedwyr laughed loudly. He stumbled his way before the queen, obviously having had plenty to drink himself. "Good night, fair Gwynevere. The welcome has been full." He slapped Peredur's arm and embraced Merlin along the way. "Good night, beautiful one," said Bedwyr, bowing before Elanor. He stopped and gazed into her eyes, before shaking his head with a laugh and saying, "Merlin the Great God has favored you highly." With that, Bedwyr staggered out of the Hall and out into the night.

"I shall look after him, my lady," Peredur said, pounding his fist to his chest and taking off after his friend.

Gwynevere stood gracefully and brushed Elanor's cheek with her hand. "It is my time as well," she said as she turned to leave.

"Let me walk you to your room, my soul," Merlin softly uttered. "I would not have you walk these tiresome halls without the support of my arm."

They meandered wearily through the passageways, arriving at Elanor's door. Clinging onto Merlin's arm, Elanor leaned into his warmth, refusing to let go.

Merlin turned to see her hand holding the pendant. His heart faltered and he lowered his forehead to rest upon hers. There they silently stood, not wanting to part. A fire ignited within him, and though he worked hard to keep it contained, Merlin struggled to suppress his desire for her—her scent, her beauty. He placed his hands into her hair, feeling the soft tendrils in his hands, then kissed her.

This kiss was fuller and more lasting than the rest had been. This kiss carried a passion like none of the others. The two stumbled as they kissed, embracing one another.

But then, Merlin stepped away, shaking himself free to sober his mind. He placed his hands over his face, rubbing his eyes and forehead, hoping to break the trance. Oh, but his heart yearned for her, and once again he reached out to wrap her in his arms. He gazed into Elanor's eyes longingly. But with a smile, he let her go reluctantly.

Elanor smiled understandingly and carefully unlatched her door, slowly slipping away into the darkness of her chamber. Merlin leaned against her door, his heart still calling for her. Part of him felt like he would rather sit outside her door all night than retreat to his own. Laughing to himself, he tentatively walked back to his room.

The night had swept them away, and he knew in his heart that he would need to make her his own forever. This thought kept his heart afloat throughout the night, thankful and surprised that he would be given such a chance of love. Truly, a second chance at life and destiny.

THE SONG OF THE BARD

Elanor and Gwynevere rode out very early into the cool morning air. The red light of the sun had only begun to rise as the sky grew light with blue. Cilaen rode along with them, hoping for the opportunity to forage herbs in the meadow, while Peredur led with his guard of three men.

The day was fresh and bright as they rode out of the Palisade through the main gate and into the open green. They ventured a mile or so to where the land became level before turning onto a wide road that entered a forest of tall, twisted oaks. Now amongst the trees, they slowed, allowing Gwynevere to pull her horse beside Elanor.

"So," Gwynevere said with a playful grin, "do you love him?"

Elanor looked startled, quickly twisting around to see if the others had heard.

"They cannot hear us. Worry not." Gwynevere leaned in closer. "Merlin is in love with you, is he not? He has never told me so, but he does not hide it well. The silent and solitary druid has changed. You have created something anew within him, I think. Before, he spoke only in riddles, but now his eyes are telling me stories I can understand." She looked sideways at Elanor as her horse walked in pace with her own. "Truth be told, Merlin was a warrior once, as well as druid. It has been said that in battle, an awen would come upon him, and he would slay all who would dared come into his fray. He was dangerous, reclusive, and magical.

That's what the world said of him—but I knew him always to be considerate and wise. That was Merlin before grief changed him, and his countenance grew old and without light. But now, I see the gentleness and wisdom returning."

Elanor sighed, laying her words out delicately. "I do not know what Merlin was like before. What I do know is that from the moment I came here, he was the only thing that made any sense. He understood something about me, something that was hidden even from myself. My whole life I have been a stranger to everyone. Known by no one. Then I found him. The fog went away, and I could see myself." Turning to look at Gwynevere, she whispered, "Yes, I love him. With my whole heart, I love him. I wish to never go back to the world I knew before if it means that I cannot be with him."

"I am glad," Gwynevere said firmly. "There could never be a thing more right. It was as if you were brought here to bring him back to life. Though I do not think you came just for Merlin. No…something lost has been given back to me as well—if I could be so bold? Something about your face the moment I saw you. You felt…" she sighed, "…familiar."

"I hardly know how any of this can be," Elanor replied. "I am only glad that I have been received by you and blessed by your friendship. I have no idea why or for what reason I am here, but I am glad if you are one of them."

Gwynevere sighed again, reaching across to touch Elanor's hand. "You know, if Merlin does not hurry up and make you his wife, I fear that Bedwyr may offer to steal you away. His focus has always been his loyalty as a warrior, but now he sees you."

Elanor gave an incredulous look, then rushed to change the subject. "Why has no man sought for your hand?"

"Ah, well…I am Arthur's, and they all know that is how it will remain. I, myself, am not ready to not be Arthur's, even though he is gone. And his men will never see me in any other way. It would take another man from a kingdom far away to look at me and not see Arthur."

Awestruck by Gwynevere's nobility and honor, Elanor nodded. If she could have an ounce of Gwynevere's strength, she would be blessed.

Abruptly, they heard a distant shout. "My queen!" Behind them, a Cymry rider barreled toward them. Dust flew up behind him, his haste creating anxiety as they awaited his arrival.

"My queen!" the rider declared, arriving breathless. "A chieftain," he heaved, "from a village north of the citadel has come to call upon you. He said you would want to hear him. It is not urgent, but important. I thought since you had not gone far, you would want to know he had come."

"Is it Rolan?"

"No, my queen, it is Chieftain Aeron."

"Oh…if it is Aeron, I do not want to keep him waiting. I am sorry, Elanor…I must return."

Elanor shrugged graciously. "It is not a worry. We can ride another day."

Cilaen countered, "All does not have to be lost. I would still enjoy riding to the meadow. I have herbs to gather."

"I would go with them," Peredur agreed, "and return the lady safely. I will keep two of my men and send the third back with you."

Gwynevere hesitated, looking at Peredur while she pondered. "Yes…y-yes. Would that suit you, Elanor? You could still see the meadow today?"

Elanor smiled. "I would dearly love to ride to the meadow. Only I would miss your company."

"We will ride again another day." Then, gazing seriously at Peredur, Gwynevere said, "Be sure to keep her safe."

Peredur placed his hand upon his chest and bowed his head to Gwynevere.

The queen nodded and turned to ride off with her new guard. They stood, watching them disappear down the road.

"Shall we go?" Peredur prompted, tossing his hand over his head to lead them forward. They kicked their horses and moved down the road. "The meadow is not far from here."

Soon they came upon the road that opened up into a beautiful meadow. It was as Gwynevere had described it. White daisies were scattered upon the grass, and patches of lavender grew up in bunches. Bees happily buzzed about the lavender blossoms, filling the air with their sweet perfume.

Elanor gasped, "What a happy place."

"Yes," Cilaen said, breathing deep the fresh air. "I knew you'd like it. There are always wild strawberries here during this time of year." Sliding down from his horse, he immediately bent down to scavenge the ground. "Ah, yes—the birds have not gotten them all." Picking one of the sweet berries, Cilaen popped it into his mouth. "Here." He smiled and handed Elanor a handful of strawberries.

Instantly, Cilaen came alive, searching around every shrub and tree for all he could find. "What a bounty!" he shouted from the ground, rising his head so Elanor could see the brightness in his cheeks.

Elanor sat down on the grass and laughed, amused by Cilaen's enthusiasm. She put a strawberry into her mouth, enjoying its sweetness and the morning's crisp, refreshing air. The wind brushed through her hair as she relished in the momentary solitude, while leaves danced on their boughs. After a while, she felt ready to join Cilaen in collecting his treasures, so she stood, dusting the remaining strawberry leaves from her dress. She loved getting her hands dirty, pulling roots and leaves from the ground. Cilaen pointed to a bushel of mushrooms that Elanor gladly gathered.

Peredur shouted, "We must leave soon or else I will not have been faithful to my word."

Cilaen quickly grabbed his collections, and Elanor helped him place them in satchels. Then they were off once again, back down the road, to return to the Caer. Happiness leaked out of the creases of Elanor's mouth as she cherished the time well spent.

As they rode back, a startling noise sounded overhead. It was the sound of bird's wings just over Elanor's head and a flash of black in her peripheral view. She looked up, spooked, thinking it must have been a large raven. As she peered up at the branches, her horse stopped abruptly, jolting her forward. Confused, she glanced at Peredur, seeing he had also halted. He sat motionless, his head hanging into his chest. The sting of fear bit at her gut.

"Is everything well?" Elanor shouted over at Peredur. She was met with eerie silence in return. She turned around and saw Cilaen was also frozen, slumped forward, as were the Cymry guards behind him. "Brynn…Brynn!" She clicked her tongue, kicking at her horse to get it to move.

Elanor tried not to panic but was steadily aware that something was amiss. She leapt down and walked in front of Brynn. The horse's eyes were closed, and it stood still as a statue. She pulled on the reins, but Brynn's head only pulled left and right as she yanked, doing nothing to rouse the horse.

"Cilaen!" She ran to him, shouting in alarm as she smacked his leg. "Wake up!" She reached up to touch his hand.

Are they wounded? she wondered, feeling helpless and unsure.

A loud thump sounded, and Elanor's heart leapt. Terrified, she turned to see one of the guards had fallen from his horse. She ran to him and shook him. "Oh, wake up. What is wrong with all of you?" Baffled, she sat in the dirt, staring at her companions while her heart beat wildly. The trees creaked, giving her a sick foreboding.

Should I find help? Is it wise to leave them?

"The guards at the front gates!" she said, panic rising in her voice. "Maybe I could reach them on foot."

Before she could leave the area, the hairs on the back of her neck stood at attention. Hot blood coursed through her, and fear rose in her stomach. Instantly, she was up on her feet in alarm. She heard footsteps moving toward her through the forest. Elanor turned to see a group of hooded figures emerge from behind the crooked trees. In terror, she started to run, tripping backwards over the hem of her dress. Scrambling to her feet, she ran, but did not get far before one of the darkly hooded men stood out before her. Screaming, she turned toward the forest. Her every instinct told her not to run into the wood, but in that instant, she could think of nowhere else to go. Running as fast as she could, she reached for the trees, and just as her foot glided past the first oak, her head was struck. Splitting pains ran through her scalp as she fell to the earth before all went dark.

She woke for brief moments at a time, hearing the crunching of footsteps as she was dragged by her arms, and then faded back into darkness. In those short moments of consciousness, her head ached while warm liquid dripped down her face.

Inescapably, she woke to find that she was lying on the cold, dry ground. Horror returned as she recalled the events that had brought her here. She kept her eyes closed as she heard the voices of strange men all around her, fearful of what might happen once they discovered her awake. Carefully, she lifted her hand to touch her throbbing head. Her matted hair was wet and sticky with blood.

"She's waking!" she heard a man yell.

"Pull her up!"

Within seconds of the order, two men violently yanked her from the ground. Her head ached and the world spun. The hooded man in front of her seized her face.

"Open your eyes!" he growled.

Her eyes snapped open at his command, while every part of her trembled. Elanor was sure these were the very men who had terrorized the villages, murdering men and children. She focused hard to not allow herself to be overcome with fear. With effort, she tried to slow her breath, but her body was already in a panic.

Angrily, he shouted at the others, "Where is the queen?"

"She was not among them." ... "There was only this one." ... "Wasn't she the one we were meant to find?"

"Shut up!" His eyes tensed as he locked eyes with Elanor. "We have been made aware that Merlin has a special attachment to you. Making us wonder who you might be…We may not be able to meet Merlin face-to-face without consequence, but we knew we could find his weakness. I care not for pretty things." Hatefully, he struck Elanor across the face. The sting sent blood flowing from Elanor's teeth down her chin. All the men surrounding her laughed while she fought back her tears of pain and terror.

"We are setting a trap, you see. One that not even the wise Merlin will be able to foresee." The man's gravelly voice moved deeply through Elanor's ears. A voice matching his malice. "Merlin has tried for the last time to bring an end to the old religion. His New Ways will be blotted out. He should have stayed on that island, hiding away with his dead king," he seethed. Then, he slid his hand into his cloak and pulled out a clear small bottle. The liquid inside was thick and dark, like old blood. "Open her mouth."

"No!" Elanor struggled, fighting to wrestle free. She twisted and was able to get an arm loose but was quickly seized again. She used every last muscle she had to break free but was dominated by the men that held her. Powerless and afraid, tears began to flow freely, dripping off her chin as she sobbed silently.

Infuriated, the hooded man unsheathed a knife, springing toward her in a rage. Like lightning, his blade tore into Elanor's flesh, just above her hip. Searing hot pain shot through her body as the men forcefully held her upright. The evil man moved to point the bloody tip of his blade at her throat.

"Open your mouth!" he said through clenched teeth.

Boldly, she refused, pressing her lips together tightly. She was determined to do everything within her power to not to swallow that vile black poison.

"Open your mouth!" he commanded, tossing the blade away, then quickly grabbing her violently around the throat. His strong hands choked her. She could feel things in her neck popping under his grip. Her body writhed as she struggled for air. Elanor gasped, unable to keep her mouth from opening, and the devil shoved the contents of the bottle into her mouth, emptying every drop before throwing her to the ground.

Elanor could feel the liquid leak down her throat. She tried not to swallow, but her throat convulsed as she heaved, forcing air back into her lungs. The hooded man dropped to his knees before her and placed his face close to hers.

Then he spoke strange, angry words she did not understand. "Marwolaeth gadw ti…Marwolaeth gadw ti…gadw ti…gadw ti." As he spoke, her whole body went cold.

He stared her in the eye. Now, Elanor could clearly see his face, red and cratered. He smiled with delight, his black eyes wild. The whites of his eyes were bloodshot and bulging from his effort and sweat beaded on his forehead. His face forced a will of anger to rise within her. She wanted to crush him into the dirt beneath her. She was frustrated by her helplessness.

"It is done," he said proudly. "You will now surely die, but not until he touches you. He will come to save you, and surely, when he reaches your cold body, the dark magic will cause the poison to fill his body, and you both will die." He laughed wildly at his success, disappearing from her view as the hooded men moved away.

Elanor groaned bitterly, and with all the strength she could muster, threatened, "You will never fool him. You will be undone for this. He will kill you." A final tear dripped from her eye.

He snapped around, seething at her words. "This will teach you to keep your mouth shut." The man kicked her as she lay on the ground, defenseless. Elanor's ribs cracked agonizingly at each blow. She coughed and lurched as they slithered away, leaving her on the ground. A supernatural wind followed behind them as if erasing their steps.

Her hands tingled while she laid weeping, utterly spent. There was nothing left for her to do. Scared and alone, the coldness of pain stole over every part of her body.

Trembling, she shouted, "Help! Help!" doubling over at every attempt. She hoped maybe Peredur would wake at her cry.

Struggling deep within herself, she thought of Merlin and wondered if she would ever see him again. Losing herself, she drifted in and out of consciousness, the flashing memories of the evil men tormenting her. She had never witnessed so much hate. The shocking violence and venom that now coursed through her body made it hard to breathe as the trauma freshly picked at her mind.

Elanor closed her eyes and began to hear the comforting voice of Merlin speaking to her. In a dreamlike state, she was back with him by the lake. He was telling stories about his father's powerful gift of song, and that he, himself, learned to hone his magic through song. Then, the scene changed, and she saw Merlin standing with his harp before the warriors and chieftains on the night of Beltaine. She heard again the sweet, mournful song he had sung, and as she heard it, something rose in her innermost being.

The song took on a life within her. Elanor opened her eyes. She lifted her head and crawled forward through the dirt, leaves, and sticks. A magical strength flooded her, and she lifted her chin and opened her mouth. Out of her flowed a sound, rich and strong. It was a song. She knew not the words that she sang but could almost feel in her heart what they meant. The song echoed through the forest, taking on an unnatural, reverberating sound.

Deep within Merlin's mind he heard her. The song she sang rang in his ears, causing him to drop the small bottles he had been holding. They shattered as they hit the floor. He leaned forward, putting his hands over his ears.

Awareness came crashing into his mind. "It is Elanor!" Merlin said, frightened, clutching his heart. *I can hear her. She's calling to me. I do not know how, but I can hear her song…She is in trouble.* He jumped toward the door, running with haste out through the Great Hall. He caught sight of Bedwyr and ran to grab hold of him.

"Something has happened in the south meadow," Merlin said wildly. "I must not delay. Elanor…the queen…we must be quick."

"But the queen has returned," Bedwyr said, alarmed. "She has left Elanor with Peredur and Cilaen."

Merlin looked at Bedwyr, struck with fear. "Gwynevere has returned without Elanor?"

"She is with Peredur!" Bedwyr said, confused, quickly becoming concerned.

"Something has happened. I must go now. Notify Gwynevere and follow behind me with the Cymbrogi. Something is terribly wrong." He ran out the door, and within moments he was upon a horse, riding out to the meadow as fast as the wind.

All the strength was leaving Elanor now, and her song ceased. She glanced up, rolling onto her back. A white light was coming toward her. It was bright and calm; she heard the light puffing and whinnying of a horse, similar to sounds she'd heard Brynn make.

Maybe, she thought, *Brynn has come to find me.*

The soft, comforting breath of the creature hovered just above Elanor's face. Images of Brynn danced in her mind as she closed her eyes. All fight had gone, and she let go.

POISON

The hooves of Merlin's horse pounded the ground. His heart ached inside his chest as he tried to push away all thoughts that something terrible had happened. Still, nothing could take away the urgency with which he rode, driving through the grounds like a blur. All his thoughts were on Elanor.

What happened?

Terrible scenarios crept into his mind; he hoped none were true. His horse breathed loudly with each pounding stride. He could see the road in the distance, urging him to push even harder while the trees whipped past on his right.

Merlin turned onto the road amidst the oaks and sped until he saw Peredur sitting atop his horse just ahead. He saw the others with him, and for a moment, he felt relief.

Elanor must be with them.

Merlin slowed his pace, but as he neared the enclosed patch of oaks, the pit of Merlin's stomach triggered. Peredur was atop his horse but sat unnaturally still.

"Peredur?" he called, receiving no response.

Surely, he can hear me.

Merlin quickened his pace as a chill air surrounded him. His eyes suspiciously searched around the forest.

"Peredur!" he shouted again, this time close enough to ride up next to him. He gazed at them, eerily still and unmoved. The riders were slouched over, and one warrior was on the ground. Elanor was missing, and the sight shot dread into his heart.

He sprang down from his horse and lifted his hand to feel the unnatural air. It was different amongst these trees, and he could sense it. There were no birds singing, and every color seemed muted and dark. Merlin recognized the enchantment and immediately shouted loud, druidic words of power, followed by, "Be broken!" He brought his hands together with a thunderous CLAP, which echoed through the forest, creating a gust of wind that blew across the sleeping riders. Then, a soft breeze came, and the sound of the rustling of leaves returned. Birds returned to sing brightly, and the clouds moved away from the sun, uncovering its light.

All the riders roused to waking, confusion etched upon their faces.

"Where is she?" Merlin said urgently. "What happened?"

Cilaen and Peredur peered at each other, becoming fearfully aware.

"You were enchanted," Merlin continued. "You would all still be asleep now if I had not come. What is the last thing you remember?"

"We were returning. It was still morning…" Cilaen said, confounded as he looked up at the sky. "It seems much later now."

"We were headed back…" Peredur leapt down from his horse. "Nothing seemed amiss. That is, until you were here in front of us…with Elanor gone." He put his hand on his head, still a bit foggy and overwhelmed, but quickly snapped into action. "Men!" he shouted. "Get on your feet. Explore the area. We must find her."

Cilaen sat upon his horse, stunned as he watched Merlin scour the ground for signs.

Merlin shouted, "I see several footprints along the road!"

"Yes," confirmed Peredur. "At least five or more men it appears. No horses."

"That means they are on foot."

"Yes." Peredur moved from Elanor's horse, following a small pair of footprints, still fresh in the dirt. "They could not have gone…" Peredur stopped abruptly at the tree line, staring at the ground.

"What is it?" Merlin ran to meet him.

"She had been running…I followed…then I saw this." He pointed to the ground and drew his finger in a line straight ahead. "She was dragged."

Merlin's heart sank as his eyes followed Peredur's finger, seeing the blood-spotted ground before them. His body shook. His heart already retreated, regretting the price of love.

Just then, the queen arrived with Bedwyr and a wake of twenty men. Gwynevere dismounted and quickly scanned the scene. Her chest stuttered with worry, and tears welled in her eyes.

"What has happened? Where is Elanor?" she asked, directing her gaze at Merlin, and then Peredur.

Merlin's countenance was tense with the beginnings of grief.

"I…I am sorry, Merlin. I left her…she…" Guilt stung Gwynevere's heart. "Chieftain Aeron had come to the citadel. It was important to hear him immediately. I let them go…Peredur was with them…" She shook her head regretfully and looked at the ground. "Aeron told me of strange hooded men that had been spotted moving through their forests. If I had known, I would have never…"

"There is a trail," Peredur interrupted, swallowing hard.

Bedwyr had been tracing the evidence while they spoke, then joined them, seeing the blood before Peredur's feet.

Peredur commanded them all, "Quietly…follow the trail. Keep your eyes peeled. Aim to not alarm the enemy."

Silently, the men spread out and moved through the darkening oaks. They focused on the ground, like predators smelling for prey. The leaves rattled like bones as the wind shook them.

Merlin's thoughts raced. Clearly, these were not thieves or bandits. The evidence of devilry upon his arrival, and Gwynevere's testimony of Aeron, was enough to tell him who had taken Elanor. His insides were in knots thinking about what men like these could do. Hope that she would even be found alive haunted him.

For what reason would they have taken only Elanor but left the men?

Soundlessly, a flash like lightning appeared, blinding them. The brightness dissolved, revealing a man dressed in blue. The men gasped, mumbling whispers at his sudden appearance.

Startled, Merlin jumped and threw his hand up, his eyes flashing like fire. "What have you here, man in blue?"

"I have been called by Elanor's song. Did you not hear it?" He spoke calmly, holding his hand up toward Merlin with gentle authority. His voice brought peace to the stunned men. "I have come to your aid, and to warn you." Merlin's heart was not eased by his words, and urgency grew in his heart. "If I had not come to you now, you would surely have died, but this is not the story I have written for you. Elanor has been significantly harmed. She has been given a poison that is enchanted. If you touch her, Merlin, the poison will kill you both."

Merlin's chest heaved at the man's words. His spirit grew disquieted, fearing there was no hope. "Where…where is she?" Unnerved by the man's warning, Merlin ached.

"She is just a little deeper in, where there is an opening in the wood. She is being protected by an ancient enaid of this forest. Her song called it. One of its kind has not been summoned for a thousand years. Enaid are messengers and gift givers. This one has come to help her if it can."

Sadly, Merlin groaned, "I heard her song."

"Only one of purity could have called such an enaid. Follow me, I will lead you to her, but I warn you: No matter how much you long for her, do not touch her. Any of you," he commanded, pointing at the men. "It will be the end of you."

Forward they went. The trail stretched a long way into the wood, with the man in blue leading them steadily. Eventually, the trees opened, and there, on the ground in a torn dress, laid Elanor. Above her, a beautiful, pure white creature hovered, its nose floating just above her face. It was not unlike a horse, but much taller and thinner. Its legs and neck were long like a deer. Its muzzle was delicate and small. Long, white eyelashes lined its blue eyes. Its hooves were cloven, and its tail was long with a tuft of silky white hair on the end. Along its neck flowed a satin mane, and then from its head, pointing down toward Elanor's heart, was a long, ivory horn. The creature was purity itself. It delicately whinnied as the men drew close.

As he approached, Merlin saw a dress stained with blood and a face red and bruised. Blood lined the side of Elanor's face and filled the creases of her mouth. But for the soft movement of her chest, he would have already thought her dead.

Merlin fell to his knees before her. He wished with all his being he could touch her and bring her close. Tear marks streaked her face, and the sight made him groan. He lifted a hand over her, pulling on whatever healing magic he had within himself, but there was a great chasm separating them that kept him from reaching her.

"I must touch her," he said weakly to the man in blue. "What am I to do?"

"This enaid will break the evil enchantment, but once he does, the poison will begin to kill her. He cannot break the enchantment and stop the poison. You must be ready to heal. The enaid will wait until you are ready."

"But what if I cannot heal her?" Merlin gazed hopelessly at the man in blue, but he had disappeared. He pounded the ground with his fist and yelled with anguish, sending the nearby birds to flight.

Gwynevere silently moved next to Merlin. Tears fell from her eyes. Unmoved they sat and the men stood still. A long moment passed without words. No one knew what to do.

Timidly from behind Merlin, Cilaen said, "If I knew the poison, I might be able to create the remedy."

"Quickly," Bedwyr shouted, as if coming awake. "Search the forest. Look for anything you might find that could help."

Bedwyr's action snapped Peredur to rally a small group of Cymbrogi to search for signs or tracks that would lead them to the villains. "Go back...gather your horses and go after them. But stay hidden and send a rider back once they're found. We will come after them with force. Go!"

Hardly a moment passed before one Cymry had found, searching amongst the leaves, a vial that still had a small bit of black liquid inside. He handed it to Cilaen, who smelt it with his eyes closed, focusing on its scent. "It smells like belladonna...nightshade. I may be able to help slow its effects if I am right. This looks to be a very concentrated form of the nightshade to be of such a black color. Merlin?" he asked, running over to him. "This concentration of poison, I could not remedy completely. But if I could give her a tincture to slow the poison, you might be able to save her with your magic."

"Yes," Merlin replied, visibly shaken. "Yes, if I could at least touch her."

"Give me but a short time," Cilaen said before taking off into the forest. He still had the fresh herbs he had collected from the morning within his pouch, and one particular root, he thought, would be helpful. He sped into the foliage of the wood, picking more leaves and stems. As quickly as he could, Cilaen returned with his hands full of green. "Somebody! Start a fire! Quickly!" he yelled, placing his findings in a bowl and pulling supplies out of his bag. His hands were fast and his heart burned with purpose. Cilaen boiled water over the fire, adding roots and leaves he had smashed. Over the steeping potion, he uttered prayers and druidic words. His eyes were closed, and his brow labored.

Merlin was losing his heart in the waiting. He looked at the condition of his beloved, remembering her sweet kiss from the evening before. Now it was all being taken away. He stared at the creature, whose face remained set above Elanor's. The enaid did not stir. Only its breath could be heard, its nostrils flaring with each breath. He wondered at it, as he discerned a power emanating from it. It seemed to never blink. Only to breathe. Completely still, but for its tail that swayed lightly behind it.

"Thank you," Merlin whispered desperately to the enaid. "Thank you for hearing her song." He closed his eyes to concentrate on the flow of his own magic, hoping that what they were about to do would be enough to save her.

"It is done!" Cilaen shouted at last, bringing an end to the pain of waiting. "Let me only cool it a moment." He poured his concoction into a smaller vessel and blew on it. Cilaen rushed to Merlin's side with the tincture in his hand. "We must be swift."

The lump of fear in Merlin's chest tightened. The moment had now come.

The enaid lifted its head, understanding that it was time. It stepped backward, and then lowered its horn to touch Elanor's mouth. The creature whinnied softly, and then a translucent wave vibrated over her body, blowing leaves and dirt that surrounded her. After completing its task, the enaid puffed loudly, shaking its head before galloping away. It disappeared quickly after diving into the trees like a bird flitting through a bough.

Now that it had gone, many of the Cymbrogi wondered whether they had seen it at all.

Merlin's eyes were on Elanor as she began to slowly move and open her eyes. "Merlin?" she murmured feebly. "I knew you'd come." As she spoke, she started to cough and choke. The skin under her eyes turned dark, and her eyes rolled back into her head.

"Quickly!" Cilaen shouted. Merlin grabbed her under her shoulders and tipped her head back. Cilaen poured the tincture into her mouth, losing some as Elanor coughed. "It's done!"

Merlin placed her down and her body started convulsing.

Gwynevere had been trying to keep herself calm but now wept bitterly. Bedwyr ran to her side and leaned her face into his shoulders, hoping to muffle the sound of her anguish from the Cymbrogi surrounding them.

Merlin placed his hands upon Elanor and spoke his words of power. His body shook as consternation formed his brow. Suddenly, Elanor collapsed into stillness. With apprehension, Merlin lifted his hands to his mouth. He had done all he could. Her stillness was deathlike.

A tear leaked out of Merlin's eye. He had lost her. Just like he lost Arthur. Just like he had lost—

A loud gasping sound came out of Elanor. Wrenching for breath, she arched her back as she filled her lungs. Merlin pulled her into his arms and brushed the hair out of her eyes. She laid in his arms, breathing long deep breaths. As her breath slowed, she opened her eyes.

"Did you see the unicorn?" she croaked roughly, her voice barely above a whisper.

Merlin looked at Elanor, confused. Tears of relief formed in his eyes to hear her speak. "Unicorn?" he asked, kissing her forehead as he caressed her.

"The hooded men," she labored. "They want to trap you…kill you."

"Shush!" Merlin rocked her in his arms. "You must rest now. All is well."

Elanor breathed weakly and reached to touch his face.

Merlin stammered, "My soul."

She closed her eyes, and he held her tightly. As he cradled her, Merlin quickly sobered as he felt warm liquid drip over his hand. "She's bleeding!" He trembled, holding his hand up for Cilaen to see.

Cilaen cautiously tore at Elanor's clothes and revealed the slash the hooded man had given her. They had been so concerned about the poison, they had neglected to examine her further.

"This wound looks deep," Cilaen said, concerned. "I can patch her the best I can, but she must be taken to the Palisade immediately. Only there can I properly mend her. She is losing blood and time." Hastily, he poured water on the wound and wrapped it tightly. "We must move her now!"

Merlin sat motionless, utterly shocked and in despair. He couldn't move and continued clinging to Elanor.

"Merlin!" Cilaen shouted.

Still, he sat unmoved.

"I've got her!" said Bedwyr, springing to action. He took her tenderly from Merlin's arms. "I am sorry, brother. I must take her."

Cilaen nodded at Bedwyr. "We must be swift, but ride delicately. We cannot cause her to lose more blood."

Merlin heard the men move off. He could hear Cilaen's voice in the distance shouting orders but could only sit stunned. His heart could handle no more, while every fear and pain rose to the surface. He wished he had stayed on the Isle of Avalon.

That would have been better, he thought. *None of this would have ever happened.* He bitterly remembered Rian, who'd encouraged him to listen to the dreams that beckoned. *For what?*

Gwynevere was still beside him. She peered at Merlin, afraid to speak, but unwilling to leave him alone.

Peredur approached him. "I found this." He pressed his clenched fist into Merlin's hand, leaving behind Elanor's blue pendant. "It must have fallen from her," he said. Peredur sniffed the air bitterly, then walked away.

"I am so sorry, Merlin." Gwynevere sobbed. "I should have taken her to ride in the fields, like you said. I could never have imagined this. Please forgive me."

Merlin nodded his head. It was all he could muster in response to her. He could not blame Gwynevere or Peredur. If anyone was to be blamed, it was himself. He should have gone with them. He should have found the evil men the first time they went to search for them. He squeezed the pendant in his hand. Maybe he should have never dreamt he could have had a gift so fair. Maybe he should have never hoped.

As if slapped in the face, the feeling of emergency returned to him. How could he have allowed another to take her from him?

22

THE THORN RETURNED

Merlin came crashing into the chamber just as Cilaen was wiping his hands clean of blood.

Cilaen's eyes were red and weary. "She is resting in your bed," he sniffed, then turned to wash his hands and face in a basin. He slumped into a chair. "I have stitched her and done all I know to do. Samara is with her now, cleaning her. When she is done, you can see her."

"How is she?"

"I have cared for injured men like this…" Cilaen's emotions squeezed his voice, stopping him. "But not our dear Elanor. Those brutes. Those evil bastards."

"What does that mean?" Merlin stared fearfully at the door Elanor laid behind.

"She has lost a lot of blood, my friend. We will have to wait and see if her body is strong enough. I have done what I know to check for internal injuries. All that is left to do is pray that the Great God will heal her where I could not."

The door opened and out stepped Samara. Her cheeks were wet with tears as she carried a basket full of red-stained linens. She did not look up but hung her head as she hastily departed.

Cilaen stood dejectedly. "Come."

Merlin glanced at Elanor laying in his bed. Her face was clean, revealing the black and red marks of her injuries. Samara had braided her hair to the side. Her brow was wrapped in clean linen to cover the wound. Elanor's breath wheezed as she exhaled. Wrapped around her delicate neck were deep purple bruises, shaped like a man's thumb and fingers. Merlin touched her throat. His anger boiled over.

"They choked her," Cilaen said, noticing Merlin's observation. "It is very swollen on the inside. The injuries to her neck alone will take time to heal. It will likely affect her voice for a while." He pointed to her side. "She has several broken ribs on her side—and a wound just there." He brought his hand where she had been cut. "But all these things will heal, as long as there is nothing more."

Merlin nodded his head, placed his hand upon hers, and quietly wept. The horror of the day continued to wash over him as he recounted every moment of it in his mind. The man in blue, the enaid. The song he had heard, and the devastation of seeing Elanor lying on the ground. Clenching his hand into a fist, he fumed, grinding his teeth in ire. He wanted to find those wicked men and crush them. Never had he felt such hate. Not even toward Morgan and Mordred had he felt such hot, uncontrollable rage. Once discovered, Merlin thought about what he would do to the man who had dared wrap his fingers around Elanor's beautiful throat.

Merlin spoke to no one, but took up a vigil night and day, hoping that Elanor would soon awaken. Cilaen believed she was not worsening, with no evidence of fever or abating breath—but it had been six days, and still she had not opened her eyes.

Merlin's thoughts choked him. Day after day, he regretted his choice. He was doomed to fail and doubted there even was a new kingdom he was called to be responsible for. He knew one thing: He would not rest until the villains were destroyed. He would kill them, and they would come to realize their mistake as his sword struck their necks.

Those dreams, Merlin agonized. *They led me astray. Why did the Great God cause me to call to her? What could the purpose be if she dies? This is my fault. I chose wrong. She would be better off without me.* The cold, grey escape of Avalon's mists comforted him. *She needs to be back in her own time, where she will be kept safe.*

Deep inside him, a still, small voice echoed, *"Do not let the thorn return."* But Merlin could not keep the bitterness and anger from growing within him, and finally, on that sixth day, he left.

Cilaen opened the window to let the air in. Merlin had been gone from Elanor's bedside for a day, leaving behind an emptiness felt by them all. Gwynevere sat beside Elanor, holding her hand when, all at once, the pace of Elanor's breathing steadily quickened, and she noiselessly screamed—her voice gone. She doubled over onto her side, a pained look on her face.

"Lie still!" Cilaen encouraged as he grabbed hold of her. "Your movements will make it worse. Lie still."
Elanor's eyes slowly opened, revealing her confusion.

Cilaen urged, "Do not try to speak. Your throat…it is recovering. You have been injured. Just rest."

Elanor's eyes gradually focused on the faces of Gwynevere and Cilaen as they leaned over her. Gwynevere soothed her, tenderly hushing while she rubbed her forehead. "Gently now…Gently."

Elanor felt every ache awaken in her body. Everywhere hurt; her throat burned, and every breath sent pain into her side. The sting only ebbed as she remembered the face of the hooded man. The memory brought the horror freshly back to her mind.

Panicking she thought, *Where is Merlin?*

Elanor's lips moved to soundlessly form his name.

"He has been by your side night and day. He will return," Gwynevere assured her.

However, two more days passed without any sign of him, until…

The door creaked open, and Merlin stood with his face long and his skin pale. Beneath his eyes were dark circles. He gazed slowly over at Samara and Cilaen before his eyes met Elanor's. She sat weakly, the red remnants of violence striping her throat and face, though her bright, hopeful eyes shined through.

Tears welled in his red eyes as he timidly approached her. He pressed her hand to his mouth, kissing it. Then, he put his hand on her face, relieved to see her conscious. "I did not know you had awoken," he said, faltering. "I had to think. Watching you laying there overwhelmed me with despair."

Even as he spoke, Elanor witnessed a shadow creep over his face and his eyes darken. He shook his head, then pushed away from her bedside. Something was wrong. She could not speak, but she could see his grief and anger. His heart was hard and far away, and he was resolute. He was leaving.

"I know you can see me, Elanor." Merlin said quietly. "I have been selfish. You do not belong here with me. There must be a way to send you home, and I will find it." Looking at the floor, he refused to look at her. "I needed to see you once more, unbroken, but now..." He closed his eyes bitterly, clenched his jaw, then turned to leave.

Cilaen rushed forward and firmly gripped Merlin's arm. "You cannot just leave!"

Merlin's eyes flashed fiercely as he yanked his arm from Cilaen's grip and walked out the door.

A knife pierced Elanor's heart. Nothing she had been through in the forest could compare to the pain that now surged into her heart. She couldn't scream, or even cry. The suffering was too deep. She had become like glass, shattered on the floor.

How could Merlin do this?

Elanor stared in utter shock. Her mind tried to understand the grief and anger she had seen within Merlin.

He can't have left. He must come back.

She wanted to hope, but the resolve she saw in him assailed her with doubt.

Slowly, she began to tremble. It was as though she was shivering, but she wasn't cold. She desperately gazed at Cilaen, who looked back at her in an angry stupor.

Samara dashed to her side. "Elanor! Elanor!" she said, lightly patting her on the cheek. "Look at me, dear one."

Gwynevere broke into the room, breathless and upset. "What has happened? I saw Merlin leaving. I tried to call to him, but he wouldn't respond. I chased after him into the stables, but he was off before I could reach him." She looked across at Elanor and saw her hollow look of shock.

Gwynevere knelt quietly before Elanor. "What has happened...What has happened?"

Cilaen spat angrily, "He has run away."

"No..." Gwynevere faltered. "He can't have left us."

Elanor tried to speak. The words barely formed on her lips as she worked to squeeze the sound out of her throat. Finally, she whispered, "Please! Please!" A tear dropped from her eye. "Take me...away from here."

Gwynevere's heart broke. "Cilaen, can she be moved?"

"If she is carried, and carefully."

"I will get Bedwyr," Gwynevere said, quickly rising to her errand.

Elanor felt lightheaded, and time lapsed. The next thing she knew,

Bedwyr was by her side, gingerly he lifted her from Merlin's bed. She wrapped her arms around him and looked at his face. His eyes were sad but strong. His solid arms held her firm, making her feel safe as she leaned into him. She slid in and out of consciousness as his steps rocked her. When she opened her eyes again, she found she was alone, lying in her own bed.

She turned to see that the green flame of the clay lantern had gone out. Probably due to being neglected, and the oil not refilled. The disappointing feeling of it crashed over her. Her thoughts drifted to the night she and Merlin danced under the green branches while the dancers twirled around them. She remembered the pendant and the kiss. Everything had felt so perfect and untouchable. She reached to her neck to feel for the pendant and realized for the first time that it was also gone. Probably lost in the forest somewhere. The pain of all the loss put a wedge a little deeper into the crack in her rejected heart.

In the forest, when all was lost, she reached deep within herself and a song came out. But now, there was nowhere she could reach to fix it. No song to sing. She did not belong back in her world anymore, but she didn't know if she belonged here without Merlin.

She did not want to despair. She did not want to be shattered and broken hearted. She wanted to fight like she had in the forest. She wanted to have hope and be free, but she couldn't muster up the strength. Her body hurt, her voice was gone, and the pain in her heart seemed infinitely stronger than she was. Her only thought was to close her eyes. Maybe then she would wake, and the world would be right again.

Just go to sleep, and all the pain will be gone.
So, she did.

The next morning when Samara brought Elanor some broth, she did not wake. Samara tried to wake her, but Elanor did not stir. Her skin was hot with fever.

Cilaen rushed to examine her. There was no infection in her wounds, or anything indicating that she should be unwell. But deep down, he knew it was her broken heart that afflicted her. Making Elanor sit up, Cilaen tried to force her awake.

"You must fight, Elanor," he said, lightly tapping her cheek.

Elanor could hear him, but she felt far away. She agreed that she needed to fight but had a hard time finding her way back. She saw the faces of those who cared for her as the days moved forward. She saw Cilaen, Samara, and sometimes Gwynevere. Always, she was glad to see them but couldn't find her strength.

But one day, Bedwyr came. He sat down in a chair beside Elanor's bed. She knew he was there, even though he sat quietly. And after some time, he cleared his throat and began to speak.

"You must get better and start eating," Bedwyr said with tender concern. "We miss those blue eyes and the brightness of your smile. The apples are turning red, and Brynn would like you to feed her some." He laughed somberly, and then sighed. "This is an awful thing that has happened. You are our hope and light, and Merlin promised you had come to us for a reason. Well...I do not think that you will have done your job if you leave us now." He breathed out again, then collapsed back silently into the chair.

"Arthur and I were young boys together. My father was the Battle Chief of Dyved, and Merlin brought Arthur to stay with us when he was just a baby. As we grew, we played together like brothers. My father taught us to wield a sword and throw a spear. We pretended to hunt and longed for the day we could hunt as men.

"When I was only twelve, my father sent me away. It is the custom of chieftains and kings to send their children to be raised in the Halls of other great men. In this way, their children grow wise of the world and its rulers. My heart was broken to be sent away. Arthur and I had never been apart up until that day. Merlin took Arthur far north to King Ector of Caer Edyn, while I went to go live with the horse masters of the west.

"Arthur met Ector's son Cai in the North. Aih," Bedwyr reminisced. "I miss Cai and his wild red hair...You know, they say Cai killed his first boar with Arthur by his side when he was only fifteen. They chased the thing down a ravine, cornering it amongst the rocks. The boar was frenzied and charged them, knocking Cai to the ground, almost killing his horse. But as it rounded, Cai took aim with his spear and skewered it through its mouth. Cai was a strong brute."

"We were reunited each year at the warriors' Gathering of Feats. It was my favorite time of the year. Each year, we were bigger and stronger, and soon, we were the champions." Bedwyr grinned proudly.

"But the day Arthur drew Aurelias's sword, we were finally reunited as brothers. Merlin proclaimed Arthur the rightful heir, though many of the lesser kings would not accept him. They were still fighting amongst themselves over which of them would be high king.

"But Merlin was brilliant, you see. He knew that all the kings understood that he was the kingmaker. None of them had rightful claim. Merlin cleverly proclaimed Arthur as Prydain's Battle Chief and knew if Arthur conquered those that invaded our lands, the kings would have to stop their squabbling and allow him his rightful place. So, Arthur, as chief over all the Cymbrogi, set up his strength of arms with me and Cai at his side. This, the beginning of Arthur's mighty strength in the land of the Britons."

Bedwyr's story sparked a new reality to awaken within Elanor. Arthur intrigued her. She remembered seeing him in her dreams. His face was familiar and secure. He inspired her and made her heart feel strong. Her eyes opened, and she reached out to Bedwyr.

Taken aback, Bedwyr took her hand. "I was so lost in my story I did not see that you were awake."

"I liked the story," Elanor whispered slowly.

"Then," Bedwyr said, pleased, "I will return with another one tomorrow. If I have your permission."

She nodded and smiled ever so slightly.

And so, he did. Every day for the next two weeks, Bedwyr came. Every day, Elanor ate a little more, and her face looked brighter. Bedwyr told of great battles and the tremendous exploits of Arthur and his men. Sometimes, he even told stories of Merlin and how he fought alongside them, moving the winds to save them.

Elanor loved all of them. His stories made her feel connected to something bigger than herself. They helped her forget, even for a moment, the pain in her heart. His kind, brown eyes and wide smile made her contented. He was not woeful, and even though he was battle scarred, he did not seem to despair.

There was pain and grief in his stories, but always he focused on the triumph.

Bedwyr told her, "Arthur saw answers when others saw problems. He was wise and fearless, while many cowered away. He sought peace with his enemies whenever he could, and even made alliances that were said to be impossible. In diplomacy, he was forgiving and merciful. But in battle, he was decisive and formidable."

With great passion, Bedwyr explained, "Arthur ran into the fray of battle, and his blade slew ten at a time. The Great God's hand was ever upon him, and he feared not the devils that rose against him. He loved his people, and he loved his men." He choked with emotion, "And he fought beside them, and gave his life for them…His love for us…was Arthur's greatest strength, and his greatest weakness."

Bedwyr's stories were the perfect distraction. Elanor's time alone made her think of Merlin, and she did not want to think of him. She hated how she longed for him. She was angry for what he had done. She could find no excuse for his choice to run. She rather preferred embracing anger than allowing herself to feel how much she missed him. She hoped that he would return, but this thinking always made her heart sting.

Only Bedwyr brought the light. His tales told of better places and times. Sometimes, he would tell her about times that were much worse, and it reminded her that she could feel thankful. Every day she waited for this, and every day she hoped Bedwyr would never leave.

UNWELCOMED RETURN

Cilaen was deep in his work when Merlin returned looking travel-worn and unsteady. Cilaen stood, surprised, but as he gazed upon Merlin, his shock quickly shifted to a fierce, unwelcome gaze.

Merlin's eyes turned away, resisting the shame that came with the conviction of Cilaen's eyes. He stood in the doorway, unsure whether to speak or storm through to his chamber.

Merlin had returned, but he remained uncertain why. He had ridden out into the wilds in search of answers. But always, thoughts of Elanor distracted him, confounding his purpose. Stubbornly, he pushed against the tide, wrestling with reason. His thoughts chased him like relentless wolves.

He scavenged the land for evidence of the evil pestilence that had torn and beaten his beloved, hoping that releasing his vengeance would heal his heartache, but he found nothing. Without rest, he wearied, never getting a foothold or gaining any ground.

He knew he was running from the pain, and finally, feeling a fool, his running had led him all the way back, ashamed and broken.

Merlin never returned Cilaen's gaze but rushed to his chamber and shut the door behind him. He had not truly slept for weeks, and now, finally home, he believed he could. He threw himself down and closed his eyes while his weariness stole him away to sleep.

The next morning, Merlin woke with a heavy heart. His guilt clawed at him, making him wish his eyes remained closed. What heartache had his lapse caused? He had been so certain that leaving was the right thing to do. The sight of Elanor, broken, made him feel like his head was plagued with angry bees. He rubbed his palms against his eyes as he tried to bring himself into some semblance of readiness.

Merlin shook his head and left his bed. Hunger was getting the best of him, so he quietly entered the main chamber. He was relieved to find Cilaen had gone. Merlin knew it was too much to wish for a glad greeting from him. He ripped a chunk of bread out of a loaf sitting on the table, and famished, he began to eat. He took a large draught of water, parching his dry lips and mouth.

On a table behind him, Merlin spotted a pile of small parchments. He could see that they had been drawn upon, and their unique beauty caught his eye. He drew the top parchment away, and underneath was a drawing depicting what could only be himself—perfectly detailed—with a dove in his hands.

Merlin fell into the chair behind him. He had never seen any of Elanor's drawings before, but he knew that these were hers. His heart pinched at the sight of them. He wasn't ready to let go, not yet. The thought of Elanor compelled the violence in his heart to surface again. The anger, the hate. But this time, it was aimed at himself.

The door clicked open, and Cilaen entered with his arms full. He saw Merlin and paused. He set his jaw, then turned to set his parcels down.

"Those are hers," Cilaen said over his shoulder. "You know… if you are going to run away again, it is best if you just don't come back." Cilaen turned to face him. "You should not see her if you are not going to stay." His face was solid and grim as he looked at Merlin, who still held Elanor's drawing in his hand.

Silence passed between them as they stared each other down. Cilaen's anger steadily rose. "This is your way though. Isn't it? When things are too hard? You just get to leave while we clean up the mess?" Cilaen's lip curled with disgust and his chin quivered. "Say something for your faults! Have you nothing to say?" He paused. "Elanor survived being beaten, slashed, and even poisoned, but she almost did not survive what you did to her. Did you think you could just leave and she would move on? Did you even think of her at all, or just yourself? You know she loves you. Her broken heart was almost the death of her, and a fever nearly took her. If it had not been for Bedwyr, she would have been lost to us."

The mention of Bedwyr's name slapped Merlin across the face. "Bedwyr?" he repeated, trying to stifle his fury.

"Oh, stop! As if you have a say. You gave her up...You gave up the one whose magic is not unlike your own. You gave up one of beauty who has been a gift to us all. And you, *Master Merlin*, have been inexcusably selfish and unwise," Cilaen scathed.

Rising to his feet, Merlin said, "You do not understand! You could not understand!"

"No! *You* do not understand," Cilaen retorted, pointing his finger as he shook with anger. "I trusted you—we all did."

Merlin could not take any more of Cilaen's accusation. He pushed passed him, blood boiling in his ears. He was not angry with Cilaen, but he refused to acknowledge the consequences that Cilaen was forcing upon him.

He knew he couldn't aim his anger at Cilaen, so he aimed elsewhere. Merlin charged through the Hall and out to the stables where he knew he would find him. And there, standing alone in the yard, was Bedwyr, having finished his work.

The instant Bedwyr saw Merlin was the instant he was struck, feeling the full force of Merlin's body slamming down upon him. Merlin grabbed Bedwyr by the neck and shoved him into the outer wall of the stables. The men slammed against the wood as they fell.

Bedwyr flung his arms up to defend himself, breaking Merlin's grip. He sent his elbow flying—CRACK—right across Merlin's mouth, forcing him back and knocking him to the ground.

Merlin got up and charged again, but Bedwyr turned to evade him, causing Merlin to careen into the wall.

"Merlin!" Bedwyr shouted, putting his hands up to keep him at bay. "My brother! Why do you attack me? Is this how you greet me after being away?"

Merlin glared, wiping blood from his lip. Still ready to fight, his teeth were bared aggressively.

"I do not want to fight you! Have you gone mad?"

At Bedwyr's words, Merlin slowly sobered as he peered at his confused friend. He grunted and collapsed back onto the hay beneath him, wearily placing his hands on his head.

"What has gotten into you?" Bedwyr said, approaching him while he rubbed his head—sore from being slammed against the stable walls. "Where have you been?" He carefully lowered himself next to his friend, now that it was apparent Merlin did not want to attack him a second time. "I would like to say, I am happy to see you, but we must work on our greetings."

Through pained breaths, Merlin spoke, "Elanor. You have been seeing her?"

"Ah!" Bedwyr mused, now understanding Merlin's rage. "Come now. You know me better than that. I am a man of honor. You should not have left her, but I know who she belongs to. You and she are meant for one another. She was brought from the stars and given to you, not me. What I have been doing, my dear friend," he said, closely eyeing Merlin, "is all I could to save her...You did her wrongly." Bedwyr's eyes narrowed. "I did for her what you did not. I stayed. I did not know if she would have me, but she liked my stories. You should be thanking me, not running me down like a bull." He rubbed his shoulder. "I was on my way to see her now. You could come...she needs you, Merlin." Picking up some straw, Bedwyr stuck one end in his mouth to chew. "Though, please understand, if you leave her now, I will make her mine," he said smiling, though his tone was serious. "Or would you rather I blackened your eye to match that lip? I could go for another tussle."

"I have been such a fool," Merlin said finally.

"Yes, that you have. Though you should not be telling me, you should be telling Elanor."

Merlin sorrowfully conceded, "Do you think she could forgive me?"

"There is one way to find out. Come now. She is waiting." Bedwyr stood from the ground before helping Merlin to his feet. Merlin pondered weakly for a moment, then followed him to Elanor.

Elanor had been waiting for Bedwyr to come. She knew it was nearing the part of the day when he visited. Samara had brushed her hair and placed a robe upon her. Everything had been set just right.

Samara was busy setting kindling on the fire when Bedwyr came waltzing in through the open door. He stopped to acknowledge Samara, and then turned to greet Elanor, bowing low and looking up at her.

"Bedwyr!" Elanor squeaked with what little voice she had.

"Elanor!" he said with surprise. "Your voice."

"Yes!" Her voice was still weak and gravelly but had tone for the first time. "I woke this morning, and my throat felt less tight. I spoke, and my voice flowed out without pain."

"And you're smiling!" Bedwyr affirmed. "Well, my heart is warmed to see you so healed. I cannot stay, however," he relayed with sincere sadness. "I have brought someone who needs to see you much more than I." He walked over and kissed her hand, squeezing it longingly.

Elanor saw disappointment in his eyes and a reluctance to let go, making her heart ache.

"Surely, they could wait, Bedwyr. This is our time."

His brown eyes locked with hers as he hesitated. He sighed heavily, then turned toward the door. He glanced into the hallway, then nodded, his lips pressed firmly together.

What is disturbing him so? Who had come? A twinge of fear lurched into Elanor's chest.

Bedwyr spread his arms, welcoming Merlin in.

Samara gasped loudly.

Rattled by the sight of him, Elanor swiftly turned away, her mouth falling open. Hurt and anger rushed through her as she stared at the wall, unwavering. She was afraid to look at him. Unwilling to acknowledge his presence.

Bedwyr promptly left the room, and Samara followed after him, shutting the door. Merlin faced Elanor uncomfortably, unsure how to begin. He gazed at the side of her face. The red remains of bruises and cuts were still evident on her skin. Elanor's chest heaved angrily, making it hard for any words to come. There was nothing he could say that would put an answer to his leaving.

Slowly, he pressed himself to humbly sit on the edge of her bedside. Tenderly, he reached to touch her hand that laid on the bed.

Elanor's heartbeat quickened, and hot emotions flooded her face. She refused to cry. He did not deserve her sorrow. With as much grace as she could muster, she held it all in.

"I know why you left," Elanor breathed in her cracked, fragile voice. "I saw what was in your mind that day you left. That thorn you let come crashing back in. So much grief and anger. You believed that you were being punished for choosing love. So, you ran and pushed me away…thinking sending me back to my time would solve your grief. You know as well as I do that I don't belong there anymore." The tears were almost too much for her to hold back. She swallowed deeply, then continued, "I just hoped that you would choose me over the pain. I trusted you."

"Is it too late for me to make that choice?" Merlin asked meekly. Her one cheek was flush, and her breath trembled. "Please…Please forgive me, Elanor. I still do not understand what drove me so hard. I have been a mad man running through the wilds. The sight of you like that…it broke me inside. You are my very heart, and I was afraid. I was afraid that I had caused it all to happen."

Elanor gave no response, and Merlin slumped over, looking down at the floor. "I was in love once before. Many, many years ago when I was a youth," he said, somberly remembering. "She was young and beautiful. I still remember the rose in her cheeks. Her hair was red like flame. She was to be my wife. I left her to go on a hunt, and when I returned, the village had been attacked, many slaughtered. I found her amongst the other maidens. The savages had wrecked them so completely. I vowed to never love again, and so I did not. Never did I need to. My purpose and mission were of a higher calling…when I saw you…bleeding…I thought I had betrayed myself. In truth…I used to know my purpose, but I do not have one anymore. At least, not apart from you. I forgot that."

His story softened Elanor's heart, and she freely wept now. She gave up the hard exterior and let the tears come rolling. "I want to be angry with you," she sobbed, embracing his hands with her fingers. "You broke my heart. I struggled to find myself again." Then, she wept even harder. "Owe!" she squealed, pulling her hand up to her side. The movement wrenched her ribs into a spasm. She doubled over, waiting for the pain to subside. Merlin reached to help, but she held her hand out to stop him. After the pain faded, she remained breathless. Still, she faced away from Merlin, refusing to look at him.

Feeling helpless, he asked, "Can I help you?"

Elanor shook her head in reply.

"Look at me," Merlin pleaded. "I tell you this story not to justify. Only in hopes that it will help you to understand. Please, Elanor."

"I forgive you. Of course…I forgive you." She held her ribs tightly, wincing.

Desperately, Merlin said, "Then why will you not look at me?"

"Because I am afraid to. I don't want to see what I saw the last time I looked into your eyes. I do not want my heart to break again. Can I really trust that you will stay?"

Delicately, Merlin lifted Elanor's chin and turned her toward him. She squeezed her eyes shut as he moved closer. Tears dripped over the curves of her mouth, and Merlin wiped them free.

He placed his forehead onto hers and breathed her in. "Please," he whispered softly, "open your eyes and see me."

Elanor slowly shook her head in refusal, but then he kissed her softly. Her eyes opened, revealing bright blue, and she saw Merlin's tears. The light had been stolen from his eyes. Now seeing him, she could no longer keep herself from caring. She wanted to lift the heaviness in his eyes and bring back the light they had before the forest stole it all away. Her anger melted away and she felt love returning. She leaned forward and kissed each of his eyes. Then, turning herself toward him, she allowed Merlin to bring her into his chest, and they rested in each other's arms, warm and whole once more. The embrace healed them, reminding them of what it had been to be in each other's arms.

THE HEALING OF SAMHAIN

Samhain had come and now the hearth fires blazed. Merlin explained, "This is the season of warm draughts and good company. The warriors will move in from the fields and fill the Hall with their rich laughter."

The thought of laughter warmed Elanor's heart. She continued to heal and needed to be reminded of life outside her room. Standing for an extended length of time was difficult; she mostly sat or remained in her bed. Cilaen surmised it may have been the enchantment and the poison that kept her from healing more rapidly, but he was pleased with her progress.

Cold wind blew through the latched windows of Elanor's room. Elanor peered out between the cracks to see the greying sky. Merlin sat at her bedside as she flipped through the pages of the blue book. The pictures beautifully detailed creatures she had never seen before. One particular image of a horse sparked her memory, and she remembered the unicorn. She had forgotten him due to the nightmares and anxious thoughts from that day in the forest. But as she gazed out at the cold grey, the unicorn returned to her thoughts like a ray of hope. She remembered the magic that came upon her and the song that she sang.

The creature shined with bright light, and it consumed her as she lost all consciousness. That was when she heard him. His voice resonated in her mind while his image became clear and alive. As a beautiful white shadow, his presence swept over her, pure and powerful. He told her his name was Grwyrthrhodd. He was a gift bringer and had heard her song.

Out of the silence of her thoughts, Elanor murmured, "He wanted to give me a gift. He said I was to call to him again."

Merlin looked at her strangely. "What do you mean? Who said this?"

"The unicorn. He came to me in the forest."

"Unicorn?" Merlin thought for a moment, trying to understand. "You mean the enaid?"

"I saw him that day in the forest. Did you see him?" Elanor wondered if maybe her memories were only a dream.

"I saw him," Merlin mused. "He stood over you. The man in blue said he was protecting you. That you had called him with your song. He said, 'No one has called such a one for a thousand years.'"

"The man in blue?" Elanor asked, taken aback.

"It was the man in blue that told me of the enchantment and led us to you."

Elanor pondered, then continued, "The unicorn's name was Gr-wyrthrhodd…he told me he would keep me safe. He asked me to return when I was well. He seemed confident I would be." She lost herself in the light of the hearth. "Would you take me to him, once the weather becomes warm and I am well enough to ride?"

Merlin nodded his head. "Of course, I will take you. How would we find him? Would you know how to call to him?"

"I don't know how I did the first time," she admitted. "It was in my memories of you, the song came. I passed into a sort of dream, and you were there. Your song in my mind pulled something deep within me. There was no thought. It just came…but when it came, it was familiar, and I knew it. It was as if all the good things that were within me pushed back the darkness."

"I heard your song." Merlin recoiled at the remembrance of it. "Your song was in my head and in my heart. That was how I knew something was wrong. Urgently, I went to find you and discovered that your song had called the enaid and the man in blue." He shook his head. "It was a powerful song."

Merlin hesitated before timidly asking, "The hooded men? Did you see them? If I found them, I would…" He stopped, working to suppress the rage that rose as he spoke. "I don't know what I would do. I must aim to be far wiser and less hateful, else we fall into another of their deceptions."

"I…I could show you," Elanor began uncertainly. "But I may not be able to control what you see. You would have to be aware of how it might affect you. I saw one man's face." Her eyes flashed fearfully as she remembered him, her mouth twisting at the memory. "They all wore hoods, but one of the men came close to me. He was probably sure I was going to die. I could see every inch of his horrible face." She clenched her teeth and closed her eyes. The unlocked memory forced her breath to quicken.

"I could not ask you to relive that."

"I am not afraid," she said promptly. "I will not suffer them to remain, if I could do my part to stop them."

Merlin stroked her cheek. "I know you are strong, but this is not required of you."

Elanor set her jaw defiantly. "I will show you his face!"

Merlin held his hands back against his chest dubiously.

Elanor took his hands tenderly and unwrapped his clenched fists. She calmly exhaled, and Merlin was transported into her memories. He saw Cilaen and Elanor laughing in the meadow, the warmth of the sunlit morning shining on their faces. Already Merlin longed to stay here, in wonderful peace, but the memory continued forward.

Dread beset him when Elanor's horse stopped, and he felt her panic rise as she stumbled helplessly. The men approached her from out of the woods, and he wished he could stop it all from happening. Merlin anxiously searched for a way to be released from the memory as each horrifying moment rolled into the next.

But the moment had come. Merlin forced himself to stare at the devil, taking in every line of his face and the sound of his wicked voice as he knelt before Elanor. He was overwhelmed by wrath as he stared at him. He yelled soundlessly at the man's murderous face, yearning to sink his fingers into his skull.

Merlin listened closely as the man released his dark enchantment, and the practiced air of his speech revealed him. This villain was not a learned sorcerer. He was parroting words he had been told. Though effective, the magic had come from another, more powerful sorcerer—this man only a puppet. Merlin was alarmed by the unsettling revelation, as these mysteries could be leading Prydain into a worse fate.

Now Elanor lay lifeless on the ground, and the sight of it made Merlin see red. His heart begged, "I have seen enough!"

The magic lifted, and he was once more with Elanor, sitting at her bedside. The torment was over.

Immediately, Merlin reached to caress her, feeling her safe within his arms. It was as though he had awoken from a horrifying nightmare, only to see that everything was right once waking. Relief washed over him, yet he knew that it had all happened just as he had seen it.

"I am so sorry," he said, his voice pinched.

The vision had taken a toll on Elanor, and she turned away from him. With tears pooling in her eyes, she whispered, "I'm tired."

"Yes…of course," Merlin said, pulling the blanket up around her shoulders.

Witnessing the attack from Elanor's perspective caused guilt to surge through him. Merlin felt ashamed having abandoned her. He placed his face into his hands as emotions drifted through him like waves upon the shore. He knew Elanor's experience had been terrible, but to see it for himself was overwhelming. Even so, the pain had been worth the glimpse of the enemy. His suspicions had been correct: The attacks in the Southlands were deliberate, and there was now a greater concern.

Merlin unwrapped the folds of his tunic to reveal Elanor's blue pendant. He pulled it out and unraveled the chain while he gazed upon it. He rubbed the blue stone with his thumb, peering over at Elanor, who lay now asleep in her bed, softly breathing. She truly was stronger than he had given her credit. He kissed the stone and began to quietly sing over it. The stone radiated bright blue as it vibrated with a dull hum. Then, it diminished back to its previous quality as he pressed it into her hand. It would be there when she woke. He was glad to have it returned to where it belonged.

Merlin whispered, "I will take you to your unicorn."

25

GRWYRTHRHODD

Merlin strapped his harp to his horse's saddle, hoping that his playing would help Elanor find her song. Now that she was well enough and the blossoms and warm weather had returned, it was time to fulfill his promise to help her seek the unicorn. He knew the power of song had a deep connection to soul and spirit, and also to those that walked in the otherworld. He was eager to help Elanor connect to that magic, knowing if she could, they would see the enaid again. Quietly, he slipped an item into the satchel while Elanor's eyes were diverted. It had been a long Samhain, and he aimed to make their venture memorable.

Elanor still limped, never having fully healed from the wound in her side. However, the brightness of the sun lifted the heaviness she felt, lessening the painful sting of the evil days of the forest. Riding silently at an easy pace, she wondered whether seeking the unicorn would amount to anything. Memories of the enaid seemed like an illusion. Had it not been for Merlin's account of the beast, she would have been certain it was a dream and nothing more.

Elanor winced as she carefully dismounted her horse. They were stopped near the two arching trees that formed a gateway to the lake. "The journey was hard for you," Merlin said with concern, seeing her limp worsen.

Elanor waved her hand. "It will ease. A glimpse of the lake will bring me all the healing I could ever need." Her brow furrowed as she watched the water lap at the shore. "How does one begin to pull on the magic to call a unicorn?"

Merlin simply smiled as he drew up his harp and settled himself on a nearby rock. He plucked the strings precisely, as though it were the breeze that blew across them, making them hum.

Elanor closed her eyes, trying to connect to the thought of the unicorn. Merlin's music made her feel at peace. She focused on the wind that blew across her face and the sound of the water running through the pebbles.

"You are trying too hard," Merlin said, breaking into her concentration. "Let the memory of the magic come. It is there."

Elanor's thoughts were still a jumble of pain and fear. It was difficult to separate the song from the pricks of dread that arose within her. She inhaled slowly, hoping she could settle into the magic, but she could not break free from the traumatic barbs that insisted on having her attention. She sighed out in frustration, rubbing her forehead as if to rub the memories away. The whole effort seemed pointless.

"Listen to my song," Merlin soothed. "It was the memories of my song that lead to the magic. It was disconnected from the fear and the desperation of the moment."

And so he sang:

Little one, little one, it was the birds that sang their song.
Long and strong, they echoed the sound of what they heard beneath.
They answered children crying loud,
They answered nature's groaning call,
They answered the days long yearning,
They answered the call of the night's calm stirrings.
Little one, little one, it was the birds that sang their song
Long and strong, long and strong, they echoed on.

Verse after verse, Merlin sang about birds, and Elanor listened. Releasing her thoughts, she focused on the birds singing around her. Their twitting and chirping sounded in rhythm. *Listen!* she heard deep within herself. *Listen!* Then, from down deep, she discovered a rousing burn in her chest, almost as if in agreement to the songs she heard around her.

Elanor's mouth opened, and her voice soared with strength. As she sang, birds flew out over the lake and Merlin stopped to listen. It was an unnatural sound streaming out of her spirit, loud but soothing.

Then, out through the trees upon the shoreline, a light broke forth, and out of it appeared the tall, white creature. It reared back on its hinds and charged toward them, tossing its head back and forth. As the enaid rushed forward, its arrival brought an awesome sense of excitement, its hooves biting the pebbles as it traveled.

The sound of falling stones made Elanor open her eyes. Upon seeing the creature, she ceased her song. The enaid slowed as it gracefully approached her, tenderly whinnying. Elanor timidly gazed at the magnificent creature, and when their eyes met, her spirit connected to his. He was in her heart and in her mind. He bowed his head and touched his muzzle to her face. Elanor delicately placed her fingers upon his cheek.

Merlin stood back, allowing space between them.

The enaid spoke to Elanor within her mind. *"I know you, child, and you know me. I am Grwyrthrhodd. I have longed for your song to call me again. Your voice has awakened me from my long slumber and has revived a new purpose. I am messenger and gift giver. Healing is what I have, for you must carry this gift also. Purity and strength I have, and so shall you. You have thought yourself weak and invisible, but your purpose and destiny are beyond what you have understood. Please...call the Emrys here, for I would speak to him also."*

Elanor responded, "Emrys?"

Merlin startled in response to hearing a name that had been long forgotten.

"He calls you Emrys...He would like to speak to you also."

"I have not been called by that name for many years," Merlin stuttered, eyes wide. He approached the enaid humbly, and Elanor placed his hand upon its muzzle.

Then, Merlin heard him. *"Her name is Gwenddydd, and you and she are one. Twins. Joined in magic. Like you were to Arthur, you are both two sides of the same coin. One the defender, and the other, healer. You cannot build the promise without the other, and Arthur's promise depends on you. Many things are waking, both good and evil—both will know your names. You, Emrys, and you, Gwenddydd. Great Emrys, what is in your heart to do this day, is right. Now, Emrys...your sight again will be restored."*

As the creature spoke, a bright flash, like a fire's spark, fell into Merlin's eye, then disappeared. He rubbed his eyes fiercely, blinking them open and shut.

"For you, Gwenddydd, this day I have come to give you a gift."

Grwyrthrhodd stepped back and placed his ivory horn over her chest, and as he did, heat radiated through Elanor's body. She fell to her knees. Her marrow shifted and changed within her. Lightly, he repeated her name, *"Gwend-dydd...Gwenddydd."* Each time she heard it, Elanor felt her mind being renewed. Blue light radiated around her.

Realizing her body no longer felt any pain, she quickly stood. For the first time in many months, Elanor felt strong and complete. She laughed and flung her arms around the great creature, whispering, "Thank you, thank you, thank you." She pressed her face into his neck.

"I will be with you when you call, Gwenddydd. I am always near you, and I can hear you when you call to me. My gifts are yours; my purpose now aligned to your destiny."

The unicorn lifted his head and galloped away, disappearing into the forest.

Elanor moved her body back and forth, shifting her legs and hips. When she pressed her skin where the cut had been, the scar underneath her dress seemed to be gone.

"Merlin!" she yelled excitedly. "I...I am healed. I have no more pain." She laughed, twirling in joyous circles, displaying her freedom.

Merlin rushed to lift her into the air and spun her around.

Then she was off, frolicking across the shore. Her dress flowed behind her. She turned back toward Merlin and leapt into his arms. "I cannot believe I have seen a unicorn." She peered up at him. "And he healed me." Her face was radiant, beaming with life. All the pain of the past season had been erased.

The moment had also melted Merlin's grief, and a youthful joy returned to his countenance—just as when Elanor had pulled the thorn from his heart. The enaid had said that what was in his heart to do, was right. And so, there was something he desired. He had longed for it, but tragedy had stolen it away. But now, on this day, there would be nothing to hold him back. Merlin gazed at the beautiful blue of Elanor's eyes and the gentle blush of her lips. Nothing else in the world mattered but her. He pulled from his coat a grey piece of myrtle wood. Tenderly, he placed it into Elanor's hands.

"What is this?" Elanor asked, rolling the wood in her hands. The object was small but long, carved with whorls, with a delicately whittled face on the top, and worn in places where it had been rubbed smooth.

"It is a gift of myrtle. It was my father's and is very old." He beamed. "This is a gift my father gave to my mother when he wanted her to be his wife, and now I give it to you."

Elanor brought the figure to her chest as Merlin's golden eyes sparkled with tears.

He placed one of his hands over hers and said, "I cannot be without you, Elanor. You are my very soul. I have already spent too many years of my life without your fullness. I would marry you. Will you be my wife?"

"With all my heart!" she exclaimed loudly. She jumped and wrapped her arms around his neck. Merlin gleefully spun her around and she kissed him as she laughed. The joyous moment had finally come, and the bright sun shined, lighting them with its fondness.

Merlin lifted his harp in celebration, singing as they walked along the shore. He sang happy songs about kings returning home and lovers reunited. His voice resounded through the air with their celebration.

The true song of the bard was never just a simple song; it was always so much more. Elanor listened to every lyric and every stroke of the harp. His voice, a powerful instrument, seemed to move the trees. She believed that every lyric, every story, was meant to shift the paradigms of her heart. The words moved, taught, and prophesied with their sound. There was purpose in every word.

Elanor now knew the song was in her, too, but she had not learned to use it as Merlin had. Her mind floated with merry thoughts of a wedding day. She imagined the faces of Gwynevere and Cilaen beaming in gladness.

She all but danced as they walked from the shore up into the forest and amongst the trees. Every tree grew large before them, the deeper they went. Elanor stooped to pick from a patch of flowers when Merlin stopped playing. She turned and saw him facing tentatively into the forest, looking and listening.

"What is it?" she whispered.

He held his hand up to calm her. "Listen."

Elanor stood quietly. Her ears captured the noise as it steadily grew louder. The crunching of sticks and leaves were unmistakably the sound of many feet roaming the forest.

Merlin grabbed hold of Elanor, his eyes set sternly ahead of him. "They are coming this way."

VILLAGERS FROM THE SOUTHLANDS

Elanor nestled into the safety of Merlin's side, grabbing hold of his arm. His presence gave her courage.

Shadows appeared between the trees. Slowly, figures began to emerge, revealing themselves as they stepped into the light. Trudging out into the open were men, women, and children, led by an old man with a long rowan staff.

"Who is there?" the old man shouted, becoming aware of them.

Merlin replied calmly, "We are only riders out for a day on the lake. You have no need to fear us."

Upon hearing his voice, the old man put out his hand to halt the people. Cautiously, he moved toward Merlin. As he moved closer, they saw the man's eyes were white with blindness. His hair was white, and his skin was tanned and deeply lined with age.

Merlin recognized the robe and staff. "Are you druid?"

The man stopped at Merlin's question and grasped his staff with both hands. "I am Marcus. I am the elder druid of these people. Our village has been ravaged, burned to the ground. We travel to Caer Lial, where we hope the High Queen will have mercy on us."

This news struck Merlin to his core. Just as the frost was melting—had the attacks begun once more?

"Where do you hail from?"

"We come from the Southlands, from a village on the very edge of Llyonesse. When our village was devastated, we had nothing. King Lugh did not even give us bread, thinking us liars. So, leaving Lugh's kingdom, we have travelled afoot, both young and old, and now we are weary and starved. Many we have lost along this long way."

The old man gazed up like a man in the dark. Merlin was baffled; how had this blind druid led these bedraggled refugees?

"I am sorry for your hardship, but you have nearly reached it. Caer Lial is a short distance from here. We will aid you by leading you the rest of the distance."

The old man said nothing, but his empty stare suddenly seemed to connect. His white eyes bore deeply into Merlin's.

"Do you have sight, Marcus?" Merlin asked.

"My eyes were burnt by the evil men who burned our village, but I have learned to use another kind of sight. And I can see that you are not just a man. You have light and purpose. And the one that is with you glows blue." The man's eyes grew large with revelation. "You are the Emrys!" he said, reaching his hand forward. A glint of hope appeared on his brow. "Who...who is this one with you?"

"She is Elanor."

"No!" the old man exclaimed, shaking his head as his awe continued to grow. "She is...She is...Gwenddydd!"

At the sound of her new name, magic rose up within Elanor. Her eyes became ablaze with blue light. Drawn by an inner voice, she walked toward the old druid.

"How do you know me?" Elanor asked mysteriously as she closed the distance between them.

Clutching his rowan staff, the old man leaned forward tentatively. "I see the light, my lady. It is all around you."

Lifting her hand gracefully, Elanor asked, "May I touch your blind eyes?" Her voice was powerful and strange. Without waiting for him to respond, she touched his cheek, slowly drawing her hand up to his eyelid. As she did, Marcus's eyes slowly changed from white to a deep, rich brown. Even the red flesh around his eyes became fresh and new.

Chapter Twenty - Six

The old man dropped his staff—it sounded hollow as it hit the ground. He reached up to touch his eyes. Tears flowed down his face as he realized he could see.

"I...I...I knew the prophecy would come. I knew this day would come," he said excitedly, looking back and forth between the two of them. "When Arthur was killed, I doubted, yet here she is. The Emrys, with his Gwenddydd. To heal our world and bring in the new kingdom." His chin quivered as he spoke. "The prophecy said she would heal us, and hope would come again. There is nothing the dark evils of the land can do now."

Merlin staggered in disbelief. "What prophecy?"

"Of course, you have not heard it," Marcus beamed. "The Great God told me, not you. I saw it in the stars and heard it in my bones years ago. I thought I would never see the day. I thought the dark powers snuffed out the promise, but I forget...oh, yes... I forget that the promise giver keeps his promises. I am all that remains of a small order of druids following the New Way who knew of this prophecy. We kept it secret and held it in our hearts."

Elanor felt a tugging on her dress and looked down to see a small boy clinging to her. He was thin and his face was dirty. His eyes were tender like a faun. The whole group of refugees began to draw near her. Their faces were weary, but their eyes were alight with new hope.

The little boy tugged again, and Elanor knelt down to him. "What is it, little one?"

"He cannot hear you," shouted a woman. "He does not hear. He is mute."

Elanor reached her hands up to the child's ears and smiled tenderly. Her eyes sparked with light. The boy startled at the light, but then grinned in wonder.

"Ma...mmm...mm!" the boy murmured and stammered, then stopped. He beamed, realizing he could hear his own voice. He clapped his hands, and his mother came running to him. The people moved in to see the boy as the mother's overwhelmed cries resounded. She threw her arms around the child while the boy laughed in delight.

The moment became rampant as the travelers pressed in around Elanor. Without warning, a young man yelled, "Be damned!" He dove through the crowd at Elanor, knocking her to the ground. The mother screamed, grabbing hold of her son as she fell to the ground. The people scattered in a panic. The man pulled from his belt a jagged knife. Elanor quickly seized his wrists as he pressed it down toward her.

Without hesitation, Merlin shouted loudly, and a sound rang out like an echo. The power of it flung the attacker through the air and into a tree, and he dropped his knife as he collided with the trunk. The man hastily gathered himself and ran away. Merlin drove after him, but then stopped.

He turned. "Elanor!"

She was already sitting up, dusting herself off.

"Are you unharmed?"

Elanor nodded quickly. Her forehead revealed her distress, however, her mind reeling as traumatic thoughts reignited in her.

"Who was that?" Merlin demanded, gazing fiercely at the druid.

The druid looked stunned. "He was the son of a simple farmer. He has been deeply troubled since the burning of our village and the loss of his father, but I cannot believe him capable of hurting anyone."

Shaken, Elanor clutched her arms to her chest. "I have not been harmed."

Merlin picked up the knife bitterly, brooding over the twisted, dented black blade. Then, he handed it to Marcus. "Was this his knife?"

Morosely, Marcus replied, "I do not know."

"Are there more amongst you that will threaten us?"

"I assure you…No!"

"Hmmm?" Merlin stared hard where the attacker had run. Then, he said sharply, "I will not go after him this day, but riders may be sent. There could be more to this story that needs to be known." He softened. "Come. You must get your people ready to move. We will see you welcomed at Caer Lial. You must be hungry and weary. The queen will want to hear your story. Let us go and retrieve our horses. We will return shortly."

Merlin grabbed Elanor by the elbow, leaving the people behind. The people silently stared as they left.

"Are you truly well?" Merlin asked, still heated.

Elanor's hands shook. "I am not hurt." Her attacker's face was seared into her memory. "The wildness of that man's eyes…Why did he attack me?"

"I do not know, but something has happened this day. Something more than we can see with our eyes."

Silently, she nodded, shaking off the fright. Her thoughts swirled. However, the miraculous moments had not been erased by the man's violent attempt. How was it she was now capable of healing?

Curiously, she asked, "That old druid—he knew me. How did he know that the unicorn had called me Gwenddydd? Why are you Emrys, and I'm

Gwenddydd? When the old druid said that name, a fire rose up in me. Suddenly, as if I had dreamt it, I knew what to do. As though I had seen it before."

"You healed Marcus and the boy," Merlin mused, lightening. "Grwyrthrhodd freed something in you. He has given you a gift. We must be aware of it and pay attention now as to how it comes." He stopped to look Elanor in the eye, placing his hands on her shoulders. "Your eyes have a new light in them." He kissed her forehead, mystified by what had unfolded. "I have not been called Emrys for many long years. It was the name I was called by the Elder Druids long ago. And now, you have been called Gwenddydd."

KING THUL OF CELYDDON

L eading the people to Caer Lial was slow. Only now had Elanor truly taken the time to observe the forsaken refugees following behind them. They were dirty and weary. The sound of a crying child rose above their thudding traipse. All of them had been led through the wilds by a blind druid with hardly any food to fill their bellies. Their homes were burned, and their people brutalized.

Merlin noticed Elanor peering somberly behind her shoulder. "Gwynevere will assist them the best she can. It is good that we found them," he comforted. "Now that Marcus can see, he will be more able to guide them…It was providence that we happened upon them on this of all days. Marcus had seen this day, and it was the Great God that revealed you to him first."

"How will these evil men be stopped?" Elanor's face twisted, disturbed by the sight. "These men seem able to evade all justice. They can do what they want, and we are left to watch as they do their worst."

"These men are agents of a greater evil. The Southlands have been greatly afflicted, but I believe the target is Caer Lial." Merlin gritted his teeth. "This is the doing of dark druids, hastened by their rebellion against the New Way. They want the old religion and refuse to understand anything else. All that was good about the old ways pointed to this new day and this new time."

"Do you know who is behind all this?"

"No, but the symptoms are revealing. Their attacks on these villages aim to weaken us; to sow doubt in the kings and chieftains of the Southlands of our strength. They have exposed their aim, though we do not know the fullness of their plan."

"Will you go after them again?"

"We may, but not until we know more. They seem impossible to track. I think there may be magic concealing them, and we cannot waste our time running after ghosts. As much as we hate these attacks, we must be wise. We cannot react in fear, but with cunning. I know that while we wait, we risk much. My hope is that Marcus will be able to tell us something more, but first, we must get them to the Palisade…and at this slow pace," Merlin clucked to the horses, "the sun will be down before we get there."

The sky was deepening into a darker blue when they rounded the top of the hill. The sight of Caer Lial sent an audible wave of relief. The people's quiet weariness became loud and jovial chatter. With their spirits now lifted, they quickened their pace, and it was not long before they arrived at the gates. Immediately upon their arrival, Merlin sent a rider to the queen with a message.

Dragging through into the Caer, the townspeople exited their homes, curious at the bedraggled lot wandering through. The newcomers created a mild disturbance as rumors coursed about the evidence of the evils in the Southlands—now appearing on their doorstep.

Crossing through the second gate, five wagons awaited, ready to carry them the rest of the way. Each wagon was tied to two large steers and had enough room for ten men. The sight of the wagons evoked a response of praise. Finally, after such a long and arduous journey, rest could now come. Mothers gratefully pulled their children up onto their laps. Men slouched forward as the world fell from their shoulders. And amongst them all, Marcus grinned widely, bowing at Elanor and Merlin with gratitude and honor.

Gwynevere stood nearby anxiously, waiting with Bedwyr and Peredur as Merlin and Elanor arrived ahead of the wagons. Before they had even dismounted, Gwynevere began, "There is food already being prepared, and the Hall is alight with a warm fire."

Elanor leapt down and bounded over to Gwynevere.

"What is this?" Gwynevere's mouth fell agape as she watched how freely Elanor moved without a limp.

Merlin came alongside. "There is much to tell."

Gwynevere looked at Elanor curiously, then continued, "Tell me of these people, Merlin. The message said they are refugees from Llyonesse? Their village burned?"

Merlin nodded. "We happened upon them walking through the forest. It is as we heard before. Their village was attacked and laid waste. These are the few that survived. They have women and children. Their elder druid, Marcus, has led them here, and I am hoping he may be able to..." Merlin stopped as the first of the wagons rolled to the top of the hill, revealing the destitute faces. The sight burned Gwynevere with grief as nearly forty displaced Cymry filled the wagons.

She hailed them. "You are welcome here! In the Hall you will find a warm fire and hot food. Please...go inside."

Eagerly, the refugees shuffled past, but the old druid hobbled over to stand before Gwynevere, bowing low. He shook with fatigue. "Thank you, High Queen of the Cymry. Blessed are we to receive such hospitality when our own king has turned us away."

"This is the elder druid, Marcus," Merlin introduced.

Gwynevere comforted, "I am sorry for what your people have suffered—traveling all this way for help. What I can do, I will do. I will hear your story, but not now. First, you must rest. My servants will bring blankets. You will eat and sleep in warmth, and then tomorrow, we will have council."

Marcus bowed as tears flooded his feeble eyes. "You are more than gracious. My people are so long without warmth and good food. We are grateful to you."

Gwynevere's heart sank as the last refugee disappeared into the Hall. "Have Cilaen see to them," she commanded a servant nearby. "Many of them are in need of medicines." She paused and placed her hand on her mouth, then breathed to Merlin, "Were these people victims of the same evil men?"

"I am without doubt. I have not heard the fullness of Marcus's tale, but my hope is he will have something that will give us an advantage. Something to stop this...this..." Merlin's lips pursed as if he had a bad taste in his mouth. "... slaughter of Prydain's people."

Disgusted, Bedwyr said, "To think Lugh did nothing for them."

Gwynevere shook her head, her eyes unsettled as she turned to climb the steps. As Elanor followed closely behind, Gwynevere paused. "What is this miracle? I have not seen you without a limp these many months. Yet here you are as though nothing happened."

"Already I am forgetting," Elanor said with a small smile. "We have seen the enaid."

"He returned to you?" Gwynevere gasped hopefully, her eyes wide.

"Yes. And what's more, he healed me." Elanor moved to display her freedom in movement. "And then…" She looked over at Merlin.

Merlin spread his arms out wide and gladly revealed, "I asked her to be my bride!"

"At last!" Gwynevere shouted, throwing her arms out to embrace Elanor. Peredur and Bedwyr erupted with gladness, beating Merlin with their hands in congratulations. "The sadness of this hour is still sweet."

"It is as it should be, my brother," Bedwyr said. He lifted Elanor in an embrace, kissing her cheek. "It is as it should be, my sister." He tenderly smiled. "And you are well? There is no pain?"

"No. No more pain." Elanor beamed.

Even Peredur whooped, "Great Esu!" with gladness at the news. "I hope this to be a sign that more joyous times are to come, and this dark misery defeated."

The next morning, they gathered in the Hall to hear Marcus's tale. The queen sat on her tall, high-backed chair—her full council in attendance.

Marcus approached with humility in his eyes.

The queen invited, "Please, druid, tell us of your village."

"Thank you for your kindness, my queen. We have been so heavy laden, but the warmth of your hall has brought us rest. Even now, I can hear the little ones playing. Such laughter I have not heard since before we were attacked. The Great God smiled on us the moment we met Merlin and Elanor in the wood."

With a pained look, Marcus continued, "It has been more than three weeks since we were forced to leave. The cold season had not even fully passed when the hooded men came. They were on foot, so we did not recognize the threat—there being so few of them. Our warriors were strong, sturdy men." He shook his fist defiantly. "We thought we had nothing to fear. But one of the villains wielded a dark magic, preventing us from defending our village. The one pushed our warriors back with a wave of his hands, while the other hooded men freely decimated everything." Marcus stopped to breathe as the anguish of the memory passed over his face. "Killing, burning, and destroying," he spat angrily. "Our animals were still in their stalls, as it was still the frozen cold of morning. They trapped them, then set them aflame."

"I have never felt a force so powerful. I did what I could to stop them. I spoke in the ancient tongues of power, but it did nothing. Defenseless, they bound me and made me watch while they beheaded our chieftain—sticking his head on a pike. Then, they took hot coals and burnt my eyes." His hands shook as he reached to touch his eyes. "They threw me to the ground in my own agony as I heard the cries and screams of my people. Finally, silence came. All I heard was the sound of crackling flames. I am glad I could not see it," he said, anguished.

"Those who survived helped me from the ground, and we ran for our lives. We fled to our king, but once arriving, he laughed at us, calling us liars and beggars. He sent us away with nothing. We knew not what else to do, so we journeyed here. We had little but the clothes on our back. Some died. The weather was just too cold for many of our little ones. Some settlements along the way aided us, but we knew we must continue on to Caer Lial."

Exasperated, Gwynevere said, "I sent message to your king to warn him, and he has done nothing." She angrily bit her lip, considering Marcus's story. "Tell me...You said your eyes were burnt, and yet I see your eyes uninjured."

Marcus pointed to Elanor. "That, my queen, is due to Gwenddydd."

"Gwenddydd?"

Merlin stood. "My lady, Elanor healed the druid's eyes. When we met him, his eyes were white with blindness. Elanor used a gift given her by the enaid and healed Marcus. And Gwenddydd is Elanor. It is the name from a prophecy that the Great God had given Marcus and is also the name given by the enaid."

All eyes looked at Elanor, astonished. She felt exposed by their attention. Though she knew the others were aware of her magic, it was not something she revealed. Now, it had been divulged to them all.

Gwynevere's mouth hung open. "What is the prophecy?"

"It is one of hope, my queen," Marcus revealed. "Many years ago, the Great God showed me a sign. I saw it first in the skies above. Two stars that fell like fire, side by side. The Ollamh, highest of our order, saw them first. We were a small order, since we had chosen to follow the New Way, breaking from the dark druids who chased the old religion."

"We decided to keep the sign secret amongst ourselves, as we did not think our darker brothers trustworthy. We sought the meaning, and it was revealed to me in a dream. Both Emrys and Gwenddydd were the names of the two stars. Emrys would hold Gwenddydd, and she would be hope and healing in our lands. These twin stars would bring in the new kingdom, but there would be a darkness that would rise up against them. But I saw a red dragon, and I knew Arthur would see the sun rising on this new day. I saw it, and we held the hope of it in our hearts. When Arthur died, I was confused and lost all hope. I thought the darkness had won and destroyed the promise, yet here they are," he said, pointing to Merlin and Elanor. "Emrys has returned, and Gwenddydd sits among us. Hope has returned."

"It seems it has," Gwynevere said, leaning back in discovery of the promise. "We welcome you and your people until a better place is found. Some homes will be prepared for you with our townspeople, and you, Marcus, are welcome in my Hall."

The doors burst open, and Uri came scrambling forward. "My lady!" he wheezed breathlessly. "My lady! The standards of Celyddon have been seen only a short way off. King Thul is coming with twenty men. He will be here soon."

Gwynevere stood. "Peredur! Bedwyr! Ride out to meet him." As quickly as Gwynevere commanded them, the two men ran from the Hall.

Merlin could sense Gwynevere's fear. "King Thul is friend to us."

Looking warily at Merlin, the queen replied, "I am only alarmed because it has been long since we heard from Thul or seen him in our citadel. I fear that him coming now, unannounced, may not be for a pleasant reason. I know he has been our ally, but when Arthur died, so much changed."

"Thul and Ector were close. It cannot have been easy for him when both Arthur and Ector were killed. Surely, he has been grieving as we all have. With two alliances lost, he probably had to look after his own. Have you heard from the kings Bram or Cormach?"

"King Bram I have heard from, but not seen…and there has been no word from Cormach. I have been told he sailed to Eire and has not returned these three years." Suddenly distracted, Gwynevere ordered, "The welcome cup must be prepared. Quickly, Uri…Go and tell the kitchens we will need to roast meats."

Uri scrambled out of the Hall, which became a buzz of activity. Servants rushed to prepare tables and light the hearth. With the great cauldron brimming and the welcome cup brought, they anxiously awaited King Thul and his men.

Merlin's eyes were bright at the thought of seeing Thul. His fortress in Celyddon was a beautiful land in the west, not far from the sea. Most of his lands were surrounded on the eastern side by dense forest, and his people were well known for being light of foot, able to traverse the forest without being seen or heard. The western edge, open lands, led to the sea, where men trained to become great horse masters.

Celyddon had been instrumental in many of Arthur's victories, and Thul supported Merlin's kingmaking of the young Pendragon. He had known Arthur as a child and was one of the trusted few that knew of his lineage and protected him.

The great doors of the hallway swung wide, and in entered the sturdy, aged king. His long hair and beard—once a fiery red—were now a mix of white and yellow, his beard braided in the style of the old Cymry warriors. His shoulders were dawned in the blue and yellow of Celyddon, and his chest bore a leather breast plate, decorated in dots and whorls. Those same whorls detailed the leather that wrapped around his arms and legs, while his strength was displayed in the silver torc around his neck.

Boldly, he entered the Hall with his arms open, chest high, and a broad smile. Warriors of Celyddon and Cair Lial followed in his wake, filling the Hall behind him. Thul's exulted mood put Gwynevere's mind at ease as he approached.

"King Thul!" Gwynevere said, picking up the bowl. "You are so welcome."

Thul smiled, gazing up at Gwynevere from her position on the platform. She handed him the bowl, and he drank long with great gulps. The golden ale dripped off his beard, and he wiped it with the side of his arm. He looked up from the bowl, refreshed, while handing the cup to the man that had drawn up beside him.

"Gwynevere," Thul said with pleasure. He placed his hand on his chest, bowing low. "Beautiful and gracious High Queen, it has been far too long since I have been in Arthur's Great Hall. I have missed it... And Merlin." He turned soberly. "Brother. To see you makes my heart swell."

Merlin leapt down from the platform, placing both of his arms on Thul's great shoulders and leaning his forehead down to meet his. The king shook Merlin's shoulders, then jovially patted his cheek.

"You have gotten older, my friend." Merlin grinned, patting Thul's arm.

"Hah!" Thul laughed. "And who is this lady who sits beside you?"

"She is soon to be my bride." Merlin opened his arm, ushering Elanor to come. The warriors gasped at the announcement. "She is Elanor."

"Merlin? A bride? Astonishing! I could never have imagined such a grand thing." Thul tenderly gazed at Elanor. "This will cause Merlin to stay where he ought," he said with a wink. "Am I right, Merlin?" Thul smacked him hard on the back.

"Hah—I have missed you, old friend."

"Old friend," Thul mused.

Gwynevere inquired, "What has brought you to us, Thul? My hope is that it is because you have missed us, but the twenty men who have accompanied you tell me there is more."

"I wish I were only here for such a happy occasion. I have come to tell you that my people have recently suffered an attack, and these Cymbrogi are here, prepared to protect their aging king on the journey here to you. I want to thank you for sending your message of warning, else we would not have been ready for the terrorizers."

"Please let your men be settled and your cups be filled while we hear what has happened." Gwynevere waved for the servants to begin filling cups, and the warriors reclined, settling themselves at the tables.

Merlin stayed beside Thul to hear the tale.

"I thank you, Gwynevere. Your husband, the great Pendragon, would be pleased to see how you carry his noble spirit." Thul breathed deeply. "In our fortress, we have watchmen who look from their high towers day and night. Never does a man set foot in our forest without us knowing it…Never!"

"A fortnight ago, eight hooded men appeared outside our walls mysteriously. They had not travelled through our forest. Out of the air they appeared. From your warning, we were prepared not to hesitate. The strangeness of their appearance triggered my warriors into action. Our watchmen speared five of them before they even knew they had been seen. The alarm was raised, positioning more warriors.

"The three remaining dark men appeared shaken but were not deterred. They attempted to burn our walls with fire, aided by the dark one's magic. My warriors defended our strong walls, but every spear was deflected supernaturally, leaving the men unharmed. They would have succeeded destroying our walls, but we attacked them from behind. Our men that lay hidden within our forest leapt upon them. The sorcerer was struck with a spear, piercing right through his shoulder. Then, we watched in disbelief as they vanished. We recovered quickly, and I prepared to come to you immediately. I wanted to deliver the message myself that we had crippled them."

With wide eyes, Merlin said, "They have only attacked small villages before this. I am glad to hear that they were not as successful attacking a fortress."

"Without the warnings from the queen, I fear we would not have been so lucky. If we had hesitated, I do not think we would have been able to ward them off as easily. The bastards did not know that we are lords of our forest. Catching them from behind gave us the advantage."

Merlin rubbed his chin. "This news is disturbing. Though, instead of eight dangerous men, we are down to three. The most dangerous of them all wounded. This means we may have time before their next attack. What worries me is that I believe these men were sent out by a greater enemy. Someone is behind them. Aiding them."

Thul threw out his arm, signaling to one of his Cymry, who presented him with an item. He unwrapped a muted yellow garment before the queen. "We searched those we had killed. There is nothing to remark about them, except these hooded cloaks. We noticed inside of them bore strange markings. Black scratches that were the same in each."

Merlin took the cloak, laid it open upon the floor, and examined the lines. "The markings are burned into the cloth…" He ruminated over the lines. "These charred lines are of dark speech. Dark curses. I believe these markings could explain how these men have kept themselves concealed."

Gwynevere moved to stand beside Merlin. Gazing at the cloak, she said bitterly to Thul, "We only just had news of another attack, just before you arrived in the Caer. We heard tale of a village in the south that was completely destroyed, with no help from King Lugh. They came to us as refugees for our aid."

Merlin interjected, "It is good to know these hooded villains can be outwitted. They are not an indestructible force and have now been weakened. Though I fear that also means they may change their tactic."

"Well," said Thul, walking over to the hearth and splashing what was left of his drink into the fire, "we must be wise and on guard. We are with you, Gwynevere, Queen of the Cymry, and we will rally against this force, just as we did when Arthur had need of us." He turned to face her and bowed low. "There has been nothing we could not defeat when we stood together. That is what Arthur taught us. Maybe King Lugh will need a reminder of that as he stands divided against you, leaving his own to suffer alone." He raised his hand up toward the warriors. "Thanul! Thangul!" Two warriors rushed to his side. Both were ruddy with bright red hair. "This is my son Thanul, my eldest. You know him, as he served here as one of Arthur's finest for these past ten years. And this," he said, turning to the other, "is my youngest son Thangul. He has served my hall and has become a fine young warrior and horse master."

"I have a request, my queen, that you would allow me to take back my eldest son. I have need of a battle chief, and Thanul has been trained well under Peredur and Bedwyr. We have been complacent since the Saecsen's were driven from our shores. This attack has awoken me to our need for preparedness. If you will allow me my eldest, I would leave with you my youngest to be raised as a strong warrior."

"Thanul!" the queen said, addressing the young strong warrior before her. "Would it be your desire to return with your father and serve him as battle chief?"

Thanul bowed low. "It would bless me greatly to serve my father in this way."

"Then," she said, "I will accept Thanul returning to his father, and we welcome Thangul to our Cymbrogi." Thangul smiled excitedly and bowed. The men behind him shouted, raising their cups at the proclamation.

Gwynevere smiled. "And I will do more. Thanul has served us well, for I know his name, and know of his strength and loyalty. Thanul, I will allow you to select two of your most faithful comrades to return with you to Celyddon. In this way, you will be returning with strength to your right and left hand."

"Thank you, my queen," Thanul said as he bowed, his face radiating with gratitude.

His father slapped him hard on his back and embraced him. "This is great generosity, Gwynevere," Thul said with honor, looking up humbly at the queen with his fist on his chest. "It shows you respect and support my son, and even more so, it shows that you are willing to sacrifice for Celyddon, and also Prydain. You are a better queen than I have given you credit, for I know Thanul to have been a valuable warrior."

"It is a happy day to have King Thul in my halls once again," Gwynevere declared. "The healing of this land will happen, whether this dark force wills it or not. We will be victorious in the name of the Great Pendragon." The Cymbrogi cheered. "I would not hoard my greatest warrior in support of all Prydain. Let food be brought, and more wood be brought to the hearth. We will feast to our friendship and drink together."

They feasted, and as the night wore on, many of the warriors wandered out to find their places of sleep.

Curiously, Thul asked, "What of these villagers you said had come to you for aid?"

Gwynevere replied with slightly slurred speech, "They are less than forty. Over half of them are women and children…with few men. They are led by Marcus…an old Druid of the New Way." Gwynevere inclined clumsily, resting her hand on her cheek.

"Well…" Thul leaned in heartily. "There is a village just outside the eastern edge of my lands. It is small, but if the men are hardworking, it could serve to benefit them. With the additional guidance of the old druid, the village would be grateful. If it would be agreeable to them, I will lead them out when we go."

Merlin lifted his cup. "Marcus and his people would be blessed."

"It is done, if they agree," King Thul said, grandly smiling.

Gwynevere asked, "How long will you be staying with us, Thul of Celyddon?"

"Well, at least long enough to see these ones wed!" Thul shoved Merlin jovially with his elbow, and then knocked back a gulp of ale, bursting into a roar of laughter.

Standing, Gwynevere declared, "The ceremony will be in two days' time. Yes…That is all the time we will need to prepare for the ceremony and feasting."

Merlin stood, raising his cup and kissing Elanor on the cheek. "In two days' time, Elanor will be my wife."

THE MARRIAGE OF EMRYS
AND GWENDDYDD

Elanor nervously twisted the myrtle figure through her fingers. She apprehensively watched the sun rise through her window, wondering if it all wasn't happening too quickly. Two days was hardly enough time to plan a wedding in her world, yet here it was—her wedding day. Every part of her wanted Merlin, yet there was a small part that feared all this good could not be meant for her. After all, she was only Elanor. The Elanor that had once sat alone in her flat and was important to no one.

Her thoughts over the past few days had returned to her father. She wished she could somehow tell him she was getting married. There was so little she missed of her world, but for him. She imagined being back out in his garden, sitting on the steps and telling him about her new life. She thought about what he would say and if he would be pleased.

Then, she pondered whether her future time even existed now that she was in the past. Was it like two planes of existence where both times played out simultaneously? Maybe none of her future family or friends had even been born yet, or could even be missing her? The more Elanor thought about it, the less she could comprehend the possibilities. And so, she returned to simpler thoughts of missing her father.

Elanor lifted the myrtle token to her chest, then placed it in a box set on her dressing table. The moment the box clicked shut, her door opened.

"Up already?" Samara said lightly, floating across the chamber. She grabbed hold of Elanor's hands. "Of course you are. Who wouldn't be on a day like today?"

"I hardly slept. All I could do was toss and turn."

Samara smiled. "Well, there will be enough excitement today to keep you going until its end."

"I am unfamiliar with what the traditions of marriage are like here. What am I to expect? I would have asked Merlin, but I have hardly seen him with all the preparation, and he was gone hunting all of yesterday."

"Likely he was hunting for today's feast. It is the duty of the groom to bring home a prize for his wedding feast." Samara filled a basin with water. "First thing that needs to be done is to bathe you."

Elanor winced, her teeth chattering as she slowly lowered herself into the basin, wishing Samara had taken the time to warm the water. Samara rubbed a scented oil that smelt like wildflowers over her skin and through her hair. "This will make your hair braid tightly," Samara explained with a grin, pouring more oil into her hands and rubbing it into Elanor's scalp. "We will be braiding your hair in the style of a Cymry bride."

Firmly, Samara twisted Elanor's hair, gripping her strands of hair between her fingers and pulling it around her head. Elanor's head yanked back and forth as braids hung down the side of her face. Then slowly, Samara gathered them, one by one, into a large braid down her back, leaving a few loose. She placed within the braids a gold ribbon and wove Elanor's hair over a gold ring that sat atop her head.

Gwynevere arrived just as Elanor was being wrapped in linens, with two servants following behind her. One carried a basket full of flowers, and the other, a tray of bread and cheese. Laid in Gwynevere's arms was the dress Elanor had worn on the day of the welcome feast. She had not worn it since that day, and it made Elanor's heart ache to see it again. She reached to touch the pendant which already lay around her neck. The blue stone matched the blue dress.

"You already look so beautiful," Gwynevere said, pressing her hand to Elanor's cheek. "Come, let us get you dressed; we only have a short time."

"A short time? What is to happen?"

"Some of the noble women have gathered and await you. They are eager to hide with you in the apple orchard."

"Hide?"

Gwynevere grinned with a sideways glance. "The men are down in the fields preparing. Once we have you safely tucked away within the trees, Merlin must search for you and find you if he is to have you as his bride."

The idea of Merlin searching for her made Elanor's heart flutter. "Am I required to do anything?"

"Only to accept him or refuse him."

Of course I would accept him, Elanor thought, nervously pulling on her pendant while Samara set lilies through her braids and cinched her dress lightly over her curves.

"You must eat!" Samara said, shoving bread and cheese into Elanor's hands. The servant girls giggled, chattering like birds in the corner. Over Elanor's head she placed a sheer veil that gracefully cascaded down to her waist. Then, a wreath of flowers was set to hold it in place.

Elanor was radiant. She breathed deeply, placing her hands upon her stomach to still the fluttering butterflies. Then, she was ushered out of the room as Samara pushed and Gwynevere pulled her out the door and down the hallway, crossing the threshold of the Great Hall and continuing out into the yard. The women of the Caer stood, pink lipped with flowering wreaths in their hair, brimming with excitement.

Gwynevere pulled Elanor along into the orchard. The women swiftly followed. The trees blossomed as the sun's rays shone through the trees. Swept up in the excitement, Elanor giggled nervously along with the rest.

The women scattered into the trees, each going in different directions, disappearing around the bends of the trail. Gwynevere held solidly onto Elanor, leading her to a familiar opening with large rocks in the center. The very same rocks where she and Gwynevere had sat those days not long ago. The memory warmed Elanor's heart. The opening was off the path, back behind a thick set of trees, which would hopefully pose a small challenge for Merlin.

All was silent. Gwynevere hid behind a tree while Elanor sat with bated breath upon a rock. All she heard was the sweet chirping of the birds as they fluttered through the boughs. The nerves in her stomach intensified as she waited.

Then she heard it. *Boom, boom, boom.* The thumping of a drum resonated through the orchard. The sound drew nearer and nearer. *Boom, boom, boom.* Then, hurried voices echoed.

They're in the orchard.

Elanor sat up taller. She resisted the urge to run deeper into the orchard to hide. She could hear the laughter and the squeals of surprise as the men discovered the others hiding amongst the trees.

Boom, boom, boom. The drumming drew nearer, and the voices mingled with excitement. Elanor turned around anxiously, begging Gwynevere to put her at ease as she peeked out from behind a tree.

Now she could feel footsteps pounding the soft earth and knew that soon she would be found. *Boom, boom, boom.* Elanor saw movement through the trees. The movement of one caught her eye. His body darted back and forth, and finally, turning in her direction, he stopped. Elanor had been discovered. She held her breath, fighting all her senses to remain still. As he approached her through the trees, she could see the others following close behind.

Breaking out from the trees was Merlin, handsome and tall, yet his golden eyes were timid. His hair was pulled back, revealing a cleanly shaven face. The outline of his jaw was strong, while the colors clasped around his shoulders highlighted the torc shining brightly around his neck.

"What are you waiting for?" Bedwyr shouted, shoving Merlin forward.

Gwynevere glided out from her hiding place to stand next to Elanor. Merlin reached down and lifted Elanor gently by her hand, searching for her concealed face and delicate frame through her veil. He swallowed deeply. "I have found the one my heart loves."

"You may have found her, but you cannot claim her," Gwynevere said resolutely. "You must meet the challenges laid before you if you are to prove your quality." Her eyes glinted with anticipation.

All at once, the men surrounded him, lifting him by his arms and legs. The women burst with pleasure, clapping their hands, while the groom was whisked away.

Shocked, Elanor grinned. "What is happening?"

"You shall see," Gwynevere said as she scooped her arm around Elanor's, leading her out of the orchard and down the hill in a jubilant, loud procession of singing to the lower fields. The women waltzed around Elanor, shielding her from sight. They crossed the field to a small tent set next to the mound and promptly pressed Elanor inside, quickly closing the canvas flaps shut.

Merlin threw a gutted doe upon the ground. "Is my bounty worthy?" he asked, presenting his prize to Thul, Bedwyr, and Peredur. "She was quick and strong, and I slew her with my own spear. Her meat will bless our day of feasting."

Merlin waited in silence as Thul prodded it with the end of his sword. He eyed closely the brindle hide and brushed his hand against the fur. He stood back, squinting at Merlin, then proclaimed, "She will do for feasting!" The men cheered, and the servants quickly came forward, grabbing up the doe to be divided and roasted. The first challenge was completed.

"And you, Bedwyr and Peredur? What challenge would you lay before me?" Merlin asked.

Peredur replied, "I thought I should challenge you to a match, hand-to-hand. But then I thought, I would easily win, and I didn't want you to be embarrassed on your wedding day." Peredur spread out his arms, inviting all around to laugh at his jest.

"But we thought better, didn't we, Peredur?" Bedwyr laughed. "We thought, as your brothers, we would want you to be successful and not utterly humiliated. So, we came up with a new challenge. And it is this...You must find what best symbolizes your love for Elanor, and when she receives it, she must recognize it as such."

"This is a worthy challenge," Merlin said, drawing his hand up to his chin to think. He gazed over where he knew Elanor sat waiting. Then, he scanned the field, carefully considering the ground. His eyes brightened, and his lips parted into a smile. "If I am lucky," he said, "I will know just where to find it. Cilaen! Saddle up with me and make haste." The two men swiftly found horses and rode out of the Caer at a great pace.

Behind the flaps of the tent, Elanor waited. Her anxious anticipation returned as she tapped her toes on the floor. "How long do we wait?"

"I know it is difficult," Gwynevere encouraged. "A worthy challenge should take time."

Finally, the sound of hooves pounding the ground and the cheering from the men and women made Elanor leap to her feet. Her eyes reached to see through the thin opening of the tent.

Gwynevere rose, prepared to go out to meet them. "You must wait here until I call to you," she said calmly, a smile hidden in her eyes. Gwynevere breathed, put on her queenly air, then opened the flap, leaving Elanor behind.

"Have you fulfilled your challenges?" Elanor heard Gwynevere ask.

Merlin's voice was breathless. "Yes, my queen."

"What were your challenges?"

"I was to deliver a worthy prize for the wedding feast. So, I hunted, and yesterday slew a beautiful doe. King Thul inspected it and found it a worthy choice. The second challenge was to find something that would represent our love, but the bride would have to recognize it as such."

"Have you found such a token?"

"I believe I have," Merlin replied hopefully.

"Elanor? You may come out and see what your groom has found for you." Elanor closed her eyes and slowly walked toward the tent opening. She lifted the flap. The bright sun blinded her against the dullness of the tent. As her eyes adjusted, she saw a sea of people. Her eyes alighted first on Cilaen, who stood with a proud smile. Then, with his hands gingerly cupped before her, she saw Merlin.

Gwynevere commanded, "Present your bride with your token."

Merlin's hands shook, and tears welled in his eyes. He moved his hands in front of her and opened them. There, before Elanor, laid a beautiful yellow primrose. She gasped as tears fell down her face. All apprehension left her mind.

"Do you receive this token as a symbol of your love?"

"W-with all my heart," Elanor's voice trembled.

The people responded with praise, and Merlin delicately placed the primrose into her hand.

"You may claim your bride," Gwynevere said joyously.

Merlin brought Elanor to his side. The crowd parted as he escorted her to the top of the mound, with Gwynevere and Cilaen trailing behind them. At the top of the hill, Marcus stood beaming. He held out before them a folded red cloth. Then, turning them to face one another, Marcus wrapped the red cloth around their hands, binding them together. He lifted his hands into the air and spoke a blessing:

Two stars I saw fall from the sky,
their names were Emrys and Gwenddydd.
Together, healing and new life would flow into our lands,

Blessing the New Way and Kingdom of the Sun.
Great God, before you I bless these ones,
Go before them and let not darkness touch them.
Today, Emrys and Gwenddydd, I bind you as one.
Never to be broken, fixing the time undone.
Once and Future you will be,
Emrys and Gwenddydd, two stars now one.

The druid let his arms fall, then said, "Merlin, unveil your bride."

Tenderly, Merlin lifted the wreath of flowers, and then delicately pulled the veil from Elanor's face, revealing his bride at last. Now he could see the blush of her cheeks and the curves of her mouth. Her eyes glistened with tears not yet fallen. She was his treasure.

"Merlin, do you accept Elanor as your bride?"

"With all my soul." His soft eyes gazed into Elanor's with tender desire.

"Elanor, do you accept Merlin as your groom?"

"With all my soul," she said. Her heart beat wildly as she pressed on the primrose still within her hands.

Marcus proclaimed with gladness, "Then you are wed!"

Without a moment's hesitation, Merlin swept Elanor up and kissed her. She caressed him, hoping the moment would last forever. They both tearfully laughed as voices lifted in celebration. Emrys and Gwenddydd, married at last.

29

THE WEDDING FEAST

The Great Hall was set with many fine meats, with Merlin's doe the center piece of the queen's table. Warm mead overflowed, and the sweet aroma of honey cakes floated through the room. Joyful laughter resounded while maids and their partners danced, surrounding the flames of the hearth.

Elanor and Merlin leaned into one another, delighted after their long and glorious day. Never had Elanor imagined a wedding so honest. The traditions of the Cymry people flooded her with awe and respect. Every moment was a gift.

Gwynevere clapped, bringing the room to attention. "I have a gift for the groom and his lovely bride." Lifting her hand, she revealed a silver torc. Beautiful, and intricately braided, it shined orange and red, reflecting the hearth's fire. "This day," she said, pausing momentarily, "things were set right in marriage. Merlin has always been the wisdom and guide to all of Prydain. He had been Arthur's right hand, just as he was with Aurelius, and Uther after him. The very backbone of the great kings of this land, and invaluable to us all. We are glad he has returned." She bowed her head, honoring Merlin, and the people cheered and banged their cups in agreement. "And…" Gwynevere continued, bringing them back to attention, "…he has brought to us hope, as has Elanor. The darkness of our hour brightened." Gwynevere turned to gaze at Elanor with a strange expression, pressing her lips and tilting her head. Then, with a haunted air, she said, "It is though Arthur had returned to us, walking through our halls once again." Her statement shook the room; all were taken aback by her words, confounded. "Our hearts have been lifted ever so slightly from the grief of Arthur's death."

Elanor looked to Merlin, baffled. *What did she mean?*

"Merlin wears a torc of silver, and through this, all know his authority in these lands. He is the kingmaker and chooses to honor me. Now, his bride shall also be established by his side." Gwynevere walked behind Elanor, bent the torc, and wrapped it around her neck. The metal was icy as it touched her skin. The cold sensation brought with it a sense of burden Elanor was unprepared for. Heavily it laid upon her collar as she doubted her own worth.

Perplexed, Merlin stood, lifting Elanor to stand beside him. "This," he declared, "is a gift of high honor." He bowed. "Gracious High Queen Gwynevere."

King Thul stood and lifted his cup. "I second that the queen is wise in her gift. Merlin is the kingmaker, and his bride should be no less his equal. Your quality, Elanor, has been seen since the moment of our meeting."

Peredur rose as well, raising his cup, and Cilaen and Bedwyr followed. The people stood silently, raising their cups high, and Gwynevere shouted, "May the Great God bless you and bring you peace!"

"May the Great God bless you and bring you peace," the people roared back.

"Let a song be raised," a man cried out from the crowd.

"Merlin, sing!" others began to chime.

Merlin nodded at the people in agreement. "I will sing a song. For this is our day, mine and Elanor's, and I would sing for my lovely bride." He cleared his throat, but this time he took no harp in hand. A single note radiated from his lips, tender and sweet. It was gentle and somber, like a lullaby, causing every ear to be stilled. Intimately, he began to weave his story.

"There once was golden warrior from the otherworld who fell in love with a mortal woman as she walked the hills by the sea. Though she was not of his world, he could not turn away from her.

"Moved by his love, he rose to meet her. His face handsome, the golden warrior bowed before her, tall and strong. He walked along the shores with her, day after day, and she, too, fell in love. So, she went with him to the otherworld to be his wife, choosing a life away from the shore.

"However, this choice caused a sorceress of the otherworld to become jealous. For she had loved the golden warrior also and did not believe a mere mortal should be rewarded with his love. The sorceress waited for the woman to be left alone to work a malevolent magic to divide them.

"The day came; the warrior went hunting, leaving his love alone. At once, the sorceress set an evil enchantment, changing the beautiful maiden into a helpless dragonfly."

Merlin stopped singing as tears welled in his eyes, but then his voiced raised high again…

"When the warrior returned home, he was devastated by what had been done to his love. Now a little dragonfly, the maiden's wings glittered as she rose to light upon his hand. The warrior could not reverse the enchantment, but he held the dragonfly close to him. Wishing no further hurt to come to her, he set her upon his shoulder during the day, and at night, he kept her in a glass box.

"The sorceress was angered that her enchantment had not forced the warrior to abandon his love. Though, one day, as the dragonfly sat upon the warrior's shoulder, the sorceress sent a great wind, blowing the dragonfly out to the sea. There she was battered, tossed by the wind, and her shiny wings became wet and broken. The maid believed she would die, but then, she woke on the pebbles of the seashore, having lost all her memory of the one she loved. So, she returned to her life, walking about the hills of the shore, while the golden warrior groaned in grief.

"A young king went in search of a bride. His servants, sent to search the land, came upon the maiden at the seashore. She was so fair, her blue eyes shined, and her hair rippled like silken waves. The king, astonished by her beauty, asked her to be his bride, and she accepted him. He was a good and handsome king, and the maid believed herself to be very fortunate.

"The warrior of the otherworld had heard about a king and his maid of great beauty. By the description, he believed it to be his lost love, so anxiously, he went to see if it might be her. Disguised as a young man, he journeyed to find her, and within the gardens of the king's hold, he saw it was, indeed, his love. He approached her, but she did not know him. He told her she was his bride, and that an evil sorceress had enchanted her. He feared she had died but had now come to bring her back with him to the otherworld.

"Still, she had no memory of him, and she said, 'Why would I leave this king that loves me for a stranger?'

"The warrior hung his head low, believing he had lost his beloved forever. But then, a clever thought occurred to him, and he decided to try again.

This time he came as himself, a golden warrior from the otherworld. Knowing the king was an avid game player, the warrior challenged him. The king accepted, believing he was the best at everything, always ready to prove before all that he could best even the greatest of warriors.

"First, they threw spears, and the warrior let the king's spear fly the farthest. Then, they played a game of riddles, and the warrior selected riddles he knew the king could easily divide, while playing the fool. Each time, the warrior gave the king whatever he wanted as his winnings. Finally, he challenged the king to a hunt. Whoever returned with the biggest boar would be the winner.

"The king laughed, knowing well where to hunt for the biggest beast, and felt the warrior at a clear disadvantage. They raced to the hunt, both returning with the boars they had slain. This time, the king was surprised to see that the warrior had bested him. His boar was by far the biggest and outweighed his own. The king, being a man of honor, offered the warrior the same offer he had given. He offered him anything he wanted.

"'I have but one request,' the warrior said to the king, 'that you would let me have just one kiss of the bride to be. That is all.'

"The king was shocked, instantly regretting his offer. He felt bound, however, and said, 'In two days…return here, and I will grant this request.'

"When the day had come, the king had all his warriors guard the palace. He believed that if he could keep the warrior out, then he would be freed from his promise. The king's warriors surrounded the gates while the king hid with the maiden inside. However, the golden warrior, being of the otherworld, simply bypassed the barricade and magically appeared before the king and his bride.

"As the maid saw him in his true form, she was captured by his beauty. She was drawn in and approached him. Slowly, she reached up and gave him the simple kiss he had requested. As she did, her memory returned.

"She yelled, 'Take me away with you! Back to our home in the otherworld!'

"The king was alarmed and commanded his warriors to attack, but in the chaos, he found that the golden warrior and the maiden had disappeared. The king's warriors searched, finding no trace of them. Only some said that they had seen two swans flying away side by side, a golden chain between them.

The song had ended, and the beautiful story of love returned had captured Elanor's heart. "Such a lovely, sweet song," she said, standing and kissing Merlin.

He retrieved two cups from the table and handed one to Elanor. "Let us fly together," he said, lifting his cup. They all drank quietly, having all been lulled by the song of the bard. Then, Merlin pressed Elanor's hand to his lips.

The feast had come to its end, and with the attention no longer on the two of them, Merlin and Elanor quietly slipped out into the courtyard. Elanor pressed into the warmth of Merlin's side while the crickets quietly chimed their songs. The moon cast shadows onto the tall, carved stones, making them appear to glow. Images of Merlin's story danced through Elanor's mind. The love of a golden warrior and his glittering dragonfly. She could hear the flutter of the dragonfly's wings in her ears.

Elanor gazed up at him. Captivated, she smiled with a spark in her eye, then grasped his hands and pulled him toward the Palisade. She danced through the hallway and glided up the stairs, keeping Merlin's hand tight in hers. She pulled him through the doorway of her chambers where a fire danced with its light, warming the room. Elanor ran in first, then stopped, facing away from Merlin.

She took the primrose and set it tenderly next to the box that held the myrtle figure. She hesitated, glancing at the yellow petals as the desire in her heart grew. Enraptured, she turned, seeing Merlin's eyes timidly peering back.

Elanor wondered what she had given. Merlin had searched for her and found her. He had won the hunt and found a token of their love. He had even sung her a beautiful song. She would not hesitate. He would have his prize. Elanor ran to him, throwing her arms around his neck, and Merlin embraced her, joyfully and fully. Now bride and groom, they no longer held back but breathed each other in, letting their love take them away into the night.

Elanor woke still wrapped in Merlin's arms. His breaths resonated deeply as he remained asleep. Elanor got up, wrapped herself in a robe, then scuffled quickly to warm herself by what was left of the fire. She stared happily into the bright coals that were still red under the grey ash. She reminisced with pleasure on the day before. She felt like she had been caught up in a fairy tale.

A light knocking at the door snapped her out of her thoughts. Samara quietly slipped in with a large platter of food, whispering, "I know you are an early riser, and thought I should come and light the fire and bring you some food."

Elanor smiled, gratefully taking the platter full of cold meats and honey cakes left over from the feast.

Samara quietly approached the hearth, careful to not make any noise. Elanor turned to embrace her, squeezed her tightly, then kissed her head. "Thank you!"

Samara nodded, and an amiable blush lighted her cheeks.

Leaning back against a bench near the fire, Elanor watched Samara gather kindling. Merlin tossed and grunted at the rattling of the wood, and Elanor and Samara giggled softly. The new wood quickly caught on the hot coals and crackled.

"In a little while, I will bring you a warm bowl of water to freshen." Samara lightly bent her knees, then left.

The door clicked closed, and Elanor heard a moaning voice say, "Why are you warming yourself by the fire when you could be warming yourself over here?"

"I wasn't sure you would want me waking you with my icy fingers and toes. You were sleeping so peacefully. I am warmer now," Elanor said, rushing back over to the bed and tossing herself in. "Maybe now I can warm you."

Merlin's lips curled at the edges, his eyes alight with pleasure, while Elanor snuggled in beside him, then sighed.

She drew her fingers across his brow. His dark curls fell over her fingers. Elanor's eyes caught hold of Merlin's, and she saw a foreboding look intermingled in his love. "What is it? What has you darkly ruminating?"

He grabbed her face, pulling it toward his, and kissed her. "I would rather not disturb our love with talk of evil…" He twisted his mouth. "But I suppose there is no hiding it from those seeing eyes." He rolled onto his back, then breathed loudly, "The dark happenings are increasing."

Elanor turned her head to gaze at him. "Thul said the hooded sorcerer has been wounded."

"Wounded, yes…wounded, but not killed. Though this dark one is not who worries me. There is a greater opposing darkness. Grwyrthrhodd spoke of things both evil and light coming awake, and Marcus prophesied a darkness rising specifically against you and me." Merlin sat up and exhaled. "We cannot be fools. These harbingers are telling us of increasing woe, and we would be fools to think it will abate."

Elanor leaned up onto her elbow, her heart nervously beating faster. "Are you leaving?" She tried to catch her disappointment, but it was already appearing in her eyes.

"Yes…" Merlin turned, looking at her from the corner of his eye. "Gwynevere and I have spoken. The Southlands have been the most afflicted, and those are the lands that seem the source of these evils. I must go and seek out King Lugh and see what I can of these lands. We cannot sit by passively. But I have a plan…" Merlin leaned over next to her and caressed her cheek. "I will not be leaving you behind. I have the strength to protect you, and I cannot if you are left. Also, you must recognize that you have a part to play in this."

"I would leave Caer Lial?" The idea struck a deeper chord of fear within her. She felt protected and safe within the Caer's walls. The world beyond them was wild and dangerous. Thoughts of the safety of her flat began to comfort her. "But what of Gwynevere? Wouldn't she need you here? What if the evil comes to attack the citadel, like it did in Celyddon?"

"That is a concern. I do not believe the enemy has become a great enough force to risk an attack on Caer Lial just yet. If they were, they would not be trying so hard to draw us out. These lands are blessed and stand prepared with the strongest Cymbrogi of all the land of Prydain. Though we should not assume the enemy wouldn't try. Therefore, Caer Lial will need to stand ready. Already our forests are being patrolled, and the outlying chieftains on the ready. I am being sent because Gwynevere knows my perception and strength of magic will go far in discovering our enemy."

"Will we go alone?"

"We will remain undiscovered and out of the enemy's view if it is just us two. I can conceal us. However, I will not be taking you to Llyonesse. I will search those lands and seek out the King alone...My mother lives in the Southlands in the Caer of Dyved. King Cormach's country. You will be safe there."

Elanor's eyes shot wide open. "Your mother is living?"

"Hah! Yes!" Merlin laughed.

Elanor's brow furrowed as she tried to settle her mind on all that Merlin revealed. "You have lived so long...I thought...since you had not mentioned her, that she was..."

"She is alive and well, and dwells in an old, Roman villa, next to the stronghold of King Cormach. The village of Dyved surrounds the villa, where the monks of the Caer tend to the people. My mother is a healer and aids the monks when people are sick. She is skilled in medicines and healing words."

Elanor was mystified. "Has it been long since you have seen your mother?"

"It has been almost seven years."

Elanor sat quietly as her mind raced. "Would the journey be long?"

"It would take us many days to reach Dyved. I have ridden there in three, but that was when I rode in haste. That would not be the way for us. We would travel more gently, so it may be six days, or more."

Elanor nodded her head slowly, and then sat up, rubbing her head. "When would we leave?" Her eyebrows lifted in worry. "What would your mother think of me? I am a stranger in these lands." Elanor's own mother flashed in her mind. The disappointment. The rejection.

Merlin sensed Elanor's stress and wrapped his arm around her. "We would not leave for a few days. We have a lot to prepare, and King Thul's son Thangul will be making his oath tomorrow. Thul would want us here for that, and then he will be returning home, and with him, Marcus and his people. They have agreed to go to Celyddon. We wouldn't want to miss saying goodbye to the old druid." He placed his fingers beneath Elanor's chin, looking into her eyes. "My mother would not hold a bad judgement of you. She'll love you."

"What if I do not want to go into the wilds?"

"I would not force you. Though I would long for my wife to be by my side. Come with me, Elanor."

The word *wife* brought back the warmth, lightening her heart. "Of course," Elanor said, forcing a smile.

"You have nothing to fear, my soul."

PART TWO

30

SO MANY GOOD-BYES

King Thul beamed with pride as Thangul stepped into the Great Hall, prepared for his day of commissioning, his eldest son Thanul by his side. The Cymbrogi of both Celyddon and Caer Lial stood, awaiting the ceremony to begin.

Under the queen's strong gaze, Thangul approached. Both Peredur and Bedwyr took up their positions beside Gwynevere, displaying their full authority as Battle Chiefs.

Thangul wore only a simple white tunic and breeches, with his soft boots tied at the knee. He held his chest high, though his eyes were nervous. Silently, he strode forward until he reached the feet of the queen, then bowed his fiery red head.

Peredur stepped forward, unsheathed his sword, then boomed, "Do you swear fealty, as a Cymry, to your queen? Do you choose to fight to protect the realms of the land of Prydain and the lives of the Britons? Will you submit yourself to me as your Battle Chief and master of training?"

Thangul lifted his chin, his strong voice echoing through the Hall, "I do swear fealty!"

Peredur walked aggressively down the steps with his sword raised. He grabbed hold of Thangul's arm, lifting it above his head, and pressed the hilt of the sword into his palm. Peredur stared him solidly in the eye with his jaw set firmly, then returned to the queen's side.

Bedwyr raised his voice, pulling forth a spear and lifting it high. "Do you swear fealty, as a Cymry, to your queen? Do you choose to fight to protect the realms of this land of Prydain and the lives of the Britons? Will you submit yourself to me as your Chief in Arms and horse master?"

"I do swear fealty!" Thangul shouted all the stronger.

At Thangul's oath, just as Peredur had done, Bedwyr charged Thangul, lifting his other arm, and placed the spear into his hand. He then returned to his station next to the queen. Thangul now held both of his arms high above him, one clutching a sword, and the other, a spear. He lowered his arms, humbly approached the queen, and bowed low before her. Thangul took the long sword and the spear and placed them on the ground in front of the queen before setting his cheek upon her feet.

"I thank you, Thangul, son of Thul, for your fealty. I know you will serve me honorably as your brother Thanul has served both me and the great Pendragon. You are a welcome warrior of the Cymbrogi, and I accept your sword and spear." The queen took up a folded linen and unfurled it, revealing the colors of red and gold. She wrapped it around Thangul's shoulders, fastening it with a silver brooch.

Thangul stood with pride while the Cymbrogi cheered in his commissioning. King Thul lifted his hand and marched to stand before the queen.

"My queen…Gwynevere." He bowed. "I want to take this moment, as you have accepted my son, to speak to you before all that are gathered here." He looked at the floor for a moment, then cleared his throat. "I should have said this the moment I arrived, but out of my own pride—I did not. Please forgive me. You have honored me greatly, and I have not returned that honor as I should have."

"I was supposed to be your support and ally, but when Arthur died, I did not come to assure you of our alliance. In truth, I was not sure I could support you as High Queen. I was so broken that I did not recognize your strength. I have realized that Arthur was strong because of you, and he was also strong because of Merlin. Forgive me if my distance has made your rulership difficult. I will do my part to rally the kings to do the same as I am doing now." In saying that, he unsheathed his sword and laid it before her feet. Thul knelt before her and declared, "I honor you as High Queen of these lands." Then, he placed his cheek upon her feet.

Gwynevere's chin trembled, and a tear escaped her eye. "Please rise, my friend," she said. "I understand the confusing times we have been through better than anyone, and I will not fault you. I only thank you, that you have come to me now and put your trust in me. I will aim to be worthy of that trust."

Merlin rushed from his seat and placed his hand on Thul's shoulders as a sign of acceptance. Peredur and Bedwyr quickly followed Merlin's lead, laying their hands upon the king. Lastly, Gwynevere rested her hand on his forehead, placing herself as High Queen before him. Thul laughed, and emotions ran high as the warriors' voices rose in song, pounding their fists in allegiance.

By the next morning, the jubilant songs of the warriors still echoed in their hearts while Thul prepared to depart for Celyddon. Gwynevere offered two wagons and four steers to take the displaced villagers to their new home.

"You will be greatly missed," Merlin said to Marcus as Elanor embraced him.

Marcus's face reddened with emotion. "It has been the privilege of my life to marry the promised two I had seen so long ago. Thank you, dear one," he said, placing his hand upon Elanor's cheek, "for giving me back my sight." Then, turning to Merlin, he said, "And we will meet again. In the happenings of these days, we will need one another."

Thul was busy slapping backs and clutching strong hands—saying his farewells. Then, he and Thanul leapt onto their horses, ready to lead the way. The remnants of Marcus's people sat waiting in the wagons at the bottom of the field with hope in their eyes. Gwynevere and her company watched from the jutting steps of the Great Hall as they departed through the first gate.

"Now you are to leave us," Gwynevere said to Merlin, her serious gaze on him. "I am hoping that something will come of your mission this time. I know Adhan will be overjoyed at the sight of you."

Elanor's nerves rose again at the mention of Merlin's mother, still concerned for their inevitable meeting.

Gwynevere looked at Merlin squarely. "We are prepared for our enemy. Though I am hopeful that the wounds inflicted by Thul's warriors will have slowed them."

"I believe an attack from the hooded monsters will not occur again in this season. Their magic requires a great amount of time to conjure. They cannot use their evils at will; they have to raise the magic into being from the depths of demons. Once spent, they must conjure it again. But that does not mean they will not use other means and haven't already summoned other dark devices. Without knowing who our enemy truly is, we are left without tools to know what devious plans could be made. This I am hoping to discover. King Lugh is no innocent, and I am hopeful I can divine some clues from his twisted words. Let nothing suspicious pass your gaze unnoticed. Let no word of my departure be spoken of, and we will be back before the season changes for harvest. Gwyenvere…" Merlin started, before leaning in, "…Dyved is in the south and still has a mighty king who is our ally. We must continue to send word to Eire for Cormach. He must return to gird up the Southlands."

Gwynevere nodded knowingly, while Cilaen came alongside Elanor.

He looped his arm around hers. "I will miss you, my sister, though I am overjoyed you will be seeing Dyved. That is my home. I wish I were going with you. I would love to see Adhan. She taught me more than Merlin has in healing, and she helped take care of my mother when my father died."

"I am sorry," Elanor said compassionately.

"I was young. He lost his life fighting for Arthur, and though his death broke my mother's heart, I have always felt proud to be his son."

"Is your mother still in Dyved?"

"She is there," Cilaen said, twisting his neck and shoulders uncomfortably at her question. "She is called Efa."

Observing his discomfort, Elanor quickly moved on. "I have not given much thought to leaving this place. It feels strange now to leave. Especially after…"

Cilaen broke in, "You will be glad you journeyed to Dyved." He squeezed her encouragingly.

Elanor followed Merlin down to the stables to prepare the horses. The air was cold, and the stable was quiet and still. Nothing but the soft puffs from the horses could be heard in the frosty grey of morning. She felt a strange pang in her heart, as the time of leaving had come. Elanor was unnerved by their plans, traveling on horseback and sleeping wherever their feet landed. The possibility of encountering the evil hooded men raced through her mind.

Elanor handed Merlin the supplies as he strapped satchels and blankets to the back of their horses. Lifting the saddle to tighten it, Elanor caught sight of two swords beneath. "Are you planning on wielding two swords at once?" she asked playfully.

Merlin gazed out of the corner of his eye with a mischievous grin. "That short sword is for you. I would not have you out in the wilds without teaching you how to defend yourself."

"I am not a warrior."

Merlin squinted. "You must become what is necessary. With the threat of evil in these wilds, you will need to know how to properly wield a weapon."

Elanor glared, feeling less prepared than she already had to embark on this venture. She brooded as she pulled herself up onto Brynn. Her lack of experience intimidated her, and she found no support from Merlin. He seemed ready to press her on every side, leaving her no space to hide herself like she had her whole life. So many fears and anxious thoughts cluttered her mind. Especially the thought of meeting Merlin's mother. She didn't like feeling weak or out of control. She had trusted too much when she left the Caer the first time, and now she was not readily willing to offer her trust again.

As if reading her mind, Merlin said, "You will be well." He patted her leg, then launched himself up onto his horse. "I can see the worry on your face. You will see such beauty, and we will be together. Trust me."

Elanor sighed, looking forward with apprehension. "I do trust you," she said, more to convince herself. She straightened up and put on an air of confidence to set Merlin at ease. Grabbing Brynn's reins, she was encouraged that at least she felt comfortable with her horse. Merlin jostled his horse forward, and Elanor followed.

Merlin smiled back at her, clicking his tongue as they galloped out of the citadel. Now that the wind was in Elanor's hair and she could hear the horse's hooves beating the ground, an excitement rose within her that she had not felt since Merlin had suggested she come with him. As they rode, she caught sight of the oak forest just ahead. Her heart raced. They turned onto the road, slowing their pace.

Traumatic memories leaked into Elanor's mind. She closed her eyes, struggling to shrug them off and focus on the bare oak trees with their few green leaves unfurling.

I have nothing to fear, she told herself. Still, a panicked urgency grew inside her stomach.

She tried to hang on to the sight of Merlin in front her, but all she could see was the hooded man's face next to hers as she laid on the ground helpless. The memory barraged her mind. Elanor heard a bird's wings flap above her head, and the startling sound provoked her to jerk her horse to a stop. The sound triggered the stark memory—the horrific moment—just before things went wrong. Her body was flush with fear. Elanor slumped forward. The ground spun, and her ears throbbed with the sound of her heartbeat.

Merlin heard Elanor's gasps and stopped abruptly. He turned and saw her panting in panic, leaning over in her saddle. Immediately, he drew up beside her, scolding himself for having brought her through this part of the forest.

"Elanor," he said calmly. "Elanor. Look at me." He continued to beckon her until she looked at him.

Her body trembled, and she couldn't focus. Merlin reached to touch her cheek and uttered druidic words. The sound of them felt like a cold wind blowing across her skin. The tingles in her feet and hands began to dissipate, and her awareness returned.

"There you are…Listen to my voice." Soothingly, he sang. His voice, like a comforting spirit, lifted her. Merlin dismounted from his horse and climbed behind Elanor, folding her in his arms. He held onto the reins of both horses and walked them forward as he continued to sing.

Elanor's panic slowly evaporated as the way became narrow, and then widened again. Finally, they reached a small stream, and Merlin helped her down from the horse to rest. He set her by a tree, then wet a cloth in the stream, still singing all the while. Returning to her, he dabbed the cool, wet cloth on her forehead.

"What happened? Why can't I stop trembling?"

"Just rest," Merlin soothed. "I should have known better than to take you through that part of the forest. This is my fault, but you will recover. This happens to warriors that have been in battle. It will pass."

"I feel so weak—such a burden. We only just started out, and already, I am slowing you down."

"Slowing me down? We are going together. You are my wife, not my burden. This is happening because of the trauma of the forest. It is still fresh, what happened there. Even I was reminded of its horrors as we passed through. I should have brought us through another way."

"I don't want a *forest* robbing me of my strength."

"This journey will work some of that out, and you will be stronger for it. The safety of Caer Lial would not have fully healed it. This is strength, Elanor."

She smiled slightly; his words had made her feel less weak.

"We have actually gone a good way. If we rest, we can continue through to reach the open plain before nightfall and camp on the forest's edge. The trails will become more jagged and narrow from here, so I want to make sure that you are recovered before we go on." He laid his hand upon her head and continued to speak healing words over her. She felt each one of them as they reached her ears, bringing waves of calm.

Merlin leaned against the tree and pulled Elanor beside him. "Close your eyes and listen to the water trickling in the stream. I know this stinging rush of fright," he began. "When I was young, barely a man, raiders attacked my village. I had been riding beside my grandfather, who was chieftain. When he saw them coming, he did not hesitate. He thrust a long sword into my hands and called for me to charge with him into the fray."

"At first, I was afraid, but I charged anyway, swinging my sword in a panic. But then, I saw ahead of me my grandfather losing ground. Men were falling upon him, overwhelming him. I leapt from my horse, and as I did, something came over me. It was like a fury. Some call it a frenzy of battle. I rushed in with my sword, heat beating up into my face.

"Like a savage wild beast, I tore through bodies, leaving a trail of blood. None that collided with me survived. More warriors from our village flew into the battle—leaving none of the enemy standing. I learned to hate the feeling of battle that day, and what it turned me into. I resented the taste of blood and the sound of metal tearing through flesh.

"My hands and arms were painted red. Never having taken human life before, this was my dismal introduction. I crumpled to the ground as waves of panic and terror seized my body. My grandfather carried me back to my mother, and she worked to bring calm to my mind, but that battle never truly left me. I could only numb the horror as I grew."

"They had a new name for me that day, and though they meant it to honor me, it pained me to hear it. They called me Dodwr Marwolaeth, Bringer of Death," he said bitterly. Merlin shook his head, then kissed Elanor's forehead. "Rest…these dark images can be replaced by the wind and stream…Rest."

Elanor nodded and closed her eyes, choosing to listen to the sound of the stream running over the rocks. The splashing and gurgling of the water made her think of a crowd of people chattering through an echoing hall. Exhausted by the panic, she drifted away.

Waking, Elanor breathed a deep sigh. "I am well." She sat up strongly and stretched herself. "It has passed."

Merlin stood, brushing himself off. "Are you sure?"

She rose and walked over to the stream, splashing her face with the cold water. "I am curious to see what lies beyond this stream."

Pleased with her resilience, Merlin helped her back onto Brynn's back. They were off again, but this time adopted a slower pace as the road had now become a rocky trail along the stream. The muddy path smelled like damp soil. As a cool breeze blew through, they felt refreshed while they passed over the trail.

Slowly, the trail turned upwards and away from the stream. Merlin instructed Elanor how to maneuver up the steep embankment. She had to duck low in order to be free of the branches above her head, and finally, at one point, they had to dismount to hike the trail on foot while leading the horses. After much climbing, they reached the top, and the trail widened. As the way became more solid, they mounted their horses again.

The sun gleamed down at them through the trees, giving them momentum to gallop faster, riding side by side on the wide road. The forest went on and on as the sun started to fade. But soon, the forest gave way, and the trees thinned. There, coming into view, was open landscape with rolling hills of tall grass.

Elanor breathed deep, allowing herself to feel the accomplishment.

"I will find us a place to bed for the night," Merlin said, pleased that they had arrived with daylight still available to them. "I know a place further in." Through the trees, veering off the road, Merlin took them deeper in off the edge of the forest, until they arrived at a small, round opening with a rock face jutting up along the back.

The night now full, Merlin sat, singing softly into the night air while throwing another piece of timber into the fire he had made. The light from the fire made his features dance as the frigid air turned his breath into ringlets of mist. Elanor wrapped herself tightly within a wool blanket, then laid her head down. She laid there but a short moment, listening to the night's noises, and then was quickly asleep.

Fresh and cold, Elanor woke in Merlin's arms. She was surprised that she had slept throughout the night, but the satisfaction of previous day's journey had completely lulled her to sleep. Maybe she was more for this world than she could have imagined. Her apprehension abated as she eagerly followed Merlin's lead, galloping forth into the green, hilly plains.

A few more days passed, and now they rode to a high hill for Merlin to have a vantage point to scan the landscape. "Nothing," he said, shaking his head. "All is quiet. Unusually so. No omen or sign of ill. This does not sit well within my spirit. The enemy has been clever at keeping themselves concealed, leaving nothing to follow. An infection always has signs." Merlin squinted his eyes while pondering.

"What of the Southlands? Marcus's village?"

"We have not gone far enough south. There, I am sure there will be something to be found. This enemy has worked hard to keep their destruction known but unconfirmed, like a rumor. This allows people a false sense of safety, and they remain unready and complacent." His eyes bounced across the plain. "We are not far from the villages that were attacked last season, but they are to the east, and we are going to the western edge of the Southlands...Aaaah!" He grunted in frustration.

Elanor stared at her hand. It had become blistered from the practice of holding a sword.

Merlin took hold of her hand, rubbing the red. "It will take more than weapons to hinder this enemy. But this discipline will do more than make you skilled with a sword. It will prepare you to fight instead of retreat. You are doing well."

Elanor was unsure that was true. She did not feel strong enough to stand against anyone, let alone a sorcerer, if it came to that.

"You must become strong of mind, Elanor." Gazing into her eyes, Merlin's handsome strength redirected her. "Your magic...yours and mine...has been prophesied. If you cannot hold a sword, then you will not believe in your strength to use your magic to derail the enemy. You are meant to overcome this darkness. But you cannot remain hidden and do so. There is still an inner strength within you that lies undiscovered. You healed Marcus upon a whim of magic, but true strength does not wait for whims. It presses in to be prepared." Merlin tightened his lips, then turned to gaze out at the sky. "Dark clouds are coming. There will be rain," he said, pointing up at the grey clouds. "There is a village not far off, and they will likely give us lodging during the rain."

Elanor nodded, seeing the dark mass moving in.

Quickly, they were on the road to beat the rain. The settlement rose before them, and as they neared, two riders came galloping out to meet them. Merlin stopped and brought Elanor alongside him, warily shielding her with his arm. The young warriors held their spears low.

"What business do you and the woman have in our realm?"

Merlin replied, "Are these not Ranok's lands? As chieftain, he has always been eager to receive Merlin into his Hall."

"Merlin?" replied one of the young riders, startled. "Are you the Emrys?"

"I am he. Is Ranok living?"

"Y-y-yes!" the rider stuttered. "Ranok would be pleased to see you. We have had to be cautious who we allow to enter our lands. There has been utterance of dangerous strangers. Please, we will lead you. Rain will be coming soon."

"This is why we have sought you out. We are journeying to Dyved and saw that the sky was growing dark. We hoped for the hospitality of Ranok's hearth to shield us from the rain."

"That he'll do," the rider said, clicking his tongue and leading the way forward.

31

THE CAER OF RANOK

Ranok's village was a large settlement, surrounded by a wall of high timbers. A large hall with a thick, heavy thatch was at its center. The Hall was built with round, wooded pillars, containing detailed carvings of ancient creatures twisting around each beam painted with red and green. A doorless entrance was covered in a large, painted canvas that whipped and flapped eerily in the wind, revealing a black void within.

"Wait here," the rider said, pushing back the flap to enter the Hall.

Merlin winked encouragingly at Elanor as they waited.

Emerging from the shadowed doorway came a plump old man in a long white tunic and a green robe. His hair was white and woolly, and his eyebrows sprang forth in tufts. It was hard to see where the hair on his head stopped and his beard began. He had but one small eye. Where his other eye should have been was a disfigured mark with a red scar across it. Blue dotted tattoos lined the sides of his face.

"Aih!" he said, tossing his hands at the surprise of seeing Merlin before him. "Lucky man am I, that the Great Merlin has brightened the doorway of my hall. Never did I think I would be so fortunate to see you once again." He patted Merlin happily on the chest, looking up at him with a smile. Seeing Elanor, he limped toward her, scanning her with his one eye. "Who is the young beauty?"

"It is good to see you, Ronok. Many years it has been. This…" he presented Elanor, "…is my wife. She is called Elanor."

"Oh my, my," he said, whistling through his teeth. "This cannot be. The old druid has married a beautiful, young blue bird. I am old, Merlin, but this fortune is beyond my reckoning. Haleth!" he shouted. "This is my grandson." He waved the young rider to his side. "Haleth, tell your wretched mother to cook up one of the goats and prepare a bed in your father's house." The young man ran off, and Ranok laughed as he patted his belly. "Now *that* is a boy who knows what is good for him. Strong he is," he said, making a fist, "but inexperienced. None of Arthur's great battles to teach him his strength. Ah, but he serves his grandfather well." He stared off toward his grandson, smacking his lips. "Come in! I am happy, so happy you have come to my house. Let us have some ale and a warm fire, eh? Your lovely will be more comfortable in one of my chairs."

As they entered the hall, gold rings jingled around Ronok's ankles and wrists. Several hounds pounced at them, barking loudly.

"Ack!" Ranok shouted at them, picking up a bone and throwing it across the floor. Happily, the hounds bounded over each other to capture it.

Elanor delighted in the rugged, wild look of the place. Bronze cups and plates laid scattered about the tables and floor. Old, chewed bones and mounds of hay occupied the corners. It was musty and smelt of old, forgotten ale, but the smile on Ranok's face made it hospitable.

"My dear wife has gone to be with the mother goddess," Ranok said sadly. "Now I rely on my son's wife for everything. I miss my dear one. I have gotten old, Merlin. Slow and sour," he laughed, with a twist of his mouth. "What say you, Merlin, of these rumors of sorcerous strangers? I fear I would not have the strength to withstand them if the rumors were true."

Merlin replied, "I am interested to know what you have heard. Have your people encountered any of these evils?"

"Only talk of villages being destroyed, though none have seen this with our eyes. We have heard telling of King Lugh's own citadel suffering due to his tyranny. Too long has he been allowed to rule without accountability. And Cormach has done little to make us feel secure, as he had abandoned these lands. Aaahh," he grumbled.

"I am sorry to confirm these rumors are indeed true. Though King Thul has recently dealt a blow to them that I hope they will not quickly recover from. It is good you are cautious in allowing strangers to pass through your gates. Keep your men ready and armed. All complacency must be done away."

Ranok nodded. "My son is a good battle chief. I would have you tell him what you know. My son honors me as chieftain, but my time is done. It will be for him to decide what to do. I have only wisdom left, and I am not sure there is even a lot of that to be relied upon these days. My wife used to say that with only one eye, half my mind had to be gone as well." Amused with himself, he slapped his knee and whistled through his teeth.

"Where is your son?" Merlin inquired.

"He is hunting. He will be told of your arrival when he returns. But you are not here for business, you are here for hospitality, and you shall have it. I will not have your good company spoiled by the woes of the land."

A woman, broad and strong, with dark hair tied back tightly, came in carrying what looked like a skinned goat leg in one hand. In her other hand, she held up a large pitcher balanced on top of her shoulder. She came in without looking at any of them and set the pitcher down roughly at Ranok's feet—giving him a very dissatisfied look as she did. Then, she went to roughly jamming an iron bar through the goat leg and hung it on a spit over the fire. She grunted, wiped her hands on the front of her apron, and then walked out of the room.

"See?" Ranok said, pointing. "Wretched, that one is." He burst into laughter and smacked Merlin's back. "You probably thought I was being unfair, but now you see, eh?"

Merlin and Elanor could not help but share in the hilarity and laughed.

Ranok picked up the pitcher at his feet and poured its contents into cups—handing one to each of them. "She brews the ale, too, and she does a damn fine job. That's what I think made my son want to marry her. She was the maid of the finest ale in Prydain. Drink!" His laugh echoed into his cup as he took in a large draught.

The pelting sound of rain started to beat on the thatch before a downpour began. Elanor was grateful to be inside and warm by the fire. When evening came, the meat was served, and Ranok's son returned home.

Halok arrived in the Hall appearing like his father, with Haleth by his side. Blue whorls tattooed his forehead and beside his eyes. His hair was dark and woolly, and his stature not tall, but firm and strong. His nose was red, and his eyes were small, but his teeth shined out white beneath his bushy, brown beard. He willingly joined in the revelry as if he had been in the Hall with them the entire day, but as the silence of the evening descended, Merlin and Halok disappeared to talk about the hooded strangers.

Elanor stared into the flickering fire, quietly listening to their dark whispers. Her head sank slowly into her palms with fatigue, and she was relieved when Merlin finally expressed that they were tired and ready for sleep.

Halok's wife lead them through the pouring rain to her home. Inside, a flickering light revealed a bed she had prepared for them—a short platform of woven hay with furs on top. Elanor thanked her, and the woman grunted with a nod.

"Will they not stay in their house also?" Elanor asked, watching her leave.

"They will all be sleeping in Ronok's hall. It is their way."

It rained throughout the night, and the sound made drifting off to sleep easy. By the next morning, the sun peeked through the clouds, and a low mist floated through the air.

"It will be a warmer day today," Merlin remarked, walking to stand beside Elanor as she peered out the door.

She reached up to kiss him. "Will we leave today?"

"As soon as we can gather ourselves and thank our hosts."

"They are different than others I have met. They seem to have an older way."

"Yes…Ranok's realms remain untouched. His ways are of an older time. In Caer Lial, the effect of Rome still lingers, but these men are Cymry, through and through. Ranok comes from a long line of chieftains that rebelled against the rule of the Romans. These rebels would have been Ranok's great-grandfathers. They fought to maintain their way of life while others became complacent, trusting that the Romans would protect them. But Rome left…" Merlin's eyes grew tense as he remembered. "Rome began their exodus when I was a boy. It was Ranok's ancestors that helped many to re-establish the old ways of the Cymry tribes. To remember who we were before Rome. There are still a few of these Cymry tribes scattered about the lands."

"Ranok's tribe quickly rose to support the new Cymry king, Aurelius. Especially one made king by the ancient way of druidic kingmaking. These old chieftains wanted their land back." Merlin pointed to the houses scattered about the Caer, many of them tent-like and not built with wood or stone. "Ranok's father and his people had been forced to wander because of their rebellion. So still, they live as nomads, even though their lands have been returned to them. It was King Cormach, ruler of these lands, that surrendered a portion of the land back to Ronok. He rules from Dyved, and he is a good king. Though he has been absent from these lands of late."

"We are not far from Dyved then?"

"Maybe another day's ride before we reach the forest of Dyved. From there, it will only be another half day's ride. Hopefully the rain will not hinder us. I can see that it might," Merlin said, clicking his tongue as he looked up at the sky. He shook his head.

"I will not be bothered by a little rain," Elanor chimed, making Merlin smile.

"Well, then, we should gather ourselves."

As they left the house, their horses stood outside, already waiting before Ranok's hall. Haleth was directing some young boys in readying their horses, tightening the saddles and getting everything properly attached.

"Aih!" Haleth said, waving them in. "We supposed you would want to be on your way. The rain should stay off for a while." He stopped to whistle, and then shouted, "Grandfather!"

Quickly exiting the Hall came Ranok, Halok, and his wife. Halok's wife had her hands full of bundles that she hurriedly shoved into Haleth's hands. "My mother has made you some food to take with you on your journey." He waved a bundle at them.

"To be so handsomely fed by my son's wife is a compliment indeed," Ranok rang loudly. "What have you done to our cantankerous woman?" Halok and Haleth responded with exuberant laughter.

Merlin grabbed Ranok's hand and arm solidly. "It has done my heart good to sit at the hearth of Ranok. Thank you, my friend. I wish we did not have to leave you so soon, but I am anxious to continue our journey."

"Yes, yes. Well, I am happy to have seen you, and both Halok and I have been glad of the warning. We will not be taken by surprise by evil enchanters." Then, bowing to Elanor, he said, "Lady blue bird, it has been a long while since a lady of your grace has been seen in Ranok's house. To meet the bride of Merlin is to be a fortunate soul indeed."

32

THE NARROW PASS

R ain dropped lightly on their shoulders, though it lifted into a light mist. The grassy plains were becoming more jagged as large, rocky hills and mountains jutted out of the ground. Their path now led them between two bluffs.

Each rock formation and boulder reminded Elanor of Merlin's songs. Some boulders laid together, appearing as sleeping giants, while others were scattered so randomly upon the grassy plans, she imagined they had to have been thrown by the huge behemoths. She enjoyed thinking of the land in this way. It brought life to all her eyes looked upon and made Merlin's mythical songs seem real. Grwyrthrhodd had resembled a unicorn, and Elanor surmised that possibly, there were many ancient creatures that could make faery stories real. Hardly did she speak, as they rode, captured by her thoughts.

"You're learning to look deeper and listen more intently," Merlin said quietly, breaking into her thoughts. "Every good druid must learn to observe and think beyond what is in front of them. They learn to train their spiritual eye when looking at the world."

Elanor straightened, snapping out of her deep contemplation. "How is it you know what I am thinking? Isn't that my gift?" She grinned. "Anyway, I am not a druid."

"Hah! Then why do you perceive and discern like one?"

"Well," she said, "since I have only known but a few, I would hardly be the best judge to know what one was."

"What did you see?"

Elanor twisted her lips to one side, unsure her fantastical imaginings weren't childish. "I was thinking that this place reminded me of giants. There's my deep, druidic thinking for you," she laughed. "I was thinking of Grwyrthrhodd, and how he is a…" She paused to find the right word, "…spirit, and not a being. As I look at these rocks and hills, I believe there is more to explain why a place is the way it is—hidden and unseen."

"You speak of the otherworld. For some, the way is veiled, while others can see right through to the other side. Some only see the otherworld in dreams or vision created by the awen. But sometimes, the otherworld breaks through into our world for all to see. That is what happened with Grwyrthrhodd. Somehow, your song broke through the shadow, revealing him to us all."

"What is the otherworld?"

"It is a place that shadows our world. We live in unison and work together for a similar purpose. There is both light and darkness there, but the Great God uses the good and can speak through it. The good spirits that dwell there are called enaid. I have seen very few, but when I have, it has been for a great purpose."

Elanor's brow creased. "There was great purpose in the forest when I sang out?"

"And there continues to be a great purpose since the moment you arrived. The man in blue has appeared in the otherworld and in ours. Though he is not like an enaid. I do not know who he is, but he has aided us in this purpose— to bring us together and protect us."

Elanor nodded as she worked to understand.

Merlin drew them to a halt at the edge of a precipice. He pointed. "Down there is the forest of Dyved. We do not have long now. We will sleep there, and then move off toward Dyved in the morning. But we will have to carefully pick our way down this rocky ledge. There is a pass leading down just a short way ahead, but it is narrow, and there are many loose stones. We will need to tread carefully, and I will need to walk the horses down."

The thought of maneuvering down the steep face of a rocky cliff made Elanor's stomach swirl, the height dizzying her when she stared down it. She tried to calm her nerves as Merlin searched for the passage down.

Chapter Thirty - Two

As they descended, the ledge turned and the steep pass was revealed, leading all the way to the bottom. The path jutted out, zigging and zagging dangerously from the sides of the cliff. A thin, silver stream sparkled from the bottom.

Elanor swallowed tensely at the sight as fear settled on her. She bit her lip, breathing deeply, and decided to conquer the descent.

Merlin tied the horses together to lead them so Elanor could walk freely. The further they descended, the steeper the path became. Elanor's ankles ached as they twisted over the rocks, but she concealed her discomfort, refusing to allow Merlin to see her suffering. She grabbed hold of the rocks and climbed down the jagged stairs, carefully placing her feet on the loose rocks.

The rush of the river sounded closer in her ears, reassuring Elanor that the bottom was near. She peered over the edge and saw that the narrow, silver stream had steadily become a wide, shallow river.

Reaching the bottom, they leapt from the final rocks, and the horses whinnied with relief, galloping down the last bit of the way. Now, for the first time, Elanor dared to look up and see the height they had descended from. She tilted her head back and gasped. Already she dreaded the long way back upon their return. Stumbling over to the river, she knelt to drink and wash the dust from her hands.

Merlin moved alongside her to do the same. A prideful expression was on his face as the wind blew the tresses of her hair across her eyes. "That was a long way," he said proudly. "And not a groan or grumble from my Elanor."

Elanor sighed long and loudly. "Sometimes, it's better to not know what you are in for until it is already over."

"Hah!" Merlin laughed while collecting some blankets to cover the ground. "Come," he said, patting the blankets, "sit down on this." He lifted Elanor's legs into his lap and began to un-wind the leather straps from around her ankles, slipping off her boots. "Soak your feet in the cool water a while, we have some time. What kind of husband would I be if I did not allow you to rest?"

The water was cold and icy, and it soothed Elanor's hot, throbbing feet. The horses were also glad for the break. They laid down on the banks of the river after having each taken a long drink.

While they rested, they shared a parcel of food from Halok's wife. It contained nut cakes and dried meats and was a welcome delight after the long trek down.

Merlin exuberantly chewed his meat. "I cannot wait to show you Dyved tomorrow. I have longed to see my mother. We will arrive not long after midday, and it will be a joyful season of rest for you in my mother's house."

The reminder of meeting Adhan pierced through Elanor. She had been so consumed with the journey itself that she had almost forgotten. She would rather descend the precipice all over again than meet her. Thoughts of escape gnawed at her like mice chewing on a rope. Maybe she could return to Ranok's and sit with his son's surly wife. Elanor turned once more to look behind her at the pass.

"What is it?" Merlin asked, sensing Elanor's worry. "What has you looking back so often? Since I mentioned Dyved, you have looked like a frightened rabbit in a trap, waiting to run away the minute I set you free."

She knew he had seen right through her but was not ready to give an explanation.

"Elanor…please tell me what is on your mind."

"I…" she groaned with frustration, "…I feel…It is hard to explain." She glared at the forest. "I am not sure I know myself. How long before you leave to travel further south?"

Merlin wrapped his arm around Elanor and held her head to his chest. "I will help you settle for a few days before leaving. You need not worry. My mother will not judge you ill. She will take good care of you. You must trust that I would not have brought you all this long way if I thought you would not be well received."

Trust. There was that word again. The one thing she wanted to have so badly but seemed to slip through her fingers. The anxious thoughts and nagging feelings
only increased.

They reached the forest, and that night was the first restless night Elanor spent on their journey. Every annoying root, rock, and bump on the ground seemed magnified. Merlin's singing and the night's noises gave her no peace. Even the warmth of Merlin's arm brought her no comfort.

She felt ridiculous for feeling so much worry, but she could not shake it, no matter how hard she tried. She laid there, wishing the morning would come— hopefully bringing a resolve to her anxiety.

What's the worst that could happen? she thought to herself. *If Adhan were to hate me, what then?*

She turned toward Merlin and buried her face in his chest, listening to his breath and trying with all her might to cast away all her bad thoughts until morning.

ADHAN

The mist of the morning descended and Elanor rose, relieved that the sun would soon be rising. Deciding to brave the cool water of a nearby stream, she silently snuck away.

The tingle of the icy water was refreshing as she splashed her face. Then, hanging over the water's edge, she rinsed her hair and neck. Her lips shivered as she wrung out her hair.

CRACK! A branch broke behind her. Elanor's head whipped around with alarm, only to see Merlin approaching the water. "Merlin!" she shouted. "You scared the life out of me!"

Merlin laughed, kneeling beside her to wash his face. "Ah, the water bites," he said, squeezing his eyes shut and sucking air between his teeth. "Did you not sleep at all?"

"Not even a little," she said, discouraged. "As hard as I tried, I could not silence my thoughts. I did try, Merlin."

"I know," he said, glancing at her as water from her hair dripped onto her shoulder. He lightly wiped the drips running down her forehead. "You trust me, Elanor, and believe that my words are true?"

Tentatively, she looked away. "I do…it's only…How can you be sure?"

"I promise that before the day's end, you will be in blessed company, and all your anxious thoughts will be nothing but a torment of the night."

Elanor nodded.

They paced themselves through the forest, as they had no need to hurry. The branches hung much higher in this wood of evergreen. The scent of pine lingered in the air while the sun warmed the earth. The ground was mossy and bright with purple clovers that laced their path. Happy red deer hopped through with their fauns, standing out against the green. It seemed almost a pity when the forest gave way and opened to reveal a yellow landscape.

Quickening their pace, they came upon a road and turned to follow it.

"We are nearly there!" Merlin yelled, breathing out with a satisfied smile. "It is just over that hill."

Peering down the road, Elanor could see a hill gradually rising. The sun had already crossed the sky and was beginning its descent to the west. Soon, the hill would be underneath them. Cresting its top revealed a large plateau with a settlement set upon it. A large stone tower jutted up from its edge. It was a lofty, turreted structure that was large enough to be seen from their distance. Behind the plateau, a backdrop of tall mountains rose like a painting, making the stone tower look all the more majestic.

"It is Dyved," Merlin declared with pleasure. He whacked the hind of his horse, leading the charge toward the plateau.

Elanor swallowed hard. The excitement of the journey was over. She tried to embrace the thought of how wonderful it would feel to finally sleep in a real bed.

Reaching the base of the plateau, they started up the road to the settlement. As they neared the top, voices rang out merrily above them.

"They know that we are here," Merlin said with a broad smile, staring up to the ledge.

"'Tis Merlin!" an excited voice echoed.

At the declaration, a group gathered over the edge, and many more filled the top of the road. A tall, sturdy man ran down the hill, waving his arms in welcome.

The warrior arrived out of breath. "Merlin! It has been too long since you have been home to us." The man had long, silver hair braided back and a cleanly shaven chin. His eyes were bright and grey. He grinned, patting Merlin's horse. "You have been well missed, my friend."

"It has been too long, Galen. Too long," Merlin said, leaping from his horse to embrace him.

Galen shook Merlin's shoulders. "Your mother has longed to see you."

"I shall not keep her waiting," he said, climbing back onto his mount. "We must see her before we are slowed with too many greetings, I think."

"Yes!" Galen nodded, looking wondrously over in Elanor's direction. "Who is the lady?"

"I shall introduce her to you all, but first, my mother."

"Yes…yes." Galen nodded, following in line behind the horses.

As they reached the top, the people surrounded them, enthusiastically shouting their greetings. Warriors slapped at Merlin's leg as he travelled past, while their eyes transfixed upon the mysterious maiden.

They moved through the green village of round, thatched houses and pens of cattle and sheep toward the stone tower at the very edge of the plateau, the length of the valley before it. Then, they turned to enter deeper into the village.

Beautifully landscaped gardens and trees lined the road. Steadily before them rose a great house. Its walls were stone and washed white, while the roof was red and angular, supported by many doors and columns. The structure was a great Roman villa with a courtyard before it. Within the courtyard stood a white fountain, aged and cracked. Cobblestone lined the ground, creating pathways decorating the yard.

Slowly, Elanor slid from her horse, her eye set upon the large main door. Her stomach twisted anxiously.

Merlin dismounted, assisting Elanor to the ground. He pulled her chin to face him. "There is nothing to fear."

Elanor's eyes flashed, reaching to find truth or comfort in his words. Within his eyes, she saw the excitement of a small boy running into his mother's arms. Her emotions rose. She had never experienced what it was to be greeted by a mother whose heart yearned for her.

Gracefully gliding out of the door came a woman, tall and lovely. Her hair was a beautiful cascade of silver that swirled in the wind as if it were floating through water, shining like silk. Her features were without lines, pure and white, and her eyes were bright and blue. Though she wore simple clothing, she looked to be a queen of the otherworld.

Adhan walked straight for her son, raising her hand to her mouth. She reached for him, her cheeks dampening with tears. "My son!" She embraced Merlin. He wrapped his arms tightly around her, turning his head into her neck. "Let me see your golden eyes," she said, placing her hands on both sides of his face. She gasped. "What has happened? You are youthful once again. The years that had been stolen from you seem to have returned."

"Mother," Merlin said, his eyes aglow. He took her wrists into his hands. "I am well beyond what I have ever been. This…" he trailed off, turning to face Elanor, "…is my wife. She is Elanor. My very soul. We have come that you would know her."

A resounded gasp escaped the people at Merlin's announcement.

Elanor froze as Adhan's tearful eyes turned to gaze at her. The heat of Elanor's fear instantly rose, and a pink flush lighted her cheeks. She turned to stroke Brynn to soothe her own discomfort, leaning her head into the horse's mane.

Elanor closed her eyes, bracing for impact as Adhan approached. A tear slipped from her eye, and she quickly wiped it away in hopes that Adhan had not seen it. Adhan's slender fingers slipped softly over her shoulders, and then, Elanor found that she was being pressed into an embrace.

"My son has returned to me, bringing me a daughter. My heart never hoped for such a blessing." Adhan stood back, grabbing Merlin's hand with one hand and Elanor's with the other. "This is why my son has life in him once again. I feared I had lost him through the final trial of Arthur's death, but now I see I have him once again renewed. Please…" she announced to the gathered people, "…I must have my children come rest in my house. I know their journey has been long. Then we will celebrate their arrival together."

The people whooped and clapped their hands, slowly dispersing back to their homes, while Adhan pulled Merlin and Elanor toward the house.

They entered the brightly lit structure. Mosaics tiled the floor, creating pictures similar to those Elanor had admired on the floor of the Palisade in Caer Lial. In the middle, yellow tiles created a large picture of the sun. On each side of the sun, lines displayed pictures of men and women harvesting wheat. The walls were decorated with paintings of bundled wheat, chipped from the once bright and vibrant colors of gold and yellow. A table set for dining stood beside a hearth, surrounded by wooden chairs and benches with silk cushions. Stone stairs ran along both sides of the chamber, leading to other parts of the house.

Adhan patted the cushions. "Please…warm yourselves and rest." She pointed to the chairs she had so lovingly prepared. She floated to a seat opposite them, her eyes still sparkling with tears. "Food and drink will be brought…I had heard word that you had returned from the isle. This gave rise to so much hope for me, but I did not know until now that it was true." Adhan reached across to grab Merlin's hand.

He lifted his mother's hand to his mouth and kissed it.

The nerves in Elanor's stomach heightened. Though she had been seemingly easily accepted, she couldn't quite soothe her feelings. She sat silently, her palms sweating, all her focus directed at projecting a calm appearance.

Merlin began to tell Adhan of the darkness and the errand that had brought him south. He spoke of Thul and the events leading up to Celyddon killing five of the eight hooded villains. His mother seemed not surprised of his stories of woe but nodded, making it plain that these happenings had not been new to her ears. But then Merlin shifted to speak of Elanor. Adhan's eyes rested upon her, making her feel uneasy. She could no longer hear Merlin's words but instead, the words of her own mother resonated in her head.

"She is worthless, David! It was never my decision to bring her here—it was yours. She's your problem."

The words of her mother still cut like a knife. For years, Elanor had shoved the memories so far down and had done well pretending the words had never been said and had never hurt her. Before all this, she had lived her life happily in denial, unbent by her mother's lack of kindness. Now, she could not keep her overwhelming sadness from seeping out.

"She is not my daughter—she's not even yours!"

Why had she always called her mother? Maybe it was because she hadn't had anyone else in her life except for Helen. She had been the only mother Elanor had ever had. Her thoughts faded into another memory…

"Going off to school finally?" Helen asked in an antagonistic tone.

Elanor looked at Helen tentatively as she packed her paints and canvases.

"Will be glad to have those hideous things gone. Really, I do not know why David continues to encourage this hobby of yours. At least now I will have this space back to put my things in. David can't argue to keep this a room for you anymore." Helen crossed the room to look Elanor straight in the eye. "Have you nothing to say to me for all the years I have given up my home for you?"

"Oh…uh…yes," Elanor stuttered. "Truly, I am thankful to you. This has been the only home I have ever known, and you are the only mo—"

"What? Mother?" Helen interrupted with a loud, jarring laugh. She bent down closer to Elanor's face. "Let's not fool ourselves, love. I was never your mother."

Adhan reached over to touch Elanor's hand, seeing her anxiousness, but her gentle touch did not pull her from the memory playing in her mind.

"David wanted you! He chose you. He saw that little baby and thought it was his life's mission to care for you—be a father to you. But don't make the mistake of thinking that I ever wanted to be your mother."

Loud and clear those words rang into Adhan's mind as she touched Elanor's hand. The pain of the words struck like lighting, searing Adhan's heart. She gasped and fell back into her chair, placing her hands over her heart.

The sound of Adhan's gasp cut through Elanor's memory, abruptly stopping it. "I'm sorry. I'm so, so sorry!" Elanor said, standing up to reach for her. "I didn't mean for that to happen!" Elanor stood awkwardly, then burst into tears and ran for the door. Bile rose up in her throat. She knew any moment she was going to vomit. She ran as fast as she could, through the door and into the courtyard. It was dark, and Elanor was disoriented, but she quickly located a row of shrubs. Racing to them, she retched.

Elanor wiped her mouth breathlessly, frantically scanning the yard around her. She didn't want to go back where she had humiliated herself. Stumbling, she walked toward the fountain. Once her hand touched the cool stone, she collapsed beside it. Feeling the supple turf beneath her, she buried her head into her arm. Her tears flowed freely. Embarrassment of the spectacle she had made overwhelmed her.

Merlin watched in shock as she ran. He leapt to go after her, but his mother grabbed his wrist.

"No, Merlin," Adhan said. "I will go. She needs a mother, not a husband right now."

"What has happened?" he asked, confused.

"Do you truly not understand?"

Merlin paused, staring at his mother with his mouth wide. "She had been anxious during the journey. She did not sleep well because she was so deeply troubled over meeting you. She worried that you might not receive her well. I told her she had nothing to fear."

"I am afraid it goes much deeper than that." Adhan peered behind Merlin at the door, "She has magic? Like you?"

Merlin nodded. "There is really so much to tell."

"I will go to her. Leave us to talk a while."

Adhan stood and drifted out the door. She saw Elanor outside, crumpled in a heap beside the fountain. She moved over to Elanor and tenderly knelt before her, taking the folds of her dress to wipe her tears.

"I am so sorry, Adhan. I did not mean to…"

Adhan silently set her hand on Elanor's and stroked it.

Elanor stared at her, baffled. Adhan's soothing nature was confusing. Especially after her unappealing dramatics, she'd braced herself for a more negative reaction. She believed Merlin would be the one to come to her, not Adhan. Yet here she was, and in all sincerity.

"I am so embarrassed," Elanor sobbed. "I hope you do not think the worst of me—running out like that. I am usually not like that."

"Usually not like what?" Adhan stroked her cheek.

Elanor's brows bent in. "This is not normally how I like to be seen."

"I touched you. You did not touch me." Adhan's eyes saddened. "I heard her awful words in my head, and I could feel your heartache. She was not your mother?"

"No." Elanor sniffed angrily. "She was not my mother, but she was the only one I've ever had." Tears dripped down her trembling chin. "I guess I have never had one, but I convinced myself she was my mother anyway. She rejected me every day, but for some reason, I kept thinking she would change her mind. Maybe she would find value in me and love me, but she didn't."

Adhan breathed out softly. "Come with me." She lifted Elanor to her feet. "It is beautiful, the edge of the Dyved at night. Let us walk and see what we can. Tell me about your father."

"Oh…he was good." Elanor wiped her eyes. "He and I spent long days together. He always made time for me. Though I always felt guilty that I had stolen him away from his real family. Since my mother, Helen, wanted nothing to do with me—him choosing me was like a slap in her face."

"He was not your father?"

Elanor sighed sadly. "He treated me as though I were his real daughter. He and Helen had two other children, Nancy and Jack, but he doted on me. Now that I look back, it is likely the reason I was never close to my brother and sister, and why Helen hated me so much. He chose me over them in a lot of things."

"He found me. He was walking in the forest with Brando—that was the name of his dog—and, according to my father, Brando sniffed me out and began to bark. There my father found me, wrapped in a blanket, set on the top of a tall stump crying. He said from the moment he saw me, he knew it was his job to care for me and protect me. At least that is the story he told. I have never known any other family, and my father has never been able to find any information on where I might have come from. Just abandoned there in the forest."

"You will not be abandoned here, Elanor," Adhan said as they moved into the open space of the plateau. The wind howled as they neared the edge to look out, and the night sky made the grass below look like a blue, rippling sea.

"Those are wheat fields. They have not grown tall yet, but soon they will be long and green. The fields are a breathtaking sight in the light of the moon." Adhan sat down in the grass and gestured for Elanor to sit down beside her. "I love my son. He is my promised one, and I feared that he was lost forever. Now I see he has returned, and not only returned, but he is whole. Many years it has been since I have seen such light in his eyes. The light is you. I cannot have a bad judgement against you for that reason alone. My son says that you are his soul, and if that is true, then truly, you are also my daughter. I do not have to know you to understand that you have a quality that is special for my son, who has never had a mate, to have chosen you. So, either you are an enchantress and have bewitched him, or you are truly as special as he says you are. Though, I do not think an enchantress could fool the pure heart that dwells within him. Morguese tried, but she could not. Darkness is never stronger than the light."

"Please be at peace. You will not have to fight for a place in my heart as you have with your own. I am glad that I heard the voice within you, accusing you. That voice lied to you about your value. That voice could not have told you the truth, or else you would not be here with my son. The Great God would have you loved."

Elanor had never heard anyone talk like Adhan. Her words were so healing and full of life. She had so much authority as she spoke, and yet it came with such tenderness and grace. Elanor felt silly for having been so anxious, and yet, the way Adhan spoke made her feel like she needed this moment. She needed to be pressed to feel the rejection and ponder the acceptance. It felt genuine. Not forced, but free.

Elanor whispered, "Thank you."

34

BLESSED DYVED

O ut of the dim light, Merlin approached. "The wind is sharp," he said, teeth chattering. "What happened back there?"

Elanor lifted her chin toward him. "When Adhan touched me, I was in deep thought about my mother and…"

Merlin nodded. "She could see your memories."

"Yes." She dropped her head. "I am sorry, Merlin."

"Come here." Merlin pulled Elanor into his arms.

Adhan stood, smoothing her dress with her hands. "There is warm food that has been prepared, and a bed made ready for you. Let us return. There are many things I want to know, but it is for tomorrow. You have travelled far, and now Elanor knows she has come to a place where she can fully rest."

Quickly they ate and were ready for sleep. Adhan led them up the staircase on the right and through a small door into a corridor. The short passage had only one door, which opened to a beautifully lit room with yellow walls amplified by the flicker of candlelight. Sheer linen curtains waved lightly in front of a large, open balcony, which provided a high view of the courtyard.

"There are doors," Adhan said, walking to the curtains and pulling them closed, "if you desire to keep more warmth inside." She grabbed Merlin's cheeks and kissed his forehead. "I am overcome with happiness to see you, my son. I already yearn for the morning. Though I will sleep in comfort knowing that you are here under my same roof." Adhan embraced Elanor, bringing her head into her chest. "Daughter, I know you will sleep in the abundance of peace tonight. I am glad to have the extra gift of you this day. Please rise no earlier than you should. No work or travel will meet you. Good night," she said quietly, slipping out of the room.

Merlin took Elanor's hand and spun her around. "Are you truly at peace?"

Elanor nodded as she walked about the room, running her fingers across every surface. "It's so beautiful here."

"Ah, yes. Many a Cymry king has ruled from this house. It was built by the Romans long ago, but has been established much longer, a house of the Britons. King Cormach and the rulers before him have aimed to keep this house strong, as it represents so many years of history. The late King built the great watch tower," Merlin said, pointing out the balcony, "and chose to give this house to my mother, and she houses many of the brothers of Esu here. My mother has a long history with the kings of Dyved. I was born in the room that my mother still occupies. This plateau was once known as Caer Myrddin."

Caer Myrddin? Elanor wondered, noting the similarity to Merlin's name as it rolled off his tongue.

"But during the early years after Rome departed, this Caer was attacked and left weakened. Still the lordship of Dyved remains. My mother is matriarch to many of the people of Dyved. I assume even more these days, as the younger Cormach has been away."

"Why has Cormach gone?"

"I do not know. I have my thoughts as to why, but until I see him again, I will not know fully. Arthur's death sent many of his faithful into darkness. I knew this, and I expected much less to have remained established when I finally returned. I did not even know if Caer Lial would still be standing. If it had collapsed, I would have blamed myself. I turned inward instead of being an aid. As did Thul and Cormach."

Merlin continued, "Cormach and his father formed strong alliances with the kings of Eire. We had many enemy kings in Eire, but Arthur had a way of turning our worst enemies into our greatest allies. Cormach was instrumental in this becoming so. Because of this strength, Eire stood with us when we needed their help. And it was an alliance with a chieftain of Eire that brought Gwynevere to meet Arthur." He paused at the recollection. After a moment of silence, he said, "I believe that our young King Cormach has found solace with his friends in Eire and has hopefully not abandoned his people. I cannot judge Cormach, as I have been guilty of the same. I only hope he returns as I have, for I feel we will need him in the coming days."

As the night went on, the freshness of the air blowing in through the open window lulled them into a deep sleep. Elanor's dreams were full of images she could not hold onto. But then, she dreamt again that she could see Merlin, high above, standing on the edge of the plateau of Dyved. As he stood, a white dove descended and landed in his hands. One wing remained up, while the other curled down around its body. Then, Elanor's stomach twisted, and the feeling of falling overwhelmed her.

Her eyes snapped wide open. Elanor was unsure why the scene in her dream had rattled her. As she calmed her breathing, she felt the warmth of Merlin beside her. Her eyes slowly focused on the linen curtains blowing gently in and out of the room. The sun had already long risen. She had not slept in beyond dawn for a long time. The freshness of the morning still hung in the air.

Elanor carefully pulled herself out from under Merlin's arm, slipping her feet out onto the floor. The stone floor felt like ice. She wrapped herself in a blanket and wandered out onto the balcony.

The air was warm, so she let the blanket fall from her shoulders to feel the sun's rays upon them. Footsteps sounded just beneath her, and she leaned over the balustrade. A silver haired man was leaving the villa. Catching his gaze, he turned to salute her with a smile. It was Galen, the man from the day before. He continued on, and Elanor watched him until he disappeared around the corner, into the village.

"Ah, Galen!" Merlin breathed, walking onto the balcony and standing beside Elanor. He peered up at the sky, standing tall and proud in only his breeches. "It is a lovely morning."

Elanor laughed, a little pleased by his freedom. She enjoyed the look of him, strongly set in the morning light. Glancing at the torc that laid around his neck, she placed her fingers insecurely upon her own. Elanor still hadn't gotten used to its weight. "I am not sure I have earned mine," she said.

"I do not think you will feel like that after all is said and done," he encouraged as he stretched his arms wide, inhaling the crisp morning air.

The new day had dawned, and their journey was complete. Elanor's anxieties momentarily silenced; she now looked forward to seeing Adhan. They took the long morning to enjoy one another and rest, but as their stomachs began to growl and the smell of food filled their noses, they dressed and ambled down to the Hall.

"Good morning! Strawberries—freshly picked, with cream and honey," Adhan said. She was dressed finely, and her eyes sparkled with excitement. "Galen has just been, and picked through the food already," she laughed. "It has been many long years since Lord Merlin has been to Dyved, and the people are anxious to meet your beautiful new bride. They're quite displeased at the thought of not celebrating your marriage and are awaiting permission to prepare a feast and bonfire—which includes the women stealing your bride for the day. Of course, I have already given them permission and care not whether you'd like it or not. They have already set the poles of ribbon and begun placing the long tables. So, my dear one," Adhan said, peering at Elanor, "eat, for you are about to be stolen away."

Merlin chuckled as Adhan pulled Elanor over to the table. "You are about to be most heartily welcomed to Dyved, my love."

Merlin tore a chunk of bread from a loaf. Grinning with his mouth full, he said, "I will go find Galen; the groom should help build the pyre. I have missed my friend anyway, and it will give me something to occupy my time with while I wait for my bride." Out the door he bounded like a little boy going out to play.

"The women are eager to get their hands on you," Adhan said gleefully. "They think you are a princess, and the thought of you has them enthralled. The last princess to come here brought them forth their Lord Myrddin."

Myrddin? The name enticed Elanor as much as it had when she'd first heard it. She desired to know more about Merlin's connection to Dyved. She wondered how much Adhan could tell her.

Adhan continued, "There have been kings and princes, chieftains and lords of battle, but few ladies of such beauty wearing a torc of nobility."

Elanor shook her head. "I know nothing of nobility or being a fine lady."

Adhan shot a confused glance at Elanor. "Well, my dear daughter, you might not think you know, but nobility is what you carry. It is what all who lays eyes upon you sees, whether you are aware of it or not. You are who you are. Maybe I can help you see that."

Elanor longed to understand what Adhan meant. Adhan mystified her. She was so delicate, yet strong. It was as though she truly was from another age and time. Much like Merlin, she was timeless, and her words bore more gravity than those of men who had not seen through time as they had both done.

Elanor was eating her last strawberry when she heard giggles coming from the doorway.

"Prepare yourself. You already have little ones adoring you—just there." Adhan pointed.

Elanor turned to spy two little girls standing in the entrance. The elder girl held the younger one's hand. The girls were soon followed by a woman, who Elanor assumed was their mother.

"Hello, little ones," Adhan said, standing to greet them. They ran to wrap their arms around her long legs, and she bent down to kiss each one. "Elanor, this is Ffion."

The blonde woman bowed toward Elanor, a slight smirk on her lips. Her green eyes were bright, and freckles dotted her face.

"Beca and Bethan are the little ones. These are the wife and children of our dear friend Galen, who is battle chief and steward of Dyved."

"Hello, Beca and Bethan." Elanor kneeled to greet them. "What lovely golden braids you both have. Did your mother do them?" The girls giggled, then gazed up at their mother. Elanor stood. "Ffion, I am very happy to meet you and your lovely daughters."

Ffion gave Elanor a sideways smile and threw her hands up on her hips. "Well, Merlin has found himself a proper one. Come with me." She grabbed Elanor by the arm and dragged her out the door. The two little girls laughed as they scampered behind.

"The women are restless. They have been waiting long while you slept the day away." Ffion winked at Elanor with a friendly grin.

Already Elanor liked Ffion; she had sass, and it reminded her of her friend Jess, whom she had left behind for what felt like a lifetime ago.

Adhan waved them on, staying behind as they scuttled down the road toward the village. Other women followed in their train, some carrying baskets of linens. As they approached the open plain, Elanor watched as villagers bustled about, preparing tables for the upcoming feast. Rounds of meat already rolled on spits, the aroma of roasting meat wafted through the air.

Elanor perked up when she saw who she thought was Merlin, but a bump on her bum drew her attention downwards. Beca and Bethan pushed her on impatiently to keep her moving. They turned into the trees behind the village.

As they moved deeper into the wood, Elanor heard trickling water, and it wasn't long before she found its source. They arrived at a spring with a crystal-clear pool underneath.

"Did you bring the soap?" Ffion shouted.

"Aih," came the reply.

Elanor was taken aback as Ffion began untangling the bust in the back of Elanor's dress.

"Wait!" Elanor yelped, holding her dress closed. "Wait—what are you doing?"

The women roared with laughter, and Elanor realized they were not going to wait for her permission.

"It will be alright, Elanor," Ffion chimed jovially. "Once you're in the water, you won't notice the cold."

What? Elanor's eyes widened as she realized what was about to happen. Now all the women were gathered around her, briskly throwing their clothes off. She felt less exposed as the women's contagious laughter grew, making Elanor smile with nervous excitement. They were all about to take this icy plunge together. Even the little girls had stripped down, prepared for the bath. Ffion had Elanor by one arm and giddily, they tiptoed toward the water.

"Just get in all at once, it's easier that way," Ffion said, jumping in all the way over her head.

She made it look so easy that Elanor decided to follow suit. She jumped in, and the icy sting stole her breath. She rose up, gasping for breath. The women burst into laughter, each jumping in one after the other.

"Quickly!" Ffion handed Elanor the soap.

Women all over the pond swiftly helped each other wash, shivering as they hastily passed the soap.

It was over almost as quickly as it had begun. Women dashed out of the water, promptly wrapping themselves in linens. The sun was warm, shining through the trees in patches. Quickly finding a sunny spot, each one laid themselves out to dry. Beca and Bethan wasted no time in getting dressed so they could run around after little grey butterflies that flitted around the clover.

Frozen, Elanor dashed for her clothes.

"Oh, no, no," Ffion said. "Not you." She gave Elanor a linen to wrap herself in, then helped her wring her hair while tying it up. "You must sit and wait." She offered Elanor a place to sit down on a rock that was warm and sunny.

"Warm yourself here, and then we will prepare you." Ffion smiled, then struggled to quickly pull on her own clothes.

It delighted Elanor to watch Ffion grapple with her daughters' heads as they moved around like squirrels. Then, she combed out her own lovely golden hair and braided it up. Elanor hoped she wasn't going to be left sitting naked on a rock while the others made themselves beautiful.

Once the women had dried and dressed, they became busy working on little tasks. Some were finishing stitches on a white dress, while others collected flowers from the clover. The women were radiant in the sunshine as they moved about the trees like magical nymphs.

Ffion grabbed up the comb and began to unwrap Elanor's hair. The women followed Ffion's lead, gathering together to do their part. As Ffion tenderly combed, others came ready with flowers in hand. Ffion braided Elanor's hair, piece by piece. The women watched and participated as if Elanor were a sculpture they were all working on together. They placed the white dress over her head. Pleased with the look of it, the woman who had made the dress went to work sewing on the final pieces. The others continued to set flowers in Elanor's hair, and finally, placed a wreath upon her head.

Elanor stood completed, and now the women were free to begin decorating each other with the remaining flowers, each setting a wreath upon their heads. Springtime itself had erupted in the display of their beauty—the brightness of their eyes, the white of their teeth as they smiled, and the sound of bird's song in their laughter.

Ffion nodded at Elanor with a wink. "Merlin will be pleased."

She lifted her voice loudly in song, signaling the rest to join her. Gladly the larks moved back out of the trees and into the village. The men sprang up brightly as the women emerged from the trees. A drum began to play, and a harp strummed. As the maids neared, a man would appear and whisk his woman away. The sight took Elanor by surprise as she watched each couple dance away onto the green. More and more kept coming until finally, Elanor saw Merlin diving toward her—lifting her up into his arms. They joined in the dance with the other happy couples, dancing around and around in a circle.

Elanor saw Galen with Ffion in his arms. She watched them spin while Galen kissed Ffion's neck. Elanor peered into Merlin's eyes, realizing that some of her happiest moments were dancing in his arms. She kissed his mouth and buried her head into his chest. All of Dyved clapped their hands as the happy couples danced. The two little girls danced hand in hand. Too quickly the song ended, and everyone threw their arms up with a loud hurrah.

The music started again, and the couples turned to take their seats. Merlin nuzzled Elanor and whispered, "You have stolen my very breath." Before setting themselves next to Adhan, he called, "Galen, let me properly introduce you to my bride." He waved Galen to come near. "This is my Elanor."

"My lady," Galen said, placing his hand over his chest, bowing low. His demeanor reminded Elanor of Bedwyr.

Ffion stood beside her husband. "A true noble lady, she is."

Elanor felt her dress being pulled and turned to see Beca and Bethan.

"Come dance with us?" Bethan chirped happily.

Beca slapped Bethan's hand. "That is not how you ask a princess to dance with you."

Merlin knelt to their level. "How, then, would you ask a princess to dance with you?" he asked, winking at them.

"You say *please*." Beca glared down at her sister.

"Please will you dance with us, Princess Elanor?" Bethan requested sweetly, staring up at Elanor.

"I'd love to." Elanor grabbed Bethan by the hand, and Beca laughed with glee as she led them forward into the dance. The people danced in circles, rotating around the big pyre waiting to be lit, with the drum tapping happily as they leapt and spun.

Ffion leaned over, smiling at Merlin. "Our daughters are happy that you have brought them a princess."

Merlin threw his head back and laughed, settling down next to Adhan as he watched Elanor being led around by her finger.

"She truly is lovely, my son. She is eager to find joy. Tell me about her?"

Merlin quietly unraveled the story of how Elanor came to Prydain. He told his mother about the dreams and how the magic had begun. He explained that though Elanor had magic, it was foreign and new to her.

Adhan listened in awe, turning her gaze toward Elanor. "This land is entirely strange to her? I thought it odd the way she described her mother and father. She is not from our time, but a world entirely different."

"Yes. She needs grace, and yet she has strength that is rare. She is not tainted or despairing like so many. She has hope and is resilient. She…" His voice broke as he remembered the horrific events that had transpired in the forest. "She spent all of Lughnasadh and Samhain broken in pieces, and I did not have the resilience to watch her suffer, so I left her."

"What happened?" Adhan leaned in.

"The hooded men, they aimed to kill me, and brutalized Elanor to ensnare me. If it had not been for the enaid and my and Cilaen's skill, she most certainly would have died. And look at her," he said, pointing to a beautifully bright Elanor dancing with the two children. "She always tries to be so strong."

"You returned to her, Merlin. Do not enter into guilt, but know that in the end, you chose what was right. She forgave you, didn't she?"

"Yes."

"These revelations of Elanor mean something more. There is a destiny in it, I can hear it in all that you say."

"There is a prophecy," Merlin continued. "An old druid named Marcus said that he and some of the New Way saw a sign of two stars falling in the sky many years ago. In a dream, he learned the names of the stars were Emrys and Gwenddydd. You have heard me called Emrys, and just before meeting Marcus, an ancient enaid named Elanor Gwenddydd. Marcus prophesied the destiny and purpose of these twin stars, but I am still seeking the Great God for understanding. I do not fully understand the role we are to play."

"I am astonished! This makes the song rise within my heart."

"I thought that the kingdom of the sun had been lost, but now I believe it may be that we are being graced a second chance."

"This has come to me, Merlin, and it is something I think you should bear in mind. If the druids of the New Way have seen the signs in the sky and received a prophecy, don't think that the dark druids did not also see the signs. For they have surely seen it as well and would have sought out their meaning."

The idea that the dark druids were aware of the prophecy had not even occurred to Merlin, but of course, this had to be true. For the druids all looked to the sky and the world around them to know what is to come, and the practice would not have changed for those who had turned to darkness.

What prophecy would they have heard?

His mother's warning made him contemplate a little more deeply the darkness he knew stood behind the hooded men and their attacks. He gazed over at Elanor, who was now sitting in the grass with the two girls as they brought her handfuls of tiny daisies. He didn't want fear or worry to steal the joy of the celebration, nor the goodness of being home with his mother. However, a new concern tugged at Merlin's mind. If the stars that fell in the prophecy were two, and if the dark druids were to discern the stars as Marcus had, then not only was his life under attack, but Elanor's would be too.

What had happened in the oak forest, Merlin thought, was an attempt to destroy him, and the druids saw Elanor as a vessel to trap him. Maybe they had not realized who Elanor was, and maybe, by some chance, the dark druids knew nothing about her. Still, this sobering idea washed over Merlin. He wanted to whisk Elanor away to safety. Anxiously, he became more eager to take his flight to Llyonesse to discover what he could.

Bethan took the handful of flowers they had collected and arranged them in Elanor's hand. After working on this for some time, Bethan declared, "We are all done. Now we have to give them away."

"Whom should we give them to?" Elanor asked.

Bethan pointed to a silent woman who sat alone on a stool, her mouth hanging open slightly, just on the edge of the celebration. She stared off into nowhere and did not move or blink. Her hair was dark and laid in strings on her shoulders. Dark circles hallowed her eyes, and her face was worn. Her hands were curled on her lap, and her shoulders slumped forward.

Beca whined, "No, we don't want to give them to her. She wouldn't know it if we gave her flowers or not."

"I want to give them to her," Bethan fought back.

After a few minutes of bickering, Bethan won the battle. She delicately took the flowers from Elanor's hand, glaring at her sister as she did. As she approached, the woman did not acknowledge the child, nor did she move. Bethan gingerly placed the flowers in her open palms, then rested her tiny hand upon the woman's cheek. "Here's some flowers for you," she said sweetly. "It will be alright now."

The woman's eyes moved toward the child, their eyes locking briefly. Seemingly unmoved, she faded back into her world of nothingness. Bethan skipped away, and Beca chased after her, giving Elanor the freedom to return to Merlin, who was glad to have her back.

"I thought I might have lost you for the rest of the day," Merlin said.

"They are dear ones. I have not often been around the laughter of children." Elanor gazed at him and saw uncertainty in his eyes. "What's wrong? You seem disturbed."

"Truly, I am just happy to have you back by my side. My mother has just said something about the dark druids and the prophecy that has made me ponder. Though, dark thoughts don't have a place between us this day." He put his fingertip on the blue stone of the pendant that laid on Elanor's chest. "You shall remain safely in my arms."

As he spoke, Elanor instantly recalled her dream from the night before. In that moment, she saw Merlin holding the white dove in his hands and felt her stomach drop as the sinking sensation of falling washed over her, just as it had in her dream.

She looked back across the long tables to see the woman that Bethan had given the flowers to, still staring off without response. Some of the flowers had fallen to the ground. "Merlin? Who is that woman? Why does she sit like that?" Elanor leaned slightly, directing him to see who she was talking about. "Bethan gave her flowers, and she gave little response."

"Yes, I saw sweet little Bethan giving them to her." Merlin stopped and leaned over to his mother. "Has she never recovered?"

"No," Adhan said sadly. "There are days where it seems she will return to us, and then she disappears again. Still, the women in the village take turns caring for her."

Merlin shook his head. "That is Efa, Elanor," he said. "That is Cilaen's mother."

"Cilaen's mother?"

"She broke when her husband was killed in battle against the Saecsans. When his colors were returned to be buried in the warrior's mound, she slowly started disappearing, little by little, year after year—more of her has gone away. It hurts Cilaen to see her, so he doesn't return to Dyved often, though I know he longs to see it, and my mother again."

Elanor understood now, why Cilaen had acted strangely when he spoke about his mother that day before they left. She wondered if her gift of healing could help her. She had seen it work on Marcus's blind eyes and on that little boy's deaf ears, but that healing just sort of happened. She thought, if given the chance, she would try.

Finally, the meat had properly cooked, and the feast was about to begin. Galen stood up on the table and shouted, "My brothers and sisters! This has been a blessed day. Merlin and his bride have come to Dyved, and we are full of joy and merriment because of it. We will light the fires and feast until the sun sets behind the hills. For today is a good day of love and of friendship. Of sons returned and hope restored, and to our beautiful brides who represent the bounty of this day, we celebrate this day in all its fullness. We celebrate you, Merlin, and your beautiful bride." He jumped down from the table and grabbed two flaming torches. "Merlin, join me, brother, and together we will light the fire of celebration."

Together they placed the torches into the pyre, and the flames licked high. The people shouted their happy cheers as the fire roared. Then out came the food, carried out by men in brown robes. Large loaves of bread and juicy cuts of meat were served. Bowls of ale were set at each table, full for the people to dip their cups into. After the tables were served, the men in robes joined in the feasting.

"Are these the brothers that live at the villa?" Elanor asked.

"Yes, that one there," Merlin said. He pointed to a bald man with a white beard who dipped his cup into a bowl. He was very old and frail, patting his knee and cackling weakly at something one of the men had said.

"He looks like a funny fellow."

"His name is Balek, and he is almost as many years as I am. I knew him when he was a druid, long before he was a monk of the ways of Esu. He went to Rome to study the Christian God, then returned here to build a community of saints. He says that Esu completes the picture of the Great God. He teaches the people here, while the brothers tend the gardens of Dyved. Many of the children know how to read Latin because of Balek." Merlin stood, placing his hands on his hips he shouted, "Balek!"

The old monk's head twisted around to face Merlin, and the smile on his face grew long, "Merlin!" Balek shouted, hobbling over to meet him.

"Why haven't you come to greet me?"

"Oh, my dear brother, I am glad to see you. I did not mean to delay my greeting. Never! But, you know, I move much more slowly these days, and that bowl of ale was of higher importance." Balek laughed, reaching up to embrace Merlin, who towered over his small frame. "And this is your bride." Bowing before her, he said, "I am amazed that this man has slowed down his all-important self long enough to have found such a one. So many other people with destinies that he had to help along the way, he forgot he had one of his own." Balek grabbed Elanor's hand and leaned in. "I can see that your destiny is one large enough. The Great God shined a light on you so bright that Merlin could not walk past it. Am I right there, Merlin?"

Merlin laughed. "I think you must be."

"Let me tell you something, my one." Balek moved closer to Elanor. "It is Esu you must know if you want to know what the Great God has for you." He stared up at Merlin. "And fear and worry will lead to only more fear and worry. I've told you before, Merlin, Esu will give you life in the place of death. You will need to know this if you are not to stumble around too long in the dark. You understand, don't you? I know all your signs and the way you see. Only north points to north. You cannot find north if your stars align over the wrong horizon, eh? I am old. I have no time to mince words." He puffed out his cheeks and waved his hand. "Anyway, you are going away. I know you aim to search out the dark. You hope to find something, but this mystery is deeper and will not be easily found on the surface. I will speak to you when you return. I can see your mind needs to be cleared. I will help you then."

"You are a prophet, my wise friend."

"Eh." Balek waved his hand again to dismiss Merlin's words. "I am off. Too much food to eat, and I am already feeling tired," he mumbled as he hobbled away, ready to greet the next man in front of him.

"Do not allow his peculiar speech to fool you," Merlin said to Elanor with a laugh. "Make no mistake, his words ring true."

The sun finally set on the feast, and the fire lit everyone's faces with a dancing red light. Bethan and Beca laid curled up with their mother as Galen told stories to all who gathered. Elanor rested in Merlin's arms while she watched Galen's animated movements make shadows before the light of the great fire. It was as if the stories came alive in the flames.

He told stories of a hunter that chased a white stag into the forest and found he had fallen into the otherworld. The man was chased by ancient hounds, and later, was turned by magic into the same white stag he had been chasing. The story ended sadly. As his men came upon him, they saw only a white stag and did not know it was the hunter—so they hunted and killed him. It was a dark story with many twists and turns, and certainly none of it came out the way the listener thought it should have, but still the story made the children giggle and gasp, to the pleasure of everyone's ears.

THE SWORD

CLANG! Merlin's sword struck Elanor's, knocking it from her hand. Her elbow twisted, and pain radiated up her arm into her shoulder.

"Hold it steady!" Merlin demanded. "Tomorrow I will be leaving, and I want your stance stronger."

Elanor glared at him, rubbing her shoulder as she lifted her sword from the ground.

"I know this is difficult, but you are stronger than you think. It will just take discipline and time. Now hold out your sword and grip it properly." He positioned her thumb and fingers on the hilt. "Like this!"

Elanor breathed. Sweat had formed on her brow, and her muscles ached as she tightened up her stance. She was frustrated, though a sense of empowerment flowed through her as she swung. The sword had felt so heavy at first, but now it was steadily becoming an extension of her arm. If only her hands could hold the grip. Determined, she launched, and Merlin struck. Again, her elbow twisted, and she buckled—wrenching in pain.

"Take it up again. Take that anger and channel it."

Elanor was unsure she could handle another strike. She gazed up at Merlin imploringly.

Merlin laughed. "Alright…alright. Let's take a rest from the strike. Instead, hold your sword with the flat of the blade running across the horizon. Just hold it steady. Aim your eye at the tip and breathe."

Awkwardly, she stood strong. Her whole body trembled as each muscle worked to hold her blade.

"Gwynevere's father trained her to be battle ready. She did not shy away from battle but fought alongside her brothers to protect the people of Eire. Gwynevere had as much spirit to crush the enemy as Arthur did in the long season of Prydain's battle-ridden past. She was quick to splatter her face blue and whiten her hair with clay…Hold…hold."

Elanor bit her lip.

"Now, she sits as a high queen," Merlin continued. "When you were taken by those evil men, it would not have just been Peredur and his men who would have fought to protect you, but Gwynevere also…Now lower your sword."

Elanor gasped. She dropped the sword like a stone. Her arm fell like a dead weight to her side. She gritted her teeth as she rubbed her shoulder. "Ah…" she grunted breathlessly. "I would…have never guessed…Gwynevere was such a fierce warrior."

"It is because she is noble. She does not have to prove herself strong in this way anymore, nor does she crave the fray of battle. You can be noble and gentle but also possess the strength and bones of a warrior."

Merlin woke early, his heart aching as the morning had come for him to depart. He hated leaving Elanor, but the urgency was strong for him to discover his adversaries, if he could.

He watched as Elanor slept, deeply breathing. Laughing to himself, he thought about how hard he had worked her the day before, teaching her the art of the sword. He admired her determination to learn, especially since he had not given her much of a choice in the matter.

Her shape was lovely underneath the blanket. Her back slowly moved up and down to the rhythm of her breath. Her dark hair was tossed around, and her arm lay rested across her face. He kissed her on her tossed and messy head. Her blue eyes fluttered awake.

"Do you really have to leave?" Elanor whispered.

"I must."

She nodded, and her eyes turned fierce. "Find them...Find them, so we can crush them."

Merlin rushed to press his lips against hers, moved by the courage that rose in her voice.

The hooves of Merlin's horse beat the ground as he took the trail to Llyonesse. Two days from Dyved he drove, determined to see Marcus's village for himself. Before the village was even in his sight, he could smell the scent of damp ash. He slowed his pace, his anger prickling. A bitter taste formed on his tongue as he readied himself for what he might see.

The mist of the morning had not fully lifted when he came upon the scene. The creaking sound of unsettled wood groaned as the wind blew. The ground became black beneath him, and large burnt spikes stood alone like giant spears. These the timbers that once had formed homes and sanctuaries.

Merlin dismounted and squinted his eyes to see through the mist. He noticed movement in the distance as his eyes focused. "Hello?" he yelled, placing his hand upon the hilt of his sword. He pressed forward cautiously as the swaying shadow took form.

"Aah!" He jumped back. Disgust and fury surged through him as he focused upon the drooping bloody head on the top of a pike. Merlin spat angrily upon the ground. The sight evoked memories of the evils left behind by the Saecsans.

Eventually, the sun burned off the mist and revealed a barren blackness. Nothing had been left. Bones remained on the ground, picked clean by birds. The morbid remnant of evil made Merlin seethe. He picked some of the ash from the ground and wrapped it in a cloth. He imagined smearing it into the face of King Lugh, who had done nothing—leaving the land to rot.

Merlin kicked over debris and rustled through fragments. Voraciously, he searched for anything that could lead him to his enemy. Thoughts brooded in his mind of Elanor, still vulnerable, possibly the aim of this burning, murdering enemy. No matter where he looked, he uncovered nothing but ash and decay. He did not want to look where the bodies laid, stripped of life, but he refused to leave any stone unturned.

As he stepped forward, he felt a lump under his foot. Assuming it was just a rock, Merlin moved to continue, but he felt compelled to look back. A small, smooth stone lay smashed into the ground, strung to a strap of leather.

Merlin peeled it from the ground and wiped it free of the black mud that clung to it. The stone was white and contained markings on one side. The same odd patternless scratches he had seen inside the yellow hooded cloak. He rolled the wicked thing into his hand. It was something. Something that might prove to be helpful.

Discovering nothing else, Merlin left for the Caer of Llyonesse to confront King Lugh and surmise what he could from him. It was another day's ride before Merlin arrived at the gates. Mysteriously, the gates stood wide open, with no guards standing watch. He trotted in slowly. The houses in the Caer were eerily quiet. An unsettling feeling weighed heavy as he continued toward the stone tower Lugh governed from. He would have thought the town abandoned had he not begun to see heads popping out from around corners and behind doorways.

Why are they hiding? Who are they afraid of?

Merlin arrived at the tower door and climbed down from his horse. The first sign of life was a warrior running to meet him, his hands free of any weapons.

"Merlin?" he called in a hopeful voice.

"It is Merlin. Who is it that calls for me?"

The warrior approached, gasping for breath. "I...I am Elian, lord," he said breathlessly, bowing low. "You would not know me, but I know you. I am battle chief of Llyonesse. I faithfully fought for Arthur during the great Saecsan battles. I am loyal still."

"Why do the people hide? Where are the Cymbrogi protecting this citadel?"

Elian shook his head. "No, lord. Not here," he said, holding up his hand to silence him. He peered over his shoulder as if expecting to find something behind him. "I am relieved to see it is true, that the Emrys has indeed returned to us. King Lu..." He stopped and straightened uneasily. Then, he whispered, "These days are dark..." Elian's eyes nervously danced around. "I hope you have come to help us. I cannot say more."

Elian's words disturbed Merlin. *How twisted these lands have become?*

"Why has no one come to Caer Lial for aid?"

Elian shook his head.

"I am here to see Lugh. Where is he?"

Elian led him forward through the doorways, into the Hall, then quietly bowed to dismiss himself, swiftly leaving the chamber.

The Hall was grey and empty. No warmth of hearth, nor tables set for feasting. A lone throne sat in the center, tall and ashen. These halls had forever been dank and bitter, but never had Merlin seen them so devoid of life. He wait-ed for a sign of anyone, feeling the creepiness of the empty hall, waiting on edge like he had been trapped. No one entered the room.

"Lugh!" Merlin called. His echo bounced off the walls with no reply.

Finally, out from the dark recesses of a doorway, a woman dressed in finery slowly emerged. "King Lugh is indisposed," she said, keeping her distance. "I am his queen. You may speak with me."

"What has the king so afraid that he refuses to speak with me?"

"Oh, no…You misunderstand. He does not refuse to speak with you. No…he just…he is not here."

Merlin grunted, then shouted, "Lugh! Do not leave me waiting. Why have you not taken care of your people? What is this darkness that has infected your lands? LUGH!" The force of Merlin's voice shook the walls, and the queen covered her ears.

A crooked, stringy-haired man wearing a dirty, animal skin robe ambled out from the doorway, his hands gripping his chest. "How dare you disturb me," he chided. "Why do you come here, Merlin? I owe you none of my loyalty."

Merlin's mouth twisted. "You are a lesser king before the Highness of Caer Lial. What do you say of your lands?"

"Hah! Gwynevere has commanded no fealty from me. These are *my* lands and *my* people."

"Your people have been murdered and their lands destroyed."

Lugh cackled. "What nonsense. Lies. Lies."

Merlin stared deeply at the king, trying to discern if Lugh had gone mad or if he was just hiding something. Out from his pocket, Merlin retrieved the ashes he had collected from Marcus's village. Uncovering them, he sprinkled the dust upon the floor. "This is all that remains of a settlement on the northern tip of Llyonesse—your lands. Its chieftain's head has been left on a pike."

"Lies."

"Your people sought your help and you gave them none."

"Lies…Lies…Lies. None of my people have asked for aid, and there are none in need."

"Why is your own Caer left afraid? They didn't dare leave their houses as I approached. Where are your warriors?"

"This Caer is on my lands," Lugh seethed, peering at Merlin ominously from under his brow. "You have no business here, Great Merlin of Caer Lial. The

Pendragon is dead. Did you think you could come back here and demand my allegiance? It is as it was before the Pendragons ruled, and my lands have been well kept. You speak nothing but lies."

"Bah!" Merlin threw the remaining ashes at the king's feet. "I may not be able to call you to account this day, but that day is coming." Merlin turned to leave but halted in his tracks. "Who is it you have made a deal with? Who do you allow to poison you?"

"There is no one who lords over me. Not even you, all powerful Merlin," said the king, a nauseating smile upon his lips.

Merlin knew he would extract no answers from Lugh, and he rode out of the gates of Caer Llyonesse in a fury. This obstinate king would let his lands crumble and do nothing to protect them. One thing Merlin knew for sure: King Lugh had not lost his mind. He was aware of the darkness defiling his lands and made no effort to intervene, for whatever reason. Perhaps he had made a deal— or at least, had convinced himself he had, for likely he was nothing more than a pawn. King Lugh was surely not the source of the evil.

36

BALEK'S GARDEN

Merlin rode straight through to Dyved without stopping. He needed more answers, but at least had collected more information on the sickness of the Southlands. However, the enemy had evaded giving him a true sense of anything, yet again.

He would search for answers as a druid and seek any signs he could derive. In the stillness of the night, Merlin rode up behind the plateau and into the forest to find a high rock that had been an old friend to him. It was in this kind of place, within the deep silence, where he often heard the voice of wisdom. In every breath of air or groaning sound of the trees existed the possibility he might find the voice he was listening for.

In the days of Arthur, Merlin would steal away until he had wisdom or understanding. Always there came a revelation or a whisper, but now, all was silent. No wisdom, no understanding, not even an awen had come to him for many years. With Elanor, there had been moments of sight, but they did not bring answers, only more questions. Grwyrthrhodd had said he would see again, but nothing of that promise had materialized.

The breeze picked up as the sun rose. The sweet scents of honey and pine floated through the air, reminding him of Elanor. Exhausted, and with no revelations to be found, Merlin shook his head and climbed down from his rock.

He hiked back down the hill, pulling his horse behind him. Now he longed to return so he could throw his arms around his beloved.

As Merlin headed back through the wood, he saw along the path the small, fragile frame of Balek leaning on his staff.

"Merlin!" Balek panted, waving his arm in the air. "I have come to find you!"

Merlin quickened his pace to meet him on the lane. "How did you know I had returned? Has something happened?"

"Heh! Look at you skip and run like a boy in his thirties, while I huff and puff up this path to find you. I tell you; I will have much to tell the Great God about this injustice when I finally see his face," Balek wheezed, trying to catch his breath.

"Please." Merlin escorted him over to a flat rock, just off the path. "Rest yourself. You have found me now."

"Yes, well, I must speak to you. I saw you in my heart as you sat up on your rock with your mind full of questions. The Great God led me to see you." Balek patted Merlin's knee. "You want to see again, but your mind is too full. It is not your heart that's the problem. Your heart is full of love, and that can never hinder sight. It's fear…so much fear." Balek leaned his head onto his staff, collecting himself; he sighed to catch his breath.

"That is exactly my plight," Merlin said, raising an eyebrow in surprise. "The druid within you still perceives."

"Hah!" Balek laughed. "That is a yes and a no and is exactly your problem. Things are changing, Merlin, and your eyes are becoming new. Listen," Balek said, shaking his head, "you can't go up a mountain asking so many questions. You want to know about the dark evil. You want to know about the mystery of your bride. You want to know about the prophecy. Maybe you don't see and hear because you want to know something that the Great God isn't speaking, and darkness wants to take hold of you and confuse your mind. You are too used to your signs. Stripped of all your old ways, you cannot perceive. The Great God will use signs of sky and earth, but your paradigm must shift."

"I do not understand."

"Of course you don't." Balek slapped Merlin on the forehead. "Listen to me. There is more to the Great God. He is the one behind all that is happening. I can see His hand upon you. He was with Arthur, and He led you in those times also, but Arthur misunderstood and sought Him in the image of the cup. The old ways kept his eyes blind, and they're blinding you as well. The Great One has removed those old ways of the past. Can't you see? These evil ones fight to keep them, and if you want this new kingdom to come, then it cannot come with old ways."

"You speak more in riddles than I do, old man."

"Shush! Listen! I will tell you a story. Long ago, there was a man named Saul. He thought he knew the right way. He went forth in all his righteousness, destroying all men who did not align with his right way. He thought his way was the way of his God, and that he was doing a holy service. But then, there came a simple prophet who spoke a good word, telling of a New Way. Saul would not listen; he still had too much of his old knowledge keeping him from hearing or perceiving. He watched as angry men stoned this prophet to death, glad that his words had been silenced. Pious he was in his rightness. One day, as he was traveling, a bright light appeared before him. This light produced a brightness so piercing; it was more than the light of the enaids of the otherworld."

Merlin was reminded of the awen that had come upon him that day when Elanor first arrived in Caer Lial. He remembered her touching him, and how he had seen in the vision the man in blue. That was the first time he had seen him. The light that radiated from him made Merlin feel like he had known nothing, and the contrast of the light was so great that it humbled him.

Balek continued, "The light revealed that Saul's actions were not in accordance with the Great God's righteousness, but in accordance with his own. Saul's heart broke because of all the wrong he had done, and as the light lifted, it left his eyes blind. He could no longer see the path before him. He needed a new path, a new direction, and new eyes. As Saul repented to this New Way, his sight was eventually returned to him." Balek placed the top of his staff over Merlin's heart. "You are like Saul. You are blind, but you are blind only because you do not recognize that the path you must take is different. The path has already been opened to you, but you do not have understanding. You and that daughter of Prydain are on new ground. Truly, both of you are still in the dark, but with each new day, your vision is clearing."

Merlin pondered a moment, then said, "I have seen a man in blue. In my awen he has appeared before me. Do you know of him?"

"Aah! He is leading you already. He will likely lead you to himself when it is time."

"I have always found the answers myself, but since I have seen him, my answers seem to come through others, but frequently not the answers to the questions I am asking."

"Maybe you are asking the wrong questions. Maybe your questions should align with the last answers you received."

Balek's words travelled through Merlin's mind at the speed of light, knocking loose what he thought he knew—aligning the pieces in his mind. Merlin replied, "What is the new path?"

"Precisely, Merlin the wise. The way you are going on in this new world, you cannot solely rely upon yourself, but must lean more on others. Elanor will help you do that. Now," Balek said, smacking his lips, "I am tired. Take me back to my garden. I think you will find the delicate hands of your mother and wife tending to it."

Merlin lifted Balek up by his arm. Setting him upon his horse, he walked from the shady darkness of the wood out into the shining, crisp air. The weight Merlin had been carrying seemed lighter after their conversation. He felt as though he had drunk from a spring—his whole body and mind brightened.

"Thank you, Balek…for finding me. The Great God indeed had purpose in it."

"Well, sometimes it is good to do the finding while others are still looking."

Merlin laughed and shook his head. The old man was as sharp as a knife with his riddled words.

They arrived at the garden where Elanor and Adhan were joyfully up to their elbows in dirt. Merlin's heart lifted at the sight of them.

"Merlin!" Without hesitation, Elanor leapt up and rushed into his arms. She repeatedly kissed him as he pulled her close. Merlin laughed as he gazed at his lovely noble lady. Dirt was smudged across her forehead, and her hair was frizzy from the activity.

Setting Elanor down, he turned to embrace Adhan.

"What news?" Elanor began. "Did you see anything?"

"The Southlands have become ill, and the mind of Lugh twisted. There is no bringing him to repentance. His own Caer was full of disease, fearful and decaying. I couldn't find much to go on, but we now have more than we did before. Gwynevere will need to deal with Lugh, but it is essential," Merlin said, turning to Adhan, "that King Cormach returns, else I fear for these lands, and Dyved."

CAER MYRDDIN

While Merlin had been away, Elanor spent her time with Adhan in the garden with the brothers of the villa. Elanor loved getting her hands dirty, picking all the beautiful green lettuces, carrots, and strawberries. There were even lovely bunches of radishes, turnips, and onions. It reminded her of her father's garden and how she used to help him pick all the pesky weeds that sprouted, attempting to take over the beautiful vegetables.

She loved watching Adhan touch every root and green leaf, as if her touch released a magic to make them grow. They laughed joyfully together as the sun warmed their backs and dirt smudged their faces. Elanor didn't feel useless here. Here, she had a place, and her worth was acknowledged. She wasn't just the girl that dropped out of the sky. She was Elanor, wife of Merlin, who was son of this Caer of Dyved.

Now that Merlin had returned, the two women set to work in the kitchen, preparing the bounty of vegetables. Turnips, carrots, and onions went into a chicken stew. Adhan peeled the turnips while Elanor diced them. Elanor had never spent time in a kitchen with her mother. She realized just how lonely a life she had spent. So many years of solitude. She had become so used to it that she never felt there was anything wrong until the light of all her friends in this world exposed it.

Sitting with Adhan, working together in this way, made Elanor feel what it must be like when a family prepares a special meal at Christmas. The laughter and the smell of good food cooking. The satisfaction of having created something for the whole family to enjoy. Adhan felt like a mother should. Warm, inviting, and unconditional.

"Adhan?" Elanor asked. "Why was this place called Caer Myrddin?"

Adhan stopped peeling her turnip, looking at Elanor with slight apprehension. "It was so named after my son, but the reason is long in the telling. The short of the story is that he was king of the lands long ago."

"King?" Elanor stopped her work, her eyes wide.

"Yes, king. But he was for only a very short time. He was barely a man in those days. The King Cormach and his son Cormach have watched over me these many years, given me this place to live, because I was the wife of the elder Cormach's father. He was not Merlin's father, but he loved me, and so I married him long after my love had died. He was a kind and loving husband, and a good king. He was King Murrian, and he ruled from this villa in peace." Adhan looked deeply at Elanor. "Has Merlin told you of Ganieda?"

"Ganieda?"

"She was his first love."

"He has, but I never knew her name."

"Merlin loved Ganieda and aimed to marry her. Murrian wanted Merlin to be established and have something to offer his bride, so he gave him a portion of his lands. Murrian gave Merlin the portion below and gave his son this plateau. He treated Merlin as his second son. But…" Adhan's eyes drifted. "Those were such unstable times. Saecsans invaded our Caer. The battle to defend Dyved lasted weeks. In the end, Merlin had slain so many that the Saecsans became afraid. They feared he was a sorcerer of unstoppable power, and they retreated."

"Sadly, as the dust cleared—King Murrian was found slain. The warriors brought Merlin back, lifted high upon their shoulders. In their eyes, the victory had been because of him. Once upon the doorsteps of this very villa, the warriors cast their swords before Merlin and placed their foreheads and cheeks upon his feet, honoring him as their new king.

"The young Cormach also bowed before Merlin, trading his lands for Merlin's. Merlin became the inheritor as an elder son, and Cormach as the younger. But his kingship was to be short lived.

"Ganieda waited a year for Merlin while he rode the lands, strengthening his name. Finally, the day before the wedding had come. Merlin and his men went hunting for the wedding feast. Upon returning, they saw smoke rising from the plateau. The Saecsans had returned once more, waiting strategically for Merlin's absence, knowing the Caer would be at its weakest without him."

"Unprepared, the warriors of Dyved did not have time to defend against the invaders. Severed heads laid scattered on the ground, ready to be set on pikes. The Saecsans had taken Ganieda, along with other maids, and brutally raped and murdered them." Adhan's chin quivered, and she dropped her head. "I will never forget the scream that rose from Merlin's throat that day. It was as though the trees shook in response to him. The Saecsans panicked and broke rank at the sound of him. Merlin charged in with fire in his eyes."

"This gave rise to the warriors of Dyved to fight back; the tide shifted so quickly that the enemy hadn't the time to collect themselves. It was as if a mighty ocean wave had come and slammed into the invaders, washing them away in red. The battle ended, and every last Saecsan laid in their own blood.

"When the battle cleared, Merlin was gone and did not return. The young Cormach rose up in his place, so naming the Plateau Caer Myrddin, and the valley below Dyved, in honor of Merlin. It was a deep time of sadness. I could not stay in Dyved, as it pained my heart to remain. It was not until years later that I returned."

A tear fell from Elanor's eye. She had hoped for a more triumphant history for Merlin's namesake of Caer Myrddin. She sat quietly while her knife moved up and down through the turnips. "I am sorry," she said finally. "I understand now, why Merlin was not eager to tell the tale. Where did he go after he left Dyved?"

"That he has never told me. I only know that he did not return until the sons of Prydain, Aurelias and Uther, returned to take back the throne from the evil King Vortigern. He returned with a spark in his golden eyes and destiny in the palm of his hand."

"I am sorry if I asked too much in the telling of the story."

"My daughter, this is now your history, as you are now part of him. It is a story that you should know. The torc that still lies wrapped around Merlin's neck is the very torc he was given as king of Dyved. Soon, the torc that rests around your neck will also tell a story, and it will be one intertwined with that of my son. One of destiny. My son was not meant to be king. He is a king-maker. And poor, sweet Ganieda would not have been able to be wife to such a man—it would have destroyed her in time. But you, Elanor, are an equal in your portion and destiny. I can see it in those blue eyes. That same strange magic that resides within my son. Never has there been anyone for my son, other than you." She pointed her knife at Elanor. "You are the reed that will bend, but not break."

Soon the stew was ready, and Merlin, Balek, and all the brothers gathered in the main hall of the villa to eat at the long table. The stew was much enjoyed, filling Merlin's emptiness with its warmth. The darkness of the previous days stung a little less as the evening turned to the brothers' joyful story telling.

Balek's eyes were becoming like dark, sunken shadows. Merlin moved to sit beside him, just as Elanor burst into rolling laughter in response to a story.

"Her laugher is like a bird song," Balek said, in a tired, stretched voice. "Pleasant to hear as it tickles your ears."

"It is very much like that," Merlin replied. "Balek? You look weary. Can I take you to your bed?"

"I would like that very much, but let us just wait. A few more stories. I do so love how my brothers are when they have an audience. And Elanor and Adhan are so wonderfully attentive to all their happy tellings."

"Yes, my friend," Merlin replied. Something was amiss as he quietly watched Balek. He appeared worn and weary; much more than the tiredness of old age.

Balek remained steadfast until even the animated brothers themselves were beginning to quiet. Through the wide-open doors, the crickets chirped, and the wind blew a serene, hushing sound.

Balek patted Merlin's back. "Now I am ready. Let us slip away quietly; I do not want to make a fuss." Merlin supported him as Balek leaned on his arms and they quietly crept out into the hallway. "Will you lead me out to my garden? I want to gaze at it in the quiet glow of night."

Merlin nodded, continuing to the garden and bringing him to stand in its full view.

Balek sighed. "Ah, look there." He pointed to a small movement amongst the lettuce. "It is a wee rabbit." He laughed. "Mm…let him be. We have proven there is more than enough to share in this bounty." Quietly, he watched the rabbit scurry for a while, and then nodded.

Merlin wrapped his arm about him and led him on.

A small bed with a single blanket, a chair, and a table, were all that sat inside Balek's tiny chamber. Merlin gently removed Balek's shoes and outer robe, then supported him down into his bed. He scooted the chair next to Balek's bedside, knowing the old man was not ready for him to leave.

Balek reached for Merlin's hand and patted it feebly. "I am ready to go now," he said in a low, confident whisper. "My life is going from me, and I am ready to see my Lord."

"I understand."

"Esu is calling my name, and my heart yearns to see him."

"You have been my friend for many long years," Merlin said, clearing his throat as emotions pushed through. "I remember you, Balek. I remember the young filidh that was hungry for knowledge. Fervently, you sought understanding. I will never forget when the druids of Eire taught us of the treasure of the triple God and the great signs they had seen. Their words were like fire. It produced such a ripple in the Order of Druids that it broke us apart at the seams. But you were not bothered, choosing to travel away with Phineas and go to Rome—giving your life to this New Way. Such brightness was in your eyes. It was as though the very light of the sun had flooded them. You were a determined young man, with your woolly red hair."

Balek chuckled lightly in response.

Merlin asked, "Did you find your answers in Rome, Balek, my friend?"

"Rome had nothing to fill me, as the Great God of glory already had. I knew I would be better used here. And as these lands became more unstable, I was able to help and heal. Remember what I said to you, Myrddin."

"I will not forget it."

"Good. Good. The brothers will be prepared for this, and all will be well. I will rest now," Balek said, closing his eyes and breathing softly.

"Rest," Merlin soothed, placing his hand on his shoulder. He quietly blessed Balek as he slept. Several hours passed, and finally, Merlin fell asleep in the nook of his arm.

By morning, when Merlin awoke, Balek had truly gone. He had become still and breathless. His life had gone in the night. Merlin wiped his eyes as tears came into them, and he leaned down and kissed Balek's fragile hand.

"Sleep well, my friend. Your morning is surely much brighter, and your gardens more bountiful now you are waking on the other side."

THE TIME FOR LEAVING

Adhan's tears drifted down her cheeks. The songs of the brothers rang high above the roaring fire of the funeral pyre, rings of smoke unfurling into the sky.

"He has been part of this place for so long," Adhan said. "So many go away and never come back. I am glad he is resting now. Lately his face seemed strained. I could not be selfish and wish that he would go on forever. I know that he was happy he was given the chance to see Merlin again."

As Adhan spoke, Elanor watched her in awe; she noticed how Adhan's silver tears matched her silver hair that blew gracefully by her face. Her eyes had the ages of the world behind them, and her voice, deep and lofty. How could she and Merlin be? How had time lost such a wondrous race? Even now, only Merlin and his mother remained, but maybe there were more hidden amongst the folk of Prydain. People in her future time would not have been able to recognize the gift that they were, but here in this slower time, they could still be seen.

This world was harsh and unforgiving, yet it was quieter. The chaos of the world still existed, but in a way that was not so close and stifling. People here were satisfied with a song and a story. They were satisfied with a dance and a fire and delighted at the return of those who had been far from them. Nothing was taken for granted. Even a life was properly remembered, and the words spoken of those lost were brimming with purpose.

Elanor thought of all the words that had no meaning. The loudness of the people of her future time. The endless babble of opinion, and all the rhetoric. All just so one could hear themselves and feel important. Was that the future this would all build to? Grace and majesty forgotten.

A pang of sadness struck Elanor's heart to know that one day, Adhan would be no longer, and all her beauty, grace, and wisdom would be gone. She felt fortunate to be one of only a few to have seen her, known her, and be loved by her.

The next morning, a chill hung in the air, and Elanor found Merlin standing at the edge of the plateau, leaning against a crooked tree. The tree was dead and leafless, twisted and knobbed.

Men bustled by, sending wagons down to the wheat fields. They had grown tall and golden, ready for harvest. Elanor stood on the edge to watch the wind blow through it in ripples. Her eyes caught a fox dash into the wheat. Its trail parted the grass as it darted through, causing little birds to fly out.

Merlin appeared watchful and grave.

Elanor asked him, "What is it?"

"Oh…" Merlin was shaken out of his hard stare. "The men are preparing the fields. They will be harvesting soon."

Elanor's spirits sank. "We will be leaving soon then."

"We cannot wait for the weather to turn. I am needed to report back to Gwynevere all that I have seen."

"I wish we did not have to leave."

Merlin gazed at her, feeling the same ache. "You know we cannot stay."

"Can we not?" she asked, her eyes earnest. However, she recognized what she already knew. "Leaving Adhan will be difficult."

"I am pleased that my mother has come to mean so much to you," he said with a pained smile. "I always feel my heart ache when I have to leave her sight. She knows the time of leaving is near, and I know she does not desire it either."

"How soon?"

"We will have tomorrow, and then we must leave."

Merlin's words made the sweetness of the morning turn into sorrow.

"Though something else troubles me." He pointed out beyond the fields, directing Elanor's eye toward a distant forest. At first, she saw nothing, but then, out from the covering of pine trees came a large raven flying straight at them. It flew swiftly, and Elanor crouched to avoid it as it alighted beside them on the dead tree.

The raven tapped at the branch with its talons, then leaned its head down and cawed loudly. Then it flew back down into the forest and disappeared. The ominous sight of the bird left Elanor with a deep, sinking feeling.

Merlin gazed at Elanor from the corner of his eye. "This raven has been flying from this tree to the forest since I came at the rising of the sun." He clicked his tongue between his teeth. "Balek dies, and now I begin to see the signs."

"What does it mean?"

"Ravens are harbingers of warning. They confide in those they deem worthy, and often seek to protect. I have been pondering this all morning. There is something unwell and dark before us. We cannot linger here. If we do, the darkness may come to Dyved, but if we leave, we may meet it along our path."

"What do we do?" Elanor said, set on edge by Merlin's warning.

"We heed the omen of our dear blessed raven, and we do not set out unaware. We must travel carefully." Then he encouraged, "You and I both have strength enough."

Merlin's words did not shake the unsettled feeling of foreboding that rose within her. "If we are being warned, shouldn't we flee somewhere else?" As Elanor spoke, the raven returned, flying out over the fields before landing as before, cawing loudly.

"We are not being shown this to fear." He turned, squaring her to stare him in the eye. "Look at me, Elanor. You have the fortitude. Signs like these are revealed to give us strategy, not doom. We must be careful how we discern signs and prophecy. They are not always as they seem. They are sign posts. Often those who receive them are the ones called upon to have the answers. We cannot fear, though I know I do...Peer out across this wide plain and into that forest. Ask the questions that you need answers to. If you can look into a person's eyes and see the truth about them, then you can look at a landscape and know what is to be seen."

Elanor glanced across the plain and held her breath. So many emotions and thoughts ran through her. They were about to abandon their safety to enter the folds of darkness. She took a deep breath and reached out for Merlin's hand.

"Close your eyes," Merlin soothed. "As I look out and see this raven, at first, I felt fear and I wanted to recoil, but then I reminded myself that the raven's call is to protect. The Great God has made us aware, and awareness is a powerful weapon."

As he spoke, Elanor's unnerving dream returned to her. The dove resting in Merlin's hands. The sensation of falling. This was how she felt now, standing on the edge of the plateau.

She wanted to hide away in Dyved forever. How did Merlin know the darkness would come to Dyved if they stayed? What if he was wrong? But she knew the hooded men were ruthless. If there was even a chance that they could regroup and come here, she would not risk it. This beautiful place, Galen, Ffion and their beautiful daughters. Adhan and the whole of the village left vulnerable without their king.

She yearned for another way, but Merlin's words rang true.

"We have been given our time here, and now the season is changing," Merlin said knowingly.

Elanor's eyes shot open, and there was a boldness in them. The raven cawed loudly from the branch overhead. "We will have tomorrow, and then we will go."

Merlin smiled proudly. He wrapped his arms tightly around her and kissed her sweetly on the mouth. "There you are, Gwenddydd."

Together they headed back to the villa.

Adhan watched as they approached. The heaviness of their steps and the expression on her son's face told her all. She placed her hand on his chest. "You are leaving?" she asked with deep sadness. "I knew it must be time, though I did not long for it. When?"

"The day after tomorrow's end."

"It is true…" Adhan nodded sorrowfully. "You must go before the season changes. Lughnasadh is already upon us. It is time for you to depart before the cold weather comes." She reached across to Elanor, pulling her into her arms.

Galen and Ffion had prepared the village for a final day of feasting before Merlin and Elanor's departure. The village was abuzz as people baked and cooked, preparing for the meal of the evening.

Elanor and Adhan joined Ffion warming the ovens and baking bread, with both Beca and Bethan running around their heels.

"I caught you!" Beca exclaimed, capturing Bethan from behind Elanor's legs.

Ffion was full of her usual delightful sass, and Elanor enjoyed every last moment she spent with each of them, knowing that the morning would not be as sweet as this.

Elanor happily carried out one of her handmade loaves to set out on the table. Her eyes were captured by Efa, who sat silently. Her heart twinged.

"Adhan?" Elanor asked. "I wonder..."

Adhan approached, standing beside her.

"Could I go to Efa? Could I speak to her?"

"Of course," Adhan said curiously. "What is within your heart, daughter?"

"I wonder...I thought maybe..."

"You want to see if you can heal her?"

"Maybe," Elanor admitted reluctantly. "I don't know if I can, but..."

"It is a good desire, Elanor. It has been in my heart to see her healed for many years. Even in the days she would still speak, I hoped and prayed to set her free. I don't think it is ever good to stop trying, and I do not think that it is wrong that you would like to try now. Come, I will take you to her."

Adhan bent down beside Efa, who sat despondent. Adhan's presence brought no response.

"Efa? This is Elanor. She is a friend of your son...Cilaen. She is soon returning to him and would like to tell him of his mother."

Adhan nodded to Elanor, inviting her to speak. "He-hello, Efa. Your son is brilliant. He has taught me to speak the language of the Cymry. He has been a brother to me...he saved my life. I am very grateful to know him. You would be proud."

Efa's eyes remained glazed, staring off.

Elanor paused, wondering if she should continue.

Adhan nodded encouragingly.

Elanor boldly reached up, touching Efa's cheek. She willed the healing magic to come, and her eyes flashed bright blue. She felt the magic lightly release through her hands, then sat back to see if anything had changed.

Efa's eyes slowly came into focus, and she noticed Elanor.

Their eyes locked, and Elanor saw what was within them. Her heart became heavy and sick with despair. A flooding sound of tears and oppressive dark clouds attacked Elanor's mind. Inside Efa's thoughts, Elanor saw her crying and screaming in despair.

Elanor ran to her and yelled back into the echoing nightmare, "I can help you! Take my hand! I can heal you!" Over and over she yelled, in hopes that

Efa would hear her. She got down on her knees and settled right in front of Efa's face. "I can help you!"

Efa looked up, her face angry and wild. She grabbed Elanor's wrist, as all else stilled around them, and said, "NO!" Her shout was so final and shocking that Elanor found herself falling backwards, and then…

Elanor came back to herself and found she was sitting in front of Efa, still gazing into her eyes. Slowly Efa's eyes unlocked from Elanor's, and she drifted back into nothingness, unresponsive. Elanor fell back on the ground, overwhelmed by the experience. A tear fell from her eye.

"What happened?" Adhan asked, anxiously lifting Elanor from the ground. Efa sat, unmoved, solid as stone.

"I could see…I could feel her pain and her despair. I have never seen into a heart so shattered and broken. I was there, and I told her I could help her. I knew I could, but…she didn't want it. She did not want to be healed. She wanted her pain instead." Elanor's mouth hung open, pondering how anyone could willfully choose pain.

"She chose, long ago, to disappear into her pain. It is as if she feels her pain is keeping the memory of her husband alive."

Elanor breathed out in disbelief.

"All of us have chosen pain, at times, over freedom. I know when I lost Merlin's father, I thought I could not go on…but the look of my baby's bright, golden eyes reminded me that I needed to fight through my grief. It is hard to see someone consumed by sadness. I had hoped Efa would find the strength to heal. I still hope, but there is no use trying to help someone that does not want it. I am glad that you wanted to try, and you should not carry the weight of her sadness."

"I wanted…so much…to tell Cilaen that his mother was well."

"Ah, well. Cilaen has given up his anger over the loss of his mother a long time ago. We will keep serving her as we do, and I will never stop praying that she will come out of her cave of despair."

Elanor imagined someone drowning in a lake, with an oar extended to help pull them out, but they choose to sink into the depths and drown. The thought was foreign to her, but, as Adhan had said, many people have moments, however small, where they choose to drown.

"Let us not spare another minute on Efa's unending grief."

Elanor could only agree. Still her heart ached for Efa as she followed Adhan back to carry out more bread.

Soon the meat was ready, and all the food was brought. Everyone ate happily together, their laughter ringing through the air. Elanor's heart would feel a little emptier leaving this happy, warm place, yet her heart had begun to long for Gwynevere, Cilaen, and Samara. She missed Bedwyr's flashy smile, and even Peredur's lumbering glare.

The sound of Dyved bubbled up in Elanor's heart as she laid down to sleep in the villa for the last time. She curled up next to Merlin, hoping that the morning would wait a while longer before coming.

Merlin woke to the sound of little voices giggling through the open balcony. He rose and peered through the linens. Beca and Bethan ran through the courtyard, while Elanor awaited with her hands cupped for the tiny, handpicked flowers.

The girls beamed as Elanor wove the flowers together to form two small crowns. Soon the little daisies would be gone—the cold sending them into hiding. And soon, he and Elanor would be gone, headed back to the land that needed them.

"Do you hear that ruckus outside?" Merlin asked with a smile as he bounded down the stairs to Adhan.

"It is a most joyful ruckus." Adhan grinned at her son, busily wrapping food for their journey home. She placed the bundles to be loaded into satchels. "The horses have been readied."

"All has been done then. I fear the hardest part will be pulling my wife away. She would stay here forever if she could."

"Yes," Adhan said longingly. "I would have you both stay if that was the right choice."

"I am sorry I stayed away so long."

"My son, I knew being your mother meant I would have to let you go. Twice I thought I had lost you forever, yet here you stand." She grabbed Merlin's neck and pulled him down to her. "I will miss you with my whole heart." Adhan kissed his forehead and tussled his hair.

His hair now a mess, Merlin leaned against the open door, watching Elanor kiss the girls goodbye before they padded home to their mother, decorated in flowers.

Elanor remained where she sat, watching the girls run down the lane.

"Elanor?" Merlin prompted.

Her shoulders winced.

"It is nearly time."

She dropped her head. With a sigh, she gradually stood.

Merlin grabbed hold of her hand. "We will return."

She smiled up at him mournfully. "I am ready."

Together they went to gather the horses and found Adhan was already leading them out with Galen. Elanor released Merlin's hand and ran to Adhan, embracing her. Adhan let her cheek rest against Elanor's, squeezing her tightly.

"We will see each other once more," Adhan said, reaching out to grab Merlin's chin, while still holding Elanor close. "Take care of my daughter." She kissed his cheek, and then brushed his forehead with her fingers.

As Galen and Merlin said their goodbyes, Elanor reluctantly pulled herself away. She did not want to leave the only mother that had ever loved her. But placing one foot in front of the other, she moved toward her horse. Adhan grabbed Elanor's hand as it laid against her horse's neck and walked beside them as it slowly strode closer to the plateau's edge.

Many had gathered to see them off as they finally reached the precipice. Adhan's eyes flooded with tears. Her chin quivered as she patted Merlin's leg.

Reluctantly, they descended, riding out past the wheat fields. Silently and steadfast past the hills and into the forest. Back the way they had come.

OMEN OF DARKNESS

"We have eyes on them, my lord. Merlin was followed from Llyonesse. He and the bright one have left Dyved and are returning to Care Lial."

"That meddlesome druid. Lugh is mine—these lands are mine. Merlin has no authority here. My eye is upon him. That blue witch must be killed." A sinister gleam sparked in his eyes, and he asked, "Which road will they take?"

The raven's warning burned in the back of their minds as they wove their way through the forest. They spent the night on the forest's edge and rode out early toward the high rocky cliff, but as they neared the river, Merlin paused.

"What is it?"

"I am wondering whether we should continue this way," Merlin mused, gazing across at the tall cliff. "We must be wise. That way is more direct, but it leads us through open lands. If we go west and then north, it will take us through thickly wooded lands—keeping us hidden from spying eyes, if our enemies are on our path. Though it is a road less traveled and would make our trek more difficult."

"If you think going west would be a safer route, then I think we should take it."

Merlin looked to the west, then back up at the cliff. He pondered up at the sky, as if waiting for an answer. Reluctant, he said, "I am not confident west will be safer." He turned a circle as he mulled over the choice. Finally, he pulled alongside Elanor. "We go west."

"Right then," Elanor assured. "We go west. Come what may, we have at least made our choice."

He nodded, eyeing the trail warily. "Then let us be off and get as much distance as we can before nightfall."

The plain they rode upon was yellow with pine and shrub. It took most of the day, but the landscape slowly became more mountainous. A shield grew around them as the density of the trees increased.

"See those two hills?" Merlin pointed in their direction. "We will need to go between them. It may take us a day or two, but we will find a small fishing village not far on the other side. It will give us lodging and a ferry across the river. A larger Caer exists, just west from that village, that harbors the sea. The home of another Southernly king. We will not go there. The smaller settlement will be a fine enough place, as it is a well-travelled route for sojourners crossing the river."

They did not make it to the forested valley before nightfall, but early the next morning, they quickly found themselves in its midst. The trees were close, with no sign of a path. Once they had pressed their way in, the air hung stale and lifeless. It was not long before Elanor hoped for open sky and fresh wind. Old and twisted, the forest smelt of rotten wood.

The deeper they went, the more uneasy Elanor felt. As night fell, the forest was devoid of night birds calling or crickets singing. Unnaturally it sat, silent and still. The only resonate sound was the deep creaking of the trees, their groans making them seem alive with ominous thoughts.

The next day, the horses raked through bumpy, uneven ground. Soon it became too challenging to navigate on horseback, so they dismounted and walked along on foot. The travel was unending, with little progress. It was all too soon that the sun began to set. The failing light made it hard to see through the thick trees, and they resigned for the night.

Merlin placed his finger to his lips, signaling for Elanor to keep her silence. He felt someone might be listening, lurking in the dark corners around them. An awareness of something more in the dark forest filled him with foreboding.

Elanor did not want to mention the creeping feeling, for she feared her words would make it become real. Leaning into Merlin, she shivered quietly in the cold, humid air. She sought comfort, but there was none to be found.

Chapter Thirty - Nine

Neither of them found sleep in the dark wood. Anxiously, they waited for the sun to rise. Staying in one place for too long seemed an unwise choice.

In the dark morning they pushed forward, walking slowly on foot. Once the sun was high enough to see, they risked getting back on their horses and moved cautiously, always watchful in the dank, grey emptiness between the trees.

"We are not alone," Merlin whispered. "I hope I have not led us astray. You must stay close to me. Something stills this forest and makes it strange. Stay on your guard and pay attention to where I lead."

Merlin strove to move quickly, but he struggled to find direction. Confusion clouded his mind. An unnatural weariness tempted them to surrender to sleep.

"It is witchcraft," Merlin warned. "Do not shut your eyes or give in to the false lullaby."

Elanor gazed longingly at the ground. It looked like a soft blanket that would surround her with its dark, dense arms. It was as if she were trudging through mud up to her knees, even though solid ground was beneath her.

Anxiously, Merlin darted his eyes, mumbling beneath his breath.

The night came once more, and again, there was no rest—only the tense waiting for light to come so they could escape.

Heavily, they rose again to another day in the wretched forest, with no hope of finding its end. Trapped, the unchanging forest gave no sign that they were breaking through. Each day was darker than the day before. Even the horses whinnied nervously, affected by the paranoia that was growing in all of them.

Elanor wanted to shut it all out and go to sleep, but when the evening came for the third time, terror kept her from rest.

In the morning, Elanor fumed. Her eyes had become grey, and Merlin's furrowed brow brought no peace. She wrestled hours with a dark force gnawing at her mind. *This is all his fault. We should have never left Dyved. Now he has led us to rot.* When these thoughts consumed her, her strength fought back. *No...no...we will be free! Merlin will find a way.*

Her resolve to resist the voices in her head was waning, but then, a gust of fresh wind blew across her face. Elanor gasped. It was like water after walking days through a desert. The confusion lifted, and she brightened. Peering before her, she saw that the trees opened wider. Hope alighted within her for the first time in days.

Maybe we have found our way out.

She turned to see if Merlin had caught the breeze, but his eyes were wide and panicked as he searched the trees.

Afraid, she pulled alongside him and whispered, "Merlin?"

"Shh!"

Startling her, Merlin shouted into the air words that vibrated with power—causing the horses to rear. He grabbed hold of Elanor's hand and leaned forward, his jaw set, ready to fight. He shouted again, "Amlygu...Datguddio!"

This time, a bodiless shadow floated between the trees beside them, causing dread to rise as they saw it.

"Ride!" Merlin shouted in alarm.

"What is it?" Distressed, Elanor grabbed her reins.

"There's no time!" He smacked the hinds of Elanor's horse. Brynn reared back, whinnying wildly, then launched into a full run. Elanor braced herself, holding tightly.

Merlin was left behind in her wake. She quickly glanced behind, and he was pounding up behind her, catching her up in the chase. Trees passed as blurs of green. The wood opened more and more, finally revealing an open landscape.

Elanor was relieved, but their pace did not slacken.

The crisis continued as Merlin bent forward in his saddle, leading them on.

Weak and tired, Elanor concentrated on remaining steadfast.

On and on they rode. Elanor worried she would not be able to carry on. Her legs were giving out, and it was becoming hard for her to catch her breath. Her grip steadily grew weaker. She thought to yell for Merlin to stop, but then a settlement came into view. Her heart leapt. They had made it.

DEMONS

Merlin slowed. The sound of hooves beating the ground became lighter. A deep relief poured out of Elanor with a heavy groan. She collapsed forward, letting go of the reins and wrapping her arms around the neck of her horse.

Brynn was wet and frothy. Elanor patted her horse compassionately, while Merlin led them straight to the river. The horses puffed loudly, eager for water.

Elanor slid from her saddle. Her legs trembled, almost unable to support her weight as they ached with exhaustion. Merlin steadied her in his arms as they tried to catch their breath.

"What was that thing?" she asked, gripping his tunic.

"No–not now…Not now," he gasped. "We are not where we can talk." Gazing down at her with seriousness on his brow, Merlin panted, "We cannot stop here, Elanor."

Her heart sank at his words, and her eyes dropped with disappointment.

He gripped her shoulders. "You can do this, Elanor. We are not safe. Stay with the horses, and I will hire a ferryman. We will cross as soon as I have secured us one." He lifted her chin, pulling her face toward his. The light had gone from her eyes. "I am sorry. I know you need rest. The horses have been pushed hard also, but we cannot stop. Not yet."

He offered her the skin of water. Thirsty, Elanor took the skin from his hand, but in her fatigue, she found it hard to drink. She forced herself to gulp some down, then handed it back to Merlin.

He drank deeply, wiping his parched mouth with his arm.

Elanor wanted to tell him that she would keep going, that she would be strong, but the weariness seemed to steal her words, and they would not come.

"I will return," he said, hurriedly walking away.

Elanor was amazed by Merlin's strength and endurance. Certainly, it must have been gained over all the years of battles and trial. She was encouraged that they would make it because of him. They would get to the other side because he would carry them through.

The horses grunted beside her, and she gazed out across the wide river. The shore on the other side was small and distant. It would take them a while to cross, and already she knew the day was more than half over.

Merlin returned quickly. "We are fortunate. There is only one more ferry going out today, and I have paid the man to take us across, but we must go now."

Elanor grabbed Brynn's reins and pulled her toward the settlement. Few round houses scattered the land, leading to a large, wooded tavern with establishments selling goods and supplies to wayfarers that travelled through. In front of them, along the river, was a landing where a man stood on a large, flat raft, waiting for them.

As they passed the ever-promising tavern, Elanor's hope for warm food and a soft bed diminished. The disappointment lingered only for a second—then, she turned to the raft.

The ferryman's face was grey with a sour frown. He had a brown leather flap that rested over his long white hair that matched the brown clothes he wore.

The man grunted, "Ye ready?"

Without a word, Merlin pulled the horses onto the raft and tied them to a hitching post. He extended his hand to Elanor, and they collapsed onto the raft's bench. The man shoved off from the landing with a large stick, pushing them out through the water.

"Where ye travellin' ta?" The man's question was foreboding, while he stared at them with his saggy, grey eyes.

Discerning the warning, Merlin responded, "Our travels are our own, sir."

"A tall man and his lady comin' out from the wilds—fleeing with some dark secret, eh?"

The man had been watching for them. Elanor now understood why they could not stay in the settlement. Eyes and ears were everywhere. Eyes for whom, neither of them knew.

The sound of the water and the warmth of Merlin's chest made it hard for Elanor to keep her eyes open. She tried to keep herself awake, knowing that the situation was still dire, but slipped away into a dark sleep. Merlin held her close, watching the ferryman closely.

The ferry arrived, scrapping alongside a landing on the other side of the river. The sun was setting, and the light grew dim. Merlin shook Elanor awake, suspiciously watching the ferryman as he stared over at them, hunched over his long stick.

Merlin quickly untied the horses. The water lapped the sides of the raft as the horses clopped off the ferry and departed onto the landing. The man drew up to the other side of the raft and pushed off to return. All the while, Merlin kept his eyes fixed upon him until he was out of sight.

"These lands are marred with the shadow of the enemy." He turned to Elanor, worry in his eyes.

"The ferryman was watching for us?"

"Yes. His eye was on us, and not just because we are strangers. In the forest, a great darkness was pressing down upon us—keeping us lost and weary. It should not have taken us so many days to get through. I recognized it and fought against it. That is how we finally found our way out. I revealed the shadow, which broke its hold. I could sense the shadow's malice for us, and it was not ready to surrender when we fled. I hoped crossing the river would put some distance between us, but the suspicious nature of that ferryman has forced me to believe that we are still not safe. Do you understand?"

Elanor nodded.

"There is a grove of trees over there. Perhaps I can find a place amongst them to rest. There, maybe we will not be easily seen. We need to eat and refresh ourselves. We cannot be wise without food in our bellies. We have already been without for too long."

The thought of food made Elanor's stomach groan. Anything would do.

Within the grove, Merlin found some thick shrubs that sheltered them.

The food had no taste, but it quickly disappeared. Now nourished, they were able to rest, but their sleep remained fitful. Thoughts of the dark shadow crept into their dreams, jolting them awake throughout the night.

Swollen eyed and silent, they rose to the road once more.

A great mountain range peeked out from above the trees. Merlin sighed with a smile. "We are getting close," he encouraged. "On the other side of those mountains is the shore of the lake near Caer Lial. It is not as close as it looks, but it is hopeful to see it."

Elanor gasped. Two snow-capped peaks stood, one higher than the other. "A happy sight. The very sign of home."

"The Caer may be another three days' ride, but we are passing out of the Southlands. Soon we will be in the Halls of the Palisade once again, where our friends will greet us."

"Does that mean no more shadows lie before us?"

"It is my hope."

Their spirits brightened. They had almost forgotten that they had anything to fear. The day was so bright and clear, and the air, warm. Maybe crossing the river had put a distance between them and their shadowed enemy. Maybe their suspicions of the ferryman were wrong. Either way, they pressed on, and the hope of home grew in their hearts.

Elanor mediated on the happy thought of being back in her chamber—Samara greeting her with a warm smile. Her eyes started to close as she dreamt.

Merlin was just ahead of her and noticed that the atmosphere of the woods suddenly shifted. The forest darkened. The clopping beat of Elanor's horse stopped. Alarmed, he turned to see Elanor's head slumped down into her saddle.

He jumped from his horse. "Elanor! Elanor! Wake up. You must not sleep."

Almost drunkenly, she slurred, "It's fine. It's nice. I can rest a while. The Caer is so close. I can see it."

"Elanor!" Swiftly, Merlin pulled her down, frantically tapping on her cheeks—forcing her to sit up. "You cannot sleep now…Elanor!"

Elanor did not want to fight the sleep. She was contented to give in and allow it to take her away. It felt peaceful. No more striving, only rest. Already she dreamt of Gwynevere and Cilaen greeting them as they rode up the hill through the apple trees. They were overjoyed to see one another again. Only Merlin seemed to be falling away. It was as if he was being pulled backward by an invisible force. He yelled, but she could not hear his words. Urgency swirled in her stomach.

She shouted, "But we are home, Merlin. Can't you see? Where are you going?"

318

Chapter Forty

Merlin held Elanor in his arms. He pulled on his magic to bring her back. Lifting his hand above his head, he snapped his fingers. "Ennyn!"

In her dream, she abandoned Gwynevere and Cilaen and started chasing after Merlin. "Merlin!" Suddenly, she was pulled through the air toward him.

She could hear his voice shouting, "You must wake up! You must wake up!"

Elanor reached her hands out to him, and her eyes shot open—finding herself laying on the ground in his arms. His eyes were still shut as he mumbled druidic words.

"Merlin?" she said lightly.

"Oh, Great God be praised," he said, drawing her into his chest. Then releasing her, he pressed his lips against hers.

"What happened?"

"Dark magic. It crept in, lulling you into sleep. There was no warning. It was upon you before I noticed it had come."

Elanor leaned to stand and gazed at the trees. Confused, fear returned to her. "I didn't even know I had fallen asleep. I dreamt of Caer Lial, Gwynevere, and Cilaen. I wanted to stay there, and I would have if you had stayed with me." She stopped, turning to Merlin. "What would have happened if I had not awoken?"

"Something is lurking. We must get clear of here. We do not have much daylight left, but what light we do have, we must use to find a safe place to rest for the night."

Merlin found a cleft under the side of a rockface for shelter. It protected them from behind and gave them an open view of what was in front of them. He kept Elanor close—his arm wrapped tightly around her. There would be no sleeping. He would have to be their eyes throughout the night. He could not risk losing focus for even a minute as the dark night fell upon them. The forest's seemingly peaceful air was oppressive as it tried to lure them into its false serenity. Merlin didn't trust it.

Elanor struggled to stay awake. She did not want to leave Merlin to stand alone, but she was too exhausted. Even with the threat, she could not keep her eyes open. But Merlin, too, was wearied by the lack of sleep. Several times he caught his head nodding into his chest. He smacked his cheeks and rubbed his face to restore himself. He battled to stay awake, but finally his eyes closed, and sleep took him.

The moment Merlin's head hit his chest, all the night's sounds silenced. The chirping crickets and rustling leaves went still. Out of the dark hollows emerged a being that slinked toward them. The leaves that laid upon the ground crackled.

Elanor laid across Merlin's lap, while his head slumped over onto her side.

Through the depths of Elanor's sleep she heard a loud resonating hiss. Her eyes shot open. Before her, she saw a black creature crawling on the ground toward her. It shined like wet tar, and the sight of it sent a streak of terror down her spine.

"Merlin," she whispered loudly, jolting herself backwards to wake him. Merlin snapped awake.

The creature shot up from the ground and opened its mouth wide with a hiss. Its head bobbed threateningly.

As their eyes took in its form, they found they were gazing into the eyes of a menacingly large snake. Its body was as black as night, as were its eyes and teeth. Its mouth hung open, ready to strike as it dared them to move. Merlin whispered cautiously, "Stay still!" Slowly, he lifted his hand. He shouted, and the serpent went flying backwards. As soon as it hit the ground, it dodged back toward them with great speed. Merlin shouted again, and this time the force of his magic split the snake's head in two. It fell to the ground, writhing where it had fallen, curling in and out of itself. It dissipated into black smoke, releasing a shriek that echoed.

Terror struck Elanor as Merlin cried out in pain. She turned to see that, latched onto Merlin's hand, was another hideous black serpent. It had bitten down hard, and Merlin struggled to shake it free. Its jaws and fangs fastened tight.

The tail of the demon whipped wildly as Merlin clutched his arm. The snake wrapped itself around Merlin's forearm. Then, the creature dissipated into black smoke, entering his hand where the fangs had pierced him. Merlin fell to his knees.

Elanor threw her arms around him as his body writhed in pain. His hand dripped with blood, and veiny black lines grew from the bite marks; up his wrist.

The horses went wild with fright, kicking and bucking against their reins. Elanor stood quickly to calm the horses, leaving Merlin to crumple to the ground. She hoped if she could calm Brynn, then the other horse would follow. She could not risk them breaking their ropes and running away. Not now.

"Sh-sh-sh...Shh, Brynn!" she soothed, approaching her calmly and holding her hands up to the horse's nose. "It's alright, girl. Shh!" The horse whinnied as it quieted, her hooves stamping more lightly. As Elanor had hoped, her efforts also calmed the other horse, and she was able to return to Merlin.

"Merlin, what do I do?" she cried fearfully, observing his pained, pinched face and the beads of sweat on his brow. She caressed his hand within her palm and willed her healing magic to flow. She breathed to calm herself and closed her eyes. Suddenly, the serpent's piercing eyes sprang inside her mind, causing her to fall back in shock. "It's not working!" she pleaded, hoping that Merlin might have an answer for her. She caressed his face as tears poured down her cheeks. Desperately, she said, "You cannot leave me, Merlin. You cannot!"

Panting, he said, "Try again."

Elanor shook her head and tried to gather herself. Kneeling beside him, she called out, "Grwyrthrhodd, help me." Then, she whispered, "Great God, give me grace. I love him. Help him." A great light flashed before her. Inside of it moved a silhouette. It looked like Grwyrthrhodd, but within the blinding light, its form changed, appearing like a dove. Whatever it was amid the brightness—it drew nearer to her. "Help me!" Elanor cried, her voice cracking and her cheeks wet with tears. Suddenly, she saw a cave. Its cavernous walls were lined with large, white crystals that glowed radiantly. Then, a voice within her said, "Go to the Crystal Cave."

The light faded, and Merlin writhed before her.

"My love," Elanor urged, "we must go now. We need to go to the Crystal Cave. You must help me find it."

Merlin's eyes grew wide, and he nodded. "Y-yes," he said, with great stress. "How do you know this place?"

"I have seen it. A light revealed it."

"Help me to st-st-stand," he stuttered. "Take me to Brynn."

Quickly, Elanor grabbed his good arm and wrapped it around her shoulder, pulling hard.

"Aah!" he screamed painfully.

Elanor pulled him anyway, feeling the urgency of their plight. She quickly dragged him over to Brynn, and Merlin placed his hand upon her muzzle. He closed his eyes, and his eyelids flickered. Elanor could sense his magic but was unsure what was happening. Then, Merlin's hand dropped, and his shoulders slumped forward.

"It is done," he said. "Brynn will take us to the caves. They are in the mountain."

With a great effort, Elanor loaded Merlin onto his horse, tying his horse to hers. He laid forward on his saddle, holding his hand in agony. The second Elanor was upon Brynn's back, the horse jolted forward and led them on.

41

THE CRYSTAL CAVE

Elanor was in turmoil. She had no idea how long it would take to journey to the cave, nor did she know how much longer Merlin could hold on. He laid on his horse motionless. Never did he groan or utter a word. There were moments Elanor feared that he was already gone. He gave her little sign of life as he laid on his saddle.

"Merlin?" she called, with no response.

She had to have faith that Brynn was leading them in the right direction. Many times, she wrestled, feeling like they weren't going anywhere at all and were wasting precious time.

Doubts constantly invited more fear and worry. Tortured and in the dark, she was on a path that never ended. Every minute passed slowly, and at every turn, she questioned whether she was doing all she could to save Merlin.

I cannot live without him.

Merlin was the strong one, the magic one, the one that was supposed to keep her safe. All night, flashes of the liquid black serpent flashed into her mind as shadows of the forest haunted her. The trees taunted her eyes, hiding darkness behind their solid, ghostly frames.

There could be more—more dark shadows, she thought.

The blue of the morning was finally breaking through the ugly black of the night. With the dull light, Elanor saw that they were climbing slightly and hoped this meant they were close. Two large stones appeared, guarding a path. The stones curved formlessly. Erosion had stolen the forms of what, Elanor guessed, had been stone warriors. Brynn led right between them, and they descended onto the path as high walls of earth rose on either side.

Moving upwards again, the path led them to a mound on the side of the mountain. Finally coming to the top, rows of stones were revealed in the dim light. Large stones formed two circles. One inside, and one outside. A mysterious, electric magic floated in the air.

The wind howled with frigid gusts, sending chills down Elanor's spine. She slid off her horse and ran over to Merlin. Anxiously, she touched him. He stirred in response, and relief cascaded through her.

"Merlin, we are on a mound with stones. Have we come to the cave? Is it nearby?"

He did not speak but put his hand out for her to help him down. Once down, he remained hunched over, his arm curled into his chest. Even in the dim light, Elanor was alarmed to see black lines had sprawled up his neck and across half of his face.

"We do not have a lot of time. We must find the entrance before the sun rises. We must…" Merlin contracted in pain. "We must enter in at the time between times."

Elanor did not understand, but she quickly perceived that they had been lucky to have arrived when they had, and that time was of the essence. Merlin pointed his finger forward. Elanor did not hesitate to pull him, limping forward, crossing through the circling stones to the rocky wall on the other side. Against the wall were three more large stones. Merlin moved toward the center stone and rubbed his fingers over it, wiping it free of the mossy overgrowth. Revealed were ancient lines of ogham writing.

Merlin placed his hand on the stone and looked to the sky. Elanor waited with anticipation as the wind swirled. Merlin's eyes met the horizon and waited as the sky became steadily lighter.

Mystified, Elanor witnessed what had been a wall of stone fade into the black mouth of a cave. A ray of sun peaked upon the horizon; instantly, Merlin read the ogham on the stone. As he spoke the words, the sound of stone rubbing against stone grated, and a great, cold, stale wind blew from the mouth of the cave.

"Now!" he shouted, shoving Elanor into the cave. She stumbled to the ground inside. Seconds later, they were on a damp stone floor in pitch darkness. The door that stood behind them had shut.

Elanor was disoriented. Everything had happened so fast. The thick darkness was nearly tangible. "Merlin?" she called out, blindly reaching for him. "Merlin!" Desperation rose in her voice. Her hand patted the ground and ran across the soft warmth of his leg. She pulled herself forward, feeling for his hand. He was unresponsive, so softly, she reached to touch his face, hoping to feel the heat of his breath. "Merlin? You have to help me. What do I do?"

Alone and helpless, the darkness surrounded her, and she felt lost. Elanor did not know what to do. Who was she without Merlin? Just a girl. A girl with nothing and no one. What could she do? She shook Merlin, frantic for him to awaken so he could save them. Afraid, she began to weep. She curled up beside him, trapped by whatever dark thing lay hidden in the blackness.

Then, Merlin groaned. The sound of his pain snapped her out of her tears of despair.

She rose up, and cried out, "I'm here! I brought him, just as you showed me. Help me... Help...Please!"

Nothing but silence came.

Elanor crumbled forward onto her hands, the cold ground beneath her offering no comfort. But then, she felt a slight vibration underneath her fingers. A dull humming sounded, and she lifted her head. The walls radiated with the subtle light of white crystals. The cavern dully illuminated by cylindrical prisms that jutted out from the floor and hung from the ceiling. Smaller, round crystals scattered the gaps between them.

Quickly, she turned to Merlin. His whole face was covered in the black, venomous lines.

"Help!" she cried out to the crystals.

The dull humming steadily grew louder. The sound reverberated from the crystals themselves—fluxing with the hum.

Captured by the sound, Elanor's fear began melting away. The vibration shifted to a sound like voices singing. Each crystal rang out in its own unique voice. Each voice, a reflection of one, resonating above them all. Like a tuning fork, Elanor's magic quickened in response, reminiscent of the day in the forest. Lightly, she started to echo the song, and as she did, the light brightened. It escaped the crystals and danced into the cave, enveloping her. Elanor lifted her hands, and the song burst forth from her lips, loud and strong. Her song created an explosion of brightness, which flooded every dark corner.

Heaving, Merlin revived. His eyes flooded with light. He saw it swirling around Elanor, causing her hair to float around her. Spreading out behind her, a light formed large wings. A crown of light spun above them, and in between stood a spirit. Looking down upon Elanor as she sang, it placed its hands upon her head. Its face seemed to gaze at both of them.

Elanor ceased her song, but the magical light sang on, bouncing around the cave. She opened her eyes as her hands floated down. Her eyes alight with blue, she took hold of a large, round crystal and peeled it out of the rock as if it were soft clay. Then she placed her other hand over Merlin. Her slow fluidity made her appear as if she were moving through water.

Tenderly, she grabbed Merlin's snake bitten hand and sang once again. The harmony created by her voice, with the crystals, was unearthly. It was as if the sweet taste of honey had become a sound.

Warm, mild heat filled Merlin's hand and moved down throughout the rest of his body. The black veins slowly disappeared. First from his face, then down his neck, through his arm, and out from his hand. Black smoke seeped from the wound, forming a dark, billowing cloud above him, until every last bit of poison had been pulled from his body. The smoke swirled, transforming back into the black, filthy serpent.

The snake hissed loudly, tainting the sweet music with its acrid sound.

Elanor pointed to the writhing serpent. Then, casting her hand toward the floor, the snake was thrown to the ground. The snake gathered itself and darted on its belly, launching at Elanor like lightning. Armed with a crystal, she brought it down hard upon the head of the snake, smashing its head into the ground and shattering the crystal into pieces.

Light sprang from the shattered crystal, sending a shockwave that knocked Merlin across the cave. As he landed, all went dark. When he opened his eyes, he was no longer in a cave, but in a room bright and colorful. Rows of shelves were lined with books, and next to him stood an old man. He was waiting for someone. And then, nearly walking straight into him, appeared a bright eyed Elanor. She was as he remembered her the day he met her, her hair tied high and cascading down her shoulders.

Curious, he watched them interact, completely unaware of his presence. This was not his world, and this was an Elanor that did not know him.

She spoke kindly, moving the old man to tears. The old man handed her a blue book. Merlin was shocked to see it was his book, his mother's book. The very same book that Elanor kept on her bedside table.

How could this be? Who was this man?

He remembered how taken aback Elanor had been when she had discovered the book amongst Cilaen's collections. This was a memory it seemed, but how? Was it Elanor's memory? Quickly, he tried to put the puzzle together as Elanor walked away. He wanted to yell at her to come back. He looked at the old man, who glanced sadly after her.

"Elanor!" he shouted, as the memory faded.

The wind blew cold across his skin as his eyes fluttered open. The cave was washed in the natural light of daytime. He slowly turned and saw the door to the cave open wide.

No doubt, he thought to himself, *the magic of the cave is allowing us a way out.*

His head ached as he sat up, rubbing the back of his head. Pieces of crystal scattered the floor—rolling down his tunic as he rose.

As his eyes focused on the scene before him. Elanor laid on the floor, her hand still over the crystal that had crushed the serpent's head. The crystal was in pieces beneath her hand. Her face and hand were covered in red cuts from the shards that had projected on impact. The sleeve of her dress was torn. The snake was completely vanquished. Nothing was left to see, except the black line of ash in the shape of its tail.

Merlin rushed over to Elanor, rolling her up into his arms. He noticed his own hands were cut, and his clothes torn.

"Elanor!" He lightly tapped her cheek, his heart thumping. "Wake up, my soul."

Her breathing quickened, and her eyes opened, as if startled by a bad dream. "Merlin...You're alive." She leaned into him, grasping his tunic as relief washed over her. "I was so scared."

"You did it ..you saved me." He squeezed her tightly.

She reached up to touch his face. "You are cut."

"I am afraid you are as well, my love. The crystal you used to smash the head of that vile thing—it shattered, cutting us both."

She touched her face and looked at her hands. "But we did it."

"You did it."

Elanor sat up slowly, feeling her aching bruises. "I hardly did anything. It was this place. There are voices here," she said, mystified. She gazed at the crystals that now sat, lifeless. "What is this place, Merlin? I can still feel the unusual vibrations of the air."

"This place is a well of deep magic. Druids used to come to this mound and hold council, but the cave was a place only some could enter. The magic here is older and wiser than the magic of any druid or sorcerer. It cannot be conjured or contained. It obeys no master, for it is the master of itself. Dark druids that returned to the old ways of sacrifice and the ways of the darker gods cannot come here. They cannot access it because it is not the same. It is other. The dark druids call this place cursed. But those of us that honor the Great God know better. No one has come here for many years. I have been here only once before. When you told me our only hope was the Crystal Cave, I had to hope that the way would be open. The doors have long been shut, giving access to no one. For even when I came to this high place, the cave opening to me was miraculous. This land is awakening in such a way I've not seen since the days of old."

"How is it that you came here?"

"I was desperate. In a deep valley of decision. Uther had died, and I knew it was Arthur's time to rise, but I was doubting my own resolve. Prydain seemed forsaken." His mouth twisted with emotion. "I came here, hoping for something, anything, to give me a sign of direction. The cave spoke to me...I looked into the crystals, and for the first time, I saw who I was, reflected in the face of my father. He appeared before me in spirit. He sang the song my mother sang over me when I was a child. The song of the Kingdom of the Sun. Then I remembered myself. I remembered it all." Tears slipped from his weary eyes as he stared into the place of his memory. "It heals me to remember."

"This place is alive with healing." Elanor picked up a shard of crystal, her mouth agape in wonder.

"Your song called the unicorn and has now opened the door of the Crystal Cave."

"I do not believe either time it was my song. It came from somewhere else. It was you who opened the door."

"Still, you doubt your strength."

Elanor looked down, pressing her lips together. "The singer of the song itself wrapped its arms around me and gave me strength. I felt no fear once I

328

began to echo its song. I was a string on a harp, vibrating against the strokes of its master."

"We are being graced with an open door; we should not leave it too long. We must go," he said softly.

Reluctantly, they turned to leave the ancient place. Both gazed over their shoulders, catching one last glimpse as they crossed the threshold. Stone scraped together, and a wind, like a mighty hand, pushed them out—the door shutting behind them. Both quickly turned around to see only a wall of stone.

Instantly, weariness and hunger pressed down upon them, reminding them of the long ordeal. The scrapes on their skin stung, and their shoulders slumped.

Merlin pulled Elanor close. "We have but to get down from this high place and find some water. Then we can rest."

Walking through the towering stones, they found their horses quietly grazing. Brynn whinnied and galloped over to nuzzle Elanor's face.

"Oh, Brynn! I am relieved to see you, too."

SANCTUARY

They stumbled toward a stream not far from the mound to wash and to water the horses. It was a small, narrow stream, with water running just above the stones below. Elanor knelt to wash the black muck and dried blood from the cuts on her hands.

"What were those things that attacked us in the dark?" she asked. "I know well enough that they were not snakes."

Merlin leaned against a tree, exhausted. He clenched his fists angrily and spat, "No, not with their black eyes and teeth. I knew the minute I saw the first one that these were creatures created by dark sorcery. Demons. These were not just dark monsters that happened upon us in the woods. None of what we have endured has been happenstance. We have been tracked and trapped. These evil spirits were set upon us. There were two. One for each of us. I cannot believe I allowed any of this to happen."

"You cannot blame yourself. How were you to know what we would encounter?"

"We had been warned!"

"And we both made the best decisions we could make, with the unknown before us."

"I have never seen such vile creations. I do not know what price or sacrifice one would have to endure to create such fallen filth. If I had not fought so

331

hard against the evil poison filling my veins, I would have surely died. Then you would have been left. All I could see…all I could feel was darkness." Merlin's lips curled over his teeth as he recalled it.

"We have made it to the mountain. We are much closer to home. Do you think we are still in danger?"

"I do not know. I only know that it would be unwise to let our guard down."

Elanor nodded. Wearily, she used every ounce of strength she had to get back up onto her horse. The hope of Caer Lial kept her going.

They continued north, their heads hanging in exhaustion. The sun was bright, but the wind was cold. They had eaten sparingly as they had not the time to stop and eat amidst that danger. They hadn't even lit any fires, as to not draw any unwanted attention. Up until now, the days and nights had been cool, but not unbearable. Now, the wind cut beyond all layers of clothing. Neither complained but kept their heads down and pressed on.

Suddenly Merlin sat straight up. The look in his eye sent tingles through Elanor's body. The pit of her stomach dropped. She would not have the strength to fight another enemy.

The heavy scent of a thunderstorm with no rain permeated the forest. Static and electric. Ominous smoke quickly moved in on all sides. Merlin anxiously sought a route of escape, but seeing none, he grabbed Elanor's hand as they pressed together, trapped. There was nowhere to go.

The smoke sparked and bit at their skin. The swirling billows enveloped them. Merlin reached across the horses to hold Elanor in his arms. On top of the horses' nervous whinnying came a loud sound, like a giant releasing its breath, and the smoke cleared away.

Revealed before them was a beautiful spring pouring out of a mossy rock into a great pool of clear blue water. The forest was no longer orange and yellow with the signs of the season, but lush with a vibrant green. The air was warm and humid. Surrounding the perimeter of the forest remained the unusual smoke. The sound of bird's song poured from the trees, and they smelled the strong scent of flower blossoms.

"What is this place?" Elanor asked, mystified.

"I do not trust it. It is a deception."

"It does not feel like darkness," she said, slowly climbing down from Brynn's back.

"What are you doing?"

She held onto the reins of her horse and looked out across the water. The light from the sun danced upon its ripples. Then, the rippling light started to change shape and hover over the surface of the water. Soon hundreds of little lights, like stars, blinked—floating up into the air.

Merlin leaned forward. "Elanor, get back up on your horse."

"Emrys!" came the echoing breath of multiple voices. "Do not fear us."

Merlin's eyes were wide as the voices reverberated off the water.

"We are servants. The Great One has invited you here. We promise you safety and mean you no harm. We are the ones that restore and minister the One's great light. The Master knows that you need rest. You and Gwenddydd have been through much turmoil. This water will restore you."

As they spoke, Elanor approached the water's edge. She gazed into the clear water and knelt down.

"Elanor, don't!" Merlin shouted.

The water seemed to smile, and she could hear its enchanting laughter inside her head, inviting her in, and she touched the tips of her finger into the water.

"Elanor!" He jumped from his horse, racing to her side.

The water's warmth moved through her whole body, and she sank her hand in deeper. She pulled her hand out of the water and revealed that her cuts were gone. She lifted her hand up high, the droplets of liquid shimmering in the sunlight.

Merlin grabbed hold of her wrist, his mouth agape. Neither redness nor scrape remained.

She smiled, then turned toward the water to splash her face. The water was like oil as it fell from her cheeks. She came back up and peered over at Merlin. He placed his hand on her cheek to examine the miracle deeply. Her skin was porcelain, and her eyes were bright—Elanor was healed!

"Emrys and Gwenddydd, you are welcome here. You may stay as long as you like," the voices rang out. "Time here is not the same. As you stay here, time will not pass in the outside world."

"How do we know that this is not some sort of trap?" Merlin yelled out to the lights.

The lights fluttered, and then slowly, one by one, disappeared. Merlin looked at Elanor uncertainly.

She stood with a gleam in her eye, then quickly began untying her tattered dress. She kicked it away and pulled her white undergarment off—laughing like one freed. She glanced at Merlin, then jumped into the water. He waited breathlessly as he watched her kick through the water, waiting for her to surface.

She sprang up with joy radiating from her pink cheeks.

"Well, then," he said, finally letting go of his suspicions. "If this is deception, I do not think I can withstand it." He pulled off all his clothes, throwing them into the trees, and dove headfirst into the water. He sprang up out of the water, shaking his head and splashing water all over Elanor. He laughed as he raised his arms, revealing his wounds were also healed, including the deep bite marks from the demon snake.

Elanor floated over to him, tenderly caressing his hand. "See?"

"I do see," he said, lowering his hand and gazing into her eyes. The sunlight jumped off her bare shoulders and lit off the tip of her nose. He pulled her close and kissed her. Connecting in the healing light of safety and purity, the birds sang above them.

Finally, refreshed by the water, they pulled themselves from the pool. Fresh linens lay folded on the ground. Next to a grand oak, not far from the water's edge, was a fleece laid out upon the ground. They wrapped themselves in the linen and laid down upon it. It was so soft, it relieved all restlessness, and before they knew, they dropped into a deep sleep.

Hours, maybe even days, passed as they laid there asleep. Occasionally, one would stir and wonder if it was time for waking, but each time, a warm presence would sing softly and lull them back to sleep. When they finally woke, they found a large leaf laid in front of them with berries, honeycomb, and cake. Hungrily, they ate every last crumb, savoring the sweet taste.

The horses gladly grazed, resting around the grassy patches around the pool. Merlin leaned forward to scoop some of the water up into his mouth to drink and was surprised that though the water was warm to his touch, it was cool when he drank.

At times, Merlin worried if they had been tricked, but each time the thought came, it was swept away by a voice ringing through his mind, *"We are servants. We offer you safety and mean you no harm."* He believed the voice to be true. Looking at Elanor affirmed his belief; she was radiant. She sat wrapped in linen, with only her blue pendant and torc round her neck. Her laughter was like a fresh drink, and her touch like the honey they ate every morning.

One day, Merlin woke with the thought of Caer Lial in his mind. He had been dreaming of Arthur, and Grwyrthrhodd was speaking the prophecy.

"You and she are one. Twins. Joined in magic. Like you were to Arthur, you are both two sides of the same coin. One on each side. One the defender, and the other healer. You cannot build the promise without the other, and Arthur's promise depends on you. He is the

once and future king."

Merlin saw Arthur holding his sword high, the hills lined with his Cymbrogi. Merlin knew that, as he woke, the time had come for them to leave. As he stretched himself awake, beside the food laid fresh clothes, cleaned and finely mended as though they were new.

Elanor sat up and saw the clothing neatly folded. "It is time to leave, isn't it?" She sighed. "I could have stayed here with you forever."

"There will come a day for that, I think, but today is not that day. Today, we return to see our friends, for they long to see us and need us."

They dressed, taking in, for one last time, the sweet smells and the beauty of the sanctuary that had been gifted them by some magic. Elanor braided her hair and stood elegantly in her new garments. No signs of wear existed on her clothes or in her eyes. There, Merlin saw the beautiful strength of a woman untouched by the dark horrors of the forest.

"What is it?" she asked.

"Nothing," he said, brushing his hand across her forehead. "It is as if nothing ever happened."

"Perhaps it is because we must be strong for what is coming."

Her remark stole away his peace, and his forehead lined with worry. "Perhaps."

"No worry," she said. "Clearly, there is one greater that has not forgotten us."

"Perhaps," he said again, a smile tugging at his lips this time.

They saddled the horses and grudgingly climbed onto their backs, preparing to leave. Walking back through the smoke, they could feel the temperature changing, the air around them getting colder. The sweet smell of blossoms disappeared, as did the tangible peace they had experienced inside the sanctuary. Finally, out of the smoke and on the other side of where their paradise once was, they turned to see that nothing of the smoke, or sanctuary, remained. If it had not been for the fresh clothes and the healed and healthy-looking skin on their faces, they would have thought it a dream. For it was true that once they had left the blessed pool, they found themselves in the exact spot, and the exact same time, as before the smoke had appeared. Almost in an instant, what had seemed like days, felt like only a short moment.

Elanor asked, "How long before we reach Caer Lial?"

"We are about two days' ride away."

She looked at him and smiled. "Let us go home."

THE RETURN OF THE DREAMS

"They have made it through, my lord."

"My shadows were upon them. Aah!" the dark man yelled in a rage, causing his servant to recoil in fear. "Merlin," he seethed, twisting the name darkly between his teeth. "And the blue one?"

Venomously he snapped, "We will kill Emrys and his beloved Pendragons." He curled his hand into a fist. "My sight…I saw her…that witch…her brightness burned my eyes. Do we still have Donnuc within Caer Lial?"

"Yes, lord," the servant said, leaning back toward his master.

"She is still weak, and Merlin is weak because of her. She does not know who she is, which makes her easily destroyed. Time is of the essence. We must begin moving into the Caer with silence and cunning if we are to not be discovered by Merlin's quick eye."

"He is always seeing…always seeing." The feeble servant wrung his hands shakily.

"We will blind him with pain. The witch Aberva has been making blood sacrifices, preparing for her usefulness. Have Donnuc ready for her. We can no longer wait to draw them out—we must attack within their safety." He turned his nasty smile to the north. "I will take the mind and the heart of Prydain's people, and there will be nothing for Merlin to save in the end. His grief will be unending, and he will beg me to rid him of his life."

Merlin and Elanor had barely reached the gates when a herald was seen running through the gates toward the Palisade. Upon hearing the news, Bedwyr did not waste a moment. He saddled his horse and sped down the hill to meet them.

Merlin was nearly knocked off his horse by the welcoming slap on the back and fierce embrace of his friend. In the next moment Elanor was met with a kiss as Bedwyr pulled her in for a squeeze. Elanor's eyes lit up with surprise, setting Merlin into a deep bout of laughter.

"My brother," Merlin said between laughter, "I assume you are as happy to see us, as we are you."

Bedwyr's face went flush, and he shook his head abashedly. "Heh…I am blessed beyond the stars to see you both."

Brynn's front hooves clopped the ground, and her head bobbed excitedly. "Of course, I am glad to see you also." Bedwyr dismounted and approached the horse, running his hand adoringly over her nose and patting her neck.

The sight of the citadel and Bedwyr's joyful face warmed them, making them even more anxious to reach the Palisade. They rode with haste, meeting glad faces upon the steps of the Great Hall.

Before Elanor's feet could hit the ground, Cilaen had swept her up, spinning her around. "Happy is my heart to see you both at last," Cilaen said, letting Elanor's feet finally touch the ground, placing his hands on her cheeks. "I have had no one to keep me company these long days you and Merlin have been gone."

Merlin embraced Cilaen next, and then turned his gaze to Gwynevere, who stood smiling, awaiting their greeting. "I told you we would return before the season changed."

She smiled. "And you have barely made it."

Peredur gripped Merlin's arms, shaking them heartily.

Gwynevere quickly grasped Elanor by the hand and pulled her into her chest, embracing her in a long moment of sweet reunion. Then, she turned a more serious eye to Merlin. "What is the news? What have you seen in the wilds?"

Merlin sighed. "The lands have become dark. There is much to tell, and much to be prepared." Merlin's words brought an instant soberness. "King Lugh is treacherous, and Llyonesse and the Southlands are riddled with spies and demons."

"Demons!" Gwynevere snapped.

"And shadow."

"Samara!" Elanor said, entering her chamber.

Samara quickly wrapped her arms around Elanor, receiving her fondly.

"Why did you not come down to see us?"

"I had to see that all was ready for you and Lord Merlin," she said, peering up at him with a bow. "We did not know when to expect you, and at the sound of your return, I hurried to set it all right."

"Well, it wouldn't have been perfect if you weren't here to greet me when we entered."

"No, my lady. I did not want to miss seeing you." She paused uncomfortably, then continued, "I have already had your things sent to be cleaned. And you have a fresh sleeping gown laid out for you there. How wonderous..." She stopped to gaze at Elanor with a perplexed expression. "You look as though you have not travelled at all."

Elanor simply smiled.

Shaking her head, Samara motioned to the table. "The water is fresh and warmed. I will leave you to rest now, and I will look in on you in the morning." She bowed and gripped Elanor's hand before scuffling out of the room.

"Strange...She was behaving differently."

Merlin shook his head. "I think it likely has more to do with my presence."

"I can braid my own hair and light my own fires. But I like her being near, more like a...."

"Friend?"

Elanor nodded.

"She only means to honor you. Cilaen was to me a servant, and filidh pupil for some years. If the one they are serving is of a kind heart, then the result should be brotherhood, and that is what Cilaen and I have. Let Samara serve you. It does not make her less to want to honor you. Speaking of Cilaen," he said, taking off his colors and coat, "I need to gather some things. I want to get him started, discovering anything in the druidic texts about the black serpents that attacked us. Those demons were of strange sorcery, and I want to know what the enemy has been willing to do to gain such cursed power. I will not be long, as I am eager to close my eyes." He leaned down and kissed her, then sailed out of the room, leaving Elanor alone.

It felt nice to be alone and amongst her things. She reminisced how this room used to feel so empty, and now it felt the very definition of comfort. She quickly readied for bed and crawled inside the warm, heavy wool. The peace of being home silenced every thought, and she fell asleep.

And Elanor began to dream. Her dreams were similar to the dreams she had before. It started out slowly with the dove, white and shining, flying up high into the sky. Always climbing, but this time it turned and soared toward land through a white plume of cloud.

The bird floated all the way down to a plateau, just like Dyved, but there were no homes or people, only green. The dove landed upon the branches of the same dead tree where the raven had crowed. The scene of the raven flashed with its cawing sounds of warning, before settling back to the dove tranquilly sitting in the branches.

Below the tree, a human shape slowly came into focus. It was Merlin, looking up with his hands outstretched. He was calling gently to the dove, "Come, come!" He softly cooed, "Come on, little one. You will be free." The bird flew down from the branches and alighted upon his hand. "That's a good girl," he said, stroking the feathers and cupping the bird in close to his chest.

As he drew the bird in, the dream switched to a man atop a black horse. It was the same tall, proud man she had dreamt of before. Only now, Elanor knew it to be Arthur. A fire was alight in his eyes, and his teeth were set as he looked down into a valley. Behind him stood a multitude of warriors, their horses puffing and grunting, their faces tense and spears lifted, battle ready. Arthur lifted his hand, and an intense cry rose from his lips, releasing the charge.

Then, she heard, *"You are two sides of the same coin. Just like Merlin and Arthur, so are Gwenddydd and Emrys."*

The dream shifted once again, and there, floating high up in this air, was a mighty shield slowly spinning in circles. As it spun, she could see on one side was Arthur, and on the other, Merlin. It spun again, and this time it was Elanor in Arthur's place, and then on the other side, Merlin. Once again it spun, and she could see herself and Arthur, standing beside each other, Merlin still appearing on the other side, only this time, Merlin held a white dove in his hands.

A terrifying scream radiated, shifting the scene. Merlin was yelling, "Run!" Terror was in his eyes. Within the dream, she was both the white bird fleeing from Merlin's hands and herself, riding on Brynn's back—running for her life. The urgency was fearful and dire. Still Merlin yelled, waving his hands wildly, urging her to run.

The shield spun faster, picking up speed. The sound of wind whipped by her ears as she rode, tearing through her wings as she flew. The shield resonated a deep ringing—spinning violently, faster and faster. Then she heard a sound.

Thwwppt!

And all the noise ceased. Simultaneously, she saw an arrow go through the bird, while an arrow pierced through her back, sending her careening off her horse to the ground. The shield stopped spinning, and there, it depicted Merlin holding a white dove in his hands with an arrow piercing through it—blood dripping through his fingers.

Elanor's shrieks reverberated in the room and echoed down the corridors, jolting Merlin awake beside her. He sprang up to see Elanor beside him wrestling with her covers, screaming and fighting. He grabbed hold of her, pinning her down to the bed.

"Elanor, wake up! Wake up! You are only dreaming. Elanor!" he repeated, until finally, her eyes snapped open, and she frantically placed her hands on her chest, feeling where the arrow had pierced her.

"It was just a dream. You are safe...You are safe."

Elanor panted, looking around frantically. Her brow beaded with sweat as she gasped to recover herself. Her eyes were still wild as Merlin pulled her into himself.

Softly she began to cry. "I'm so...so sorry. I..."

Merlin soothed, "Shh! You were only dreaming."

"It was not like a dream. I felt an arrow pierce my skin. It was so real. Merlin..." She glanced up at him sincerely. "It was...real...or at least it seemed real. You and Arthur. I..."

A sharp knock rattled the door.

"Your waking screams were loud. I fear someone has come to check we are safe."

Sure enough, by torchlight stood Peredur, with his hand on the hilt of his sword. His eyes were set to attack.

"Peredur, have no fear, my friend. Elanor has only had a dream."

Relaxing, Peredur dropped his hand from his hilt. "Screaming could be heard all through the corridors. Look," he said, pulling Merlin out into the hall-way. Several servants had gathered outside, and even the queen stood by her door wrapped in her robe.

"Please forgive. Elanor has only had a frightful dream. We did not mean to wake you. All is well, I promise you."

Peredur leaned his torch into the chamber to gaze into the room and saw Elanor sitting up in her bed with a look of shock. He breathed out, setting his jaw. "All is well!" Reluctantly, he moved to return to his room, waving at the others to do the same.

Gwynevere came, patting the floor with her bare feet. She pushed past Merlin to enter the room, going straight to Elanor to soothe her. Seeing her flush face, Gwynevere wet a cloth to dab her face and neck.

"I am so sorry. I did not mean to wake everyone in the late hours of the night."

Merlin leaned down with concern. "Tell me this dream."

"It was not a normal dream. It was more than images; I could feel pain. Like—like in the dream I had when I found myself here with you."

Calmly, Gwynevere said, "Tell us."

Elanor reluctantly relayed every detail. Every moment was imprinted into her mind. Merlin steadily became unsettled as Elanor revealed it. He worked to not come to any hasty conclusions, but as he listened, he knew that what she had dreamt meant something, provoking fears within him of what it could mean.

"It could have been our long journey that has induced this nightmare. We certainly met our fair share of horrors upon the road." Merlin comforted, "You are safe, Elanor. Death has not come to you."

However, night after night, Elanor continued to see the nightmare. An unhappiness settled over her, as the doom brought on by the dream never abated. Always, every night, as she closed her eyes, it was there like a torment.

In hopes to help her sleep, Cilaen created a sleeping tincture, but nothing seemed to stop the dreaming. What was this dream leading to, her ultimate death?

It all rose to a peak, one night, as Elanor dreamt once again, and Merlin woke to find her struggling beside him. This time, he did not try to wake her. This time, he closed his eyes and touched her forehead. Immediately, just as he had hoped, he could see the dream, every moment playing out in front of him. He saw every detail and every sign. The dove in the tree, a warning, just like the raven. In the final moments, he saw the dread in his own face as he yelled for Elanor to run. It made his stomach lurch as he watched her go. The swift sound of the arrow hitting flesh, and then the numb shock as he watched Elanor fall from her horse. The blood dripping from his hands.

He lifted his hand from his wife, and Elanor jolted awake. She had learned to manage her terror in waking and started breathing to calm her beating heart. As she breathed, she noticed Merlin sitting with his hands over his eyes.

"I'm sorry, Merlin. I am stealing your sleep as well as my own."

"No," he whispered. "I saw your dream. I saw it." And then again, he mournfully repeated, "I saw it."

Elanor sat up to comfort him and placed her hand upon his shoulder, but he pulled away. He didn't want her comfort, for in Merlin's mind, all he saw was the blood in his hands. The stabbing fear wrestling within him, he stood and stormed over to the hearth.

"Merlin?"

It had always been this way. His first love murdered by Saecsans. His anger flared as he thought of all who had been sacrificed in his fight for destiny. He imagined taking the kingdom within his grasp and crumpling it into dust.

This Kingdom of the Sun, he ruminated. *Was it worth the price? Was it worth Arthur's life? What of his men? Mine and Arthur's brothers—were they the purchased price? Maybe if I just let the old ways return, no more blood would be spent. Maybe I was right when I left Elanor that day. I should not have returned. Was I weak to think I could love? Wouldn't my torture of separating myself from Elanor forever be better than her death?*

His thoughts gnawed at the wound that was reopening in his heart. The guilt of the blood—Elanor's blood—dripping from his hands. He fell to his knees and wept.

Elanor ran to him, wrapping her arms around him from behind. He resisted her affections, but she refused to let him go.

Suddenly, like a light, words, entered into his dark meditation. *"The prophecy was of two stars."* The man in blue flashed before him. *"Darkness cannot prevail against you if your heart is full. You assume too much and bear burdens not your own. NO MORE, EMRYS!"*

The echoing voice split through the weight of his grief and fear. Merlin's heart softened, and he reached behind him to grab hold of his wife.

Elanor whispered somberly, "Is the dream a prophecy?"

"Yes," Merlin breathed, "but we must be careful to not assume that the doom is a promise. It is a warning. We cannot live in fear of what may come and have it steal our strength. You are before me now, and I choose you. We must remember that we are two." He kissed her head. "Emrys and Gwenddydd."

"Will the dreams come to an end, do you think?"

"I don't know, but I am not sure the dreams are meant to frighten you. We must seek answers within them and not hide in the recesses of the fear they bring."

44

THE EAST IS COMING

The apples on the trees were all picked or fallen, the leaves on the trees had turned orange and yellow, and there were fewer days without rain when the queen received message that King Bram of Caer Edyn was traveling to Caer Lial. Caer Edyn was far north upon the craggy rocks of the eastern shores. This kingdom had always kept an eye on those who sailed from other lands and had been vital in keeping the wild Picti of the north at bay, as their lands ran not far from the Great Wall.

Bram was the young nephew of the great King Ector and cousin to the mighty Cai. He had taken the crown when Ector and Cai were slain at Camlan. Bram was a faithful warrior and fought for Arthur in many battles, but there had been little to no history built between Caer Lial and Caer Edyn since his kingship.

Bram's visit, Gwynevere hoped, would be in an effort to establish that relationship anew. Tensions had risen as news had spread of the darkness in the Southlands. An alliance with King Bram would bring solidarity to them all.

Elanor strolled through the orchard, keeping Gwynevere and Bedwyr company as the Queen spoke of politics. She digressed, "Arthur always had a way of turning councils with kings into great alliances. Sometimes I fear I lack his talent. I have not had many dealings with kings since Arthur's death, but now with the attacks, the kings are making their appearance, one by one—first Thul, and now Bram. If only Cormach would return, we would be stronger."

Bedwyr interjected, "King Lugh has always been out for himself. He and Croighcat are a troublesome pair."

"Who is Croighcat?" Elanor asked.

"He is the Sea King of the western edge of the Southlands. He and Lugh have been in league for many years. Neither of them has ever been trustworthy allies. King Croighcat is divisive and had set many traps to prevent Arthur's kingship, but all his treason was discovered."

"There are six kings in Prydain?"

"Yes." Gwynevere nodded. "Six kings there are now. King Lot of the High North died long ago, before the great battle of Badon Hill. His kingdom has since fallen into ruin. No king ever took his place."

The leaves crunched beneath their feet as Gwynevere's voice droned in and out of Elanor's ears. Details of chieftains and lords were being lost as Elanor's head began to throb.

"When King Bram arrives, I…" Gwynevere stopped and turned to see Elanor holding her head in her hands. "What has happened?"

"My head…It has been aching since I woke this morning. I was hoping the fresh air would help, but…" Elanor cringed at the sharp pain. "It feels like it's getting worse."

Bedwyr held Elanor firmly by the arm to support her.

"I'm fine, Bedwyr. Only I am tired. I think I need to lie down. I'm sorry, Gwynevere."

"No, please…You need rest."

Bedwyr volunteered, "I will walk you to your chamber."

"No, no! You need to be beside Gwynevere. I will be alright. It's not far, I will walk myself." As she stepped forward, her knee buckled, and she fell.

"Bedwyr, take her back to her chamber," Gwynevere commanded. "I will fetch Cilaen."

"No need to get Cilaen. He has already seen me. I just need some rest. I lost my balance, that is all."

"Cilaen will be told to check on you a second time," Gwynevere put firmly. "Go…take her now."

Bedwyr quickly lifted Elanor up by her arm, and before she knew it, she was safely back in her chamber, where Samara helped get her into bed. She hit the cushion, her head heavy as her eyelids closed. She sank deeply into the blankets, relieved to be off her feet. She was asleep in moments, remembering nothing more until she felt a soft tapping on her arm.

346

The sky was already dark, and the room was lit with candles as her eyes blinked open, then focused on a beautiful pair of golden eyes.

"How are you feeling?" Merlin whispered softly. "I am sorry I have been gone this whole day, only to find that you have been unwell."

Elanor moaned and slowly lifted herself up. She rubbed her eyes and temples, wondering whether she had improved.

"It is nothing serious." Feeling thirsty, she said, "I need some water."

Merlin poured her a cup, and quickly, she drank it down.

"I could drink more," she said, slowly drawing her legs over the side of the bed to stand. She felt ready to crawl right back into bed to return to sleep, her head still aching and heavy.

Merlin grabbed a hold of her. "Not so fast."

"I am well," she snapped. "It's just a headache, and I have slept too long."

"Cilaen said he was with you this morning, and then this afternoon. He said you should rest. I'll have Samara sit with you while we hold council with Bram. He arrived a few hours ago."

"I would like to be at the council. Please, Merlin. I have rested. I am feeling much better."

"It is not worth pushing yourself to be there."

"Truly, I feel fine. I am feeling only like I could drink an entire well dry. I am so thirsty." She poured herself another cup full of water, sucking it down quickly.

"If you say you are well, then I will not stop you, but be sure, Elanor. There is no reason to overreach for this."

"If I begin to feel unwell, I will leave and return to rest. I promise." She gazed at him earnestly. "I would hear what King Bram has come for."

Merlin walked over to her and placed his hands upon her cheek, and Elanor smiled lightly at his touch. Her cheeks were pink and not pale. Her eyes, though tired, were not dark.

"There is time for you to ready yourself, only you must be swift. I shall fetch Samara." Turning to leave, he stopped and said, "But I will have you by my side, with Cilaen nearby."

"If that brings you comfort, it shall be done."

Bram's eyes widened and his mouth gaped as Merlin and Elanor entered the Hall. He stood back, with his Cymbrogi behind him, bowing his head as their eyes met.

Merlin and Elanor took their seats. The room was still, with an uncertain atmosphere.

Gwynevere sat stern, as a High Queen to a lesser king. Her strength was on display with no sign of weakness. Fully ornamented, with her golden torc shining bright, she spoke, "King Bram, you and your men are most welcome." She gazed down upon them with an unfeeling air. "Please speak, for we would hear what has brought you before us in council."

Bram presented himself before her with an uncertain yet humble air. He was tall, and his face was young. He wore his dark hair tied back and donned the clothing of a simple warrior, with no torc around his neck or sign of authority upon him.

He bowed, placing his hand upon his chest. "My lady, High Queen of Prydain, thank you for receiving me." He then bowed toward Merlin. "I am happy to see the Great Merlin also before me. I fought for Arthur, led many times, by your wisdom. To see you once again causes me to re-call memories of proud men and great victories. My lady," he said, turning his gaze to Elanor, "we have heard of you through the mouths of many men. Hope, they say, has come with you. They call you sister of the queen and daughter of Prydain." Bram stopped to clear his throat.

"I have come representing the lands left to me by my uncle, King Ector. I have stared high up into the eyes of Ector and Cai. I am fortunate to be counted amongst their kin. We received your warnings, and of late, have begun to hear more disturbing rumors from the Southlands. Stories of murderous men and mysterious happenings. I have been a warrior all my life, and as such, I have prepared my men to be ready and watchful.

"But I am an inexperienced king, and I lack the full wisdom of my uncle, though I am determined to protect my people. So, I have come to you, High Queen, because my uncle has shown me that wise kings establish alliances. All the lands must be defended, if any one kingdom hopes to remain." As he spoke, he unsheathed a long knife that attached to his belt and laid it out flat upon his hands. He knelt, presenting it to Gwynevere.

"I am with you, Gwynevere, High Queen of the Cymry people. This knife, I offer to you as a gift, representing my high honor of you. This knife was a gift to me from the spoils of our victory at Badon Hill. Arthur gave each warrior a token. This was what he gave to me. I could never forget the honor."

His eyes shone as he gazed at the knife in his hand. The blade was long and silver, with an ornamented handle inlaid with gold. "I felt like a king that day, receiving such a handsome prize. The pride in Arthur's face as he looked upon me. This...this is the best gift I could think of to show you the trueness of my heart. We would fight for these lands and would follow you into battle. I align myself with Peredur and Bedwyr—Battle Chieftains I have followed in the past. A good leader knows when it is best to follow. I fear I have been made weaker by not coming here sooner. I can see that not all has been lost without Arthur, and that we are not alone. When the time comes, and you need us, we will ride out, just as Ector and Cai, and we will be for the High Queen. Only..." he said meekly, "...please forgive, that I needed to see for myself that the Great Merlin had indeed come back, for without him, I fear we would not have had enough faith."

"Have you so little faith in me?" Gwynevere asked sharply.

"No, my lady. Forgive me. You mistake my meaning. I meant only that, because I have been in battle with both Arthur and Merlin, I know that Merlin has swayed the tide as Arthur's eyes, as much as Arthur swayed the tide with his cunning and strength. If Merlin is with us, we are stronger for it. It brings me hope to see him."

"You speak more like a loyal warrior than a king." Gwynevere gazed at him more kindly. She approached him, taking the knife from his hand, and looked closely at its features—running her fingers down the smooth side of the blade. "I cannot take from you what Arthur has given. Let me honor you by returning your blade. Set it back within the sheath of your belt, for it pleases me to know a piece of Arthur goes with you. I had much hoped in my heart that you had come to make alliance, and this I will gladly do."

The Cymbrogi welcomed the young king by pounding their fists. Bram smiled and stood, sliding his knife back into his sheath.

Gwynevere raised her hand to silence them. "It seems to me, though you are eager for battle, there is none to be had as of yet. We do not know enough about our enemy, and the darkness is hard to corner. But I am glad to know that King Bram, along with King Thul, are prepared to defend our lands."

Elanor admired Bram for not putting on a show of strength, but coming in low, as a man serving his people. This man would be a valiant ally and reminded her of the knights she had heard of in the stories she was told as a child. Though there were no knights here, surely, she had seen their reflection in Peredur, Bedwyr, Galen, and now Bram.

Gwynevere shouted, "Let ale be poured!"

Servants dipped their pitchers in the full cauldrons, serving out drink, starting with Bram and his men. Within minutes, Elanor had a cup within her own hand, the ale splashing over the sides as they poured. She looked at the swirling froth in her cup, and immediately, sick began to rise up in her throat. She leaned back to settle herself, but the nausea had already roused in her stomach, threatening to come up.

IT IS A GIFT

Aiming to leave the room with grace, Elanor swiftly stood, lifting her head high, and tried to force a smile as though nothing were wrong. She rounded her chair, and headed for the doorway, quickening her pace. She hoped, if she could just make it to the courtyard, she wouldn't embarrass herself. She could hear Merlin asking after her but didn't dare turn around. She pushed through the door and darted for the nearest bronze urn.

Merlin looked to Cilaen, whose eyes had already followed Elanor out the door.

"I will tend to her," Cilaen mouthed silently to Merlin.

Samara was also already headed out the door.

On the other side of the door, the two of them spied Elanor leaning over an urn. Samara rushed to assist her, while Cilaen returned to Merlin.

"You have nothing to worry," he whispered to Merlin. "Just come when you can."

Merlin nodded and watched with concern as Cilaen walked back out the door.

As he returned to the courtyard, he found Samara wiping Elanor's face with her tunic, and knelt beside her. "How are you?"

Elanor nodded, feeling a little embarrassed. "I am feeling much better now."

"Let us take you to my chambers where I can examine you."

Samara helped Elanor to stand, her eyes still watering. The nausea had gone, though she remained slightly dizzy. She couldn't believe the nausea had sprung on her so quickly.

Once in his chamber, Cilaen sat her down and examined her face and eyes. "Are you still feeling sick?"

"No," Elanor said quietly. "Only a bit shaky."

He leaned back and pressed his lips together. "Elanor? How do I say this…have you…" Cilaen sighed deeply.

Samara interjected, "Have you had your time of bleeding?"

"My time of blee…my what? Why would you—" Elanor stopped, quickly understanding the question. "I, uh…" She put her hand to her mouth as she thought through the question.

Of course, this could have been a possibility. Why had she not thought of it until now?

Finally, Elanor replied, "It has been a while. I am not sure."

Samara offered a cup of water.

"I believe it is possible you are with child," Cilaen said, watching her eyes intently for her reaction.

Pregnant?

Confused emotion wrapped around her every thought as the horrors of her dream flashed in her mind. Every night she dreamt of her impending doom. The thought of it choked her. Hopeless, she sat there stunned with no response.

"This cannot be."

The metal latch scraped open, and Merlin walked through the door.

Elanor stood abruptly, her eyes wide and shaken.

"Are you well…Elanor?" Merlin waited as Elanor stared blankly at him. Nervously, he looked back and forth between Cilaen and Samara. "What has happened? Is she ill?"

Everyone stood in silence, waiting for Elanor to speak first.

Elanor fidgeted with her hands nervously. She did not want to tell him. The possibility of being pregnant would be burdensome, frightful, and ill timed. Her head was pounding, and her heart raced. Fear invaded her every sense of reason.

"Elanor, what is it? You're scaring me."

Holding his hand up to Merlin, Cilaen carefully said, "There is nothing alarming to know. I promise you. Elanor is well." He urged Elanor, "Tell him."

Elanor felt like she was a pot of water boiling and spitting out over the top. Everything screamed inside her mind. Throwing her arms down, she clenched her fists and ran for the door—pushing past Merlin. The door shut behind her, slamming with a supernatural force. Merlin began pulling on the door, but it would not budge.

Samara shouted, "Has she locked it?"

"It only locks from the inside," Cilaen replied, stunned.

Merlin shook his head. "No, this…this is a force of will, manifesting through her magic. The door will loosen once she is far enough away." Merlin looked at the door with concern, though anger sparked. "What is going on? I would have you tell me."

Cilaen responded with fragility, "It would take me some time to confirm. I had my suspicions this morning and told as much to Samara. I believe, my dear Merlin, that your wife is with child."

Merlin eyes rounded as the revelation of Cilaen's words sunk in. His face lifted in surprise. "Hah!" A single tear fell from his eye as he exclaimed, "I would be a father?" He pulled his hands through his hair and laughed while practically turning a circle. "She is carrying my child? This is what ails her?" He walked to Cilaen and embraced him, before shaking him steadily by the shoulders.

"Please, my lord," Samara interjected. "Why is she upset?"

Merlin put his hand up onto his forehead, his mouth hanging open. He turned to the door and tried to contain himself to think. "I will go to her." Merlin nodded, then, taking a deep breath, headed for the door. He pulled it, and it swung open. He turned toward them both and smiled. "Tomorrow we will celebrate the news properly."

Merlin stopped outside the door, wondering where Elanor had run to. He knew she would want to be alone. He assumed she had gone back to her chamber, but when he arrived, he found the room vacant. Immediately, he thought of the terrace, and he raced through the hallways, through corridors, and up the stairs, bursting onto the platform. But there was no sign of her.

Where could she have gone?

He did not want her to be alone with her thoughts. He put his hands down upon the wall and closed his eyes. Inside his mind he heard her. The sound of her tears echoed in his ears, and he saw her crying, kneeling beside a stone. Instantly, he knew where she had gone.

Merlin ran back behind the walls of the terrace and down into the dark chamber within. He stopped quietly at the entrance, and slowly walked toward the sound of Elanor's tears in the dark. He turned aside to grab an unlit torch and blew upon it. Flames licked to life, filling the room with bright, yellow light.

Elanor did not move. She was aware that he had entered the tomb but remained leaning against Arthur's stone on her knees. One hand in her lap, the other upon the image of the mighty king.

"What are you doing here?"

"I am not sure," Elanor said, gazing up at the stone. "I just ran and found myself here."

Merlin knelt in front of her, wiping her tears. "Why are you so sad? This day I have found that I am to be a father. My heart erupts with joy, while I find that you are here on a stone floor, weeping in a room full of sorrows."

Elanor collapsed forward and sobbed into Merlin's chest, her tears wetting his shirt.

"When you locked me inside with Cilaen, leaving me clueless as to why you were so distraught, I obligated Cilaen to tell me." He brushed through her hair with his fingers. "Is it the dreams that have caused you to fear?"

"Arthur is in my dreams, night after night. I thought maybe he could tell me something." She patted the stone with her hand. "How can I be joyful when I dream a prophecy of my death? I do not know if my time is near. If it is, will it steal this child's life, too? Or will I die, unable to raise my own child? The dreams, Merlin!" Elanor shouted. "They are so real! How can I have this hope?"

"Is this a prophecy or is it just torment?" he asked, his mouth twisting. "I remember waking in torment and anger because of the dreams I had of you, night after night. I knew that the dreams were leading me, but I never imagined that they meant to bring me you. The dreams are only one piece of a puzzle, with many other pieces missing. I wish I could make the dreams stop, but you should not assume that this dream means your death, nor that this child is not a piece that will bring us a fuller picture. And…" Merlin said, cupping her cheek in his hand, "…we cannot stop living our lives or live in fear of something we do not fully understand. If I have learned anything since knowing you…my beautiful one…it is that I must trust the Great God is doing something bigger than us both. And it is He that has chosen to give us the gift of a child."

"You are happy then?" She sniffed, sitting up taller.

"I feel like a king that has been given a gift of highest quality."

Elanor smiled, feeling encouraged, and for the first in many days, a small bit of joy began to fill her heart.

FROM THE WITCHES MOUTH

The days leading up to Beltaine were exciting. The Great Hall crowded every day with the arrival of warriors and chieftains. The towns and the fields were full of activity. Even outside the walls, large encampments grew in anticipation of the events. For both Merlin and Elanor, their hearts rose with the arrival of Marcus. The Druid stood taller and with a greater confidence than he had when they had last seen him. Then, just on the heels of Marcus's arrival, came Thul with his son Thangul.

Ahead of the celebration, games took place in the fields below. Horsemen rode across the fields, holding up the gold and red standards of Caer Lial, and people cheered as they passed.

Elanor marveled that people came excited, not only for the festivities, but also over the word of the new life that grew within her. Merlin's child gave them hope.

Elanor and Gwynevere stood outside on the steps of the Great Hall, watching the people below. They looked like a colorful swirl of ants from where she stood, and it made Elanor happy to see them as she wrapped her arms about her now round stomach.

Finally, the day of ceremony came. It was a grand day. All had been done just like in seasons past, but this time, it was amplified. The champions were brighter, and the games more triumphant. Some of the finest warriors from Caer Edyn and Celyddon, and even King Bram, had come to compete, along with Bedwyr and Peredur. They slapped themselves with blue and wrapped their hair in white clay. The sound of the warriors' wild roars intimidated in the best sort of way.

Bedwyr competed on horseback. In the midst of the game, his spear was knocked from his hand. He stood in his stirrups, grabbing his opponent by his shirt, and threw him to the ground without losing a stride. Bedwyr proved he was certainly not a force to be reckoned with.

Peredur met Bram in a mighty display of sword and shield. Peredur towered over him, and the strength of his arms and legs reminded Elanor of oaks. The battle was long and hard as sweat formed on the warriors' brows. Both were focused, waiting for the other to take one misstep, to reveal a weakness. The force with which they hit sounded like mighty hammering, and those assembled gasped at each strike.

Bram lost his footing for a split second and Peredur was there, knocking Bram's shield into his chin. Blood gushed from Bram's mouth. He spit on the ground and laughed, but Peredur knew he had weakened him. Pummeling his sword down once again, Peredur knocked Bram's shield to the ground, and then swept him to his back, pointing his sword at his throat.

Bram opened his hand to let his sword fall in surrender, and the people roared with delight. Peredur grabbed Bram by the hand, helping him to stand, then slapped his back pridefully. Both smiled and held their hands high as the game ended.

And so, the day continued into the evening as the fires were lit once again, and the people dispersed to their homes to light their own. That night was a feast for the kings and warriors, and all went to bed tired and full, but by the light of the next morning, singing and dancing could still be heard throughout the Caer.

This day was to be the dance and feast to honor the coming of Merlin's child. Only the kings and chieftains, along with their wives, and warriors of high renown were welcomed into the Great Hall, dressed in their finest.

Elanor watched the people dance from the platform. Most times, she and Gwynevere sat alone together while the rest mingled. Elanor loved seeing the people in their fine clothes, dancing and smiling. She herself was dressed in a beautiful, golden-yellow dress that had been made special for this day. Her hair hung like silk upon her shoulders, while braids wrapped tightly around the top of her head. She watched with a smile on her face as many looked her way. Many curious faces gazed at the one carrying Merlin's child. Throughout the day, many approached her to bow with a blessing, and she gladly received them.

A woman stared at her from across the room, capturing Elanor's attention. The woman was blonde and had her hair done up high. Her eyes were piercing, and her dress extravagant. Elanor wondered who she could be.

But after a while, her gaze made Elanor ill at ease—she smiled with an eerie dullness. Her eyes were a strange light green that seemed colorless from afar. She never broke her stare, not even to blink. Elanor would turn away uncomfortably, aiming to focus on something else, but somehow her eyes would find the strange woman still staring back at her.

Elanor tried to convince herself it was just her own fear making this woman's stare so bothersome. She rationalized that the woman was merely seeing her as the object of the celebration, and nothing more. But then, a familiar man with stringy black hair offered the woman some drink. An icy feeling shot through Elanor. She had seen this man before—on the day of the welcome feast long ago. The sight of him rekindled a dark foreboding. He leaned to whisper into the woman's ear. Elanor's heartbeat quickened. The woman's eyes pierced her as she leaned in to hear the pale, greasy man's words.

With a wide smile, Merlin came springing back to his seat beside her. He looked at Elanor, who sat solid and pale like a stone.

"What has happened?" He leaned in, grabbing hold of Elanor's hand. "You look like you have seen a demon."

Breaking her gaze, she turned to him and said, "That woman over there." Elanor indicated the direction with her eyes. "And the man next to her. Do you know either of them?"

Merlin scanned the room—settling his eyes upon them.

"That woman has been staring at me, and it has been giving me a bad feeling, and then that man. He's the one I saw that frightened me at the welcome feast."

Immediately Merlin discerned something off about the two of them. The man was unaware that he had the attention of both Elanor and Merlin as he continued to whisper into the woman's ear, then slowly slank away. The woman still held Elanor with her lifeless eyes.

"She moves about the room, but always her eyes are upon me. At first, I thought, she was only gazing, along with everyone else, but something sinister about her has my blood turning cold."

Merlin leaned forward in his chair and began mumbling words lightly into the air. Elanor put her hand upon his back, and he said suspiciously, "Look closely, and do not be distracted. There is something not right. There is something, like a shade."

"What is a shade?" Elanor asked nervously, but before he could answer her, the woman slowly walked toward them. She seemed so noble and less ghostly as she came closer. The strange woman's chin was held high as they both rose from their seats in preparation for her.

Merlin put on a smile. He grabbed Elanor's hand and pulled her close— still whispering words behind his teeth.

The woman stood before them and bowed low. Her smile seemed false, as though it were painted on her face.

"Great blessing to you both!" she said, lifting her head.

Elanor felt put at ease to hear her speak. The woman's voice made her feel foolish, as though her mind had run away with her. Elanor returned her bow.

However, Merlin's mind was not relieved, for as the woman spoke, he heard what sounded like two voices speaking at once.

The woman took a step closer, and Merlin squeezed Elanor into his side.

"We are blessed to be receiving this child into Prydain. I hope that the gods will give you a son."

Her eyes seemed less colorless to Elanor now that she could see them. They were bright green, warm and welcoming.

"That blue pendant that hangs from your neck…" The woman lifted her hand toward Elanor. "It is so beautiful."

As the woman reached her hand forward, Merlin saw two right arms. One reaching to touch the pendant, and one haggard, twisted hand lifting above her head with a dagger poised to strike Elanor.

Quickly, Merlin snapped to grab hold of the wrist gripping the dagger and shouted powerfully. The woman shrieked loudly. She dropped the dagger, and it clanged to the floor. Instantly, she was revealed, no longer a blonde, noble woman, but an ashen, sunken woman with missing teeth and long, stringy grey hair hanging down around her shoulders.

Elanor jumped back while the woman heaved, dangling from Merlin's grip.

"Death to the Pendragon!" she squealed in a crackled voice, struggling to pull herself free. "Let me go…let me go!"

The music stopped as the shouts commanded the attention of the whole room. Some stared, while others gave looks of disgust at the writhing, haggard woman.

"Everyone! Please move out to the yard!" came Peredur's booming voice.

"Now!" commanded Bedwyr, moving people out quickly. "Get out! Move!"

The guards took over, and both Peredur and Bedwyr darted across the room to aid Merlin. As they reached him, a loud scream stormed the Hall, causing all who remained to fall to their knees and cover their ears.

Elanor stood with her arm outstretched, her eyes fiercely ablaze with blue light. The haggard woman lifted into the air while her arms buckled stiffly to her sides.

Bedwyr and Peredur looked to Gwynevere and Merlin, as if waiting for orders.

Merlin shook his head slowly, warning them to remain still.

Cilaen still leaned silently in the corner, with Marcus gripping his arm.

The room vibrated as Elanor held the woman aloft. "Who are you?" Elanor spoke, filling the room with a powerful, unfamiliar voice that echoed through the Hall.

The woman released a tortured screech as Elanor's power forced her to speak. Her head rolled from side to side. "I am Aberva." She writhed in the air. "Aberva, witch and servant to the triple goddess. Servant of the old religion. Old religion!"

"Aberva, you will tell me the truth!" Elanor commanded. The witch recoiled, letting out a deafening scream.

"Death! Death! Death!" she screamed. "Death to you, filthy Pendragon." She spit the name from her mouth. "Death! To stop you from fulfilling the prophecy. Aaah! Stop it…stop it…Stop! You cannot…make me…tell you."

"You will tell me!"

"No…He'll kill me…He'll kill me."

"Who will kill you? What is his name?"

"He is master. Master. He is the silent, patient one!"

"His name!"

"Lord…Lord Osian. He will kill you! He will kill you," the witch cried ecstatically. "Osian will destroy you. He will stop the two stars. They will not fulfill…the prophecy if he kills them."

Merlin's heart sank inside his chest. Osian. He looked to Gwynevere to see if she had recognized it also.

Elanor pressed, "What is the prophecy? What will he stop? Tell me!"

"Only you can wake him. Wake him up. If you wake him up, all could be lost. Only she can do it…only she can."

"Wake who?"

"The Great Pendragon. He sleeps. He only sleeps for a thousand years, then she will wake him. The poison did not kill him. It did not. His wounds were not fatal. They make him sleep as the cursed one he is to these lands. Young Pendragon must not wake him."

Elanor gasped; reeling from what the witch had just announced. Could the witch be talking about her?

"I am not a Pendragon!"

The witch cackled a gurgling, throaty laugh. The sound of it made Elanor's face twist with disgust.

"She doesn't know. No...she doesn't. They send you away one day. They will send you far, far away to protect you...but not yet. You will be one day born the child of Arthur and Gwynevere. You are Pendragon. But not yet...not yet... not if we stop you. You will never be born. You will never wake him, and you will never become. You and he and Merlin cannot bring in the new age."

"Shut up!" Elanor said, as tears formed in her eyes. She clutched at her side, refusing to understand the witch's words. "You are lying."

"You make me tell the truth? And I shouldn't...I shouldn't tell secrets. Let me go! Let me go!" The witch screamed and contorted. "He will kill me!"

Elanor dropped her hand down, letting the witch fall to a clump on the floor.

Peredur shouted, "Take her!" Warriors grabbed the screaming witch and dragged her out from the Hall.

Elanor stood in shock, facing away from the rest of them. "It's impossible," she breathed, her voice barely above a whisper.

The silence lingered heavy in the room and remained unbroken until a gentle voice arose from the back corner of the room. "I do not know how," said Marcus timidly, "but it is true. That is why I thought the promised prophecy would not come once Arthur had been slain. I thought it was impossible. The prophecy foretold the second star would be a younger Pendragon. But...I thought...when I discovered that Elanor was Gwenddydd, that someone else had risen up to fulfill the prophecy."

"It is true," Gwynevere said suddenly. "The moment I saw her, she was known to me. It was her face." She gazed around the room at all the stunned faces. "She is his very image. Say you have not seen it! The way she speaks and moves. I saw it right away, though I could not understand how. I thought maybe the Great God had returned Arthur to me. Her eyes are Arthur's. Her spirit is his own." She stepped down from the platform and walked over to stand in front of Elanor, whose eyes dripped silent tears. "Arthur is dead, and I have never been with child…and yet you are here, and I could never deny it. You are my own, and you carry a true Pendragon within you." Gwynevere's chin quivered as she reached up to touch Elanor's cheek. "Could it be? That my Arthur will return to me? Tell me, Merlin. Isn't Elanor the one who has travelled to us through time?"

Elanor collapsed to her knees, and Gwynevere knelt, throwing her arms around her as she wept.

Merlin could hardly move or even breathe. The revelation ran through his mind so fast, he could hardly catch up. She was every inch Arthur, except that her hair, mouth, and hands were that of Gwynevere. He thought of what Elanor had dreamt. The shield, with her and Arthur on one side, and he on the other. He thought of the evil poison that had taken Arthur, having only spelled him to sleep for a thousand years. But it had only been six years since he had been entombed in the Hill of the Kings. If Elanor had come from a future time, then maybe this could all be possible, but to think she had not even been born yet, and here she was. One day to be born and hidden away, far from harm's reach, to grow up in a future land. And in all of this, he was even more overwhelmed at that thought that he and Elanor should be the destined ones. That Arthur's daughter would be his one love.

Slowly he moved to her. The shock of it all made his arms and legs feel like leaded weights. He knelt and grabbed Elanor's hand, staring off, confounded.

Could they hope that Arthur would wake? Could they believe that the words of the witch were even true? They all agreed, at the declaration of Gwynevere, that there was no doubting the resemblance. It was as if blinders had been taken off their eyes, and what they already knew to be true was revealed. Was this the reason it was so easy to accept this strange, magical visitor? Maybe they had not just accepted her because of Merlin. Maybe it was because it had felt like Arthur had returned the moment they met her. The kingdom returned to life when she came, and now, maybe they knew a little of the reason why.

47

OSIAN

"L ord?" *said the feeble servant presenting himself within the darkness of the cham-ber. "Dunnoc has come, and he wishes to see you."*

"Donnuc?" said the voice. The figure leaned forward from his chair into the smallness of light that revealed his face. Shrouded in the shadows, only the whites of his eyes and teeth could be seen clearly.

"Yes, Lord. Dunnoc says that he comes to you from Caer Lial."

Out from the darkness, an object came flying toward the face of the servant. The object, barely missing his face, clanged onto the floor behind him—its contents splattering the floor.

"I should rip out his spine for coming here. He brings me ill news. Let him come in."

The servant bowed and scuffled out of the chamber, returning only moments later with a greasy, black-haired man.

The master squinted his eyes into small slits as the man entered nervously. "How dare you come here? Do you have any idea the risk you have incurred? No one can know where I am. You are one of the few who does, and now you violate this trust by coming here so openly."

"Lord Osian," Donnuc said, his voice trembling. "I was very careful to be sure that I was not watched or followed. I used magic to conceal myself." He rifled with his hands anxiously in front of him.

"Speak!" Osian shouted.

"Aberva was caught. Merlin discovered her. Her shade did not blind his eyes. She did not kill the Pendragon, and she was executed. She's dead…Dead."

"Dead?" Provoked, Osian stood from his great chair, his teeth clenched. "Do you have any idea the years it took? The blood that was poured to give her the power to deceive the eye and sway emotions? The cutting and the solitude to prepare her—and she failed. Aah!" he yelled in a rage. Charging forward, he grabbed Dunnoc by the throat.

"Please," he choked. "Master. I have served you faithfully. I have spied. I have done well setting up your devices of devastation. It is not I who fails you."

Osian let go, throwing him onto his back.

"Why are you here, Donnuc? You could have sent me a message in the ways I have shown you," he said, looming over him.

"I have been discovered. The girl had her suspicions a long time ago, so I remained out of her sight. But then, she saw me speaking to Aberva and pointed me out to Merlin. When Aberva failed, Merlin had men seek me out. I ran. I am no longer of any use in Caer Lial. They know I am untrustworthy."

"You drew attention to yourself."

"I underestimated the young Pendragon. She can see," Donnuc said as he slowly pulled himself from the ground, but as his body came upright, Osian's hand came down across his face—slapping him back to the floor. Blood drained from his mouth onto the floor. This time Donnuc remained down with his head low, afraid to lift his eyes.

Osian swung himself around angrily and threw himself back into his chair. He leaned back, placing his hands on his head and rubbing his temples. "If you say you serve me faithfully, then you will do this task for me."

"Anything, Master."

He pulled out a large, wooden box that laid tucked in the darkness behind his chair. As he brought it close, Donnuc saw iron hinges and a lock. Osain set the box before him. As Dunnoc gazed at the box, a sick darkness radiated from it, sending fear into his blood. His every instinct willed him to escape from whatever evil it contained.

Osian jammed an iron key into his face. "Take it!" he seethed. "Take this box and key to my servant Bevon. He will take the box to Caer Lial and open it there. There has been much dark magic sown into this. Do not fail me. This dark spirit will surely destroy them." He brushed his hand over the top of the box. "This foul breath will not be easily stopped. It is death itself to all who see it."

With great trepidation, Donnuc wrapped his arms around the box. He knew to say nothing more if he wanted to leave with his life. He would take the box and obey.

"You are fortunate, Dunnoc," he heard Osian say as he walked out of the chamber, "that you are not the one I am asking to open the box."

364

"Explain who Osian is so that we may all know and understand," Gwynevere said to Merlin as he stood among the council within her chambers. All sat on edge to hear why the declaration of this name had precipitated such worry.

"Osian and his mother lived in Caer Lial not many years back. Osian's mother was a servant within the Palisade, while Osian served the men, much like Uri does now. He was a tall, lumbering child, not very well liked amongst the other children his age. He was always angry and often set the other children against him on purpose. It was such that we could no longer allow Osian to serve in the Hall, as he was always instigating trouble. He delighted in it.

"Osian and his mother were invited to serve in the Palisade because Gwynevere took pity on them when his father was killed.

"His father was a druid but chose to marry. It is not against the druidic way for one to marry, but in this case, Osian's father no longer desired the druidic ways of life. But his father had been given a powerful talisman by his ollamh. He was assigned the task of keeping it secret and hidden. Even though he was no longer part of the druidic order, Osian's father remained its guardian.

"The talisman was a medallion, shaped in a half moon and made of bronze. In the center of the moon was a white stone. No one knew where this talisman had originally come from. Some thought it may have travelled from lands far in the east and arrived here with the Romans, carried by priests of one of their gods. It was discovered that this talisman could be used to sway people's minds and thoughts—especially those minds that had no foundation to pull on for truth. It was decided to hide it and keep it safe, away from those who would use it to manipulate others.

"Osian's father kept it hidden from all, even Osian. Osian had been very vocal about how he thought his father to be weak for not using it to give their family advantages in their lives. He tried to teach his son that things are not gained in life that way, but Osian never learned and resented his father for it. When his father died, he searched for the talisman but never found it.

"That was all until his mother became ill. She sent for me as she was dying and relayed to me the truth about where her husband had kept the talisman. She warned that her son should never know where it was and should never have access to it, for she said his heart had gone wrong.

"Osian must have been listening, neither of us aware of his presence. For as I sat with his mother, he seized the talisman from its spot. After I left his mother, I believe he returned, and he did not spare her life.

"Men were sent to seek after him, thinking they would easily find him, as he was still young and foolish—a mere adolescent—but no man found him. This is the man that the witch spoke of, and the one behind the murderous devastations of these days. He wields a talisman designed to control and manipulate, which makes him very dangerous. He would be now, not much older than our very own Cilaen."

"I remember him," Cilaen said.

Bedwyr grumbled, "I also remember the menace."

Peredur nodded his head, his eyes focused on the ground. "If only we could discover his plan, then we could do something. Be ahead of him."

Peredur's final comment revealed what they all already knew—that they were still clueless as to what to do about any of it. Knowing the name of their enemy was helpful but gave them little direction.

They now had hope that somehow Arthur would return to them, though they did not know how, as the mystery of a thousand years still loomed before them. For any strides that this new information helped them take forward, the truth was, it felt more like they were pushing against a stone that was leaned against them.

Days passed quickly after the revelation of Elanor being a Pendragon, and Elanor watched as Merlin grew distant, leaving her to be with his own thoughts. She also grappled with the witch's prophecy, the weight of her sinister words hanging heavily on Elanor's shoulders. With the baby coming soon and the recurring nightmares, she did not have the strength to pull Merlin back to her. The days bore a heaviness, and most were spent watching him sit in deep thought. The reclusive wizard had returned, and he spent his days away, seeking answers, leaving Elanor alone and confused.

The sun had only just set beyond the horizon—Merlin had fallen asleep by the hearth and Elanor had just gotten into bed when there came a knock at the door.

Elanor sat up.

"Not to worry. I will go see." Merlin threw his tunic on over his head and rushed to the door.

The Cymbrogi on the other side of the door spoke in rapid whispers. Merlin closed the door, then turned to dress himself.

"Are you leaving? What has happened?"

"Nothing for you to worry about," he replied as he laced his soft leather boots. "We have men patrolling the forest around the citadel during the nights. They have come across something suspicious. Nothing alarming. We have instructed them to report all things out of the ordinary."

"Oh," Elanor breathed sadly. Though they shared a space, it felt like Merlin was miles away.

Merlin rose, peering at her through the dark. He dropped his head, then approached her; kneeling at Elanor's bedside. "Please do not concern yourself. You need your rest." He placed his hand on her pregnant belly. "I am sorry. I have been... I don't want you to..." He closed his eyes, squeezing his brow tight. "I will return to you shortly." Quickly he stood, leaning down to kiss her head, before turning to leave.

Merlin and Peredur, along with two other men, rode out not far beyond the boundary of the great outer wall, carrying torches into the darkness—just past the edge of the forest to the head of a narrow road. They cut through to reach a part of the road deeper in and came upon a broken-down, mangled heap of what used to be a wagon. As they dismounted, Merlin saw that it had been turned on its side, the wood on the wheel splintered.

"Did they crash?" Peredur asked. "It does not seem like there is anything the wagon could have hit to be so damaged...Did the horse break free and run off?"

The young warrior beside him pointed. "There are tracks leading away that appear to be from the horse. But that is not the whole mystery. Come." He waved them around to the other side of the wagon.

Merlin spotted splinters of wood scattering the ground. He waved his torch around the forest floor, looking for a pothole or rock that could explain the damage.

As they rounded the wagon, a sight came into view that caused Merlin's insides to twist. The smell came first before his eyes could take in the scene before him. A man lay shredded and blood soaked on the ground—his chest and stomach flayed open and his face unrecognizable. His hand was clenched around an iron key, and beside him were the remains of a wooden chest splintered into pieces.

Peredur held his hand over his mouth. "What could have done this?"

Merlin knelt close to glimpse the key but dared not touch it. He looked up with foreboding. "This is not good."

Peredur began to track the hoof prints into the forest, off the road. Not far ahead, he discovered a lump through the trees, barely lit by his torch. There lay the horse. He picked up his pace to get a closer look, and the utter devastation created little doubt that the same thing that had attacked the man had also killed the horse. It laid shredded upon the ground, completely disemboweled.

He ran back to where Merlin sat inspecting the remains of the box. "I have found the horse. It has been killed in the same way, but strangely…" he said oddly, "there were no tracks anywhere that I can see of any other creature. There isn't even any trail of dripped blood. Nothing."

Merlin shot straight up, a look of horror crossing his face. "We must return to the Palisade. Now!" he shouted. "If I am right" —he hastily lifted himself onto his horse—"this is a gwyllgi. A demon hound of smoke, fire, and darkness."

48

THE FOUL DEATH

"I know of this creature," said the warrior with them as he raced for his mount. "Stories I heard as a child. The gwyllgi hunts you on the roads of the night. This creature will steal your soul with a gaze of its red eyes."

"It is much more than that," Merlin replied. "Its intentions are that which its master places upon it. I do not believe it has been sent to roam these roads. No. It is an attack from Osian. I am certain of it. The Palisade…Elanor is not safe." He clicked his tongue and commanded, "Yah!" kicking his horse's sides and launching him forward.

They ran as if the gwyllgi were on their very heels. They pressed through the first gate, undaunted, through the town, keeping their eyes peeled.

Osian must have delved deep to have conjured a demon unseen for an age. But Merlin encouraged himself that the Great God had also awakened great spirits to help them. It gave him hope amidst the fear that grew in his belly as they burst through the second gate, crossing the fields.

Death gripped at Merlin's heart, for as they reached the Great Hall, three horses laid massacred just off the side of the road. Their heads still hung from the ropes that bound them to their posts.

"Check the stall," Peredur commanded in a whisper. "Latch the doors shut."

"Doors do not stop this creature," said Merlin, warily climbing down from his horse. He watchfully glared at the Great Hall. "Wake the men to the ready and send Bedwyr to the queen's chamber. I will go to Elanor. Go!"

Both men ran into the Hall as screams echoed out from the courtyard, increasing their alarm. Peredur bolted ahead and crashed through into the courtyard. A few higher-ranking men had already been awakened by the scream and were filing out their doors. Bedwyr appeared, armed and ready with a spear.

"Great God!" came a shout.

The men scrambled to where a warrior had been found, torn open on the ground.

"Who is it?" Bedwyr said, pressing his way through. "What could have done this?"

Peredur grabbed hold of Bedwyr. "Go to the queen. Now! It is a demon."

Bedwyr's eyes shot wide open, and he instantly disappeared into the Palisade.

Peredur drew the attention of the men and commanded, "Be vigilant! Be armed! We are dealing with something that is not animal or man."

Cilaen hung over the balustrade, witnessing the commotion from the upper floor, and took off in a snap toward Elanor. He ran down the stairs to enter the Palisade and tripped over a large mass that he had not seen in the dark—falling onto his stomach. As he gathered himself, he discovered a warm wetness all over the front of him. Confused, Cilaen felt around. The stairs were slippery and sticky to the touch. The metallic smell was all he needed to confirm the horror that was already filling his mind. It was blood, and he had tripped over a man, killed in the darkness of the stairwell.

Another scream resonated through the corridor. Cilaen sprang up in dread. Panicked, he ran down the stairs through darkness and out into the Palisade. The torch light of the room revealed the smear of blood that ran down the front of him and all over his hands. He swallowed deeply, seeing nothing else in front of him, and pressed on.

The screams woke Gwynevere out of a deep sleep. A warm wind blew in from her window. *Had I only been dreaming?* she wondered, the white light of the moon dimly lighting her room. From the foot of her bed, she caught a mass of fur moving across her chamber. Tingles went through her as she heard a dull, guttural growl.

Slowly, she reached for the dagger at her bedside, becoming alert and ready to fight. The noise and the ominous shape seemed to disappear. She rose cautiously, clutching the dagger. Her eyes darted back and forth at every corner. With deep, anxious breaths, she waited. Then, she lowered her hand and stood taller, thinking she must have been seeing things. Yet the prickle in her spine kept her alert. The only sound was the silent breath of the wind.

The gurgling growl returned behind her. Gwynevere turned to face the corner of the room, where two red, glowing eyes appeared in front of a growing shadow. The eyes were small but bright, searing into her soul as if hot coals were burning through her eyes. Petrified, she was unable to move. Her eyes were transfixed on the fearful malice. The shadow moved toward her like a cloud of smoke with eyes, sharp and clear.

The door burst open, and Bedwyr dashed through with a spear in one hand and a blazing torch in the other. He shouted out, threatening the air. His cry broke Gwynevere's trance, and she stepped back, lifting her knife. Bedwyr stabbed his torch's flame toward the shadow, diving in between it and Gwynevere. Sharp claws stretched out of the smoke, black and long, with a force that knocked both Bedwyr and Gwynevere back onto the floor. As they collapsed, Bedwyr raised his spear in anticipation of an attack. But the creature had gone.

Immediately, he stood to his feet. He scanned the room, ready to for an attack. His face and neck dripped with thick blood.

The frightening commotion outside of her chamber caused Elanor to get out of bed. The sound of people running through the hallway and loud screams roused her fear as she wrapped her arms around her pregnant belly. She quietly moved toward her door when Merlin charged into the room breathlessly.

"Aah!" she screamed.

Merlin let out a long sigh of relief, seeing Elanor unharmed, and collapsed forward, putting his hand on his heart.

"Merlin!" Elanor shouted fearfully. "What is happening?"

He put his arm up to reply as Cilaen burst in behind him, covered in blood. Elanor gasped at the sight of him.

"Great God!" Merlin yelled, reaching for him.

"No! I am not injured…I am well," Cilaen said, shaking his head. "A warrior has fallen in the passageway."

Merlin dropped his arms, breathing heavily. He moved toward Elanor, every part of him yearning to wrap her into his arms, relieved that she was safe. But before he could reach her, the sound of panting breath stopped him in his tracks. The sound came from one corner, then moved to another.

"Sshh!" Merlin whispered, halting them. "Cilaen, grab a torch from the hallway. Quickly!" Merlin grabbed Elanor by the arm and pulled her into his chest, frantically listening as the invisible demon panted.

Cilaen returned, waving the torch into the corners, its light rippling off empty stone corners.

Merlin mumbled words under his breath, but this time Elanor understood them, and they sounded like a prayer. "Great God, hear me. Save us from this demon. Let your might overcome the dark."

In through the open door entered Gwynevere, followed by a very wild-looking Bedwyr. His hands and arms trembled ferociously as he gripped his spear and torch, and his eyes bulged like a mad warrior about to spring. The right side of his face and neck bled from deep scratch wounds the size of a bear claw.

Bedwyr growled, "There are two more dead in the corridor."

"What is it?" Gwynevere asked, clutching the dagger at her side.

"It is a gwyllgi. An ancient demonic hound. Our only weapon against it is fire and the light of morning, Great God help us."

"Osian?" Gwynevere asked, her voice pinched with anger.

Merlin nodded, his eyes alert. "It will have been sent with a purpose," he said, looking down at Elanor.

A loud howl resounded just outside the chamber. The sound pierced Elanor's heart with dread. The howl was followed by several barking jackal-like noises, and then another long howl. The haunting yips were moving closer.

Around the corner of the door, a black, thick smoke rolled into the room. It moved quickly, growing into a large form in front of Elanor.

Bedwyr and Cilaen pressed their torches into the evil vapor, making it shift back. A solid force materialized out of the smoke, knocking Merlin to the floor, leaving scrapes across his stomach, and flinging Elanor into the wall—slashing her arm and tearing her clothes.

The smoke gathered in the center of the room as the beast slowly took shape. Four black legs formed monstrous paws with sharp black claws. The body became a crouching wolf with large shoulders, lined with prickly quills like sharp branches poking out from its body, mingling into the blackness of the smoke. Its face was formed with pointed ears and snarling lips that revealed a mouth full of pointed grey teeth. Its small red eyes floated within the smoke.

Elanor coughed from the impact as she fell to the floor. Chills prickled her nerves as the gwyllgi's eyes set upon her and voiced an angry bark. The wolf-like creature reared back against its haunches—ready to pounce.

Bedwyr and Cilaen's flames did little to daunt the looming creature. Bedwyr rammed his spear into it, while he shoved his flame into its face. The spear sliced through the center of the creature's body, but only seemed to lodge into the smoke and branches that formed its body, causing no damage to the creature. The gwyllgi jumped back from the flame, and Bedwyr stood strong, holding his ground against it. Cilaen stood beside him, using his torch to push the creature further back.

"Do something!" Gwynevere screamed at Merlin.

Merlin stood up quickly, feeling at a loss. His mind was jumbled, and he could not think clearly. His sole focus was ensuring Elanor's safety, but once he'd found her, he, along with everyone else, was caught up in a frenzy of fear. The creature seemed to paralyze the thoughts of its victims.

He turned to see Elanor, who gazed at the gwyllgi with terror, holding her stomach and bleeding from her arm. His thoughts refused to form. Everything moved slowly as if he were muted and half asleep.

The creature jumped to the side, out of range of the two flames. Bedwyr tried to head the creature off again, but he would not make it in time. The creature reared, ready to leap at Elanor. Without a clear thought in his mind, Merlin spoke out of the magic that was within him.

A burst of wind erupted in Elanor's direction as the heavy claws of the creature fell upon her. Her clothes crumpled to the ground, seemingly emptied as the great hound dug in, its teeth ripping and tearing at the garments on the floor. The frenzied creature did not notice that Elanor no longer remained. All of them watched in horror as the creature tore.

Merlin looked around the room in a stupor, searching for where Elanor had disappeared to. Somewhere safe, he hoped.

The gwyllgi stopped, heavily panting, and sniffed at the clothing on the floor. Upon realizing nothing laid beneath its claws, it threw its head up and howled. Then, it whipped its murderous head toward the door and dissolved swiftly into smoke. Bedwyr's spear fell onto the floor with a clang.

"What have you done with her?" Gwynevere asked to Merlin tearfully. Cilaen gasped, "Is the demon gone?"

"No," Merlin spat. "It knows she is alive. We must find her before the gwyllgi does, or else hope that she finds a place to hide." He gritted his teeth. "My mind has cleared now that it has left us…I know I can kill it. If we do not, the creature will return night after night until it has obeyed its master and licked its thirst for blood." Merlin approached Gwynevere and embraced her. "I do not know what happened. I wanted to save her, but something else…" Merlin shook his head. "Come! We must find her quickly."

They rushed into the hallway, collecting more torches as they went.

"Do not shout for her," Merlin cautioned. "We must keep her concealed."

"Where would she have gone?" Bedwyr asked. "How are we to find her without leading the creature to her?"

In all their haste, Merlin stopped. He tried to remember what had happened. He had started to release whatever power was within him against the creature, but before he could, an unexplainable wind came.

He tried to focus on what was at hand. They had to find Elanor.

They all stared at Merlin, their flames making the shadows on the walls dance.

Merlin breathed, concentrating his mind as he reached out to Elanor within his heart. He imagined her, for a split second, laying on the cold, stone floor of his chamber. He almost brushed away the thought, but then he realized that in the suddenness of the moment—that was exactly where he would have sent her.

49

GWENDOLEN

T he wild gwyllgi howled, and its hacking bark resounded through the Palisade as the creature hunted for his prey. Merlin hoped he wasn't leading the foul beast straight to Elanor but was unwilling to leave her for the hound to discover first. Either way, they would have to confront the beast. They could not allow it to continue its rampage, slaughtering men, or worse, the innocent people in the towns below, who Gwynevere hoped knew nothing of the evil upon the hill.

Up the stairs, now lit with their torches, they discovered the body of a man strewn over the steps. Cilaen now had a clear view of whose blood covered his tunic.

Gwynevere gasped, turning her head away as they picked their way around gore.

Rage sparked in Bedwyr's eyes.

They could not linger with sorrow but pressed through onto the balcony. The courtyard was ablaze with warriors gathered with torches and weapons drawn. Gwynevere's heart was strengthened by the sight of so many still standing strong, ready to fight to protect their Caer. The voice of Peredur rang out, bolstering their courage, calling out to the men through the perimeter of the hill.

Pushing open Cilaen's door, Merlin called out, "Elanor…Elanor." He strove to not panic as he pressed into the room. There was no sign of her. He began to fear his fleeting thought sent them in the wrong direction. Frantically he rushed, knocking over anything that stood in his way, reaching for his chamber door.

"Is she there?" Bedwyr asked, ready to launch back out the door in search for her.

Merlin pushed the door open, pressing his torch into the darkness. There, lying naked, curled on her side, was Elanor. Her dark hair cascaded delicately down her back. Merlin breathed out in relief, slowing his haste, and quietly approached her. He shook a blanket free and laid it upon her, caressing her shoulder and placing his hand upon her stomach.

Softly, Merlin whispered, "Elanor." But she laid there, unresponsive and unconscious.

Stepping through the door, Gwynevere entered.

"We have found her. She is here."

"How did she come to be here?" Gwynevere knelt beside Elanor, brushing her fingers over her head.

"I would not know how. This is not the work of my magic."

"It wasn't you?"

"I do not know who or what it was. Only that it saved her."

"Who could have done this magic?"

Merlin shook his head. "I am only relieved that she appears unharmed."

A looming howl sounded, pulling them back into their plight. They sprang to their feet. Merlin ran back in through the door, hearing the chuff of the demon's breath. Both Cilaen and Bedwyr steadied themselves, preparing for the attack.

Merlin turned back and whispered to Gwynevere, "Stay with her," then shut the door.

The sound of sharp claws scratched on stone, closer and closer. The creature's violent panting grew louder. It snarled as its large body slowly lurched through the doorframe, its small, red eyes revealing its impending will.

It bared its teeth at the sight of them, and a deep, guttural growl made the air in the room vibrate. Unshaken, the three stood ready with their fiery torches blazing, their eyes fixed on the beast. The atmosphere was thick with the power created by its bloodthirsty presence.

Merlin stepped forward in defiance of the menacing hound. He lowered his head as a low hum resonated from his throat. Suddenly, he cast out his arms, and his eyes flashed with a fierce, golden light.

The beast winced back, barking threateningly at Merlin's display.

"Come at me, beast!" Merlin's voiced echoed.

The gwyllgi surged, rising with its teeth chattering and biting at the air. Merlin glared, his body shaking with great power, and declared, "You and your master fail. You are nothing."

The hound lifted its head, howling loudly, then leapt toward Merlin with its claws and teeth bared. Merlin brought his hands together as the creature flew at him, and light brighter than the sun sprang out of him, filling the room with its luminance.

Blinded, Cilaen and Bedwyr fell to the floor, covering their eyes.

Within the light, Merlin heard voices and saw the faint, white silhouettes of otherworldly men. They were moving and talking to one another, whispering in words he could not decipher.

"Do not fear time," boomed a voice above the rest, breaking into Merlin's spirit. The man in blue walked out from the light, approaching Merlin with his hand outstretched, pointing at his heart. He touched Merlin, and there was a flash.

Merlin opened his eyes and found he was lying on the floor. His head ached, and he blinked his eyes, trying to focus. His ears rang with a shrill whistle. Cilaen knelt next to him, speaking to him, but Merlin could not hear his words. His whole body stung as though he had been struck by lightning.

Cilaen blotted Merlin's head and mouth with a damp cloth, but Merlin pushed his hand away and slowly rolled to sit up. The gwyllgi was gone, and Bedwyr sat not far from him, holding a cloth, damp with blood, to his face and neck.

The ringing gradually began to dissipate, and he heard the muffled sound of Cilaen's voice. "You've killed it. It's gone. It burned up into flame when the light hit it. Nothing is left of it, not even its smoke."

Merlin noticed a sulfuric smell in the air. Tables had been blown across the room, and glass laid shattered all over the floor.

"Elanor?" Merlin said. The sound of his own voice was dull in his ears. He quickly stood, stumbling dizzily as he approached his chamber. He crashed into the door, pushing it open, while supporting himself against its frame. Elanor lay wrapped in a blanket, still unconscious, in Gwynevere's arms. Her white shoulders glowed like pearls.

In relief, Merlin collapsed onto the floor, sitting in between the two rooms. He turned his head. The room before him was in shambles, but free of the hideous monster. Merlin looked the other way, and there was his wife, safe in the arms of the queen. A smile grew on his face as he breathed in the calm of reprieve.

Cilaen returned to address his wounds once again. Merlin looked like he had run through fire. His body was covered in a black soot, and his head bled from striking it on the floor when he fell. His nose was bleeding, and his hands were burnt.

Cilaen stepped over Merlin to more closely examine Elanor. He pulled the blanket down to expose the three stripes left by the gwyllgi on her arm—they were not deep. With a clean cloth, he dabbed at the wound.

"Ai!" Elanor jumped, pulling her arm away. She looked up into Gwynevere's face, and then over at Cilaen in surprise. "How did I get here?" Gwynevere pulled up on the blanket to cover her, and Elanor gasped, tightening the blanket as she realized it was all that covered her nakedness.

Merlin pulled himself over to her on the floor and reached for her. "It is gone."

"The demon? What happened?" She peered up at him weakly. "You look terrible."

Merlin laughed, pulling her into his chest. "Are you well?"

"I think so."

"And the baby?"

"Fine, I think," Elanor said, gazing down at her stomach.

Bedwyr came into the room and leaned against the door with a smile, still holding a cloth to his face.

Elanor winced at the sight of his rough appearance. "You look terrible, too."

"Apparently, these are the spoils of wrestling with a hound of smoke and death," Bedwyr said, taking the cloth down to reveal his wounds. "In truth," his smile turned downward, "I do not think that there is any reward in this day, save those of us that survived it. I fear to know all those that lost their lives this night."

"The men who still stand ready will need to be told," Gwynevere interjected, "that the creature has been destroyed. There will be a lot to recover. Merlin, do you know how this happened? How did such an evil come?"

"It was awakened by dark sorcery. Osian would have had to take lives to have resurrected this power."

"You know it to be Osian?" Bedwyr asked.

"I am certain. He is staining the land with all his wickedness, though I know that all of this evil has cost him. His soul will be rent from him as he gains these powers. Our defeat of his creature will scar him, and I hope he may not be able to recover from it."

"Are we never to have an upper hand with this enemy? Osian sends his worst, and we have no way to be prepared for it."

"Oh, but, my lady," Merlin said, "if we had not had a watch in the forest, we would have had no warning, and we would not have been ahead of this creature's wrath. Our vigilance has helped us, with the loss of fewer lives."

"This is little comfort to me."

Bedwyr bowed and said, "I will find Peredur, and—"

"Aaaahhhh!" Elanor cried out, buckling forward in pain.

Gwynevere grabbed Elanor's face. "Is it the baby?"

"All of this trauma has not been good for her." Cilaen started pushing them back. "It is too early. Bedwyr, find Samara and bring her here immediately. Hopefully we can—"

"Aaaahhhh!" Elanor cried. The floor beneath her became wet with blood and water.

"There is nothing for it," Cilaen said. "This baby is coming. Bedwyr, go! Bring me Samara, and Merlin, you should not be in here." Cilaen sprang into action, shoving the two men out of the room. "Go!" he commanded, gazing into Merlin's eyes. "I will take care of her. I promise."

He shoved Merlin once more and shut the door.

Merlin heard Elanor crying out, and it sent him reeling. He stared at the door as adrenaline burst through him, unsure if he should remain or bust back through to be by her side.

The yells and screams of labor brought him back into memory:

There he stood on the other side of a doorway while Igraine was in her chamber with her midwives delivering her baby. In front of him, a very worried and conflicted Uther paced the room uneasily.

"You will remove yourself from that doorway, Merlin," Uther commanded. "That child is not my son."

"No! It is your late brother's child, and heir to your throne. I will not allow you to kill it."

"My child, and only mine, will sit upon the throne. Not this…this…"

"This is your brother's very own. Do you care so little about his memory? He who held you aloft so highly."

"She deceived me to not tell me she was with child when we wed."

"You love her, could you not love the child?" Merlin asked in earnest. "You know me, Uther. I would not stand against you, but I will not allow you harm this child. You know my strength, and I will use it if I must."

Igraine cried out from the other room, and both men cringed anxiously. Uther did love Igraine, but he was a prideful man, set on his own sons being heir to the throne. He was blinded by all other reason. Finally, a cry rose from Igraine's chambers. The sound of a baby crying out in full health.

"Come with me, Uther. Come see the child. Maybe then your humanity will return to you."

Slowly the door opened, and they entered inside. Igraine lay in bed, sweaty and tired from her labor, but with a look of utter peace and joy, holding her swaddled baby in her arms. Uther softened at the sight of his wife holding the child.

However, that night, Uther's heart grew cold once more as he tossed and turned in his bed. Murderous thoughts returned, and he was determined that this child should never become heir. So, in the night he lurched out of his chamber and down to where he saw Igraine gazing out a window as the wind blew her hair.

The baby was gone. She had given the child to Merlin to hide far from Uther's reach, but before she let her baby go, she named him Arthur. Kissing him on his head, she gently laid him into the arms of the druid who would one day make him king.

The door swung open, snapping Merlin out of his thoughts. Samara entered the room hastily. Merlin quickly pointed her to his chamber, as more sounds of screaming rolled through the cracks of the door. She nodded and ran to the door, letting light escape as she did.

The sun was rising, and light slowly crept into the room. Merlin looked down and noticed his hands were shaking. He wasn't sure how much more his heart could take as it thumped through his chest.

Bedwyr returned beside Merlin, staring over at the door as he heard the muffled sounds of Elanor wailing in the pangs of labor.

"Unsettling, this," Bedwyr said finally. "How are you faring, my friend?"

Gulping down some air, Merlin said, "I feel more anxious and helpless now than I did when we knew that the gwyllgi was at our backs."

"You need water," Bedwyr said, pouring his friend a drink to wet his mouth, and then pouring another for himself. He drank deeply, staring at the door warily.

Merlin was glad for the distraction. "Your face and neck need attending to."

Pointing at the door, Bedwyr laughed. "Yes, well, apparently my healer is busy." He hesitated before soberly stating, "Twenty-eight men."

"Twenty-eight?"

"Twenty-eight men slaughtered throughout the Palisade halls. The sun is rising, and I am glad, as the evils of this night will haunt me."

All at once, the screaming stopped, and all went silent. Merlin hoped to hear the blessed cry of a baby. Both he and Bedwyr waited anxiously, anticipating the moment. As the silence lingered, alarm rose within Merlin's chest. How long should he wait before breaking the door down? Every part of him ached to know what was happening with his wife and child.

"Please, God, please," he whispered underneath his breath.

Bedwyr reached his hand slowly to Merlin's shoulder, as he unknowingly leaned toward the door.

The door unlatched with a crack, and Cilaen stepped out. He had a fatigued look in his eye and sweat on his brow. He sighed and looked at Merlin with a tender smile. "All is well, my friend. All is well. Elanor has done well. Would you like to meet your child?"

Blessed relief filtered down from Merlin's head to his tingling fingertips. "My child?"

"Come," Cilaen said graciously. "We have won both of the battles brought us this night."

An unexpected fear and apprehension washed over Merlin, but this was a fear he had never felt before. One of awe and excitement. The moment was immense, and he felt ill equipped to accept it. Timidly, he moved through the door to see Elanor's eyes brighter than he had ever seen them, and her cheeks wonderfully flushed with rose. She smiled down at a little bundle wrapped in her arms. Out of the swaddle, little pink hands flailed, grabbing at the air— softly murmuring.

Elanor peered up with joy in her eyes. "Would you like to meet your daughter?"

Deep inside Merlin's heart, a spring was uncapped at the sound of the word *daughter*. A laugh of joy came bubbling, and tears floated down his cheeks. Tenderly, he wrapped his hands around the tiny bundle and brought it to his chest. He gazed at the child's tiny frame, perfect and whole. There was a swirl of dark brown hair on top of her head, and as her little eyes blinked open and shut, he could see the blue in them. He never knew he could have so much room in his heart.

"She has not raised her voice to cry," Elanor said, brushing her hand across the baby's plump cheek.

Merlin pressed his lips on the forehead of his baby.

"Gwendolen," Elanor said, looking up at Merlin.

"Yes, yes…Gwendolen. Gwendolen."

DRAGONS AND THE MAGIC OF TIME

The birth of Gwendolen marked a new season. With her birth, much of the darkness seemed to dissipate. Vanquishing the gwyllgi had done more damage to their adversary than any of them could have ever imagined. With the enemy crippled, many of the dark rumors from the Southlands quieted. Even Elanor's nightmares were no more, giving Merlin the belief that the dreams had been a device of darkness and not the promise of a tragic future.

None but the company surrounding the queen knew about the witch's revelations of Elanor being a Pendragon. Keeping much of Elanor's origins a mystery seemed like wisdom—keeping the truth away from prying ears. Merlin believed Osian remained still hidden in some dark corner, licking his wounds, waiting patiently for his next move. Time had been Osian's gift before, and it would be his advantage once again.

The height of this new season came with the arrival of Adhan from Dyved. She had come at the reception of the message that her son's child had been born. But even more, she brought with her news that King Cormach had finally returned home. He had received word of Merlin, which had given him rise to look toward Prydain once again. He returned with a beautiful new bride— bringing Dyved much joy. With Adhan, he sent a message of fealty to Gwynevere, as well as a promised visit to the citadel.

This now offered strength in the south, should Osian lift his finger to wound the lands, and gave Lugh and Croighcat less of a foothold. Even if the two southerly kings gave Gwynevere no sign of support, they would not have the strength to oppose her now. They would have to fall in line, or else come against Prydain's most powerful kings.

Patrols were sent out from the four kingdoms to scour the lands, their aim to be watchful of the enemy arising as they kept the villages safe and set their eyes upon any shift that gave them warning.

Meanwhile, Gwendolen grew from a small infant to a chubby-cheeked toddler, with black curls upon her head. It was surprisingly Peredur who seized the many opportunities to sweep her up into his arms and shower her with affection. Most evenings Gwendolen spent lying on her mother's chest until she fell asleep, with the calming sound of her father's harp and song.

Two years passed this way, as they fell into a contented rhythm. The light of Gwendolen's face made them forget their turbulent existence after Elanor's arrival. What had once caused alarm no longer plagued their minds.

Then, one night, Elanor heard a rising note deep within her heart as she dreamt. It was a song that carried the tremblings of magic. Calling her. Pulling her.

She snapped awake, rising to her feet in urgency.

Merlin woke, startled. "What is it?"

With her eyes wild, she said, "Dragon!"

"Dragon?"

She threw her robe around her. "I've heard her...she calls me. She's here. She needs our help."

"Wait. Elanor, I..."

"Merlin." She paused, staring hard into his eyes. "She called to me in a dream. Only it was not a dream. We have to go to her."

"Now?" He stood, shaking his head. "Dragons are old ancient creatures. I did not believe there to be any left."

"We must go," she urged.

"We? Elanor...Dragons are dangerous and unpredictable creatures. They have deep wisdom, but usually care little for humans. We cannot just go running out to face one if there is one to be seen."

"Merlin, I understand, but trust me when I say we must go. It is as Grwyrthrhodd speaks. It was magic. There is no time...please."

Merlin gazed at Elanor, confounded. She was convinced and would not be stopped. Apprehensively, he nodded, and quickly, they dressed before stealing out into the night, wrapped in their cloaks. The slap of the cold night air on Merlin's face woke him fully, and strangely, he also began to discern magic.

"Where are we headed?" he asked.

"To the open plain between the two forests."

They silently slipped their way into the stables. "Lord Merlin?" It was Uri, who rolled out from a pile of warm straw on the floor. Uri was much taller now and had been moved from being an errand boy to a stableman. This was his hope, that as he served faithfully in the stables, he would one day earn a place to train as a Cymbrogi warrior.

"Yes, Uri...it is Merlin. Elanor and I are riding out on an important task. There is no time to explain, but all is well. You are free to sleep."

Uri looked at them curiously. If it had been anyone other than one of the lords of the Palisade, he would not have allowed them to take the horses, but as it was Merlin himself, he let them through. He watched them strangely, hoping that he had not been fooled in some way, but stood, dumbfounded as they raced past him on horseback.

The air was cold and frosty. It bit at their cheeks and hands as they rode. The cold, white vapor of their breath blew behind them.

Arriving at the open plain, they were surrounded by forest, except for the hills that broke out before them. They dismounted, and Elanor searched the darkness as she held her reins. The night was clear, illuminating the hills in blue light. The trees were a backdrop of pointed blackness, revealing nothing.

Elanor furrowed her brow, glaring into the distance. "This is the place, but I do not see anything."

"What did you hear when she called?"

"I heard her voice in my head, then I saw of flash of dragon's wings, and this place. The wings were golden, and...she said she was called Gwyliwr Aures Draigen."

"Guardian. That is her name. Call to her."

Elanor stepped out into the empty darkness. The wind sounded with an empty howl, blowing her cloak and hair gracefully as she listened intently. She took a deep breath and called out, "Gwyliwr Aures!" The sound of her voice rolled out, and then was stolen away by the wind. She called again, "Gwyliwr Aures!"

Merlin stood beside her, watching with his keen eyes.

"Gwyliwr Aures...I have come! I heard your call! I am here!"

From the corner of her eye, Elanor saw a flicker. She turned to face the hills.

"Gwyliwr…" She saw it again, and now, she stared right at it. She pointed for Merlin to see, and there appeared a lonely blue hill, moving ever so slightly. The pit of Elanor's stomach triggered with fear at the imposing size of the hill. Merlin's warning of dragons' unpredictability and dangerous nature now seemed real. She took another deep breath, pushing past her fear. "Gwyliwr Aures."

This time when the hill moved, its shape shifted, and it appeared less like a hill. Its size seemed to grow as it moved toward them. Slowly it slinked, making them feel as though their eyes were deceiving them in the darkness. It walked with an unsteady pace, almost as if it were limping. Then it stopped. The creature seemed undecided whether to approach them or remain still, fading back into the shape of a hillside. Elanor called out again, "Gwyliwr Aures!"

The creature snapped violently, rushing toward them as it let out an earth-shaking roar. They covered their ears as the splitting sound rumbled, almost knocking them backwards.

The dragon shouted with a reverberating echo, "Who are you? Why do you disturb my slumber?"

Its long neck grew longer, towering high above them. The darkness made it appear black as it unfurled its wings. Its nostrils flared, its head rising with the terrible sound of sucking breath.

Merlin acted quickly. He held his hands above them both and shouted, "Amddiffyn!" just before a cloud of smoke and fire came hurdling down upon them. Merlin's strength shielded them, deflecting the fire off an invisible barrier.

The horses took off running as the flames licked down. Merlin gritted his teeth to hold off the inferno, while the heat of it radiated down upon them.

The flame ceased, and Merlin gasped in relief. The arms of his cloak smoked, filling the air with the smell of singed cloth.

"What is this?" the dragon boomed. "You cannot stop me, sorcerer."

Merlin yelled back, "We are not here to harm you, Gwyliwr."

"Who are you? And who is this woman that calls my name?"

"I am Merlin, and this is Elanor. We have come at your call, dragon."

"I did not call you, Emrys," the dragon hissed. "Yes, I know you, and your purpose has nothing to do with me. You should not have meddled with me."

Elanor could see the heaving of the mighty beast's chest and the vibrations of her throat as she spoke. As her eyes adjusted in the darkness, she saw the dragon's scales were tattered and sparse. Her color was green and dull. Her legs were twisted and lame, and her wings were torn.

The dragon continued, "Why have you awakened me? I wish to diminish. I was to become one of those hills—forgotten and asleep like the rest of my kind. I am all that remains. My magic is gone, and my usefulness, spent. I live no longer for a broken world that has forgotten me. Now there is only silence as man does what he wants. Their drought of spirit has broken my body, and I am guardian no longer. It is time for me to sleep. Go, and bother me no longer."

"It is not your time to sleep, Gwyliwr Aures," Elanor said, pressing her way past Merlin.

The dragon lowered her great head to look down at the small woman that dared defy her words.

"Elanor!" Merlin warned, fearing the dragon would roast her or smash her with its teeth.

"You may not know that you have called me, but your spirit is alive and has done so without you. You are Gwyliwr, and there is still need of you."

As Elanor spoke, she looked into the glowing green and yellow of the dragon's eyes. Within her, magic sparked, but this magic felt stronger, and much deeper. An icy gust whipped at Elanor's clothes. Her eyes flashed bright blue. She opened her mouth, and a song rose high and loud. The song itself floated through the swirls of the wind as it moved around the mighty creature, whose head alone stood tall like a tower over the feeble woman below her.

The dragon became lulled by the song and bowed its head. Elanor moved closer to the dragon, placing her hand upon its mighty nose. Light and sparks began to pop out from where she touched the creature, moving up past its nose, crackling and snapping as it continued over its face, and then down its neck. At each crack, a golden green scale was revealed—brightly shining and new. The magic flowed over the dragon, from wingtip to the end of its powerful tail.

Elanor ceased her song and lifted her hand, collapsing to the ground. She gazed up from the ground at the magnificent golden creature above her. Each scale was bright and alive with light. Its legs were straight and full of muscle. Then, the dragon spread its wings wide, appearing like green fire.

The dragon lifted its head high up into the sky and roared. The tremble of its voice rang with brightness—strong and vibrant like the blast of many trumpets.

The dragon burst up from the ground, shaking the earth, soaring as high as the moon. She danced and twirled like the dragon Merlin's magic had made so long ago. Flying high, she disappeared out of their sight. Both Merlin and Elanor were left amazed and shaken by the sight.

Elanor said weakly, "Is she gone?"

Before Merlin could reply, the wind from the creature's wings blew down upon them heavily as the dragon descended, landing lightly upon the ground.

The dragon spoke, "I remember myself. I had forgotten. My magic flows freely in me once again. How has this been done?" She gazed at her wings and jumped up and down on her strong sturdy legs. "I thought my purpose was over, but now I can see," she said, peering at the two of them. "And I know you, Emrys and Gwenddydd. The Great One reminds me. How much I have forgotten." She threw her head back and laughed, making a sound like horns mixed with the great purr of a lion. "You wait for Arthur. Only the three can do it. Only the three. That means it is time for your gift. That is why I called you. I must have called you so long ago, I lost the memory. You healed me, Gwenddydd, so now I will give you what makes all that must be done possible. Only a dragon can gift magic like this. Emrys, hold your twin close. The Great One would have me give you this."

Gwyliwr took a deep breath, pulling the curve of her neck back. Merlin grabbed Elanor, standing her up, and bracing her into his side. He could hear the roar of the fire coming up from the dragon's throat, and for a split second, felt like a fool, fearing they were about to be burned alive. However, the thought came too late, as fire spilled out of the dragon's mouth and surrounded them.

The fire came out white and hot. The heat stung and stabbed and felt like it was ripping off their flesh, but as they dared opened their eyes, they saw that they were not consumed. They held each other tightly as they were yanked and pulled.

Elanor heard many voices. One moment she was next to Merlin, the next she was in her favorite café back home, and Bill was offering her a cup of a coffee and talking about her paintings. Then, she was standing in front of Merlin in the apple orchard on their wedding day. Faces flashed by that she did not recognize, but then she saw her father David—overflowing with joy at the sight of her. All the while she was ripped by the flames. The flames were strangely similar to the wind in the dream that tore her through time.

Merlin was also seeing people and places, in rapid succession. He saw himself standing with his grandfather, learning to wield the spear. He saw Arthur holding the sword of Aurelius high above his head. But then he saw an older version of Gwendolen calling out for him.

The fire went deep inside of them, and then out to all the places and people they had known. It burned deep down into every muscle and fiber. They screamed out in pain. Elanor buried her head into Merlin's chest as he clung to her. It felt as though they stood inside the flames for an eternity, but it had only been a moment, when the fire stopped. They crumpled to the ground in each other's arms, gasping for breath.

"You will recover," the dragon said. "You have gone a long, long way in a very short time. You will feel tired now. Dragons' magic is hard for humans to carry. Most cannot. But you are special. The Great One has gifted me with time, and time is the gift I have given to you. You will understand how to use it when you have need of it. Know that you will see me again, as we are now joined in time together." Then, leaning her large head toward Elanor, she said, "Thank you, Gwenddydd. For now, I see time again. It was not the season for me to diminish—you were right." She turned to Merlin, her breath blowing his hair back. "The Great One would remind you, Emrys, not to fear time."

With that, she extended her wings and lifted into the air. She rose as lightly as a dragonfly, and unlike the giant creature Merlin and Elanor saw before them. She flew off, leaving them there in the dark, stunned. The pathway into mystery was opening wide, and their lives were about to change once more.

THE WHITE AND RED DRAGON

Exhaustion from the dragon's magic made them fall into a deep sleep. It wasn't until the sun rose that Merlin opened his eyes. Fog and the stillness of morning rested in the open field. He slept so soundly, he expected to wake in his own bed, discovering it all to have been an unusual dream. Instead, he awoke, frozen and cold, with the frost of the morning on his clothes, and Elanor lying asleep in his arms. The thoughts of the dragon and its strange, white fire flashed in his mind. What had they been given? A magic of time? He was unsure whether it was a gift, as every part of him ached.

"Elanor." Merlin gently roused her. Her lips were blue with cold, and her eyes were red as she slowly blinked them open. She pulled herself up, immediately feeling the cold, and drew her cloak tighter.

She weakly croaked, "I thought it had all been a dream."

"As did I, but the burnt grass tells me there was fire. And I can feel..." he looked at her strangely, "...the new magic. It is uncomfortable...like pins underneath my skin."

Elanor moved her shoulders awkwardly and placed her hand on her chest. "It is almost like it knows it doesn't belong."

"It will adjust if the dragon spoke truth. I heard the man in blue tell me...that night that Gwendolen was born. He said I was not to fear time. I did not know what he meant. I still don't, but now..."

Elanor's teeth chattered, and Merlin quickly wrapped her in his arms. "We must get home. It is likely our horses have gone back without us, and we will have to return on foot. It will warm us to move."

He helped Elanor to stand, and they began their trek, plodding silently. As she pondered, her heart leapt at her encounter with a dragon. She thought of the beautiful, golden-green scales and the flash of the dragon's eyes.

She asked, "Have you ever seen a dragon before?"

"In a way, I have seen two other dragons. A white and a red one," Merlin said. "But they were spirits under the ground and above me in the sky. Not like this. I have heard many men say they had seen them in the mountains. I have also known druids to tell stories of them, but dragons do not often interact with people. They keep to themselves, and I thought all had become legend."

Elanor's eyes sparked. "Tell me about the white and red dragons."

"I saw them in the days that the Saecsans still plagued our lands. Shortly after I left Dyved in my grief." He swallowed deeply, the sting of remembrance running through him. "I lost myself then. I went running deep into the wilds, losing all of my sense of reason for a long time. While I hid away, a king named Vortigern rose to power. He was a greedy coward. He gutlessly traded much of Prydain's land to the Saecsans, aiming only to preserve himself. He cared nothing for the Cymry who were losing their land and their lives.

"He set to establish himself high on a hill—to be able to see a Saecsan invasion if they turned on him. So, he commissioned his men to build a great wall and tower atop a hill; however, as they set stone upon stone, the wall would collapse, and they would have to start again.

"Vortigern was angry that his builders were unable to prevent the walls from tumbling. So, he consulted dark druids, and they declared that the triple goddess was angry, and he would need to make a sacrifice to appease her. This sacrifice needed to be a young boy that had not been conceived by mortal man. The druids knew of such a boy. They came in search of me, as my father had been a mystery to them, and they foolishly divined that he was not mortal.

"I knew that my time of hiddenness had come to an end. I had a reckoning with the Great God, and it was time for my gifts to have purpose. So, when they came for me, I was not afraid. This was to be the first step I took toward the kingdom that was but a seed within my heart.

"When the druids came upon me, I presented myself willingly. They did not like my boldness because it made them feel powerless. In truth, they were fools," Merlin said, shaking his head with a broad smile. "Powerless fools. As was Vortigern."

"I arrived to see Vortigern standing outside his mighty encampment. He was regal with gold wrapped around his neck and his wrists. He stood there, so pious, ready to spill my blood so he could have his hill.

"The moment I stood before him I spoke boldly, 'Your priests are fools! They tell you lies to protect themselves. You can spill my blood, but still your walls will collapse. You will never take this hill.'

"'How dare you speak to me,' Vortigern said. 'Who are you that I should allow you to contradict the words of my priests, who have faithfully served me?'

"'I am Emrys Wyllt. Myrddin, some call me,' I said. 'You would be wise to listen. You build your walls over an underground lake. There is no witchcraft here. No angry gods. The foundations simply cannot carry the weight of your stones.'

"'You are only a boy. What do you know of any of this? How could you know of a lake beneath our feet? That would be impossible to tell.'

"'It is not impossible, and I can tell you it is true. The spirit that has revealed to me this lake is a greater God than the one that has spoken to your priests. The voice of your priests' god would have you fall into destruction and cares not about you nor your walls. At least have your men dig, and then you can know who is telling you falsely.'

"King Vortigern was moved by such bold speech, and immediately had his men dig. He declared death to his druids if they had lied to him. It took them all of three days, but at the end of the third day, to the surprise of all, they found a cavernous lake, just as I had said.

"The ground naturally gave way once the lake was revealed, and we had to scramble away from its edge. As the ground settled and we peered inside, there beneath our feet were two mighty dragons. One white and one red. They were spirit, and when I saw them, I understood what they were. Vortigern saw them, as did all that were there that day.

"The dragons woke and began to wrestle, and as they fought, the ground shook, causing more earth to give way. The red dragon rose up against the white, but the red was weak and sleepy. The white dragon easily dominated and would defeat the red. But then, the red dragon suddenly roused. It stood taller, rising with strength. It retaliated against the white dragon, and this time, the red dragon overpowered it. The white fled, flying up out of the hole and into the sky. The red dragon pursued, until they both disappeared into a cloud of white.

The red dragon returned, victorious. Circling back, it flew low over the land with its mouth wide—then faded into the air.

"King Vortigern fell to his knees and begged, 'Please, Emrys Wyllt, tell me, what does all of this mean?'

"'This lake,' I declared, 'is the land of Prydain. The very soul of the Britons. The white and the red dragons are authorities fighting over this land. The white dragon represents the invaders, and those who would suffer them to remain. The red is the guardian and soul of the Cymry people. They have been left weak and sleepy by their years ruled by Rome, but no longer. The red dragon will rise up and crush the other.

"'The red dragon also represents a man returning to his people, who will drive out the invaders. He will be known as the Great Pendragon, and he will set up the rule of a New Way and new kingdom age for the Cymry peoples.

"'You, Vortigern, will be cast down with the rest who aim to injure these lands.'

"Vortigern shook in his cowardice. He ordered his priests to be executed, and then fled to find a new corner to build his tower. It wasn't but a few weeks later that I encountered the two sons of Prydain returning from their banishment. They were brothers and heirs of the high throne, before the demise of their father by Vortigern. Their names were Aurelius and Uther. Aurelius the older, and Uther the younger. The three of us together gathered forces from around the land of Prydain and cut down the Saecsans on the western shores. Side by side, I fought with them in many battles, intimidating the enemy as we went. Then finally, we burnt Vortigern and his tower to the ground."

"Wasn't Uther named the Pendragon?" Elanor asked. The story had awoken so much curiosity. If it was true that Arthur was her father, then these men would have been her kin. "Was Uther my grandfather?"

"Hah!" Merlin laughed. "No, Elanor. It was Aurelius that was crowned king and married the young Igraine of the southern kingdom. Though she loved Uther, her father wanted her to be married to the king, and not the king's brother. Uther remained High Battle Chief and charged the lands of Prydain and continued to battle the invaders, earning him the name Pendragon. It is Aurelius who was Arthur's father, though he was killed before he could be known as such, and then Uther became king and married Igraine. This is why Arthur had to be hidden. Uther did not want his brother's seed sitting on his throne."

"Aurelius was strong and kind," Merlin said with a calm sadness. "He was my friend. Our battle cries rose as one as we cut down our foes. His hair was dark and raven like yours. Unlike Arthur, who had the golden hair of Igraine. Aurelius had courage, but in the end, he was too gentle in spirit, and he was dashed for it. Uther had a hard, firm hand. Arthur became the embodiment of them both. A formidable battle chief, and yet his strength was in his love for his men and his unwillingness to crush unless mercy had first been offered. It was Arthur that the prophecy of the red dragon was truly about. He was the Great Pendragon."

Elanor was baffled. To think she was related to such mighty men, and yet here she was, married to Emrys Wyllt himself. The stories made her feel connected and alive. She wished she could have known them all, just as Merlin had. Oh, to see Arthur would be glorious! Would she see him awakened? Was he truly her father? She longed with everything to see herself in his eyes.

It took the entirety of the morning before the Palisade finally came into view, and with that came Peredur, leading Cymbrogi in search for them.

THE BLACK PLAGUE

W hen the horses had returned without them, an alarm had been raised. Very quickly, Uri reported that Merlin and Elanor had left during the night.

Peredur breathed out in relief as he caught sight of them, wandering bedraggled over the hill. "What in Esu's great name are the two of you doing out here? You both look like you have been through a storm. You left us beside ourselves in worry."

"Gwendolen?" Elanor asked.

"Adhan has had her well-kept. You mother seemed to not worry a lick about either of you."

Merlin laughed, exhausted. "She knows her son all too well, my friend. Needless are ever the deeds of Merlin Ambrosias." He winked. "Truly sorry to worry you all. We had not predicted our horses leaving us. I suppose we should have thought as much encountering a dragon."

"A dragon?" Peredur scoffed. "Surely you have lost your mind in the cold."

"Lost mind or not, I am certainly glad you have come to find us. We are beyond cold and tired, and our bellies are crying out for some hot food."

Peredur laughed, shaking his head, and quickly Merlin was atop a horse with Elanor positioned behind him, heading home to a warm fire and a hot meal.

The encounter with the dragon had left both Merlin and Elanor expectant. The gift from the dragon would be a timely one, and it would not stay hidden within them for long. They both struggled with unease, as the magic was unusual. It felt as if they had something stuck in their throat, or a thorn sticking in their side, and could find no relief. Always there was a nagging feeling, like there wasn't enough room to breathe, and they felt squeezed.

It was the middle of the cold season, and flurries of ice and snow had come from the north. A man came seeking the queen from a village in the east. Gwynevere knew this man must be in great need to brave the cold and frigid air that was unkind to travelers.

The man looked roughly worn, calloused from hard labor, grizzled and weathered.

"Please," Gwynevere said to the man, who stood contrite, gazing at the floor, "you have come to speak—I would hear you."

"I am Haldin," he said timidly. "I am but a simple farmer. I come from a village only a short way east of here. We are a small settlement, and mind ourselves most of the time, without need of help from others." Nervously, he kicked at the floor. "But some kind of witchery has befallen us, and we do not know what else to do. I come here to ask for help from the Lord Merlin. He knows the ways of magic and such."

Merlin leaned forward.

Gwynevere's nerves rose. "Haldin, what has happened that makes you believe that there has been witchery?"

"It happened first to my daughter, you see. We thought it a sickness brought on by the season of cold. She came back to us after gatherin' wood for the fire. She said she felt tired, but by the evening her face had turned a pale white—her lips turned grey, almost black. I have never seen anything of its like. I thought she might have eaten some poison, but she would know better," he said, choked with emotion. "The next morning, she did not wake. Her skin was cold and hard like stone. Her fingers bent crooked, like the grip you get when you feel pain. She was only the first, for four others have been afflicted. All women. Just the day before yesterday, one of our small ones came back with a handful of thorns, calling them flowers. Then, by morning, she too was like the others." The man sighed as tears fell from his eyes. "They are all still alive...but the breathin' gets weaker and weaker. Our healer knows not what to do, and we are all afraid to drink from our well, for fear that it has been poisoned. They lay there quietly fading away. We searched the trees, and we have searched our fields. It is like there is some invisible creature we cannot see lurking on our land, waiting for one to stray into its trap. It is not just a sickness. It is something else. Please...Can you help us?"

"How far is your village?" Merlin asked.

"It is less than a day's ride. Please, we know not what to do."

"Get this man some warm food," Gwynevere commanded, waving her hand at a servant girl who was standing ready. "We will discuss your plight and have you returned shortly. Please do not be troubled; you have done right to come here."

The man nodded as the servant girl came, taking him by the arm. As she led him away, he peered up at Merlin imploringly as he passed.

"Cilaen," Gwynevere said, "do you know of a sickness of this kind?"

Cilaen stepped out from his corner of the room. "No. I have heard of nothing like this. The descriptions of the afflicted are strange."

Gwynevere asked, "Merlin?"

"No," Merlin returned, pressing his brows together. "I do not want to be quick to say that this is sorcery, but I have never heard tale of a plague like this. This man comes because he does not believe this is a plague. Otherwise, they would suffer it out and burn the afflicted."

"Do we help him at the risk of our own? It is the cold season, and this illness could infect those we send."

"I am not afraid to help them," Elanor declared suddenly. "I understand it could be a risk, but what if the healing that is in my hands could help them? I would not want to withhold it for risk of myself. What if it is some kind of evil enchantment, and they are left to deal with something that destroys them like the other villages, decimated by those evil hooded men? What if we could do something to stop an evil, but we chose not to?"

"Truly," Cilaen agreed. "I could at least go with my medicines to aid them."

"Merlin?" Gwynevere asked again.

Merlin knew the answer was not a simple one, but he did agree with Elanor that if something could be done, they should not ignore the chance. This was a village within their realm. Finally, he said, "I think I know the village Haldin comes from. It is not far from here. Peredur, Bedwyr, and I have been through it on our travels to Caer Edyn."

Bedwyr nodded, giving a knowing look.

"It doesn't make sense," Merlin continued, "that a plague should start in so small a village with hardly any contact with other places. It is always the ports, and more specifically, in the grime of cities like Lindonium that reek of disease and plague. I think it is worth investigating. It does seem a strange thing. If this is a sorcery, or even a sorcerous poison, then we must do what we can."

Gwynevere breathed out heavily. "This feels dangerous. I cannot help but feel a foreboding. Certainly, we do not want to risk plague. Things have been so quiet since the vanquishing of the gwyllgi." She drifted sadly into thought, then continued, "The kingdom has become so much stronger, yet if this has anything to do with Osian, we cannot run the risk of doing nothing. Merlin and Cilaen both know how to contain plague, but it does not set right to let you go," she said to Elanor.

Elanor leaned back. "I have magic that could save them."

Gwynevere exhaled again, questioning her decision even as she made it. "If you will go, Merlin and Cilaen, I would have you aid this village. I will send Bedwyr also, with a few men of his choosing. This village is within the reach of Caer Lial, and they will be helped by us. Though I caution you to be careful. Merlin has always had wisdom to guide, so I beseech you all to heed him." Gwynevere shook her head and sat back into her chair, disturbed. She looked over at Elanor. "It is never wise to hold a horse back in its stall." She opened her hands. "You have the grace to heal, and so you should go with them also."

Elanor sighed, but did not celebrate, for she was keenly aware of the ominous tone, and was unsure whether she truly wanted to go. Her powers of healing had been so fickle.

The horses were readied early the next morning before the sun had risen. The riders were bundled in wool for the cold journey that lay ahead. Haldin shifted on his horse, anxious for them to set out.

Elanor had kissed Gwendolen as she left, feeling a great pain in her heart at her choice to leave her. Still, it felt important for her to go. There was a gift within her that was not meant to be hidden, but as she stood before her horse's saddle, her stomach twisted at the thought of pulling herself up and departing.

"What is it?" Merlin asked, noticing Elanor's pained look. He gripped her wool-wrapped hand and squeezed it.

"I don't know. It's not the mission that bothers me. It's the leaving." She looked up into his eyes. "I have never really left Gwendolen before, and...I don't know, I have a strange feeling."

"I know your heart. I feel it, too. You could still stay."

She breathed, "Do you think it is right that I want to help?"

Merlin leaned down and kissed her. "Your spirit is so bright. It is meant to help lift the darkness, and you and I are also meant to stand in the gap of these dark times. So yes, I do think it is right that you would want to help."

The journey was made colder by a wet mist that lasted most of the morning, and then by the afternoon, a biting wind seared through their damp clothes. The land was mostly flat, which gave them little trouble. The cold kept them moving at a faster pace, helping them make good time.

They arrived just after the sunset. As they approached the village, fires burned brightly.

Haldin spared not a moment, leaping down from his horse as a sturdy, plump woman came running to greet him, embracing him.

"They have come!" she exclaimed hopefully.

"Yes, yes!" he said triumphantly, lifting her off the ground as he hugged her. "How is she?"

"Still breathing, but sadly unchanged. There is a warm place prepared for you," she said, turning to the waiting riders. "I will take you there to rest. There is nothing for you to do after your long day's ride in the cold. We will give you some hot food, and then in the morning, you can see them."

"I would see them presently." Cilaen jumped down from his horse, immediately untying his medicine bag. "For I have prepared herbs that may be helpful."

"Yes," Haldin responded with a nod. "This is my wife, Eddna. She will take you to them."

The party was willing to help that very evening, but were relieved at the welcome of a warm fire and food after the chill of the day. Haldin brought them to a round house with a roaring fire on the hearth.

Shortly, Eddna returned, bringing them a warm pot of stew. "We had prepared it on the chance that you would come."

Inviting mounds of hay were set about the room, laid with blankets, and Bedwyr and his men settled themselves quickly down onto them as they ate their stew. Elanor sat close to the fire to warm herself, but soon found herself next to Merlin on the hay and fell asleep to the wonderful sound of the fire cracking and popping.

53

THE SCENT OF PRIMROSE

The next morning, Elanor woke feeling recovered from their cold trek. The fire had warmed the small space, leaving her cheeks warm and rosy.

Bedwyr had already woken with his men and were rallied around the flames, adding dried wood. There was stew and bread left from the night before, and they helped themselves.

Cilaen was still not with them, having spent the whole night with the sick.

Merlin spoke sleepily from behind Elanor. "This house is so warm I could keep sleeping happily. It will make the morning air that much colder." He sighed. "Ah, but we are here to help Haldin. Bedwyr?" he said, standing to stretch himself. "Elanor and I will go to see the afflicted. You and your men should spread out around the fields and the forest surrounding the village. Anything out of the ordinary should be taken into account."

Quickly they ate, and walked out into the cold, dark morning and misting rain. Haldin had been waiting for them and ran over to meet them.

Stressed, Haldin eagerly said, "I hope you slept well."

Merlin breathed through his teeth, huffing in the cold, "We slept so warmly it helped us to forget about this cold."

"Can I take you to them?"

"We are ready. Lead us."

Haldin raced them through a muddy road with wagon tracks made hard in the frozen cold. It was difficult to see through the fog—making it grey and dark. Finally, they arrived at a door at the end of a row of thatched houses. Quietly, the door creaked open, and the warmth from inside thawed their chill.

The room was strangely still as they entered. Before them were five small flats, each with a girl laid in blankets. On the other side of the room, sitting at a small table, was Cilaen, fast asleep with his head in his arms. In front of him lay all his bottles and a grinding stone. His fingers were stained an orang-ish-brown from the juice of herbs and plants he had been smashing and grinding.

Elanor walked over to him and gently placed her hand on his back. Cilaen awoke with a start, knocking his bottles onto the floor.

"Oh…" he said, rubbing his face tiredly. "Did I fall asleep?"

"It is alright, my friend," Merlin said. "It appears you have worked long into the night, which is more than the rest of us have done."

Cilaen smacked his cheeks, forcing his eyes to open wide. Haldin ladled a hot liquid into a cup from a pot set by the fire and handed it to Cilaen.

"Here, drink this. Something warm ought to do the trick."

"Ah, yes." Cilaen gratefully accepted the cup from his hand.

Merlin walked over to the girl nearest to him and observed her closely. He touched the grey skin on her face and found it frigid like ice. Her lips were black, just as Haldin had described, and her skin felt hard like stone.

"Cilaen?" Merlin asked. "Have you discovered anything?"

"No. I have never seen anything like it. I gave them each a tincture that would increase the flow of blood, in hopes that would do something, but there is no change."

"This one is my daughter," Haldin said sorrowfully, placing his hand on her forehead. "She is only twenty. She has such a beautiful smile." A tear slipped from his eye.

Merlin grabbed an oil lamp and handed it to Elanor.

"Hold this near for me. I want to look at her eyes."

Carefully, he lifted the girl's eyelid and leaned down. Underneath were grey, lifeless orbs. The sight made his heart jump. Merlin restrained his alarm, gazing sideways at Haldin. By all appearances, the girl seemed to be dead. He leaned down and placed his ear on her chest, and sure enough, within her breast there was a light thump. Though strangely, it sounded far away.

Elanor's eyes floated down the line of sick maids, her eyes settling on the youngest one, who was probably not even in her fifth year. She lay petrified, with an expression of pain frozen upon her face. The silence grew eerily frightening; not even the sound of breath could be heard from them. Elanor squinted, watching their chests barely move as they slowly sucked in breath.

Merlin closed his eyes and placed his hand on the girl's chest. He focused in deep and began to chant under his breath, the effort of his chant growing on his brow. A low, muffled growl resonated in his mind, and the smell of foul breath filled his nostrils. Gasping in alarm, Merlin snapped open his eyes and yanked his hand away.

"What happened?" Elanor said, startled, nearly dropping the clay lamp.

"This, this…" Merlin spat out the words with disgust. "This is sorcery. This is not some plague or disease. No, Haldin, you have been right to call this witchery. It is as though their souls are being held captive by a foul demon."

Haldin asked desperately, "Do you know the curse?"

"I do not. I do not suffer dark magic, and do not know all its fallen ways. But with every darkness, it takes but a little light to shine and it is dispelled. We just need to find the source that has created this. Has this happened to any others?"

"No, lord. None. We have gone to keeping the women inside."

"Keep them in their houses. Whatever has caused this ill will be found outside." Merlin walked away from the girl and placed his hands on the table, pondering what he had just seen. "From which direction did these girls return from when they came home sick?"

"Our back fields, there," Haldin said, pointing east. "That is why we have not drunk from our well. It is located in that field. We have searched it and found nothing unusual, but many of our people are afraid to go out there and refuse to look further, afraid they will be cursed."

At Haldin's final words, a rooster crowed just outside. The room slowly flooded with light as the sun rose, and the misty rain beginning to lift. The room brightened, revealing fine, web-like lines running across the faces of the sick girls. Their faces appeared marbled, making Elanor's stomach turn.

"Merlin?" Elanor asked. "Might I try?"

Suddenly, awareness returned to Merlin, and he peered up out of his dark thinking. He had almost forgotten that Elanor was in the room, and he responded with a jerk. "Haldin, have any of the women that have cared for these ones become ill themselves?"

"No, none, my lord. My wife and the other women have been here to care for them, and none have fallen ill."

Merlin breathed out a sigh of relief. "I am sorry. I do not mean to be on edge. This room has caused me to feel strangely. Elanor, try to help them if you can."

Elanor warily placed her hands on the icy head of the girl. It sent tingles down her spine to feel the unnatural texture and temperature of the girl's skin. She tried to focus and kept reminding herself that these ones were worth doing all she could to save them. Breathing deeply, she focused on the magic within her. All eyes were on her, hoping that at least Elanor could break the curse and set them free.

She felt the magic stir and move down through her arms. Then, a stinging, icy pain burned the tips of her fingers. She yanked her hand away. "Aaahhh!" Her fingertips had become grey like stone.

Merlin ran immediately to her side, grabbing hold of her hand. He watched fearfully as Elanor's fingers slowly returned to their natural color. Warmth returned to them, and she rubbed her fingers together. Her heart beat fast, and she felt as if she had been bitten by a snake, lucky to find that the teeth had no venom.

Merlin grabbed her face frantically. "Elanor…Are you well?"

"I think so." She breathed heavily.

Cilaen walked over and grabbed at her hands. "Let me see."

"I'm fine. I'm really fine. It was like it was resisting me. I feel as I ever did." She struggled to convince them.

Merlin slapped his hand onto his forehead, then let his hand drop slowly down his face. "I need to get out of this room. Haldin, now that the light is up, can you show us this well? Maybe with my eyes, I will see more clearly. Cilaen will know how to test the water for poisons." Merlin glanced over at Elanor and lifted his chin. "Stay beside me, hum?"

Elanor nodded, still rattled.

Haldin took them to the well that laid underneath a tall, stone cairn. Inside the dome was a wooden crank that held the rope to the bucket. The bucket rested just outside the dank hole, smelling of wet soil. Beyond the well was a field with briars, and then a thick line of trees. Everything was dried and frozen.

Haldin left them there to do their work, giving them a sense of relief. His worry and fear added an uneasy pressure, and it was nice to have their own sense while they searched for answers. Being out of the house with the afflicted lifted their increasing fright.

Cilaen even laughed to himself, feeling caught up in it all.

While Cilaen pulled out a few empty vials from his satchel, Merlin sent the bucket down the well to retrieve some of its water. The liquid came back up looking and smelling as it should, and he helped Cilaen to fill some vials. Merlin boldly sipped some of the water, swishing it through his teeth, then spat it back out on the ground.

"I do not believe this water to be tainted. So many of the people here had been steadily drinking the water while the girls fell sick. Still, we will wait to see what you find, Cilaen. I think there is some other answer to this riddle." Merlin stuck his head inside the well's stone cairn, examining the inside to see if there was anything strange.

Elanor gazed out across the field. Everything seemed to be as it should be. Not far off she could see a heifer and two sheep happily grazing on a small pile of wet hay. Wind blew across the plain, and the trees creaked in response. How could evil have befallen such a simple place? If it hadn't been for the afflicted girls, she wouldn't have believed there was anything to fear.

Cilaen shouted toward her, "Elanor, could you grab me my satchel, just there?" He pointed. "I need some more of my things."

Elanor turned to retrieve Cilaen his satchel when an unexpected warm breeze blew across her face. It was calm and inviting. It was the sort of breeze one would feel when sitting under a tree on a warm summer's day.

"E-l-a-nor!" she heard a soothing whisper say, almost as if someone stood whispering right into her ear. As it spoke, she halted, smelling the fresh scent of honey and primrose. She looked out toward the wind, her eyes scanning for the source of the sweet fragrance and the mysterious voice.

"Are you going to get me my satchel?" Cilaen asked. He looked up, watching as Elanor stared eerily off toward the trees. He tugged Merlin by the arm, then pointed at Elanor.

"Elanor?" Merlin asked, noticing his wife's strange behavior.

She answered him without turning her head away. "Isn't it strange, though? Do you smell it?"

Alarm pricked at Merlin, and he moved to stand beside her. "What is it?"

"There." She pointed ahead of her. "It is Samhain, and yet a large patch of them is growing, just there. Isn't it impossible that primrose should grow this time of year?"

Merlin stared yet could see nothing. Ahead there were only briars and brambles, with no green in them. Immediately, he became aware that something was happening that might explain the dark devilry of this place.

Elanor chimed, "The scent is so sweet."

Merlin stood in front of her and grabbed her by her arms. "Look at me!" He shook her lightly. "Look at me."

As if shaken out of trance, Elanor's eyes settled upon him. "What's wrong, my love?"

"What do you see now?"

"What do you mean? I was going to get Cilaen his satchel."

"Over there." He pointed. "What do you see?"

"Is there something I am meant to see? There is yellow dried grass and some briars. Trees?" She gave Merlin an odd look.

Merlin sighed, then let her go. He glanced back at the brambles, squinting his eyes suspiciously, and then looked back at Elanor. "Stay away from that place. There is something there, and I need to take a closer look. Stand back with Cilaen where it is safe.

Mystified, Elanor stood in place, wondering what it was that she must have missed that had provoked Merlin.

"Come now. I will go look...Stay here." He halted to look around him. "First, I need to find myself a long stick of some kind."

Cilaen stared at her with his hand out, ready for her to come closer.

"E-l-a-nor," the voice whispered again, the warm wind brushing her face. She could see them in front of her, an entire patch of beautiful primrose. "E-l-a-nor."

Why was this voice so familiar? She had heard it before.

The sound of the voice warmed her as it whispered in her ears, pulling on something deep in her heart. It was her father's voice. Without even a thought, she quickly charged toward the primrose. Her father was there, somewhere, and the primrose—the primrose was important. She had to pick some. Her father would want some. He would want some for his garden.

Merlin glanced up just in time to see Elanor running toward the briar patch. Cilaen had already taken off after her, but she would reach it before he would get to her.

"Elanor...stop!" Merlin shouted. "Stop!"

Her hand was outstretched, reaching ahead of her. Merlin did not know what would happen if she touched the briar and was unwilling to find out. He threw out his hand and released a loud cracking sound from his throat. The force of his magic threw Elanor back through the air, away from the bramble. She fell hard, hitting her head on the ground.

Merlin ran over to her, lifting her into his arms. A small amount of blood trickled down the side of her head where she'd struck the ground.

"Elanor!" he gasped. "Please be alright." He cradled her in his arms. Her eyes slowly opened, and she sat up.

Still stunned, Merlin reached for her as she rubbed her head. She pulled her hand away, blood on her fingertips.

"I am so sorry. I didn't know what else to do."

She looked at Merlin, confused, then she flashed with anger. She jerked away from him and made a run for the briar. Merlin quickly grabbed hold of her arm, pulling her back down. Elanor shrieked, fighting his grip as she kicked against him. He pinned her arms down, binding her tightly in his arms. He struggled to maintain a hold of her without hurting her.

"Let me go!" she screamed, her voice violent and high pitched. "You cannot stop me. Why would you stop me? Father? Father? I'm coming!" She turned toward Merlin with a fierce, unrecognizable glare. "I hate you; I hate you, let me go!"

"Cysgasech!" Merlin shouted with authority, his eyes flashing with golden light. As his voice boomed, her eyes closed and she slumped over in his arms, asleep. On the ground, Merlin panted, working to regain his breath. His eyes were wide as he peered up at Cilaen, and then over at the briar. "This is strong sorcery," he said between breaths. "Elanor is strong, but there was more aiding the violence of her strength and will. I knew not what else to do. I did not want to hurt her." He pulled Elanor closer as she lay heavy in his arms.

"I think you did all that you could," Cilaen said uneasily, kneeling in front of them. "Let me see her head." He leaned in to look at the wound. "It is only minor. Merlin, if you had not done what you did, Elanor may have met the same fate as the ones we saw this morning."

"Yes, well..." Merlin panted, "...I need you to take her to the house, and then find Bedwyr and send him to me. I have sent her into a deep sleep, and she will not awaken for a while. Keep her far from this place until I discover what is to be done."

Cilaen took Elanor up into his arms and carried her away. Merlin sat with his head in his hands, trying to catch his breath and calm down. Slowly, he turned his head over to look at the briar. His anger seethed. He lifted himself to stand, his shoulders slumping forward. Staring over at the bush, Merlin was unsure he wanted to get any closer. From where he stood, he could see nothing strange.

He sucked in his breath, wiping his brow with his sleeve and ponder what he would do next. He looked over at the oak trees nearby with low hanging branches. He walked over to one and broke off a long branch, then continued back over to the briar. As he neared it, the sound of buzzing flies captured his attention. A pungent smell slammed his senses. No—not the smell of primrose, but a stinking, foul smell of bile and rotting flesh. The sorcery had kept the stench and flies from being easily discerned.

"Merlin!" Bedwyr shouted as he came running. "Cilaen has told me I must come find you. What has happened? He was carrying Elanor in his arms and said you had found the cursed thing."

"Yes. Be watchful." Merlin held his hand up to keep Bedwyr back. "Elanor has helped us to find it. She is only sleeping. I put her into a sleep for her protection. This…" he said, reaching his stick forward, "…is not as it seems."

Merlin approached the briar. With one hand holding the long stick, he poked into it, covering his mouth and nose.

As Merlin nudged at the briar, Bedwyr caught the repulsive scent, and yelled out, quickly covering his face with his arm.

The briar was dense and hard to see through, but as Merlin pulled back the branches, he noticed that the thorns were wet with red, as if the illusion were lifting. Breaking the briars back with his stick, he saw bits of white and red on the ground between the twisted brambles. He knelt closer.

"Aahhh!" Merlin leapt back in shock. The sight forced vomit to rise up into his throat.

"What is it?"

Merlin reached his stick forward and pulled the branches back for Bedwyr to see. On the ground underneath the briar was the severed head of a young girl, and beside it, human fingers and body parts with innards. Blood and vomit, as well as human excrement defiled the ground. Whatever cursed evil thing this was, it was ugly and horrifying. Merlin recognized that it was likely the blood of this poor one that coated the thorns and branches.

He turned his back angrily to walk away and distance himself from it. His face twisted in disgust.

"Do you think it was Osian?"

"Yes," Merlin said firmly. "I know it is not just Osian that does evil in this world. But this…this is his handy work. My question is why? To what advantage would this gain him? If the farmer had not come to see us, only their daughters would have paid the price, and we would never have known about it."

"Aih! What would it gain him? Except that the farmer did come to us, and now we are here?" Bedwyr mused with a suspicious gaze.

Merlin squinted at Bedwyr.

"The farmer asked for your help, Merlin. Yours. Do you think he did not hope that the lady would come with you also?"

"You mean you think we may have been lured here. That this was not about the village, but a trap."

"I do not know, but it makes my blood boil to think of it." Bedwyr pointed at the defilement in front of them. "Can you break this devilry?"

"Whatever dark magic that has been done to create this curse, I know not of, but I do hope that if this unholy thing is destroyed, it will break the hold and the poison it has released."

"Then let us be rid of it," Bedwyr spat.

"Get your men. Let us set a pyre around it so that we are sure that every last bit of it is burned."

They set to work setting long sticks high around the briar, clearing the ground of grass and other dry plants and twigs. They were careful not to touch the vile mass of death.

Merlin angrily stewed over what Bedwyr had said.

Could this have all just been part of an elaborate plan to lure them? And if it was, was this cursed plague of witchcraft the only part of that plan?

Who, other than Osian, would have gone through all the pains to create such an abhorrent scene? Evil like this had a high price, and not just the price paid by the poor girl whose remains had been used to desecrate ground beneath the briar. This type of dark magic would cost the witch that delivered the curse. All signs pointed to what he knew in his heart to be true. They would have to be careful, and the farmer himself was likely no innocent if Bedwyr's suspicions were true.

54

THE TRAP

Merlin ignited the fire upon the pyre as the sun dropped down into the dark. He watched it burn, making sure all of the cursed mass was entirely consumed.

The people from the village stood outside their houses, looking on as the red flames rose higher. "Stay back," Merlin commanded them with little grace. "Stay away from even the smoke. It would be best if you all returned to your houses." But most stayed, anxious to watch the burning.

Finally, the flames began to break the pyre down into hot coals, and there came a sizzling sound as it burned the rotten flesh below. A foul odor floated through the air, and the flames burst into a bright yellow. Wailing forth from the depths of the fire, an ear-piercing shriek blared as if the curse itself was screaming.

Merlin knew it was the dying cry of whatever witch had created the filthy plague for Osian. The cost of their life now paid.

Merlin set his jaw, glaring tensely as the hideous sound echoed. Bedwyr and his men ran to get away from it, covering their ears. Slowly the sound dissipated, and as it did, the flame instantly returned to the natural red of fire.

It continued burning deep into the night. Merlin worked with the men, laying more wood as it burnt down to ensure all that was left would be ash. By morning, the coals were still smoking, and Bedwyr called on the men to dig a hole where they buried the ashes.

Merlin's clothes and face were black with soot. His eyes blazed furiously, still kindled with the sparks of the flames. The evil work had given him a dark mood. He turned to walk back toward the house where the afflicted girls still laid.

Cilaen ran out to meet him. "There is change." He swallowed, taking a breath. "Now even my medicines seem to be having an effect on them. Their skin is soft and pink once more, and warm to the touch. The little one has even begun to open her eyes."

Merlin quickened his pace. He entered the house, feeling warmth on his skin. Throughout the long night he had become numb to the cold, and the warmth from inside made him realize how long he had toiled without it.

Darkness no longer loomed, but the girls lay silently sleeping. Haldin and his wife leaned over their daughter with distress. She did not seem to be improving like the others. Her cheeks and lips were the color of flesh once again but were pale and not pink.

Cilaen pushed toward her, seeing the concern. He put his ear to her chest and could hear her breaths were stressed and shallow—her heart beating weakly. He lifted up his head sadly. Haldin and his wife searched his face for assurance of hope. But before Cilaen could even speak, the young girl breathed out a long, last breath that did not return to her.

Eddna let out a wail of grief, throwing herself over her daughter, while Haldin fell back. Tears streamed down his weathered face, dripping onto his chest.

Merlin stared into his eyes. He wanted to have compassion but was unsure if this hadn't all been in Haldin's hands to stop.

He gazed back at Merlin as his chin quivered. "She wasn't supposed to die. None of them were."

Cilaen looked at Merlin, unsure of what Haldin meant.

Merlin raged and hissed, "What was the price, Haldin? Who was it you bargained with?"

His wife looked up from her tears. "What does he mean?"

"It is not as he says!" Haldin said to his wife, his voice rising as he tried to appeal to her. "I was confused. I cannot say how it happened. I…I was to convince Merlin to come here. I knew not why. Only the threat that my daughter and these ones would surely die if I did not. There was no price. Only the life of my child."

"Who was he? His name?" Merlin demanded.

"He was a man with a crooked tongue. His name…was Donnuc."

"Did he create this evil that we spent the whole of the night burning?"

"I do not know. I do not think he did, but he knew it had been made. He threatened me with it. My daughter had already become ill. I …" he swallowed, "…wanted to save her. He told me that she would be saved but that I must beseech you and the lady to come. I would not risk the Lady Elanor, but she came on her own. I did not try to stop her."

"Donnuc." The name burned on Merlin's tongue as though he had poison in his mouth. "Is there more? Why did he want us to come?"

"Please," Haldin groveled. "I do not know any more. I was only trying to save my daughter."

"Bah!" Merlin said, turning around and bursting out the door, leaving Haldin slumped over in his grief. His anger overflowed, not knowing if there was another trap awaiting them. He stormed down the uneven road toward the house where Elanor lay sleeping, unsure of what to do—only knowing that they could not stay.

There would be no wasting time, waiting for a trap to be sprung. Merlin wanted to hold Haldin responsible for it all, but he knew better. The enemy was cunning, picking on a simple, weak-minded farmer. Haldin had been manipulated, but Merlin wasn't going to allow Haldin's weakness to kill more innocent lives.

Blazing through the door, he saw Elanor perfectly at peace, lovingly wrapped in a blanket on the straw. The sight of her was like water poured on hot coals. He knelt beside her, soothed in his heart as he watched her sleep. He didn't want to wake her but knew he must. Reluctantly, he waved his hand over her eyes and spoke, "Dihuno."

Elanor softly batted her eyes, focusing on the blurry shape leaning over her. She rubbed her eyes to adjust and saw Merlin's face beaming down at her, black all over his cheeks and forehead.

"This is strange." She smiled. "Why am I here? Didn't I already rise from my slumber today, or was I only dreaming? Why do you have black on your face?"

"There is too much to tell, and I do not want to yet."

"Why not?"

"Because the sight of you has brought me joy. I do not want the vileness to get in the way."

"Have I missed something?"

415

"Yes." He laughed. "Many ugly and hateful things. But now, I look at you, and I am reminded about the good."

"Oh!" Elanor grinned at him, sitting up and stroking her fingers softly across his forehead. She leaned forward and kissed him, and he quickly wrapped his arms around her, bringing her in tightly. He never wanted to let her go.

Maybe this once, he thought, *they could get lost in each other's embrace and go somewhere where no one could find them. Far from all the madness and the darkness.*

She was his other, and without her, his world made no sense. Even this long day was chased away by one glance at her lovely face and the glint of joy in the corner of her mouth.

Why did the world need them? Why couldn't they only need each other?

But even the two stars couldn't stay up in the heavens. They came crashing down into the midst of all these troubles.

Caught up in their love, they danced, for in this single moment they forgot all else.

"I love you, Emrys!" she whispered as their foreheads met and their eyes locked.

"And I, you, Gwenddydd." His lips were bright, uncovering his smile. "You know," he mused, "just yesterday you told me you hated me."

"What?" she gasped. Elanor worked to recollect the last thing she could remember. "I cannot have said that. I remember...the girls like stone." She cringed at the memory. "And then we went outside, and... now I'm here. Oh, Merlin, what happened?"

"You bumped your head just there, and...that might have been my fault."

She winced as she reached up to touch her wound.

"You do not remember, and I am glad. Because of you we found what had been plaguing these people. It had captured your mind, but I pulled you out of its grasp and sent you to sleep."

"You sent me to sleep? I fear I have been no help at all on this task. Was it a creature?"

"No! It was a thorn briar, poisoned with witchery. We burned it, and all the girls seem to be recovering, save the one. Haldin's daughter has died.

"Oh...I am so sorry she died."

"Elanor," Merlin said seriously, "we must leave. And quickly. Things are not as they seem. Haldin was manipulated by Donnuc."

"Dunnoc!"

"Yes, Donnuc. Donnuc sent Haldin to lure us here, and I do not believe that the cursed briar is all we should expect from the twisted soul of Osian. He may have some evil for us—"

"A trap?"

"Yes, maybe. I hope not. We cannot stay here. We must gather the men and leave, immediately. Maybe if we leave now, we will have evaded the enemy. We may have already done so by destroying the briar. I have thought that, ultimately, the briar was meant for you, but I know nothing for certain."

Elanor was instantly up on her feet. Merlin took her by the hand, and together they gathered Cilaen. They did not even say goodbye as they prepared to depart, for there was no time to wait for whatever menacing scheme might come next.

As they turned to leave, Merlin grabbed Bedwyr's arm. "We must be wary. We are not safe. If Donnuc had his hand in bringing us here, then Osian may still have some evil plan that we do not see. We cannot be careless, and..." Merlin gazed at Elanor as she pulled herself onto Brynn. "We must cover her and keep her safe. None of this bodes well with me, and I fear for her. She was the aim of the witch, and she was the aim of the gwyllgi. I am not entirely sure that the cursed briar wasn't aimed at her also. Be on your guard as we go."

"On my life," Bedwyr breathed tensely. "She is daughter of the Great Pendragon, love of the wise Emrys, and is my friend. I love her also..." He straightened. "...with my life." He gripped Merlin's shoulders in a solid lock of brotherhood.

"Good man!" Merlin said with heartfelt sincerity, and both of them rose to lead them out of the village.

The weather was kinder, without rain or wind as they cautiously drove their horses forward. Their eyes steadily watched each hill, horizon, and tree line. They stayed in the wide open, hoping to prevent being taken unaware.

Even if they moved quickly, they would not arrive before the sun had set over the hills, but they did not want to move too hastily as to miss important signs of the enemy. Their hope was at least to make it to familiar territory before they lost the light.

They stopped frequently so they could scout ahead. It made Elanor uneasy, every step looking behind, feeling like they were being hunted. There had been no signs to alarm them, and they were getting comfortably closer to home.

As they continued forward, the soaring sound of an arrow flying pierced their ears. There was a soft thud as it met its target. Merlin's horse whinnied loudly, rearing back with its front legs high up into the air. An arrow had pierced its flank and sent it toppling over with Merlin still on its back. He rolled, just before the large creature fell onto his leg.

Thwfft! Another arrow landed on the ground just in front of him, and then again, and still another into one of the warriors, causing him to fall from his horse.

The sound of Bedwyr's spear rang out as he lifted it high, looking in the direction of the flying arrows. Already he could see shadowy figures flying toward them on horseback, their bows pulled back, ready to release more arrows.

Thwfft! Thwfft! went the sound of two more arrows. One whizzed past Elanor's ear, narrowly missing its mark. Her horse was startled and stamped nervously. Quickly, Elanor pulled on her reins to get the horse to settle, as it yanked back and forth in the turmoil.

There was a frenzy of movement as more arrows came sailing toward them. Bedwyr rode toward Elanor to shield her as Merlin stood to his feet.

Merlin turned to Elanor and shouted, "Run!"

Terror struck his heart as he watched her whip the reins on her horse and speed off in the direction of the tree line. In a moment, she peered over her shoulder at him, and the familiar scene from Elanor's dream played out before him. The dove was flying right out of his hands, and he couldn't get her back. Helpless. All he could do was stand there and watch.

Bedwyr reared and sped off after her, but it was too late. Merlin's golden eyes had already laid hold of the trap. There, out of the tree line, came another rider with his bow string pulled taut.

"NO!" he cried, shaking to his toes as the archer let his arrow fly. It was the nightmare. The arrow pierced through Elanor's chest, sending her flying backwards off her horse and onto the ground.

Bedwyr shouted, tearing past Elanor after the villain who loosed his arrow upon her. His cry rose above the clash of weapons and the sounds of the men fighting behind him.

Merlin's feet could not run fast enough to reach her. His heart beat loudly in his ears as he said to himself, "This cannot be true? She'll be alright?"

She laid on her side, gasping for breath when he found her. Carefully he rolled her into his arms as panic and pain rushed out of his heart. Blood dripped from her mouth, and she coughed in gasps. Her eyes connected with his; they were already weak and dull.

"No...no!" he gasped as tears flooded his cheeks, making it hard for him to breathe. "Please—there has to be something. CILAEN!" he yelled. "He's going to help you. You'll be alright. You'll be alright. We have things to do, you and I."

"Merlin," she breathed, wincing in pain. "Shhh! Don't...be afraid." One lonely tear fell from her eye. "Gwendolen...Aah."

"Yes! Gwendolen will need you...Please, please...CILAEN!"

Cilaen was before them, gasping for breath. He was holding his own shoulder where blood streamed down over his fingers. Cilaen could see the wound and the arrow through Elanor's chest. It had likely not pierced her heart, but the sound of her sputtering breath was not a good sign. Bubbles seeped out through the blood around the arrow. He sat back on his knees and dropped his head, only lifting his eyes, heavy with sorrow, at Merlin.

"No. We can figure this out. Please." Desperately, Merlin placed his hand over Elanor's chest and grasped at the arrow and whatever magic he might possess to save her.

"Aaahhh!" she cried in pain. "Merlin...stop. Stop. D-don't be afraid. Don't be afraid." She touched his cheek, making him look at her, and whispered, "You...are...my soul."

Merlin sobbed, kissing her mouth as he lifted her closer. Out of the corner of his eye, he caught a flash of blue, and lifted his eyes to see Elanor shining brightly.

"The magic of time!" She coughed, gasping for air. "I know how to use it. Merlin, Aah.... It is going to be alright...you cannot fear time."

There were those words—*You cannot fear time*. As though those words meant anything to him or could help him save her.

"Merlin...listen...to...me. You have to find me there."

"Where?" he asked through his tears.

"In time. Once and future. Arthur. You will find me...in the future. Your time..." Her breath was labored. "Your time will tell you."

"I don't understand."

"You will find me. Don't fear," Elanor said as her body was consumed with white light, like the white flames of the dragon's fire. When the light dissipated, she was gone, having left behind a bloody, black arrow laying in the grass in front of him. Merlin leaned forward, grasping the arrow in his hands with a look of stupor and grief. His chest heaved as tears fell from his eyes, unable to understand what had just happened to his beloved. Where had she gone? Was she still alive?

THE DISCOVERY OF TIME

Bedwyr chased the archer like a hound hunting after the scent of blood—wild and frenzied. The archer fled into the forest, running through the trees, with Bedwyr behind him, undaunted.

He dashed through the low hanging branches, leaning forward in his saddle. The trees became a blur as he veered dangerously, deflecting them as he pounded ahead. Bedwyr's focus would not be disturbed. His eyes were locked onto his target as he gained on him.

The villain was not the horseman that Bedwyr was and was quickly losing ground. Peering over his shoulder, his eyes were wide with alarm.

Bedwyr saw the trees opening and reached for his spear. Holding it above his shoulder, aiming its tip straight, he launched his spear with the strength of a mighty boar. It soared through the air, ringing with death—lodging between the archer's shoulder blades and ripping out through his chest.

The man fell from his horse and landed on his side, heaving with painful groans sputtering up from his mouth.

Bedwyr halted, dismounted, and stood over his foe. Bedwyr's face shook with hate, a single tear hanging from his eye, trapped in his fierce anguish. He panted while the archer writhed, scooting back away from Bedwyr's formidable frame.

"AAaaaahhhh!" Bedwyr yelled. He lifted his sword and hammered it down upon his adversary—severing his head from his body in one swift stroke. Bedwyr's rage had bubbled over, and he fell to his knees, his weapon falling to the ground beside him. His anger wiped from him, he wept.

Once the attackers dared come within reach of Bedwyr's Cymbrogi, they were destroyed, leaving their horses without riders and their arrows without shooters. Black arrows laid upon the ground, along with the dead attackers—wearing the familiar yellow hoods that had been seen on the eight.

They trudged back to the Caer like men being led to the slaughter. Cilaen's arm hung heavily at his side, bleeding. He lacked the strength to care or feel the ache of his wound. Two men were lost, and Elanor was gone.

Merlin squeezed the arrow in his hand, challenging himself to believe she still lived. He rehearsed the tragic events in his mind, wishing he could undo it all.

Their return without Elanor sent a wave of grief that rolled through the Palisade.

"You will find her," Gwynevere pleaded. "You must. She cannot be lost. If she is gone then…what of Arthur?" she gasped. "She is…I should never have let her go. I should have…" Gwynevere refused to allow word to be released that Elanor had died. Merlin would find her. He would bring her back home; however, there was a prevailing fear in all their minds that the worst had happened.

Merlin struggled, wanting to believe that he could find her, and spent his days striving to kindle the magic of time that seemed laid dormant within him. He was hoping beyond hope that he would find the answers.

He fled into the wilderness seeking the dragon for help, but she could not be found. He felt a fool, yet without answers, he could not let her go. He could not live with the thought that Elanor could still be alive and he had given up—so he never would. As long as it took, he would press on to find his way to her.

Mocking him, in the back of his mind, was the prophecy of the two stars and the new kingdom. It felt all too familiar to the very promises that had been spoken over him and Arthur, yet he too, was dead. Or was he? The insanity of it all robbed him of all peace. He couldn't even look into Gwendolen's eyes without thoughts of Elanor gripping his heart.

Out of desperation, he rode to the village on the edge of Celyddon to find Marcus. He hoped maybe the old druid would have some wisdom regarding the gift the dragon had given him. Maybe he had heard of the magic of time and would know how to unlock its powers.

He was greeted mournfully by Marcus, who had heard tale of the missing lady of Caer Lial. Quickly, Merlin set him to the true and grievous events.

"I do not know of this magic of time," Marcus said, shaking his head sorrowfully. "But from what you have told me, I do not believe our princess is dead. Rare is a dragon's magic ever given to men, and when it is, it is always for a great purpose. Never given idly. If this dragon gave Elanor this power, and she used it, this gives me great hope."

"How will I find her? I have no way of knowing where she has gone."

"Elanor said future. And the dragon said you would know how to use the magic when you needed it—did she not?"

Merlin nodded contritely.

"The answer has to be within the time that the dragon has given you."

"Yes…but what does that mean? What time? Where in the future? How can I use a magic that eludes me?" Merlin grumbled in frustration.

"Perhaps it is because you have too many questions and too much sorrow. How can you hear properly when your mind is so full?"

"I have heard that before," Merlin said. The gentle memory of Balek flashed in his mind. "To empty my mind is difficult." Emotions choked him—reddening his face. "All I can see is Elanor, gasping for breath—while I deceive myself that she is not dead. I cannot even embrace our daughter without grief knocking at my door. I fear I hope for nothing, as I did with Arthur."

"You are hoping not at all, my friend. You fear hope is a liar, and so you do not even listen."

"Huh," Merlin mused darkly. "I have been betrayed by hope before. Too many times."

Marcus leaned forward, placing his hands upon his knees and closing his eyes. "We are druids of the New Way, my friend, and what we have learned is that it is not in magic we find our answers. That is what the dark ones do." He lifted his hands up into the air, turning them like cups ready to receive rain. "We are not the dark ones. No…No, we are not. Magic does not lead us." He opened his eyes and placed his finger onto Merlin's chest. "Who leads you, Merlin? Pride? Elanor? Love? Yes…maybe love. Love of the ones placed in front of you has not been your weakness. Not the love of Arthur, nor the love of Elanor, but this has been your strength. And still, it is that love that clouds your mind. So, who leads you now, Myrddin Emrys?"

"How is it that I have lived so long and find my wisdom from others but never myself?"

"That is how the Great God intends it. No matter how old you are, you will still need people to tell you when you are being an idiot."

"Hah!" Merlin laughed, gripping the old man's shoulder. "Yes, Marcus, you are one of the few brave enough." He then sighed, "It is the Great God who must be my guide."

"Then the Great God will have your answers."

Merlin grunted, still dissatisfied with the answer. In many ways, he felt it not an answer at all. Marcus's simple and wise direction left him feeling the same way he had felt long ago on the shores of Avalon when young Rian prodded at him with his hope. Merlin had learned his lesson then, and he knew what he should do. He must face the Great God if he was going to have any answers.

He drove toward the glass lake, his secret place of contemplation. It was there he had taken Elanor and had seen Grwyrthrhodd. The lake had always been a thin place where the otherworld and its magic never seemed very far away.

Sitting on the banks, Merlin watched the sun go down. His cries rose out above the quietly rippling waters. He wept while tears wet his beard and neck. He shouted out his fear and accused the Great God of setting up trials that he couldn't bear.

"Why won't you speak to me?" he shouted. "Here I am, alone…I have come to you. Where is my wife? Why do you send me prophecy and promise, and then withhold your hand from me? Why?" Merlin waited, gazing up at the sky, tasting salty bitterness on his lips. "What is this magic of time, and why should I not fear it?" He paused, then admitted, "I am afraid."

The sound of the wind angered him as it blew, bringing him nothing but emptiness. Even the stillness of the water rebuked him with its peace. Every rock and every tree made him burn as he seethed and wept.

Finally, through all his anguish and pain, he ceased. The storm within him was spent. Weary, he settled himself to finally agree with the stillness surrounding him. He could fight it no longer. The wind blew, cooling his wet eyes. The soothing feeling of his surrender, when he had no more rocks to throw, made him rest.

"I've been here before," he said to the stillness. Merlin closed his eyes and embraced the nothingness that was left. He breathed it in deep and let it fill him. His sobriety comforted him, and as it did, the long awaited awen fell upon his eyes. He found himself in the otherworld, sitting on the shores of a new lake. Here, the wind blew, but it was warm—the water blue and ethereal.

A light flashed, like a ray of sunshine blinding him. Merlin quickly rubbed his eyes to regain his sight, and as his eyes readjusted, he found, sitting beside him, the man in blue. He peered out at the water serenely, his lips parted in a half smile.

Merlin asked, "Who are you?"

"You will know me." The man in blue smiled even wider.

"Can you help me? The magic of time—I do not know what it is or how to use it. My love, she is…somewhere," Merlin confessed sadly.

"Memories," the man in blue replied.

"Memories?"

He nodded. "Memories. That is the magic of time. Where did your love say she would be found?"

"She said I would find her in the future."

"Do you have memory of the future?"

"How can I have memory of the future? One can only have memory of the past."

"Is that so?"

Merlin tipped his head back with a confused expression on his face. He scanned his mind—sifting through what little he knew of the future. He thought of prophecy, and then he recalled memories Elanor had shown him of her time.

"How do you use the memories?"

"You do not use them. There are right ones, for the right season. When you have the right one, you will know." The man in blue gazed at Merlin, who was completely perplexed. "You fight so hard because you have passion, but also you fight because you do not trust the path you have been given. You wrestle more than you ought. If you could learn to trust, you would find rest. You think everything will be taken away from you. You must learn to have more faith in the promise than what you see with your eyes."

"It is hard to trust what you cannot see."

"Ah, but you trusted that Arthur would be king, and you set him on his path to glory, though impossible was this task. You only doubt when you are left alone and have no one to lift you toward purpose but yourself. You are not as alone as you suppose. You have been set to a purpose. Trust this, and trust me."

"Who are you, Lord? Are you the Great God?"

As Merlin asked this final question, the brightness of the lake faded, and he found he was sitting alone. The man in blue was gone, and Merlin was on the shore as the water lightly lapped at the pebbles. He did not comprehend all that the man in blue had said, yet in his heart, he felt lighter. He had hope and courage once again.

"Memories," he pondered. He leaned back as he let memories of Elanor flicker to life in his mind. He reminisced about the sun gleaning off her in the enchanted pool and remembered the healing and the beauty of the sanctuary. Then, he thought about the crystal cave, and the desperate moment when Elanor transformed and crushed the head of that vile, black serpent. And then…and then….

Merlin gasped, leaning forward as he remembered it. His heart began to pound. Unlocking within him was a strong magic, connecting him to the memory. It felt like he had lived it. He thought he had been only a bystander observing the memory, but now he realized, he had actually been there—or at least he would be. As it unfolded, white flames appeared around him. He had discovered it. The magic of time.

"Wait!" He halted the memory, causing the magic to fade. He stood up in readiness. "I must put my affairs in order."

Swiftly he was upon his horse, riding toward Caer Lial. He would not leave them without knowing his mission. Late into the night he prepared as his mother sat beside him in his chamber, holding Gwendolen as she slept. He had no idea what would happen once he walked through that door of time, nor did he know if he would find his way back, but the sight of the face of his beloved was all he needed to be willing to try.

Adhan asked, "You have prepared Gwynevere with what you are about to do?"

"Yes. I have spoken to them all. They have hope, as I do, that something good will come of this. That maybe I will find her and bring her home."

"You believe she lives?"

"I believe more now than I ever have. Now that I have felt the magic,

I can also feel its purpose giving me strength. There is a force that is beyond me, aligning fate to bring in the promises that have rung true in our hearts." He stopped, peering down at the blue book that rested on the bedside table. Gathering it up, he laughed to himself, then placed it inside his leather satchel.

Adhan stroked the cheek of the small child in her arms, then said, "I will seek the Great God for you, my son, and for my daughter, that we will see her once again."

"You will care for her?" Merlin gazed tenderly at his sleeping child.

"We all will."

"I will miss her. So small and sweet." He squeezed her tiny hand.

"She will be well."

Merlin tried to sleep, but thoughts of what he would do come morning kept him awake. Would he see Elanor once again? The thought of her made his heart ache. He tossed and turned until finally morning did come. He sat on the edge of his bed and watched as the sun rose from the view of the window.

Gwendolen's little eyes peaked up from over the top of her sleeping grandmother's shoulder. Catching her father's eye, she slid to the ground and waddled over to him, placing her little cherub hands upon his knee.

Adhan woke, watching Gwendolen stare at her father.

She lifted her arms up, and Merlin reached down to scoop her up. Then, she put her hands upon his face and tapped his cheeks.

"Pappa!" She smiled. "Pappa bring Mamma home."

Merlin looked up at Adhan, bewildered.

"I have told her nothing of your leaving," Adhan said.

"Yes, my dove," he said, kissing Gwendolen's nose. "I go to bring your mother home. And…I will miss you. But I hope it will be for only a short while."

"Mamma miss me," Gwendolen spoke brightly with assuredness. "She will come home."

Merlin eyes dampened as he pulled on the little black curls that poked out from underneath her bonnet. She snuggled into Merlin's chest and clung to the folds of his tunic. Happy to rest there, Merlin rocked her, desiring not to leave her sooner than he needed to.

He did not know when he would return, or even if he would find Elanor. But the sweet words of his daughter encouraged him to think that maybe she knew something he did not. Slowly, Gwendolen's eyes became heavy, and she fell back to sleep. Her warm little body comforted Merlin, and he loathed the idea of letting her go, but finally, he knew it was time. He tenderly handed her back to the loving arms of Adhan, and he leaned down and kissed his mother's cheek.

"It is time."

Adhan simply nodded as her chin quivered.

He grabbed his satchel from the floor and wrapped it around himself. He grabbed his soft leather vest and his cape of colors, pinning them neatly with his brooch. Then, he stepped back and closed his eyes, meditating on the memory. It did not take long before the white flames burst onto his hands, then danced up from his feet, consuming him. He opened his bright eyes as they sparked brightly with gold, and then he was gone.

When Merlin opened his eyes, colors mingled as his eyes slowly came into focus, seeing the unfamiliar world around him. People raced while iron chariots flew loudly past.

The scene he had seen so long ago in Elanor's memory was now before him in real time. This time it was vibrant, and the noises sharp and unfamiliar. Even the smells were strange. People eyed him, giving him odd stares, while others pushed past him like he was invisible.

One man laughed and yelled out, "You cracked git! What do you think this is, a fancy medieval dress party?"

Merlin was taken aback that he understood the man's speech. He looked down at his clothing, realizing how strange he must appear to all of them.

Dazed, he tried to reel himself in. This new world was perplexing and otherworldly. He scanned his surroundings, gazing up at the buildings, in hopes of centering himself on where he was and where he needed to go.

His heart beat nervously as fear and insecurity overwhelmed him. Never in his life had he felt so foreign and displaced. He looked down the path in front of him, and then turned to look at the path behind him. Nothing but a sea of moving people and clashing loud colors.

Finally, he turned to look directly behind him, and there through a window he saw shelf after shelf of books. He sighed in relief as an excited smile lifted his cheeks. This was a place he knew. He had been there, or was about to be. He turned toward the door, his heart skipping a beat, as he reached for the unusual handle. The bell jingled as he pushed open the door. Expectant, he hoped, that when he heard that bell again, it would be Elanor walking through the doors of the book shop.

Chapter Fifty - Five

ACKNOWLEDGEMENTS

To my husband, Clay Hughes. You supported my fantastic imagination and believed in this story from the get-go. You cheered me on, never letting me give up. You are the most generous person I know—your sacrifice to make this book happen will never be forgotten.

Thank you to my kids, Ezra and Brielle, for allowing Mommy the time to write, and your willingness to be fascinated at every turn. You are a couple of dragon slayers.

I would like to give a special and significant *shout out* to Brae and Jill Wyckoff. Your undying willingness to champion others is the VERY reason I dared to be brave enough to write this story. The course of my life has been changed because you told me I was a FANTASTIC STORYTELLER. The value of your encouragement is immeasurable. Every breakthrough, opportunity, and story I write from here on out is because of you.

Thank you to my author friends, Stephanie Cotta and Nathan Keys. You were willing to give your valuable time to the rough draft mess I started with. I learned so much from you both. It was your input that significantly helped my idea grow and mature into a story I am proud of.

To the *Square Tree Publishing* team, you are a bunch of ROCK STARS. Thank you!

ABOUT THE AUTHOR

ANGELA R HUGHES

is a historical fantasy author based in Waco, Texas. Her ambition is to write stories that grip and inspire readers, alluring them into her fascinating world of myth and legend.

Angela believes in the power of dynamic, inspired storytelling. She has always been intrigued by folklore and legend, and desired to create her own. Particularly drawn to Arthurian legend and its ancient roots in the history of the Cymraeg (Welsh) people, she has extensively studied Arthurian legend and Celtic mythology.

Much of her fascination with the Celtic world began during her time living in Ireland, where she fell in love with the history and landscapes of Ireland, Wales, Scotland, and England.

In addition to writing, Angela spends her time researching ancient histories and languages—which led her to learn to speak the Welsh language. She also enjoys painting, inspiring others, being with her family, chatting with fellow fantasy nerds over coffee, baking, visiting wineries, and traveling.

The Once and Future Chronicles, Book One: Elanor and the Song of the Bard is her first published novel. She is currently working on sequels including *Book Two: Merlin and the Magic of Time*, and *Book Three: Arthur and the Golden Dragon*.

Learn more about *Elanor and the Song of the Bard* by visiting www.angelarhughes.com. You are also invited to follow Angela's author journey on Facebook, Instagram, and Amazon.

LET'S BE LEGENDARY!

 @onceandfuturechronicles

 @angela.r.hughes

 @angela.r.hughes

 @ARHughesAuthor

ALSO BY ANGELA
COMING SOON

MERLIN AND THE MAGIC OF TIME

Sent through time in desperate hopes of finding Elanor, Merlin discovers more than he bargained for in modern day Wales. Hidden amongst the crowded city streets lurk dark shadows and vengeful demons bent on destroying the promise of the new kingdom and threatening to stop Merlin from awakening the king. Will Merlin find his true love Elanor on the other side of time? Will Arthur be returned to his rightful place as king of Prydain? Unlock the mystery in *Angela R. Hughes'* next exciting installment of *The Once and Future Chronicles, Merlin & the Magic of Time.*